SUZANNAH ROWNTREE

A Stranger in the Land

Watchers of Outremer, Book Six

Chapter I.

Beirut, AD 1290

Eschiva of Ibelin stretched a little further, trying to keep her balance on the springy bough beneath her foot. The fingers of her right hand dug into the rough bark of the orange-tree; those of her left merely brushed against the dew-wet rind of the season's first orange for a long, tantalising moment before, with a grunt, she scrabbled the fruit into her hand and yanked. For a long time the fruit resisted her, its stem green and springy with new sap. Then it sprang free. The branch that bore it rebounded, scattering petals from its clusters of spring blossom.

"That *hurt*," said an accusing voice from the foot of the trunk. Eschiva jumped; she had thought herself safe from the watching eyes of any of her small army of attendants, nurses, tutors, and playfellows. When she peered through the green branches to the foot of the great tree, she found a boy staring up at her with accusing eyes.

He had to be her own age, but he did not look like any of her playfellows; he had black eyes, softly rounded features and a skin that glowed richly dark beneath the overcast sky. He looked exactly like the Abyssinian merchants who lived in the city, trading purest gold and ivory for pottery, glassware and books; or like the Nubian ambassador who had come to propose a war with Egypt in the year the great comet predicted disaster—the year her father died.

Eschiva might only be a child and the younger sister of the great Lady of Beirut, but that made her the equal of any prince or lordling in the world.

So she said, sugary-sweet: "I am so very sorry. Were you bruised by a falling blossom?"

The boy laughed and said, "I'm Ibrahim. What's your name?"

Eschiva put her back to the trunk of the old orange-tree and crouched down, digging her fingernails into the orange-rind. A spray, rich with the scent of citrus, burst into her face. She licked her lips and savoured the bitter oils as a prelude to the cold sweetness that awaited her.

"I'm Eschiva," she said. "My sister is Isabella of Ibelin, the Lady of Beirut, and I am her only heir." She swept out a hand yellow with citrus oil, flicking drops of scent towards the orange-tree, the pleasure-garden tucked like a secret into the great wall, and above all the great palace that overshadowed them, its pale stone ornamented with long galleries of airy open windows. "This is *my* home. What are *you* doing here?"

"I came to warn you," Ibrahim said. Eschiva startled, for his voice had changed. It now seemed to echo in the very stones of the fortress around them; it boomed like thunder in a suddenly-darkened sky. "They are within the palace, seeking my life. In God's name, Eschiva, awake."

Her heart bucked like a frightened horse.

* * *

It must be the dead of night; her ladies breathed steadily from their couches along the wall, and she could not even hear the chant of Vigils from the chapel. Her chamber was lit only by a glimmer of moonlight. Eschiva was on her feet, clutching her racing heart. It took her a moment to recall where she was—*who* she was. She was a grown woman and no child—she had two sons of her own. Her sister was dead and now she was the Lady of Beirut, a title which lay as heavy on her as the eyes of her enemies and the hopes of her people. And Ibrahim—Ibrahim was a memory she had not dared to stir up in years.

They are within the palace, seeking my life.

It was only a dream. Her weary body begged for more sleep. If she left now, her bed would be cold when she returned. Eschiva shivered, feeling the nip in the late October air that promised frosts to come. She should lie down again. She should find rest while she could, for God knew the day would bring none.

I came to warn you. In God's name, awake.

And if it wasn't merely a dream? Eschiva shivered, not wanting to believe. She recalled the terror in her mother's eyes whenever she spoke of the boy that no one else could see. The boy her uncle had explained as a child's fancy, but the chaplain had called a fiend...

Eschiva had never been able to understand how Ibrahim could have been either. He was quite different to the friends of her imagination, which had never shown such a vexing mind of their own; neither was there anything even slightly fiendish about him—no horns, no lies, no face growing in his belly or groin.

Sighing, Eschiva reached for the robe at the foot of her bed. As her hands sank into the luxurious pile of grey squirrel fur, the words echoed in her mind once more.

They are within the palace.

Her whole body turned cold. Eschiva dropped the robe and found a plain woollen cote to pull on over her shift. A garment she'd had her ladies lay out for the morrow's journey into the mountains, a penitential visit to the Monastery of the Holy Saviour where orgulous raiment would not be appropriate. Dressed like a shadow, Eschiva slipped from the dark sanctuary of her chamber. There was a deadly hush upon the air: none of her ladies stirred.

The chamber opened onto a long gallery that ran the length of the wall in which the palace had been built, jutting north from the city of Beirut along a promontory towards the sea. On this side of the wall, the gallery overlooked the small pleasure-garden, a terrace tucked into the space between palace and harbour. Beyond, fitful moonlight straggled between the clouds to illuminate the rooves and domes of the city to her left. There was little to reveal the sea to her left, or the distant mountains to her right.

Eschiva bent from the arched gallery to gaze down upon the the garden, where the ancient tree was still in bloom. All seemed peaceful. A faint scent of orange-blossom drifted up towards her. Then, after a moment, she caught a snatch of talk from further down the gallery.

"What do you think? If we pull this off, will the master grant your boon?"

It was a woman's voice, which might have set Eschiva at her ease, except that it was speaking the tongue of the Saracens. Of course there were few, even in Christian Beirut, who did not speak the Arabic tongue; whether by accident or design, centuries of Saracen occupation had eradicated the native languages, driving them into the churches where they survived only as liturgical relics.

But the occupiers now were Eschiva and her kin, and they spoke a type of Frankish. The harder the Saracens pressed on her borders, and the more demands they made, for lands and rents, the less inclined she was to hear Arabic spoken in her own palace. So a bolt of fear and outrage ran through her when she heard that voice.

"Who are you, to speak that tongue in the very house of the Ibelins?" she called out.

The murmurs paused, and Eschiva swept towards the two dark shapes that stood by the threshold of the great audience-hall which was the wonder of the East. A man and a woman, she judged from their dim silhouettes, and from the low mutter which had answered the woman. For a moment there was a watchful stillness about the intruders. Then the woman said, "Lord, madame, I thought I should die of fright! Are you a servant of the Lady's?"

The intruder's Frankish was fair, but still heavily accented; and, Eschiva thought, a little archaic, as though it had been learned from someone who had not been in Christian lands many years. That, together with the woman's talk of masters and boons, had her thoroughly on her guard. Surely the sultan of Egypt would not have sent a *woman* as a hired killer—but perhaps she was a former servant in the palace who had been subverted. As for the man who hovering at the woman's shoulder, he did not speak. But there was a silent menace in the very fact of his presence.

In Acre barely twenty years ago, the son of the king of England had nearly been stabbed to death in his own bedchamber. A strong and vigorous knight, the prince had managed to defend himself with fist and steel. Eschiva must trust to other weapons: her voice, which she must make as light and careless as she might, and her wits, which she must file to a razor sharpness. She might call for her guards, of course. There ought to be at least one man on duty at the far end of the gallery, and more in the guardhouse above the main entrance. Had this happened to her father, or to any other of her glorious forbears, they would only have had to lift their voice to summon the lances of all the East to their aid.

But the Ibelin fortunes had declined since her father's day: Eschiva was no longer undisputed mistress in her own city. She had an Egyptian minister in her council, and an Egyptian garrison stationed within the walls of Beirut itself. The days were past that the Lady of Beirut could order passing Saracens seized and flogged on suspicion of being Assassins, even if they had intruded upon her privy chambers.

Think of it as a game, she told herself, with a wry inward smile.

"You have no notion what a hard taskmistress she is," said Eschiva, with a sigh. "Here it is not yet Vigils, and my lady lies awake worrying over her pet bitch which is to whelp at any moment, and sends me running down to the kennels to see if the creature is yet living. What's *your* business here? Don't tell me you're here on a wager to steal fruit from the Old Lord's orange-tree. That's the third time in as many years."

There was another breathless silence. In Eschiva's mind, she repeated a few lines of the Our Father, feeling that she needed to make up for her lies.

Then, thank heaven, the Saracen woman accepted the explanation she had offered. "They say the fruit bestows long life, madame. And there is sickness in our household."

The Old Lord, John of Ibelin, Eschiva's great-grandfather, had planted the tree seventy years ago when he was building the palace. It had been a gift from his foster-sister, Marta the Knight, the White Watcher. Seventy years was a long life for an orange-tree, but the tree showed no signs of age or weakness. In this regard, it seemed likely to outdo the Ibelins themselves.

Perhaps these spies really did have business with her family's most enduring talisman. Eschiva bit her lip, weighing once more her courses of action. No: she could not call her guards, could not lay violent hands on these people, until she knew for certain what they planned to do.

"Come along, then," she said. "The tree grows here in the garden beneath. You may pluck a fruit, but then you must go."

In the shadows, the shape of the man moved to follow her. It was only then that Eschiva perceived how tense had been his stance a moment before.

It was only then that she saw a glint of steel from the lance in his hands.

Chapter II.

For Saif's sake, Soraya was glad to see him come off his guard. Had this servant woman suspected them—or worse, called the guards—then they might have had to kill her, rather than fail in their mission. And despite all the orders their mutual master could give, Soraya knew that her friend loathed shedding blood nearly as much as she did.

They might yet be forced to kill the Frankish woman. She and Saif had indeed come to steal a fruit from the Old Lord's orange-tree; but it was no part of their master's plan to leave the orange-tree standing once they had done so. In the satchel slung across Soraya's shoulder was a pot of naphtha; nestled beside that was steel and flint. No part of the tree must be left intact, save the single fruit it was their mission to carry back to Cairo.

Another dangerous mission, steeped in blood, carried out to some greater end they would never be permitted to know. She and Saif were merely blind tools in the hands of the sorcerer who now called himself al-Ashraf Khalil, the prince who stood ready to seize the throne of Egypt whenever the sultan himself should perish. There was no reward for themselves in such business. They must tiptoe into the territory of their enemies, drink blood, and set a trail of fire behind them as they made their retreat. Back in Egypt, no high office, no glory, no thanks would await them. Only boredom, anonymity, and the next deadly mission, whenever the sorcerer chose to make use of them.

Had it been Soraya's choice, she would have rebelled. She would have flown for the desert, or across the sea, or into Tartar-held Khorasan. Cairo might be the greatest city of the world, but Soraya dreamed of seeing distant lands—the gold fields of Great Zimbabwe, the palaces of Xanadu, the grand jousts of Paris. A djinn like herself had a thousand lifetimes and a thousand forms in which to explore them; she might become a nun in Thibet, a pearl-fisher in Ceylon, or a pirate in the far, icy Baltic.

But she could never leave Cairo while Khalil had her and Saif bound together on such a short leash. Nor could she divert herself with some cunning subversion of their mission. If she should by accident raise the alarm, or in a moment of mischief eat the orange, she would only harm her friend.

A shame. There was nothing better than a freshly-plucked orange, cold with dew.

Therefore, as Soraya followed the Frankish woman down a flight of sandstone steps into the palace's small pleasure-garden, she kept her thoughts on the mission.

"Why are you helping us?" she asked the servant, rather suspiciously. Even if the Lady of Beirut *was* a hard task-mistress, it seemed strange that a servant on a midnight errand should turn aside to help a pair of strangers steal a fruit.

"What else am I going to do?" the servant asked. With the cat-like eyes Soraya had crafted for tonight's work, she could see the woman as a pale grey shadow wearing a smile that was more than a little cat-like itself. "Call the guards and have you thrown into prison? Flogged, perhaps? Don't be foolish. My mistress has enough trouble-makers in her cells as it is."

Saif accompanied them blindly in the dark, tapping with the iron-shod butt of the Lance as he felt his way down the steps. The mortal eyes he was born with must barely be able to see in this fitful light; but Soraya noticed them flicking towards her all the same. She felt his incredulity, yet the woman's amusement seemed perfectly sincere. Likely the Lady of Beirut was a querulous, anxious sort of person, who kept her servants so much on the run that they would be glad to let slip what they could.

At any rate…Soraya sighed. If the woman tried to make trouble later, Saif carried the Lance. She ran her tongue over her teeth, bracing herself against the impending taste of blood. As an enslaved djinn, Soraya was bound to the vessel of Saif's lance. Not only was she bound to obey his every command and render him her own strength and immortality through the soul tether that linked them, but she also tasted every drop of blood he shed.

They *had* to get free of this torment—free of Khalil. Somehow. Sometime.

In the gallery the air had been still, but in the garden it stirred with strong and fitful breezes. Hot and cold they blew, salty and citrus; for an instant, Soraya had the wild notion that there was a great beast coiled in the garden with them, breathing down their necks. A cloud drifted from the face of the waxing moon, revealing thick turf, low fragrant hedges of rosemary and lavender, pencil cypresses, and in the very midst of the garden the great orange-tree itself, reigning like a king. Its broad-spreading branches were still white with blossom, despite the swelling fruit peeping here and there from the boughs. At the sight of the noble old tree, Soraya felt a pang of helpless rage. Was it not enough that she and Saif should be forced to shed the blood of mortals? Must they destroy the very fruit-trees, also?

"This is the tree," the servant-woman said, coming to a halt.

Saif sent Soraya another glance. "Can you pluck it?" he asked, careful not to phrase it as a command. Seeing his fist tight around the Lance, Soraya wished she could send the servant on her way in ignorant safety. But how would she do so without arousing suspicion? With a sigh, she moved towards the tree.

A cloud moved over the moon. A hot breath lifted her hair—and in the darkness, she *knew*.

There *was* Something in the garden with them. Some*one*.

Soraya's heart slid into her throat, slow and sickening. She knew now the meaning of their bizarre quest; she knew they had been sent, all blind and unprepared,, into greater peril than they had imagined.

"Saif," she said, turning to her friend.

"Hurry," he told her, not hearing the sound of warning in her voice. It wasn't meant as a command; but the magic that bound them knew no better. It picked up her feet, marching her nearer the tree, stretching out her fingers.

Steal a fruit from a palace? Soraya had scoffed, when Saif first told her of their mission. *Why does Khalil need an immortal and a djinn to do* that?

Except that she wasn't stealing a fruit from a palace.

She was stealing it from a fellow djinn.

The command closed her hand around a smooth, aromatic globe. She thought the tree fought her, clinging stubbornly to its burden. She thought the branches groaned as she tugged. She thought the air took on an angry hush…

Briefly, the fruit glowed hot and golden, a lamp in her hand that traced every bone within the flesh and sent stark black shadows racing through the garden. Then the globe snapped from its branch, shaking blossoms down on her face. In the same instant the light was snuffed out.

There was a muffled exclamation from Saif behind her. The sound was swallowed by a wailing wind as cold as malice.

Soraya recoiled from the tree as the command released her. For an instant she had no notion what to do next. Run? Shout? Fling her pot of naphtha at the tree and hope the other djinn's outrage summoned an ill-judged bolt of lightning? Throw herself on her face, begging for mercy, until the djinn reduced them to ashes and consumed their spirits?

There was barely time to list her choices, and none to choose among them. The wind shrieked about them, whipping a cloud from the earth to blot out the moonlight. In the midst of that seething cloud the tree's fruits illuminated like lanterns. There in the darkness loomed a great shadowy figure like a man.

Soraya looked up into a gigantic, oddly calm face. For a moment her mind was nearly a blank. She had the sudden horrible certainty that something like this had happened to her before: she felt the sticky tug of a malicious spirit sinking its teeth into hers, attempting to absorb her. The lost memory rose up and ambushed her; she could neither move nor speak.

Then Saif was beside her, brandishing the Lance. "There is no God but God!" he exclaimed. "Surrender, afrit, and do not imagine that you frighten us!"

It was almost as thought he *expected* to face such a being.

Before she could recover from that surprise, another followed fast on its heels: "I know you, John Bessarion," rumbled the djinn.

Soraya's heart leapt; she felt as though it was about to be dragged from her body. That *name!* Why did that name touch her like flame to naphtha?

Saif said in a ragged voice, "You know *nothing* about me, afrit. I slay Bessarions wherever I find them."

"And I know *you*," the giant boomed. Soraya flinched as his eyes fixed upon her—but there was nothing threatening in his gaze, nothing voracious or angry. There was only pity—and not a little awe. "The seventh sister, who has fallen from the stars."

Again, the djinn's words touched her to the quick—save that this time, she felt as though words were on the tip of her tongue, heavy with import, incapable of utterance. *The stars.* Wasn't that the meaning of her own name?

Who was he, this djinn who could undo her with a word?

"Don't listen, Soraya," Saif said, urgently, in her ear. His own hands were white on the haft of the Lance. "Quickly, the naphtha. There's nothing it can do to stop us."

Soraya was not so certain. Perhaps the djinn could not touch Saif; mortals were less vulnerable to spirits. But she was no mortal.

"I was a slave of Khalil's once, mortal," said the djinn, with a dogged kind of weariness, "until your own mother set me free and planted me in this garden. You can burn my tree, but you cannot force me to take refuge in the fruit. Better a hell of my own choosing than captivity in that house."

"He's lying," Saif said. "The naphtha, Soraya!"

But this was more than Soraya could bear. "Saif," she choked. "We can't. Not when he's already escaped once."

"He's a djinn—you can't believe him!"

"*I'm* a djinn!" she responded, stung. "And even if he's lying, how can we do it to him, when we're so desperate to escape ourselves? Besides, didn't you hear? *He knew your mother.*"

"He's *lying!*" Saif roared—had she ever heard him raise his voice before? In the same moment he reached for the strap of her satchel, issuing a rare intentional command. "Give me the naphtha! Quickly!"

"I speak only truth," the djinn said. "Disregard me at your peril. I will accept death, and gladly."

"And what will Khalil say to that?" Soraya put in, even as the command forced her to surrender the satchel. *"Think, Saif."*

Pot of naphtha in his hand, he paused, staring with wild eyes from herself to the djinn of the orange tree.

"Al-Ashraf will make it worth your while," Saif told the djinn. "His service is not so bad."

The djinn made a derisive sound. "Spoken like one who has never known freedom."

For a moment there was silence. Then from the wall above the garden came the sound of tramping feet.

"They're after us," Soraya said. It struck her that they were now alone in the garden. "Where did that servant go?"

The light of the orange-tree snuffed out as a gust of wind dissipated the dust-cloud that had shrouded them from view. The djinn vanished. A column of soldiers hurried down the narrow stair into the garden.

With an angry mutter, Saif threw the pot towards her. "Set the fire," he ordered, brandishing the Lance. He turned to face the soldiers as his command forced her to uncork the jar, to empty it upon the earth. Soraya bit her lip under her breath as she fumbled within the bag for steel and flint. Saif *knew* what effect his words had upon her. He must be terribly frightened, if he had forgotten himself so far as to command her, not once, but twice…

"I'm sorry," she whispered to the djinn. "We suffer too, if we try to defy Khalil."

"What's the meaning of this?" The voice that cut across the garden, to Soraya's surprise, spoke Arabic like a Cairene. "You—woman! Cease that at once!"

Soraya only wished that she could. In her hands the stone and flint cracked. A spark caught in the oil-laden grass, in the boughs overhead. The flames roared suddenly high. She snatched her hands away as the command left her.

At the rushing sound of flames, Saif turned to see the fire devouring a rosemary-bush at some distance from the orange-tree itself.

"What have you done?" he demanded. "We were supposed to burn the *tree!*"

"You told me to set a fire—you didn't say where. I've *asked* you not to command me. Look—that djinn is right. It's better this way."

"As God wills it, but we'll speak of this later," Saif said with grim resignation as the guards surrounded them. Soraya shrugged. If he hadn't insisted on her setting the fire, they might already have made their escape. Then they would have been free to consider their options, consult with their master, and try again if there was no other way. It was Saif's fault they were in this fix; she had only saved him from making the mess worse. He would admit it himself once he had had the chance to cool his wits.

The night was not done with surprises. In the glare of the fire, the guards that surrounded them wore the silken tunics and white turbans of Egyptian mamluks. There was also a plump official in the blue turban of a Copt—doubtless one of the many Egyptian Christians who served in the sultan's bureaucracy. Only three Franks accompanied him: the serving-woman from before and two Frankish guards that accompanied her.

The Copt uttered a grunt of surprise when he saw Saif's face.

"Al-Rafiq!" he exclaimed in bewilderment. "Al-Rafiq Saif al-Din! What is a mamluk of al-Ashraf doing in Beirut? Setting fires to a pleasure-garden, no less?"

Saif, who had dropped into a fluid fighting-stance, seemed to congeal in amazement.

Soraya herself was curious as to the presence of an Egyptian garrison, and an Egyptian minister, in Frankish-ruled Beirut. But now was not the time to ask.

"Is this man a friend of yours?" asked the serving-woman, with cool amusement. Or not a serving-woman, Soraya thought, now that she saw her by firelight. The tone of her voice was too authoritative, the wool of her gown too fine, her skin too white and soft for that. A lady in waiting, perhaps. Or...

Surely not.

"I beg your pardon, my lady Eschiva," the Copt said, bowing to the Frankish woman. "Please be assured that I had no notion of this man's coming. I am as mystified as you. But you must rest assured that Sultan Qalawun will take the matter very seriously; very seriously indeed."

Eschiva. That name Soraya had heard, and recently. Eschiva of Ibelin, the ruling Lady of Beirut, cousin to the king of Cyprus and Jerusalem. Now savouring the prisoners' evident astonishment with another small, catlike smile.

"In that case, I'll turn them over to your people," said the Lady with a lazy flutter of her hand. She must have taken advantage of the djinn's appearance just now to run and call—not her own guards, but the Egyptians quartered upon her. Soraya had to admire the mortal's presence of mind—not only to make good her escape in the face of an angry djinn, but to summon guards Saif could not possibly lift a hand against.

"They've done no irreparable damage," the Lady added. "But I'll expect a good explanation as to why a man from the household of—al-Ashraf, did you say? The sultan's heir?—should be committing arson upon my poor rosemary bushes. Thank you; you may go."

Chapter III.

It seemed that there was a Mamluk barracks in Beirut, in the city itself not far from the castle. The amir in command was not in a good mood to begin with, having been dragged from his bed in the dead hours. When he heard Saif's excuses, he was further enraged.

"Beirut is not ours *yet*," the amir thundered. "Nor is al-Ashraf yet sultan! Perhaps he never will be, as God wills it! Who does he think he is, sending his mamluks to trample all over the sultan's peace with Beirut? Take them away!"

They were parted, of course, and Soraya was sent to a cell of her own, where she tapped her foot in some impatience until she felt the soul tether snap tight, tearing her spirit free of its temporarily-assumed mortal body. For a moment she was adrift in the shadowy world of the spirit, surrounded by lights; on the east horizon was a restless glow she guessed to be the djinn of the orange-tree. Then she was snatched into her vessel, the Lance; and a moment later Saif summoned her out again into the lamplight of a bare but comparatively comfortable guest-room.

"Look who's getting special treatment! They put *me* in a feed-storeroom," Soraya greeted him, putting her hands on her hips. In order to create a body, she had been forced to use the soil from a potted lemon-tree in the arched window; she was in consequence a little undersized.

"I'm not sure they knew what to do with a female prisoner," Saif replied. He pulled his black turban from his shaved head and tossed it onto his bed, then dragged both his long, sinewy hands down his face with a gesture of defeat. "Do you really think that creature would have chosen *Hell* over slavery?"

Soraya couldn't understand his perplexity, but it was better than outrage. Then she wondered, with a jolt of confusion, why she should fear his outrage. For as long as she remembered, Saif had only ever been a kind and gentle friend to her.

Hadn't he?

"Of course he would," she said, a little impatiently. "Wouldn't you? Terrible as Hell might be, at least one would always know that it was one's own choice. But you've been a slave, the same as me. You *know* what it's like."

Saif only looked more puzzled still. "But it's *Hell*," he said earnestly. "God is merciful! Who in their right mind would choose such a thing? Wait—is this another of the things you say that sound serious but are not?"

"I'm not being *sarcastic*, Saif! Slavery is the hell he *knows*. Of course he won't go back to it." Soraya ran a hand through the short hair she had given her dwarfish form. She had truly expected him to understand better than this. "I don't know—maybe he isn't in his right mind. Maybe slavery *does* that to you."

Saif threw up his hands. "Perhaps you are right. Better to play it safe, anyway. I can't afford to disappoint al-Ashraf—not this time. He wanted the afrit brought safely to Cairo; if it chose Hell instead..."

His voice trailed away, as though the alternative was too terrible to contemplate. Soraya watched him, wondering whether he was simply lost for words...or whether there was something he was hiding from her.

Such as, for instance, the truth of what they had been ordered to steal.

"You knew," she said in a low voice. "You *knew* that the mission was never simply about an *orange*."

The fruit was still in the satchel, which lay upon the bed. With a sound of disgust, Soraya fished it out and tore it apart. Cold juice spurted over her hands, and then her chin, as she tore into the flesh within.

Saif made no move to stop her. But he gave her no explanation, either—and even the fruit, shockingly sweet and shockingly cold, turned to dust in her mouth.

"Why didn't you *tell* me?" she asked, angry at herself for sounding so upset. "I could have advised you. I could have spared you *this*," and she waved her hand around the locked room.

"I couldn't," he muttered. "Al-Ashraf forbade it."

"Then al-Ashraf is a fool, and you're another, for obeying him!" The silence swept out, and it was only in the stillness that Soraya knew why the thing had upset her so much. "I thought we were *friends*."

"We *are*," he replied at once. "Can't you trust me, just this once? How long have we known each other?"

She had been about to soften. To say that she *did* trust him—because she did, because there was a vast longing welling up inside her that had only *him* to fix upon. But that last question arrested her.

"Less than a year," she said. He looked a little taken aback at that. "Or did you forget that your master wiped all my memories clean? All I have is...*feelings*. And I don't know where they come from, or who they're for." She gave a shaky laugh, unable to describe how those feelings of terror had ambushed her beneath the orange-tree, when she was so sure that the djinn would consume her.

"Sometimes," she whispered, "I wonder whether it's really you that is my friend at all." Or whether there was someone else, someone she had lost...

Saif paled until his skin, even in the gilded lamplight, appeared the colour of putty. "Soraya," he protested. "I can't—I don't pretend to replace the friends you've lost. You've lived a long life, after all. But believe that I *am* your friend."

She felt sorry, then, for her distrust. "I know you are. But you commanded me tonight; more than once. And you kept things from me. Am I your friend, or is Khalil?"

He blinked at her, as though the question had caught him entirely unawares. Then he struck his forehead and said, "Khalil! I promised to report to him at dawn."

She knew that it was a distraction, but she sighed and allowed it. "Then you'd best hurry," she said, nodding towards the grey light creeping in at the window. Saif needed no urging: he reached into his satchel and drew out the silver scrying-bowl, filling it with water from the jug. For a moment they waited in silence, and then Soraya felt the slightly nauseating tug of power as the bowl's mate in Cairo connected with this one.

Al-Ashraf Khalil's voice echoed, slightly muffled, from the water. "You're late."

Saif had stiffened, watchful and nervous as always when speaking to his master. "I apologise, my lord. We ran into trouble and had to withdraw."

"Trouble? What trouble? I was reliably informed that the tree was in fruit."

"It was, my lord, and we secured a fruit. However…" Saif sent Soraya an appealing look, but she only made an innocent face and stuffed another segment of orange into her mouth. It was, praise God, none of *her* business to keep their master happy. "The afrit itself refused to take up residence within, even on pain of death. After what happened in Tripoli, I didn't want to risk driving it out of the world."

There was a long, seething silence. "Say the word," Saif added, "and, God willing, I will return and destroy the tree."

"No," Khalil said at once. "You did well. Some things cannot be forced. No matter. Beirut itself will be ours soon enough, and the djinn Ibrahim along with it."

"The sultan is planning an assault on Beirut, then?"

"On Beirut? Don't be stupid. He already has a garrison in the city and the lion's share of the rents. No. Thanks to us, the amirs have given Qalawun permission to march against Acre."

Thanks to Saif and herself, Soraya thought, recalling last month's mission. The taste of blood was metallic in her memory… So that was the point of all that bloodshed: to give the sultan a pretext for his excursion against Acre. She wondered whether Qalawun would ever know the extent to which his heir—or the sorcerer who now wore the face of that heir—was quietly manipulating his actions.

Acre, she remembered well: a great sprawling port city that had outgrown one set of walls and was busy outgrowing a second. Spices, textiles, sugar, pottery, and slaves poured through its markets from Asia to Europe, leaving its king richer than some emperors. Of course, it was the slaves Qalawun was most worried about, for they were the greatest weakness of his empire. Without slaves, there could be no mamluks, and without mamluks, there could be no sultan. With the Tartars and Genoese tightening their grip on the other slave routes running north through the Black Sea, Acre's slave market could not be left to Christian masters.

At their master's words of approval, Saif bowed his head. "I am glad," he said in a stifled voice, "to be of some poor service to my lord."

From across the room, Soraya waved her hands and mouthed exaggerated words: *Ask him!* With his eyes, Saif begged her not to interrupt.

"Return at once to Cairo," Khalil directed, apparently unaware of these signals. "Qalawun is ailing. There are great matters afoot, and little time for me to see to them."

"*Saif!*" Soraya hissed, when the light faded from the depths of the silver bowl, and they found themselves once more alone in the room. "Why didn't you ask that boon of yours? Have *you* ever seen the old sphincter in a better mood?"

"Soraya! You can't call him that!"

Soraya made an elaborate dumb-show of looking about her, as though expecting to find Khalil lurking in some corner of the room, and failing to do so.

"It's not *like* that," Saif said, not quite managing not to laugh. "I know *he* isn't here, but you never know what invisible servants he may have watching us."

"People who eavesdrop deserve what they hear," Soraya said. "Anyway, it's true. He *is* a tight-fisted old—"

"I already asked him, anyway," Saif said; and that stopped her.

"What? When?"

"After Acre," Saif said in a low voice. "The mission was such a success—I was sure that he would grant it."

"And he said no?" Soraya ran a hand through her hair. "He should have *seen* it," she muttered. She remembered the mission well. The way the violence had caught and spread. The blood everywhere, armed Franks from across the sea killing with abandon anyone who *looked* Saracen, even their own co-religionists. She shuddered, recalling the stench of blood and entrails… "Do you think he has *any* idea—any notion at all—how we've bloodied our hands for him?"

He made no reply, and she could bear it no longer.

"Why do it?" she demanded. "Why keep dancing to his tune?"

Saif swallowed. "I don't expect you to understand, but Khalil has been like a father to me—"

"You're joking."

He flushed. "It's true. This is the first thing he's ever denied me—"

"Because you've asked so *many* things of him." He didn't answer that. "What is it, anyway? This boon he won't grant you?"

From the look of exasperation Saif gave her, she thought he would not answer. But then his shoulders slumped in defeat. "God forgive me, it's my wife."

"Your *wife?*" Saif had mentioned several times that he had a wife; always as though drawing a line around his feet and warning her not to cross it. It took her a moment to dredge up this faceless woman's name. "Ghaliyah?"

Saif nodded; and every line in his youthful-looking face was suddenly heavy and sad and old beyond his years. "That is why we couldn't afford to fail in Acre. Not when the mission to Tripoli last year was such a disaster."

* * *

The mission to Acre had been a simple one: instigate trouble between the Christians and Muslims. All the same, Saif's first two efforts had failed. A fire set at the palace had been detected and snuffed out with little difficulty, and an attempt to bribe an official to ban Muslims from worshipping in the chapel set apart for their use in the cathedral of St John had also failed. It was then, with time growing short, that he had turned to Soraya for help.

The city's population was swollen that August. A Venetian fleet, stocked with fighting-men from across the sea, had arrived ostensibly to help reinforce the Acre garrison, but perhaps intended to recapture some of the city's outlying fortresses seized, in recent years, by the Egyptian sultan. Certainly the Franks of the Coast had reason to worry, since first Antioch and then Tripoli had been besieged, captured, and put to the sword. Like most newcomers from the west, the men signed with the cross were spoiling for a fight. In addition, a great number of farmers from the fertile plains that surrounded the city, Christians and Muslims alike, had reaped a good harvest. In Acre they scented profit: the city was always hungry.

The city, like any hungry man, was always ready for a brawl. Soraya proved to be the lever Saif needed. Posing with a rather troubling capability as one of Acre's many fine courtesans, she quickly struck up an affair with one of the newly-arrived Italian knights. The trap was sprung a week or two later, when the knight and his mistress happened to attend a feast in honour of a caravan of Damascene slave-merchants. Soraya swore that it had not taken much more than a little eyelash-fluttering and a whisper in the Damascene merchant's ear as she passed behind his seat at table. In barely less time than Saif would have taken to perform a single prostration in his evening prayers, suspicion turned to murder, and murder turned to a riot. The Damascene merchant was dead; and so, by morning, were hundreds of the poor farmers, whatever their religion. To the Italians, anyone wearing a beard was a Saracen.

"I tried to protect our co-religionists," Saif had told his master, when he and Soraya returned to Cairo. Describing the black business was harder than he thought; he had to thrust his hands into his belt to stop them shaking. "I remembered that you requested a riot, not a massacre. But I am only one man."

"Don't be foolish," al-Ashraf said brusquely. Saif looked up, then, and found his master wearing a look of fierce triumph. They were in the mews, and al-Ashraf bared his teeth in a grin as he fed another strip of raw flesh to his falcon. "This is excellent news. The death of one slaver—that's a pretext. The deaths of a hundred peasants—ah, now! *That* is a provocation. If Qalawun does not send an army there will be riots in Cairo as well as in Acre."

"You are pleased, then?" Saif asked, somewhat timidly. His master had always been generous, in a careless, off-hand way; he was always ready with a purse of gold or a fine new horse. As al-Ashraf's most trusted mamluk—trained as a slave in his own household, given the inestimable gift of the Lance and its djinn, which made him invincible in battle, and finally freed to serve him as a noble amir—Saif had never wanted for anything.

Except this.

Khalil now shot a shrewd look at him. "Something you want, boy? How much?"

It was too late now to draw back, and his master seemed to be in a giving mood. Saif swallowed. "It isn't gold, my lord. It's—Ghaliyah has been coughing. The doctor says there's no hope. A year, or perhaps two at the most."

His master frowned. "Ghaliyah? The *wife?*"

"*My* wife," Saif elucidated. "I know it is a great thing to ask—but if there's anything you can do to prolong her life…"

Khalil's lips tightened. "Haven't I warned you against letting your women hold such sway over you?"

Saif's stomach was a nest of snakes, but Ghaliyah needed him to be brave, and so he said: "Haven't I served you faithfully, my lord? And have I ever asked anything else of you?"

Khalil waved an impatient hand. "Of course, of course. But I can give you two or three fresh young wives, lovely and biddable. When Acre falls there will be prizes to spare."

Saif concealed his inner repugnance. A multiplicity of wives was something that suited a great many men wiser and better than himself, but they were not for him. For one thing, it was one of the few requests Ghaliyah had ever made of him, and he could not find it in himself to hurt her. For another, what would he *do* with more wives? He had so little time left with Ghaliyah that he had turned into a miser, counting every lost hour, every lost minute that he was away from her. Why had he not spent more time with her when she was strong?

Perhaps that was a weakness he ought to overcome, but how could he overcome it now, when Ghaliyah was dying and a word from him could save her?

"Thank you, my lord," he said, as humbly as he could, "but I think that unless Ghaliyah can be saved, I would prefer to take you as an example, and keep no wives at all."

Khalil, the sultan's son, did have wives—before he was quietly captured and bled in a Cairo cellar to the chant of dark magic. As for al-Ashraf the sorcerer, who had used the magic of shared names to take his place and his face—*he* never visited the harem of his predecessor, and Saif did not know what had become of them. The wives and children there must not interest his master; and as for the cousins and aunts, their sharp eyes might have noticed some lack of resemblance between al-Ashraf the sorcerer and the sultan's rash second son.

Al-Ashraf was not pleased by Saif's attempt at flattery. "Is this your wish, or your wife's?"

"It is mine, my lord," Saif said, with a sinking heart. "If I cannot have Ghaliyah, I will have no one at all."

"Then make up your mind to have no one," Khalil snapped. "That woman has long been a bad influence upon you, and the sooner she is gone, the better. I keep away from women because they are dangerous, and it will please me to see you do the same. Don't you know that you are the laughing-stock of Cairo? Al-Rafiq Saif al-Din, who is too frightened of his first wife to take a second."

For a moment Saif was speechless. Then he clasped his hands in supplication. "My lord, please! Do not be so cruel. Even God is merciful—"

"How dare you compare me to God?" Khalil asked, and the mews was suddenly cold. Saif nearly swallowed his tongue, horrified at the blasphemy he had so nearly committed. Khalil returned the bird to its perch and stalked across the room to the door, leaving Saif staring in horror at the coloured marble pavement beneath him.

What had he done wrong? How had all their hopes been dashed in a moment!

At the door, Khalil paused. "You have always been like a son to me," he tossed back, over his shoulder. "If nothing else, you should trust that I have your best interests at heart."

***

"He really said that?" Soraya snorted. *"Trust me*—oh, yes! An easy thing for a master to tell a slave!"

Saif shrugged, but did not speak; as though telling the story had exhausted him. Soraya understood, then, the reason why there had seemed to be a dark cloud hanging over her friend for the past weeks; why there was now defeat in every line of his body where he sat slumped at the foot of his bed.

Her heart struck her. She hadn't known that his wife was *dying*. She hadn't known that he felt like *that* about her, nor that he had already asked his boon and been refused. "I'm sorry," she said, putting a hand on his arm. "I had no notion."

He jumped a little when she touched him, but then he seemed to get himself in hand, and relaxed a little beneath her touch. Soraya took her hand away, not wanting to try him further than he could bear.

"Who needs Khalil, anyway?" she growled. *"I* can help you. We'll think of something. We'll hunt down the spring where the water flows that cures all ill…"

He scoffed. "That's only a story."

"Of course it is," she said, "but look at us. *You're* immortal. *I'm* immortal. Why shouldn't Ghaliyah be immortal, too? We'll find a way. We'll find a sorcerer with a better disposition—"

"Don't," Saif begged. "Do you think I haven't racked my wits for a solution? But it can't be done without al-Ashraf, and he refuses. It's the Will of God. I've resigned myself now."

"The Will of God!" Soraya repeated, with scorn. "You're always talking about the Will of God. A fig for the Will of God! If it isn't God's will to rescue me from servitude, then I want nothing to do with Him."

Saif sent her a terrified look. "Soraya! Don't say such wicked things!"

"Am I wicked, or is God, to deprive me of what even a sparrow on the housetop may have?"

Saif passed a hand over his face, and Soraya knew she was in for a lecture.

"Khalil was right," he said. "I was wrong to suggest that he act as God might act. As *you* are wrong to dictate God's actions. Surely God must be absolutely free in his decisions, his judgements bound to no standard. Otherwise, mankind would dictate God's actions, and this is unthinkable."

"In that case, it's no wonder that Khalil should turn to forbidden magic," Soraya retorted. "How else is he to have any say over his life, if God's very nature is arbitrary? I'll wager he finds it convenient to believe in a God who can never be called upon by the weak for succor."

"Soraya," Saif begged. "Please. Don't say such things…"

Her heart struck her: he might have commanded her, but did not. "All right, then—I won't." But she refused to be like Saif; she refused to live crawling when she might die running. If God could not be relied upon to help her—why, then, shouldn't she help herself?

She said none of this. Instead: "I've never met your wife. Is she really so ill?"

Saif blinked up at her, evidently relieved by the change of topic. "She's become so weak. These days she can scarcely leave her bed."

"Let me look at her. I'm a djinn; there may be something I can do for her. Some alien influence within her body that I could purge."

"It isn't—an alien influence."

"There might still be something I could help with. I can't know unless I see her."

"I don't want you to see her, Soraya."

He looked pale: she knew that she must have forced the words out of him, all unwilling. She still couldn't help feeling stung by them. "I thought we were friends."

"What am I doing?" he muttered in an undertone, to himself. Then he blinked up at her and said, "Ghaliyah doesn't know about—us. About what we do."

Soraya's face went stiff, like a mask. "You think she'd be *jealous?*"

He flushed. "No, that's not what I—Ghaliyah doesn't know what we do for *Khalil.*"

For a moment she didn't understand. Then she did. "Oh, God. Your wife doesn't know that you're a killer."

Saif flushed even hotter.

"For someone who worries *so much* about doing the right thing, Saif, you are marvellously deceitful."

That put a haunted look on his face. "I am. I know." Again, he stared at the window with eyes that were a hundred miles away. "This is my fault. I should never have done what I did in Tripoli. I should never have let that man slip through my fingers."

"Which man?"

"The one that creature mistook me for tonight." His tongue flicked out to touch his lips; his voice sank to a whisper. "John Bessarion…"

That was her second time hearing that name. The second time she felt a great welling *something* within her. Like she might break out into laughter— or into tears. Her voice, like Saif's, was a whisper: "I know that name. How do I know that name?"

"You know it because you were in Tripoli, too. You don't remember; you lost your memories since. He's the man I warned you about—the one who tried to steal the Lance."

The Lance, Soraya well knew, was her vessel. Had the Bessarion stolen it, she might have been his to command. Had he then succeeded in breaking the soul tether, Saif would be left alone—without power, without immortality; vulnerable to any enemy.

"No fear," she said. "I have no desire to trade one master for another."

"Promise me you won't even repeat his name," Saif added, hastily.

"I promise," Soraya said, and when the compulsion left her, she added, "Saif! Be careful with your words!"

"Oh—I forgot. But please. Don't tell Khalil; he won't be pleased if he knows I've let a Bessarion live." And then Saif looked heavy again. "Perhaps he is right. Perhaps Ghaliyah *is* a bad influence on me. Look what I have become for her sake. I call Khalil my father, and I lie to him."

"He calls you a son, and treats you like a slave," Soraya retorted. "I think he'll never give you what you ask; not unless you force him to it."

Saif looked blank. "How?" Then, when she opened her mouth to reply, he answered hastily— "No! I can't do it. I have you to look after, as well as Ghaliyah. If I defy Khalil and fail, how will I keep either of you safe?"

Soraya scowled, because the question was a good one. "So long as Khalil has his afrit familiar, neither of us will ever be able to escape. Qeteb made the Lance, and the Lance binds you and me together. Until the Lance is broken and Qeteb is cast out, Khalil is our master." She let her words hang in the air a heavy moment, before adding: "So let us cast out Qeteb, break the Lance, take Ghaliyah and depart. The world is wide for a free man."

It was a plan she had already suggested once or twice; and as before, Saif looked tempted.

"But *how?*" he asked. "And what good would it do me to spirit Ghaliyah to Sicily or Baghdad, only to watch her die anyway? No—as long as I'm in Khalil's service, there's hope. I *have* to have hope."

Soraya bit her lip. The argument *always* went the same way—around in a circle, before arriving back in the same place: Saif would not leave Khalil. Today, for the first time, she felt the bite of the cold fear that perhaps he never would.

"You promised," she said. "You *promised* that you would find a way to set us both free. Did you not mean it?"

Was he really the friend he claimed to be? —Soraya hated herself for the thought the moment it drifted through her mind. If he was not truly her friend, he would never have told her about his wife.

I didn't know you were married, she heard her own voice say, from far away in a memory that was lost. *Not like this.*

And she saw eyes, grey eyes as pale as steel, looking into her own; she heard a voice say, *I forgive you.*

"You did promise, didn't you?" she stammered, feeling her heart quicken in a sudden panic. "That *was* you who promised? Saif? Saif!"

He caught the hand she flung out. She looked up into eyes so like the eyes in her memory that she felt at once the folly of her doubt.

"Soraya," he pleaded. "It was me. It was the first day you remember. We were sparring in the lower room in Cairo. I told you you were one of seven sisters. I told you the Lance was your vessel. I promised you I would free you from it. Do you remember?"

Soraya struggled to regulate her breathing. "Yes…I'm sorry. I remember now."

"Good." But his pale eyes didn't waver. "I promise you again, Soraya: one day, I *will* find a way to free us both. But please. Not until Ghaliyah is safe. Or dead."

She squeezed her eyes shut. It was always like this, she knew, with a certainty that went beyond memory. Saif would never put her good before his own. Why should he? She was not even his wife, the way Ghaliyah was.

She bent her head. "I know. It's more than I can ask…Ya, Saif! I'm glad to have at least *one* friend in this world!"

He swallowed hard, as though it cost him something to say it. "So am I, Soraya."

Chapter IV.

Evening had lessened the day's heat, and the Tentmakers' Market outside Bab Zuweilah—Cairo's south city gate—stirred into life again with the sinking of the sun. A narrow, covered alley tunneling through the sprawling suburbs south of the city, the market was lined with the booths of textile artisans of every sort. One or two craftsmen were still hard at work on the colourful appliqué hangings which would be used to screen rooms or line tents, but with the sun sinking, most had now abandoned their work and put all their effort towards selling their wares to the shoppers who had emerged with the evening breeze. Itinerant food vendors had emerged from their bakehouses and were now doing a brisk trade in hot bread and fragrant meat from the city's licensed ovens—forbidden to the ordinary citizen for fear of fires. Occasionally a donkey approached carrying fresh water from the Nile to cool throats parched from hours of crying wares in dust-laden air, and the foot traffic had to squeeze up against the stalls until it had passed.

John Bessarion picked his way through the crowd, keeping a sharp watch for the stall to which he had been directed. In Acre before he was sent south, his superiors had told him that when he wanted to send news north, he must find the booth with a blue glass lamp hanging over it. Thanks to the falling darkness, he soon spotted the rich cerulean flicker some way off. But before he could reach it, the traffic came to a halt altogether.

A lute-player was strumming and singing to the tunefully melancholic accompaniment of a flute and a drum At first it was only music. And then John heard the words and they went through him like an arrow through the body, like the arrow he had taken the day he met Rahel…

A wanderer! and I roam the lands, a wanderer…
And the step between me and my beloved is ever so vast—
A long journey and I'm wounded from it,
And the night fast approaches,
And the day is quick to vanish.

Now he, too, was helping to block the traffic. The music wound about him like a net. He ought to have been watching over his shoulder, making sure that no one had followed him from the church where he had met with the Nubians—but it was hard to watch your back when you couldn't see for tears.

And should you see my beloved, greet her on my behalf.
Reassure me and say: how is my brown-skinned girl doing, so very far away?
Wanderer! and I roam the lands, a wanderer.
I forget to tend myself, a wanderer.
All because of the separation, O my dear, a wanderer.
What has happened to me, a wanderer?

Wiping his eyes with his sleeve, John glanced over his shoulder—only to be startled by a flash of impossibly green silk.

Soraya, he thought—and then he could have wept again, for how many months had it been since he saw a friendly face?

He pushed through the crowd towards the green veil—green as rich as a powdered emerald. She must have been following him. Perhaps he ought to have kept better watch. Although, knowing Soraya, a moment ago she might have been slinking through the dark, stifling alleys in a cat's guise; he might never have seen her.

The woman in the green veil turned her head and John hesitated, suddenly doubting himself. The green was Soraya's green, but the face was an old woman's, disfigured by sorrow and messy with tears. The djinn he knew might adopt an old woman's face, but she did not weep—Soraya barely knew the meaning of tears. If she yearned for a missing beloved, she had never spoken of it to *him.*

Her head bent again. She had not caught sight of John. For a moment he wanted more than anything else to go to the woman, to ask her what distressed her. To tell her how keenly he understood her pain.

Years upon years and I am torn by affection and longing
I only want to know which road will lead to her...
And should you see my beloved, greet her on my behalf.
Reassure me and say: how is my brown-skinned girl doing, so very far away?

The crowd shifted and jostled as a donkey shoved through, briefly opening up a way through the alley to the cerulean lamp. There was no time to exchange sorrows with an old woman. John scrubbed his sleeve across his eyes again, slipped through the opening, and a moment later sought refuge within the darkness of the booth.

* * *

Abdu the pottery merchant stared at John with his solemn black eyes and said, "The story goes that the great Amr, conqueror of Egypt, camped here between Cairo and Fustat before he marched on Alexandria. Before he set off to subdue the Romans, a dove laid an egg in his tent. Taking this as a sign from God, Amr ordered his tent to be left standing in the desert. Alexandria fell, and Amr returned as he had vowed, ordering his men to pitch their tents here. The place was known to the Romans as Babylon. But we called it Fustat, the Pavilion of Egypt; and later, when the city spread north, Cairo, the Victorious."

Inside the small, cramped house behind the booth with the blue lamp, the thick walls shut out much of the lingering heat and the sound of the market's bustle. One of the *khayamiya* hangings—an appliqué design in a riot of geometrical knot-work, all scarlet, black, and turquoise—divided the front of the room from the back, lending some privacy to Abdu's wife. John had not seen her, of course; the Bedouin were generally more careful about their privacy than the women of the city. But he had heard the soft grunts of a baby feeding; and now a very soft voice spoke from behind the hanging.

"The doves," said Abdu's wife, "still lay their eggs in Cairo."

"And God is still good to us," Abdu said, handing John a cup of cold sherbert fresh from the vendor's urn. "My wife's brother has this shop in the middle of Cairo making hangings for weddings and funerals, and Saida and I go to and fro between Cairo and Acre, trading in fabrics and pottery. Terra cotta from Sicily, cobalt from Persia, white and gold lustre-ware from here in Egypt. But times are not so good for the Franks, hmm? The sultan beats the war-drums, and it becomes more dangerous and less profitable for honest merchants to go to Acre, especially after these killings. The trade is moving north, through the Black Sea, to the Tartars."

"The killings in Acre…" John sighed, dipping a stick of cucumber into thick goat yoghurt. He had not been in Acre that day; he had been in Tyre, running an errand for the Master of the Temple, and now he would never know whether he might have done anything to stop the frenzy.

He and Soraya might have succeeded in exorcising Lilith in Tripoli last year, but it seemed plain now that chaos and bloodshed still dogged the dwindling Frankish enclaves of the Coast. "The Franks of Acre never wished to see such a thing happen. Now the bloodstained garments of the slain are displayed in the mosques of Cairo, and the sultan has a reason to go to war. It is all thanks to those useless brawlers from across the sea, but—"

A murmur from behind the hanging interrupted him. Abdu nodded.

"My wife says that the Frankish lords have not run mad, suddenly, all together," he said. "We know that. *They* are not the danger we fear."

"If not them, then who?"

"The story," said Abdu happily. Smiling, John helped himself to a stuffed eggplant. Abdu was dreamy; his wife shrewd. Together, they must make a formidable pair. He could not help liking them instinctively.

"The story is that when Hulegu the Tartar had subdued Damascus, he sent his envoys to the sultan in Cairo telling him to surrender or else watch his wives and children taken into slavery. The sultan cut off their heads and displayed them on that very gate, the Bab Zuweilah." Abdu gestured vaguely in the direction of the city. "Then he sent the great Baybars to Damascus with the whole Egyptian army. And Baybars taught the Tartars the taste of defeat, which they had never known before."

Abdu opened his eyes wide at John. "What did the Franks do? They allied themselves with the Tartars. What a mistake!"

"Hulegu was no Muslim," said John.

"Hulegu was no Christian, either," Abdu countered, "yet he still favours the Christians within his dominions."

There came another murmur from Saida, behind the screen.

"My wife says," Abdu added, "that since the Tartars came, who knows which of the Christians may be spying for them? Now it is as much as anyone's life is worth to be found dealing with a Christian. And now, with the killings in Acre, and the sultan mustering his armies, well…" Abdu gave an eloquent shrug. "Trade in Acre is simply not so good as it used to be."

John looked at the screen, which wavered gently in the breeze that flowed from the open door behind, at the back of the room. There was a wail from the baby, and then a renewed sucking.

"How much?" John asked, speaking clearly so that Saida would hear.

Abdu ran his thumb along his fingertips, as though counting. "I have not three-quarters the amount of lustre-ware I should need for a journey to Acre, and that means more purchases. Also the summer is dry this year; which will mean a need for more camels."

John kept his eyes on the screen. At length Saida spoke softly, and Abdu repeated her words: "Twice what it was last time." And he named a generous sum in dinars.

John considered this. He could always commission a single messenger to run by himself—but a small trading caravan would have more security and a better excuse, should one be required. "I'll give you half the sum now, and the Master of the Temple will pay the other half once you reach Acre," he said. "But the message must go at once and you must not stop to buy more pots. My news is of the utmost importance."

"You will ruin me," Abdu protested. There was a prompting murmur from the screen, and he added: "If we go without the pots, the Temple must pay extra."

John reached into his money-belt and extracted the roll of gold within, planting it on the mat before Abdu. "Tell Beaujeu I offered four times this, if you will. He will not haggle with you. Without this information, all the gold in Acre will not profit us."

There was a moment's silence, and then Abdul darted out a hand to snatch up and weigh the coins in his palm, before slipping them beneath the screen to his wife. "Done!" he said. "May God repay us for our kindness to you, and ward off any harm!"

"Amen to that," John said, extracting the letter from his robe and putting it directly into Abdu's hand. "It is ciphered, but its presence may give you away. Try not to be caught with it."

Everything was in the letter—the whole story as it had unfolded here in Cairo: the protests in the mosques, the muster of the sultan's army north of the city, the confirmation, from more than one source, that the target of this gathering storm was indeed Acre, rather than Nubia or Tartar-held Baghdad. John's stomach tightened, thinking of the strange places he had gone to gather this information. The carpenter's workshop in the shadow of the city's immense dungheap, where a nervous workman newly returned from Baalbek had described the massive siege engines commissioned by the sultan after the fall of Tripoli, and their slow progress south to Damascus. A palace near the gate of the Citadel, fragrant with starflowers, where a courtier of venerable age and irreproachable reputation had confirmed that the sultan had at last received his amirs' assent to assault Acre. Last of all, a tumbledown church where scarified scholars from the kingdom of Nubia confirmed that they had seen no signs on their borders of a new Egyptian incursion.

John would breathe more easily once this information was out of his hands and well on its way to Acre. And it struck him that his anxiety was not merely for his own sake—stranded in a hostile city, in a hostile future, earning his bread as a spy. He worried for the Christian enclaves of the coast, now whittled down to a few isolated cities: Beirut, Tyre…and Acre, queen of them all… How could they survive the combined might of Egypt and Damascus, however well fore-warned?

John gave himself a shake. This was not *his* failing kingdom to rescue. His task was to free Soraya, the one being in the world who might be able to help him escape this terrifying future and make his way back to his own native time to fight the battle on familiar ground. Better if the Saracen heresiarchs had never built their empire at all; never erased native languages, never crushed their subjects slowly beneath a weight of taxes and indignities.

Abdu and Saida were murmuring together. Now Abdu said: "There will be no more journeys to Acre after this, John Zakar."

Although he used the name he had adopted for the journey, the grave certainty in the Egyptian's voice reminded him of his beloved Rahel. John felt as though a cold drip had run down his neck. "Why do you say that?"

"Times are changing," Abdu said. "The winds of fate blow here and there as they will, and so does the will of God."

"Do you know something that I don't?" he asked on impulse, but Abdu gave him a cool, level stare.

"You don't always have to lick your thumb to figure out which way the wind is blowing, my friend."

"Indeed not," John said, forcing a laugh. The night beyond the house had grown dark, but within there was light and good food, and he felt himself reluctant to leave. He knew that he should, of course—that he should hurry away and watch his back, lest he had been followed, lest he had left Abdu and Saida, and the all-important letter, in danger. The last thing he should do was linger here with the only people in the city to whom he could speak freely.

And the step between me and my beloved is ever so vast, he thought, with a bitter pang.

Perhaps it was because he really needed to know; and perhaps it was because he wanted an excuse to linger. He cleared his throat, and said,

"Does the name *Qeteb* mean anything to you?"

"Five and Thursday!" Abdu muttered, at once raising his hand, palm outward, in the sign against the evil eye. "Don't you know better than to speak that name aloud?"

"What is his business with *that* afrit?" Saida asked, startled into loud speech. And John, feeling their terror like a physical presence, wondered whether the shadows in the house had become suddenly thicker and blacker, and the sounds from the street more muffled.

"No forbidden arts, if that's your fear," he reassured them. "The Hairy One is an enemy of mine." And he could only go home when Soraya was freed, and Soraya could only be freed once Qeteb was exorcised, for it was his power that bound her.

"An enemy of yours!" Abdu repeated, chewing the end of his moustache doubtfully. "No man ought to have doings with afrits, for good *or* for ill!"

His whisper was interrupted by the sudden, piercing sound of a donkey's bray—not from the street, but from the other side of the screen, where a door stood open to admit the evening breeze drifting from the courtyard. The baby startled with a cry, and Abdu, sounding as though he was glad for the interruption, said, "What is the matter with the creature *now?*"

"Any doings with the Hairy One were none of mine," John added, as the movement of a shadow beneath the screen indicated that Saida was going out to tend the animals. "A friend of mine is oppressed by the demon. I swore an oath to set her free."

Abdu nodded, but before he could say anything, there came a scuffle from behind the screen, and a gasp.

"Beloved?" Abdu said, nervously.

There was no sound at all now, not even from the street. A muffled silence had fallen all about them. Abdu rose to his feet and gazed down at John with terrified eyes. "Were you followed?" he asked in a whisper.

"No." And he had not been. He was sure of it. He had watched his back all the way from the church of St Demiana, and had never seen the same face twice. "Not by any mortal," he added, for the thought occurred to him that perhaps he had not known Soraya as well as he supposed.

Perhaps she *did* have a lost beloved, to mourn in the street.

Abdu was still standing motionless, searching his face with a faint line between his brows, when the screen behind him fell. John watched it as in a dream—saw the dim glimmer of evening from the open doorway beyond the screen; saw the intense colours of two veils side by side, emerald and black; saw the face of Abdu's wife with huge, terrified eyes above the fine-boned brown hand that clutched a damascened blade to her throat.

Speechless with horror, neither of the men said a word. Saida dragged her baby closer to her bosom; and then there was silence again, and stillness.

Soraya stared at John from over Saida's shoulder. *Now* she wore the face he knew her by: ageless and unearthly beautiful. Her black eyes, immense in the lamplight, fixed on John.

"What did you say?" she hissed.

Chapter V.

The woman was holding a child, which made the second man in the room foolish. With a face as grey as putty, he pulled out a long dagger with hands that trembled. "Let go of them!" he blustered. "I'll call the muhtasib!"

Soraya barely heard him. Her own hands were trembling so much that she was amazed she did not draw blood purely by accident. Perhaps the desert woman herself could be thanked for that: she put up her free hand and seized Soraya's wrist, and that held the knife steady.

For a long moment Soraya could only look *him* in the eye—the man she had followed here, the Templar spy. The piercing, iron-grey eyes. The iron-grey hair. The spare, wiry frame. At this first clear sight of him, a sense of bone-deep recognition overwhelmed her.

What was *wrong* with her? A moment ago, when she had shed the mangy, flea-bitten mongrel shape with which she had followed him all the way from the church of St Demiana, Soraya had been ambushed by the last thing she expected: a troupe of street musicians. A few words of their song, and she had been blind and helpless. The welling emotion had broken out into *salt-water* on her face.

I've lost something. What have I lost? she had asked herself, at last distilling the feeling into words. But there was no answer. It had taken a little while to compose herself, and then the spy she had followed was gone, and only a frantic search of the shops and houses lining the market enabled her to track him down.

Now, one look at his face had her drowning again, helpless in the certainty that she *knew* this man.

And that did not even reckon with the fact that, even as she lingered in the courtyard, she had heard him speak the name of her worst enemy. Declare that that worst enemy must be destroyed.

Now, her captive's husband was backing, inch by slow inch, for the door; doubtless planning to call for help. The woman clung to her wrist with a grip like steel. And the spy, rising to his feet, looked upon her with recognition and dawning—was he *glad* to see her?

Was *she* glad to see *him?*

"Soraya," he said in a voice choked with joy. "Now behold—summer has come!"

Summer? she thought, disbelievingly. And then: *Oh, God! Is* he *weeping now?* Gently, before she could move, he took the knife from her unresisting hand. Her captive squirmed free. Soraya backed a step, her heart thundering with something that was either love or terror, her mind too fuzzy to respond appropriately before the man reached out and pulled her into a fierce embrace.

His touch was like the Nile flood across parched earth. The life which a moment before had seemed scorched and desolate became utterly cool and pleasant. All was well. She was wanted. She was *loved.*

A gasp of pure relief escaped her. Even Saif took care, even when accepting a piece of bread from her hands, not to let his fingers brush her skin. He said that he was her friend, but she did not know how that *felt.* Now, in the crushing tension of the stranger's arms, she could read an incomprehensible truth.

"It's all right!" the spy declared to his fellow conspirators. "She's a friend!"

A friend. That pierced the utter disarray of her being; her thoughts ceased to drown and began to flail. A friend—to the sort of vile and shameless fellow that would abandon himself to such intimacies? To a Templar *spy?* What would Saif say? She was *supposed* to stay out of sight. She was *supposed* to report back to him. How would she explain any of this? Why had the spy been asking about *Qeteb?* Which was the friend he meant to free from that afrit? What would she tell Saif?

Why did he still have his arms around her?

As a djinn, Soraya had greater strength than any mortal alive; and now she freed herself from the embrace with a forceful shove that made the stranger grunt with pain. Her knife was still locked in his hand, but she twisted it easily from his grip and put it to his throat.

"Who *are* you?" she hissed.

The joy in his eyes faded. Her heart twisted. She didn't want to see it go.

"You don't remember," he said softly, sadly. There was an endless, unbearable moment when she wanted to shout at him again, if only to prevent herself from reaching out. Then he said:

"I am John Bessarion."

It was the third time she'd heard the name since that night in the garden at Beirut a fortnight ago—the third time it went through her like a knife. Now, a bitter taste filled her mouth. Of course it was John Bessarion. Of course it was the man Saif had warned her against, the thief who wanted the Lance. Who wanted *her*.

"Of course," she hissed, pressing a little closer with the knife. Her knuckles brushed against the pulse at his throat, telling her that his heart was beating a good deal faster now. He was afraid. *Good.* "Tell me what you want with the sun god."

"With whom?"

"That afrit," she repeated, impatient. "The Hairy One." *Qeteb*, she did not say.

Perhaps the knife to his throat forced him to be truthful. "Soraya," he said—how did he know her *name?* "I promised to free you from him."

"So that *you* can be my master instead?"

For the first time he looked angry—outraged, in fact. "Is that what al-Mukhtar has told you? And you *believed* him?"

"Al-Mukhtar is my *friend.*"

"Oh, God," he said, and looked sick. Soraya did not know what to think about that look. Then he snarled, "You aren't his *friend*, Soraya. You're his *slave.*"

That was too much. Soraya's left hand flew. The spy staggered away, falling back against the stone wall.

His hand slipped into his robe and just like that, Soraya realised it had all been a gambit. The anger. The way he'd baited her.

She knew, somehow, even before the same hand emerged, the peculiar weapon it would be holding—a crossbow, small enough to be concealed beneath a scholar's robe, ready-loaded with a small but wicked dart.

Soraya was already moving, seizing him by the throat, pulling back her dagger to strike. Saif had warned her not to trust the Bessarion, but he'd never warned her against killing him.

Those iron-grey eyes, intense with concentration, looked into hers. Soraya faltered. Her knife-hand felt absolutely nerveless. For a moment she was wide open, defenceless.

"I'm going to free you, my summer," he said, kindly. "You'll see."

Then he put the dart through her. Soraya felt a moment of agony as her labouring body was torn apart; then oblivion as her soul drifted free and was drawn back, as quick as thought, to the vessel of the Lance.

The dissolution of her body brought no relief. Within the narrow confines of the Lance, Soraya seethed voicelessly over her own failure. She'd been sent to follow the spy—to follow *John Bessarion* himself!—and what had she done? Let him see her, fail to glean any useful information, and then fail either to kill or capture him?

What sorcery had he used against her? But no, he'd had no afrit at his command, not even a lesser djinn. Surely she would have sensed such a familiar, had the man been in possession of one. It was her own nature, Soraya determined. She was a spirit, unfitted for the heady experience of embodiment, and this proved it. …But no, she knew what it was to be touched; helping Saif often meant bartering embraces. Why was this one so different?

To her relief, Saif did not leave her long in the Lance. At his summons, she burst forth and clothed herself in flesh. It was night, and the lamps were burning in a courtyard with a fountain at the centre of it. She recognised the palace at once, not just by the muted black-and-white courses of stone that banded the walls, but also by the great blackened spirit-light that roiled nearby as she donned bodily form, by the creeping of her mortal skin afterward at the feeling of oppression in the air.

Al-Ashraf Khalil's dwelling was hushed and silent, as ever; its master did not approve of sound or bustle. Soraya turned to find Saif vigilant beside her, watching over the two Nubians who knelt on the pavement with bound hands and the rank scent of nervous sweat hanging over them. She recognised them at once, of course; they were the scholars who had met with John Bessarion in the church of St Demiana. Unable to catch them in time to hear their talk, Saif had sent her to track the Templar spy while he followed the Nubians. Following them must have yielded no helpful information, either. Which was why he had snatched them up and brought them here for questioning.

How desperate must he be to curry favour with his master? Soraya sniffed. "God be thanked! Khalil will surely change his mind and grant your every wish, once you present him with a pair of Nubian spies."

Saif looked hopeful. "Do you really think so?"

"You're *hopeless*. Nubian spies are everywhere in Cairo. I have bad news."

"Report. If you please," he added, as an afterthought, to remove the sting of command from his words.

Soraya glanced up and down the peristyle, reassuring herself that Khalil was nowhere within earshot. She sank her voice low. "I got close enough to the spy to overhear his talk. First, he's the man you warned me about."

Saif stiffened. "Not—John Bessarion?"

He spoke the words in a whisper. Soraya swallowed hard, wondering how much to give away. Something warned her not to tell Saif just how much the stranger had affected her. "Yes. He did more or less as you said he would."

"Thank God. He can't surprise us now," Saif said.

Again, Soraya bit back a wild laugh. What John Bessarion had done to her tonight went far beyond *surprise*—and the worst part was that she had no way to prevent it happening again.

"He was asking for news of the Hairy One," she whispered.

"Are you sure of that? You did not mishear?" Saif seemed to be possessed by a strange, repressed excitement.

Soraya tore her thoughts from the way that Saif's hands tightened and loosened upon the haft of the Lance. Well: the Bessarion *said* that he wished to cast out Qeteb, to set her free. Did he really mean it? He might lose her, if he did that. He must have some other way to control her.

"I heard correctly. But *why?*"

Instead of answering, Saif paced away from her a step or two. Restlessly, he turned back. "Listen," he said, "all is as God wills it, but we can't let *him* know anything of this."

Him. Their master.

Soraya shivered at the thought that they were here in the master's very palace, plotting against him.

Saif glanced at the two men kneeling at their feet. *"They* can't let him know anything of this," he muttered. Soraya opened her mouth to protest, but Saif moved with unnatural speed, in one fluid stroke drawing his knife across two unsuspecting throats.

The Nubians slid to the pavement and died with a horrible gurgle.

"Saif," Soraya choked in shock.

He turned to her, raising between them the blood-slick blade. The scent, hot and metallic, oppressed her senses. Soraya clamped a hand across her mouth, wondering for a moment whether he had gone out of his mind. But of course Saif could never risk Khalil knowing that his enemy had been allowed to live, and was now plotting to exorcise his familiar.

"Soraya, you have to trust me," he hissed. The whites of his eyes were blinding in the torchlight. "Whatever he says—whatever he makes you feel—that man is *not* your friend."

She struck away his wrist, the threatening blade, red with the stench of death. "I'm not a *fool.*"

"We have to kill him. We have to bring Khalil his head. All right?"

"All right. Don't put *blood* in my face, Saif. You know the smell makes me sick."

He threw the dagger blade-down into the soft grass beside them; little good it did, given the thickening pool of blood at her feet. "You're my only friend, Soraya," he said, pleadingly. "The only one I can trust. Please—don't let that man drive a wedge between us."

"You should trust me better," she snapped, stepping away. It was impossible not to notice that the coming of John Bessarion had had an effect upon Saif nearly as profound as upon herself. He was not ordinarily so quick with his knife; in the city, which did not know al-Ashraf's most trusted mamluk as the killer al-Mukhtar, he was called al-Rafiq, *the Gentle.*

She knew that he disliked killing; but he did it anyway—just now, because he thought his wife's life might depend upon it. Because he could not trust them to keep their silence, not to buy life and freedom at the price of betraying him to Khalil.

At her words, Saif's shoulders sagged with relief. "I'm sorry," he said, glancing down at the bodies. "Can you..."

Soraya snorted, but she raised a hand and exerted her power, dissipating the bodies into the dust and moisture that composed them. In another moment, there was no sign that the Nubians had ever been there.

She felt uneasy, all the same. Saif had trusted *her* with a great many things, any of them enough to win their master's hatred. He might not cut her throat, or pierce her with a crossbow-bolt; but he might take it into his head to command her; and that thought was scarcely more appealing.

A door opened above them. They both heard Khalil's voice speaking to an attendant, and his footsteps descending the stair from the loggia above. Saif straightened, snatching up his dagger and wiping the remaining traces of blood away. Soraya shrank behind him, pulling a fold of her veil up to conceal all of her face but the eyes, and darkening the fibres of her clothes until she blended into the shadows.

She barely heard as Saif made his report—and his excuses. He described only the most routine mission—that, following a hint from a beggar at the monastery of St Simon the Tanner, they had arrived at the church of St Demiana only in time to see the Templar spy and the Nubians leaving it; that Saif had followed and captured the Nubians, but that both of them had chosen death rather than face questioning at Khalil's hands. As for the Templar spy, Soraya had followed him back to his lodgings at the monastery beneath the cliffs of Muqattam, before returning to the city. There was, in other words, nothing particularly noteworthy about the meeting, nor the Templar. Only the Nubians had something to hide.

It was a skilful tale, deflecting all attention from John Bessarion and towards the southerners. Half of Soraya's mind did not bother to listen to it, instead once again rehearsing the scene in the Tentmakers' Market, trying to find some sense in it.

The other half heard, and marvelled once again that Saif should be such a skilled deceiver.

Chapter VI.

"You said that was a *friend!*" Saida breathed, her voice high-pitched with terror. *"Don't you think you might have been mistaken!?"*

John Bessarion lowered his crossbow, shaking as the tension of the past few minutes bled out of him. Soraya's body had fallen into a damp slurry of sand and ashes upon the rug, leaving Abdu gaping in astonishment, raising his palm against the evil eye. Saida's baby jumped in her arms and began to wail, high and thin.

With a gasp, Saida snatched for a discarded mask—woven in flame-coloured linen and hung with brass spangles—amidst the cushions where she had sat. John averted his eyes, embarrassed to have breached her privacy, however unintentionally.

"She *is* a friend," he said, when the wailing quieted and Abdu had restored the screen and his wife's sense of dignity. "Only she's forgotten me. They robbed her even of that." No, it was worse than that. *Al-Mukhtar is my friend.* He shook his head in disbelief. They'd robbed her even of her hatred of the man who enslaved her. The real Soraya, *his* Soraya, would be furious. *He* was furious. Little good though it would do, he wished the Chosen was here in the sights of his crossbows.

Abdu pointed at the dust-heap on the carpet. "You *said* you had no unlawful dealings with the Unseen!"

"Nor do I." Not that his bare word would mean anything to these people, especially after seeing a body disintegrate on their carpet. John sighed. "Forgive me. It isn't safe for you here any more: you should go to Acre, *now.* Take your brother-in-law with you. No—go now, and leave a message for him to follow you once he returns. I'm sorry."

Leaving them to prepare for their hurried journey, John slipped out by the rear courtyard. Immediately south of the city gate was a cluster of markets, now walled in and, in many cases, roofed over. He walked south-east, away from the gate towards Saladin's great citadel, with many vigilant glances around him. But of course it made no difference *now.* Soraya was the one who had followed him to the tentmaker's house, and he had dealt with her.

All the same, he kept his crossbow ready in his hand, tucked beneath the thick shawl over his shoulders which marked him as a travelling scholar. A Syrian priest, come to read manuscripts in the venerable monasteries of Egypt—that was the pretended identity under which he travelled. Tonight he was glad that he had risked his identity by carrying the crossbow, but if he was caught by the sultan's enforcers in the streets after curfew, he would find the weapons difficult to explain.

Night had fallen, and there were few lamps to light his way. The crowds in the streets were thinning, whether because the hour of curfew was approaching, or because he was now out of the markets and among the palaces that surrounded the citadel, John did not know. His road took him past the citadel itself—a high fortress with honey-coloured towers at the corners, crowned with a domed palace and the spires of a mosque—and up the steep road beyond it that led to his lodgings, a small monastery tucked beneath the great cliffs of the Muqattam mountain. The dust in the air, kicked up by the traffic, cleared away to allow the light of the stars to illuminate his journey. Some minutes later he was knocking at the gate to the monastery of St Simon the Tanner. The doorkeeper, reluctant to admit latecomers after dark, demanded to see his wrist. The instruction puzzled John for a moment, but then a thought struck him; he rolled up his sleeve and showed the man his Watcher's Mark, an *I* superimposed upon an *X*, inked into the skin on his forearm. That did the trick. The door opened.

The monastery was a small walled enclosure, containing a tower over the gate, two or three churches and a handful of minuscule chapels, and in addition to these a refectory, a library, and several tall buildings containing the cells of the monks. One of the smaller of these buildings operated as a guest-house for travellers, and it was here that John had found lodging.

At this hour, most of the monks were busy in the main church, chanting the Kyrie in the day's last office. With the sound of the distant voices, and the solid *thud* of the gate closing behind him, a weight seemed to roll from John's shoulders. He took a deep breath. The air smelled fresh and green here, for there were palm-trees and a profusion of green shrubs growing in the far corners of the courtyard, and in the one long bed that bisected it.

Then he went briskly across the gravel, *crunch-crunch*, towards the guesthouse. Like the rest of the monastery, it was built of mud brick with a white stucco, yellowed by the desert's dust; there were grilles across the windows of graceful wrought-iron, bent into the shape of crosses and painted white to match the walls. A stair led up into the high portico of the guest-house. John had nearly reached the door when a scuffle from the shadows brought his heart into his mouth and his crossbow into his hand.

"There you are!" said the youngster who had been sitting in the portico like an ambush of one. He jumped to his feet and John saw the flash of friendly teeth within his luxuriant black beard. "I beg your pardon for not being on hand to guide you into the city, earlier, as I promised. I must have overslept. Did you find your way to your destination?"

John was quite sure the young novice had not overslept. Lads of his eager and conscientious disposition did not, as a rule; which was why John had taken care to be on the road to the city that morning two hours before the appointed time.

"Brother Simon," he said, thankful that the boy had taken a name easy to remember, since it was the same as that of the saint to which the monastery was dedicated. "I had no trouble, thanks to the directions you gave me last night at dinner."

"Wonderful!" The monk pushed open the double door that led to the guest-house, allowing a stream of light to flow out. "There's a tray for you on the side table, if you haven't eaten."

"Thanks, I have. Help yourself," John added, as he saw the look of longing that at once entered the youth's eyes.

Brother Simon sighed wistfully. "Saint Anthony fed but once a day, and fasted often."

"It would be the greater sin to waste good bread and cucumbers," John said gravely, not wanting to insult the young monk with a reference to his youth. He pulled open the door to the cramped cell, barely large enough for a bed and a desk, which had been allotted him. "Besides, you must sit and answer my questions, and I would not have you go away unrewarded."

"You are a man of great learning, Father John, and I will do as you say," Simon said willingly, seating himself cross-legged by the low desk, and taking an enormous bite of the bread.

John's attention was arrested by the sight of the monk's wrist as he reached for the food. Beneath the black hem of his sleeve, Simon's wrist was tattooed with a small cross—a Watcher's Mark, surely, in the Coptic style.

There had been a time when the sight of a Coptic Mark would have excited his suspicions. In Jerusalem, where he had once ruled as Praetorian Prefect for the emperor in Constantinople, it was said that the Copts were heretics, believing that the humanity of Christ had been subsumed by his deity. It had been John's task, accordingly, to imprison and persecute them in the name of the emperor and of orthodoxy. It was a past he had come to repent; and it was doubtful whether anyone now, more than six centuries later, still remembered it.

He remembered it, however, with shame. Rahel, who had been born in Alexandria, had always insisted that the Copts were practically orthodox: Miaphysites, not Monophysites. He had not believed her until far too late— until he had already begun to doubt whether it was right at all to persecute heretics in the emperor's name.

Still, John doubted whether Watchers who had lived so long and so contentedly beneath Saracen rule were truly capable of performing the exorcism for which he had come all the way to Cairo. They were a powerless people. And that, he thought with a shiver, recalling the previous exorcism he had performed with the help of the Watchers in Tripoli, was a problem.

He cleared his throat and touched his wrist. "Is it safe to wear one of those in Egypt?"

Mouth full, Brother Simon sent him a quizzical look. John added, "I heard that al-Mukhtar, the Chosen, has been killing anyone found wearing a Watcher's Mark."

The monk swallowed quickly. "Assuredly he has! Why else should so many of the Copts wear them so openly?"

It was John's turn to look puzzled. "They *want* to die, then?"

"If God wills it! The glory of the Copts is in our martyrs. The more martyrs we have, the stronger those who are left become—and to become a martyr oneself, what privilege! To have the honour of dying for the Lord and going to see him face to face!" Brother Simon sent him a cheerful grin. "But this is what I meant to have warned you about today. If you go into Cairo, be sure to return to the monastery by the hour of curfew. Wear the blue turban of the Christians, and do not think to ride a horse. And there are troublemakers who will try to quarrel with you when they see that you are a Christian; just keep your head down and appeal to the sultan's enforcers."

"I'm unlikely to find myself stealing a horse," John said drily, but inwardly he felt sickened. So this was the sort of humiliation the Saracens inflicted upon their Christian subjects. Distinctive clothing, public opprobrium, and other visible marks of subjection; all of them to be borne in silent humility, with the head down, as if they were Jews.

His thoughts turned to his wife. Rahel still appeared in his dreams, his only link with the past in which he had been born. After he had been snatched away from her across the vast reaches of time, she and the children had been left without him in a Jerusalem forced to surrender to the Saracen heretics. Had Rahel, too, been subjected to humiliation and public harassment? Was she, too, forced to submit without lifting hand or voice in self-defence?

"How do you bear it?" he asked softly. "Six hundred years of humiliation?"

"Humiliation?" Brother Simon gulped another mouthful of bread. "Why, Father John, don't you know that no one is better at humiliation than us Copts? Humility is what we do best—humility, suffering, and repentance! Where else in the world will you find so many saints and martyrs? And it isn't as though we don't have things to take pride in. Our forefathers are the ones who built the Pyramids! It was we who became the first church outside the Holy Land itself. It was we who suffered martyrdoms by the thousand under the ancient emperors, Nero and Diocletian. It was *our* Saint Athanasius who defended the holy faith against Arius at Nicaea. The whole world knows what it owes to the Copts!"

John could not help smiling. Perhaps the boy was right; even John could admit that Egypt had once been the cradle of the faith. Yet, evidently something had been lost along the way. He settled for tact: "It is a shame you have lost so much. I recall a time—that is, I have read of a time—when Egypt was a Christian land." Now, perhaps only one in five of the turbans he had seen in the marketplaces of Cairo was blue, and perhaps one in ten among the palaces in the vicinity of the citadel, none of them great lords.

"But undoubtedly we have become stronger!" said the incorrigible Simon. "The blood of the martyrs sustains us, and the removal of false believers purifies us."

"I suppose, then, that there must be a great many Gifts among your Watchers," said John, somewhat disingenuously.

"Ah, you cannot imagine how many!" Simon waved his hands, indicating the monastery and perhaps the entire landscape: "Have you not heard of the miracle worked by the good Saint Simon, here on this very spot?"

"I have not."

"Then I will tell you, for your encouragement. Three hundred years ago in Cairo there was a caliph who wished to persecute the Christians. He summoned the pope of the Copts before him and asked, 'I read in your Gospels that a person of faith can move a mountain and order it be thrown into the sea. Is this true?' The pope said that it was true, and the caliph asked him to prove it by moving the Muqattam mountain. If the mountain did not move, then the word of God was not true, and therefore all the Copts would be killed.

"The pope called all the Copts to pray and fast for three days. During the fast, the good Saint Simon, who was a shoemaker, had a dream from God instructing the Copts to pray in a certain manner. So, on the third day of their fast, all the Copts gathered to pray together, according to Saint

Simon's instructions. Their prayer was only this: 'God, have mercy.' They repeated the prayer four hundred times in each direction, and by the end of the prayer, the ground began to shake. The mountain rose high into the air—so high that they actually saw the sun beneath the mountain!

"But on that day the caliph said, 'Enough! Enough, or else the city will be turned upside down!' And at the end of his life it is said that he became insane. They cannot say that he became a Christian, for it would be a shame to them. Now, can anyone say that we do not have great saints and mighty Watchers among us?"

There was absolute conviction in the boy's voice, but John thought of the great solid mass of rock that overshadowed the monastery and dwarfed the city below, and he found it difficult to believe that the faith of Copts was quite up to the task. Certainly, *he* had never seen such a miracle worked by any Portentor.

"That is a great encouragement," he said, and tried his best to sound as though he meant it.

* * *

"Soraya will surely recover her memories," Rahel said, "once Qeteb has been cast out."

"Yes, but until then she might as well be a stranger. Al-Mukhtar even has her believing that she's *his* friend. That cur." John was silent a moment before finding the words for his deepest fear. "What if *I* didn't know the real Soraya, either? What if I retrieve her memories, and she…changes?"

"John," Rahel soothed him, her voice doing what he wished her touch still could. "We've had many friends turn on us, I know. Don't listen to your fears."

He sighed. Normally this was the best part of every day—the time when he and Rahel met in their dreams, the one thing that made their long separation bearable—more bearable, indeed, than the other, briefer separations of their marriage. Each night, she brought him news of the children, of the unfolding drama of life under heretic occupation six hundred years before. He could only hope that he brought her a fraction of the counsel, companionship and comfort she brought him.

Tonight, he felt less calm. The distance between them ached like a wound. Rahel and he were seated side by side in the monastery courtyard, watching the stars, their hands overlapping but not touching. Never touching; and therefore never at rest.

"She gave me one clue," he said, because talk was more use than shouting; and action, which was better than either, required counsel. "She overheard me speaking to the Bedouin pottery merchant about Qeteb, and she called him *the sun god.* I can't try an exorcism if I can't get to grips with the creature. If Qeteb is a sun god, then perhaps somewhere there's a temple to which he will come when summoned."

"Heliopolis," Rahel said, promptly. She had grown up in Alexandria; she knew the land better than he did. "They used to call it the House of Ra, the sun god. The city has been deserted for centuries already, of course, but whatever's left of it ought to lie just north of you. An easy walk, perhaps a few hours. Possibly there are still ruins there to which Qeteb was once bound… Or," she added, "if there's nothing left of Heliopolis, try the ruins of Memphis next. Those will be south of you, past Babylon. At a long stretch there may be some temples or monuments dedicated to the sun on the west bank of the river, among the Pyramids. But those are mainly monuments to the dead. How *are* the Pyramids, anyway? Still there?"

"Still there," John said. Even on the far side of the river from Cairo, the three mountains of stone loomed over the city like a manmade version of the Muqattam mountain. No doubt in another six hundred years they would still be there; it would take more than a few millennia to reduce them to rubble. He hoped that Heliopolis was equally reliable… "I'll set out for Heliopolis in the morning."

"Not alone? John," she reproached him when he nodded. "Qeteb is at least as powerful as Lilith ever was, and this is his place of power. You need other Watchers."

"I don't know if I can find any."

"Not among the Copts?"

John sighed. Brother Simon boasted of the Egyptian martyrs, but surely most of his co-religionists must be content to hug their revelation to their bosoms, loath to endanger themselves by bearing witness to their faith. John could not accept that this was how it had to be, when Christ had preached a world filled with a knowledge of God that ran deep as ocean water. "Beloved, they've spent centuries genuflecting to the Saracens. Would true Watchers humble themselves in such a way?"

"I don't know," Rahel said, with a glimmer of laughter. "At present we're all genuflecting to the Saracens, John. Even me. Even you."

John felt his jaw tighten. "Temporarily," he insisted.

"Does that make us false Watchers? Or weak?"

"No, but…" Remembering the fears that had seized him earlier that evening, he turned to look into her dark, mirthful eyes. "Rahel. Do you know what it is like these days to be a Christian in Egypt? They must wear clothing that marks them out as Christian. They are forbidden certain dignities. There are steep taxes, and they are barred from high office, and forbidden to speak their native tongue. And let them comply never so carefully, they may still be set upon by brawlers, or forced out of the offices they do hold, at the sultan's pleasure." He searched her face. "My love, if things like that were happening in Jerusalem—"

"John," she said steadily. "Nothing of that sort is happening in Jerusalem."

"But if it was, you'd tell me?"

"If it was, I'd tell you. But it hasn't been so bad, truly. The Saracens are only a small garrison here, and they don't conduct themselves the way the Persians did when they captured Jerusalem—rounding up priests and bishops, inciting the Jews to riot against the Christians and slaughter them. Everything is peaceful. Indeed, it's said that—"

She caught herself.

"Go on," John said, watching her bite her lower lip.

"It's said that the Nestorians and Monophysites in this city are better at peace than they ever have been," Rahel said.

John uttered a ragged laugh. "My fault, I suppose!"

"It's not your name they curse, dear. It's that of the emperor."

"I warned them," John growled. "At Oliveta—I warned the Watchers. After what we'd done to the heretics, of course they'd prefer the rule of other heretics to the rule of the orthodox. But they'll find out their mistake in time. The Saracens must know they can't transform an entire country in a few months. Wait until they feel secure in their conquests; then you'll feel how heavy their hand can be."

"And how long will *that* take?" Rahel asked him. "Six hundred years?"

John glanced at her sidelong. "Don't laugh," he said.

"I am not laughing," she said. "But don't you believe? No matter who rules on the earth, is Christ not Lord? Does he not bless his people, even when they are ruled over by strangers?"

"Of course he does," John said. "I do believe it."

But it *mattered* who ruled on the earth. It *mattered* that his children, his people should not be humiliated and persecuted. It *mattered* that they should be spared centuries of suffering.

So much was riding on him. *So* much. There were nights when the task felt impossible: exorcise Qeteb, liberate Soraya, return to the past. Undo the invasion. Save the Christian East.

But he had to do it, because there was no one else who could.

Chapter VII.

It was scarcely mannerly, but Eschiva's impatience had been mounting for months. When Margaret, the Lady of Tyre, at last disembarked from the lateen-rigged nava by which she had arrived at Beirut's port, Eschiva lost no time in prying her friend away from the smiles and speeches of the self-important kinsman who had escorted her to the palace.

"Come away to the privy garden; I'm dying to speak with you, my dear," she said, winding her arm through Margaret's. To the attendants who had gathered to meet the Lady in the great audience-hall, with its splendid marble panels and the dragon presiding over the fountain at the centre, she said, "You may have the afternoon to yourselves. And no, Balian. I'm aware that the minstrels have been practicing for days, but I'll hear them tonight at supper. What! are they a dish of oysters, to go bad in the heat? Plaisance, if you will bring the things I asked you to arrange, we shall require no other attendants."

That shook off the officious Balian, and a moment later they were alone, arm in arm in the garden. The air was fragrant with the scent of citrus and lavender, blended in with the salty smell of the sea. Above them, the orange-tree stirred in the breeze. In the two weeks since the Egyptians had made their attempt upon it, Eschiva had doubled her guard and set an additional sentry to watch the tree by night, like the angel with the flaming sword who had guarded Paradise; but no further attempt had been made, and she was just beginning to feel at ease again.

Margaret was laughing.

"I didn't even have a good look at your sons," she said. Amaury and Rupen had been assembled with other attendants and family members to welcome the Lady of Tyre. "They *are* my nephews, you know, if only by marriage."

"The boys are not a dish of oysters, either," Eschiva reminded her friend with a laugh. Now that she had Margaret with her in the garden she felt a little less fevered with anticipation. The two of them had married the Montfort brothers of Tyre; now both brothers were dead, but the friendship between the widows remained. "I'm sorry; I've barely asked how you are."

Margaret, who was as fat and guileless as Eschiva was lean and ironical, fluttered a gracefully bejewelled hand. "Oh! much the same as ever, as you can see. But what's all this fever of hurry? There isn't a *man*, is there?"

Eschiva opened her eyes wide in amazement. "Oh, yes! Because this blessed city leaves me all the time in the world for philandering! My good gossip, you're mistaking me for my sister Isabella, God grant her rest."

Margaret shrugged. "So you say, my dear, but *I* expect one day some absolutely unsuitable scholar, possibly in rags, will ask you whether you have cast any interesting horoscopes lately. Then you will fall into a passion on the spot, and it will be up to me to talk some sense into you. I am prepared for anything!"

Eschiva could not repress a laugh. "Well! I call *that* hypocritical, from a woman who has sworn not to marry again."

"Not to marry Sir Gerard of Montreal, at any rate. But why should *you* not find another husband, with love or without it? Someone to take the running of this city off your hands, and give you delight and comfort."

"Or care during my life, more likely, and tears and dolour when battle takes him away from me," Eschiva retorted. "Who is there, anyway, that *would* be suitable? A poor knight like your Sir Gerard, with half his attention on the rich prize of Beirut? Or one of the Cypriot princelings, still wet with his mother's milk?"

"Ah," said Margaret, seeing at once. "Don't tell me King Henry has offered you his brother, too!"

"My dear! A *child*," Eschiva said, laughing. "Amaury's age. Can you imagine? No, thank you! I have two sons already; I don't require another."

Margaret shuddered. "Boys that age," she said, "*smell.*"

"Well. I have my heirs. Why should I look for more trouble? Any man who marries me will only be interested in the lordship, anyway. Even my sister was never sure of her paramours. I shall live the life of the angels, *neither marrying nor being given in marriage.*"

"Not even to a ragged scholar?"

"Even ragged scholars may wish to change their rags for a furred gown. Besides, I've far more important things to do, as I said." Eschiva heaved a sigh. "I am the Old Lord's heiress. It falls to me to save Beirut from her enemies. That was why I called you here, as the Oliver to my Roland, so to speak."

Margaret's eyes opened wide. "My dear, you know that I am ready to do you good knight-service, at any hour or season you shall name, so long as we can find a suit of mail cut to my figure. But is the situation so desperate? In Acre they seem quite certain that the sultan's expedition is meant for Nubia."

Eschiva frowned. "That's what my council said, just this morning."

The memory was not a very pleasant one. Eschiva had been a few minutes late for the morning council, which was held in the audience-chamber, airy with the sea-breezes that flowed in through the galleried windows and musical with the trickle of water through the channel in the floor. She had lingered at her chapel, deciding to make confession after hearing Mass, for she had an idea that the task ahead of her required the cleanest possible conscience. The session of her own court ought not to have begun without her: but when she arrived she found her second cousin Balian already proposing, as the nearest male relative resident in Beirut, to take the chair in her stead.

"I am not *dead,* cuz," she had drawled, prowling to his side with a silent tread, just for the pleasure of seeing his guilty start. It was not the first time she had had to reprove her cousin for presuming too much upon his position. As a nobleman long bereft of his lordship, he had more ambitions and more time on his hands than he knew what to do with. As the nearest male Ibelin relative in Beirut, moreover, Balian never ceased to remind her that propriety dictated that certain matters of state ought to be left to a man. Worst of all, as the titular Prince of Galilee, he fancied himself as her liege lord, and therefore due her deference.

That was ridiculous. It was more than a hundred years since the lords of Beirut had done homage to the princes of Galilee, and never during the reign of Eschiva's family. For that matter, it had been more than a hundred years since Galilee had been in Christian hands at all, having been lost at the dreadful battle of Hattin. Cousin Balian was only clinging, fiercely, to a hoary legal fiction.

As he stepped aside, letting her take the seat that was hers by right, Eschiva had wondered whether she, too, might cling to her title and privileges long after the reality had slipped from her hands…

It was not an auspicious beginning to the council, and the sequel was little better. Her constable relayed a report from his spies in Damascus: the great siege engines that had been preparing all year in Baalbek were now on their way south. But, having reached Damascus, they advanced no further. Had they been destined for a new assault on Nubia, they ought certainly to have rolled on.

"Who's to say they won't?" someone asked, and then the argument went around and around in well-worn circles.

Eschiva cleared her throat. "If I may interject."

A silence fell upon the hall. She nodded towards the domed ceiling above the fountain, where the figure of Helios, the Sun, presided among allegorical figures representing the signs of the Zodiac, the seasons, and the hours of the day. "You know that I am learned in the interpretation of the stars," she told them. "You may have heard that a Great Conjunction took place some time ago in the house of Aquarius, presaging some great alteration in the fortunes of princes, which has not yet come to pass…"

"Five years ago, wasn't it?" asked her chancellor—a bishop, as usual. "Are we quite certain the expected alteration has not yet occurred?"

The Church did not always approve of the astrological arts, acknowledging that although the heavens undoubtedly ruled over affairs on earth, it was unwise to inquire too closely into their power. Eschiva did not allow the bishop's scepticism to trouble her. The heavens were orderly, readable, comforting: abiding by certain mathematical rules. Reading them gave her knowledge, and therefore power—a power to which her birthright entitled her, as much as it fitted her to command the Ibelin name and fortune.

"There was a Great Comet the year my father died," she reminded the chancellor serenely. "Many great lords perished that year, not just my father. I merely ask you to recall that it is *not* beyond the bounds of imagination that we may face the sultan of Egypt once more, and soon. We must take counsel."

"*Would* the sultan go so far?" her cousin asked. "With all the profits he draws from the rents of *our* fiefs and the tariffs from *our* ports, we do him more good than harm. And then, what threat do we pose? Even if we were to ally with Nubia and Tartary together, how many men could we possibly field?"

"It's a good question," Eschiva said—Balian might be a thorn in her flesh, but she must not be too proud to acknowledge when he had a point. "One which Countess Lucy of Tripoli asked herself only last year, when the Master of the Temple sent to warn her that the sultan was about to attack *her* city."

There was a brief, heavy silence. Some of her own councillors had been present at that siege, and the ghastly slaughter that ended it.

"You may be unaware," Eschiva added, "that the Templars have access to a spy *very* highly placed at the sultan's court. According to this Saracen lord, the sultan's decision to attack Tripoli had to do with trade, not war. In order to consolidate her control of Tripoli, Countess Lucy promised unheard-of trading rights to the Republic of Genoa. You know that Genoa has emerged triumphant from the merchant wars. They control all the trade in the Black Sea; they are tightening their grip on the Mediterranean; now they have sent emissaries to Baghdad. With control of all the major trade routes, it now lies in Genoa's power to deal a mortal blow to the sultan of Egypt."

"In what way?" Balian asked, laughing.

"By cutting off Egypt's supply of slaves," Eschiva said. The words echoed around the council-chamber, quiet but powerful. Everyone knew the significance of *that*. In Egypt, a man gained power by gaining slaves. Turkish boys from the vast plains of Asia were conveyed as slaves to the markets of Ayas, Acre and Cairo, then raised and trained as elite mamluk troops belonging to the sultan and his great amirs. Once a mamluk was fully trained and thoroughly loyal to his master, he might be freed, now ready to become an amir himself and begin anew the process of amassing slaves and power.

So entrenched had the practice become that upon the sultan's death, the throne of Egypt was now more likely to pass to one of his brother mamluks than to one of his sons. Sultan Qalawun himself had begun his career as a slave in the service of a former sultan.

"Imagine how frightened Qalawun must be," Eschiva went on. "His slave recruits are brought to him by Christian merchants in Christian vessels. All Genoa needs to do is stop the trade, and within a generation there will be no more mamluk army, and no more mamluk amirs."

"They'll never do that," said her chancellor, the corners of his mouth drawing down. "Genoa now has almost a monopoly on the slave trade. It's too profitable for them ever to stop."

"Would *you* wager an entire empire on that?" Eschiva asked. "Qalawun's best course now is to take Acre, which houses the largest slave-market in the East. That opens a crack in the Genoese wall. From there he might move north against Cilician Armenia, to take Ayas. Then the crack becomes a breach." She shook her head. "The recent slaughter in Acre was too perfect a provocation. Qalawun wouldn't have gone to war for the lives of a few Syrian peasants, even if their deaths *did* provoke riots in Cairo. No: it's the fact that slavers were the target that would have worried him."

Eschiva glanced around the room, seeing furrowed brows and hands tugging at beards. "To conclude: All our information indicates that Qalawun is planning a major campaign, and Acre is the most likely target. I propose that we ought to set aside money-fiefs for as many knights as can be found, and send them to Acre for the defence of the city."

She sat back, feeling confident for just a moment that she had put her case so strongly, no one might contest it.

Then Balian cleared his throat and said, "You still haven't proved that Acre is the most likely target, cousin. Qalawun might equally well be going south, to Nubia, to source his slaves there."

He had not listened to a word she said.

Eschiva restrained herself, with some difficulty, from pronouncing an instant sentence of banishment and exile upon her kinsman. She had noticed on several previous occasions that his tactic for winning arguments had nothing to do with fact or reason. Instead, he remained silent throughout all her closely-reasoned argumentation, before descending serenely from the heavens to re-state his own position as though she had not *just* demolished it.

"Every last time, my dear," she now told Margaret, making light of it, since she could hardly exile her cousin for the crime of bad argumentation. "He never has to present his own arguments; he simply rejects mine as insufficient. And because he gets the last word, the whole council puts more faith in his unsupported assertions than they do in their own lady, who labours day and night to preserve them. It would never happen if I were a man. I've a good mind to confer a new dignity upon him. My Lord Pain in the Neck."

"A man like that needs a good political marriage to keep him busy," said Margaret. "Can't you ship him off to bother some heiress in Cyprus or Greece?"

"He's married. A sad loss to all ladies." Eschiva sighed.

"And the council's decision?"

"I proposed that we should send knights to aid in the defence of Acre, but they refused. If we raise knights for the defence of the kingdom, it will come to the sultan's ears and turn him against us. So we are thrown back upon the Watchers."

"Ah! The Watchers!" Margaret said, her eyes dancing. "I wondered whether you had forgotten about them!"

A kind of lay brotherhood, the Watchers devoted themselves to practical good deeds. At one time, the Ibelin family had been well-nigh synonymous with the Watchers in the kingdom of Jerusalem. Her great ancestor John, the Old Lord of Beirut, had also been a Prester of the Watchers, foster-brother to Marta the Knight herself. It was his good deeds, Eschiva felt certain, that had laid the foundations of the Ibelin clan's greatness. Even if no Ibelin had ever actually sat on the throne of Jerusalem or Cyprus, they had become something greater—makers of kings, breakers of emperors.

They had left her, Eschiva, with a legacy both burdensome and glorious. A legacy she was determined to preserve for her sons.

"I haven't forgotten," she said, mildly. "But I've had much to occupy me. And everything has had to be done in strict secrecy. If I'm going to revive the Watchers who made my great-grandfather, for all practical purposes, the king of the East, then I can't risk the Egyptians in my own garrison getting wind of it. And I certainly don't want Balian to know; he'd try to make himself Prester."

"If you need a Prester," Margaret said, "there was one in Tripoli a year ago during the siege. Don't you remember? You were very keen to take him away with you, and he insisted on staying. But I've no notion whether he survived the sacking."

It would have taken more than a sacking to snuff out a man like the Old Lord, and if this Prester was of the same quality, Eschiva thought it was likely that he had survived. All the same—she noticed that her waiting-woman Plaisance had entered the garden with a knight and now stood waiting at the foot of the steps, a pair of cloaks folded over her arm.

"I remember the man, but if all goes well, we won't need him." Eschiva nodded towards the gentlewoman and the knight. "It's taken me much discreet inquiry, but I've found an old merchant who was once one of the Old Lord's Watchers. Shall we go to meet him?"

"In disguise?" Margaret asked, divining at once the meaning of the cloaks and the discreetly-attired knight. "Oh, Eschiva! It's been *ages* since we went somewhere in disguise together. Do you think we could stop for sherbert on the way?"

* * *

They did not stop for sherbert on the way, because Eschiva insisted upon business before pleasure; and besides, she was in a fever of anticipation. "It's taken me months to find someone who was present at the Old Lord's councils," she told Margaret, by way of excuse. "And of course he's grown old."

"Weren't there any newer Watchers you could ask?" Margaret inquired, puffing slightly with the effort of keeping up with Eschiva's long stride. Much of the width of the city's main street was taken up with shopkeepers' booths, and the presence of the knight at their back, and the black silk veils which marked them out as ladies of noble birth, did not greatly deter the crush of people. Eschiva supposed that they might have travelled equally well in litters; but that would have attracted too much attention.

"There were, but they came after the Old Lord's time." Eschiva was too proud to say it, but by the time of the second John—her father—the Ibelin fortunes had already been on the wane. When her father died, and her sister Isabella became the Lady of Beirut, it was said that no woman had ever been a Prester of the Watchers, and Isabella was too fond of paramours to insist upon keeping up her membership in a devotional brotherhood. She had quarrelled with the Pope in order to keep her first paramour, and upon the death of her second husband, she had quarreled with the king to avoid being made to take a third. That was when she had put herself and her fief under the protection of the Egyptian sultan, and the humiliation of the Ibelins was complete.

Eschiva, a young girl watching her sister's adventures, had taken warning. Love affairs were politically as well as morally dangerous. No breath of scandal had ever attached to *her* name. Yet the new king, himself barely half her age, *still* thought she ought to be safely married off to his younger brother—and she only a few years shy of forty!

Eschiva meant to revive the Watchers, but not as they had been in her father's day, nor her sister's. If they were to do her any good at all, they must be the sort of Watchers who had brought the Old Lord to power.

"I take it you heard about the riots in Acre," she said, now, to distract Margaret from thoughts of the decline of the house of Ibelin. "What did *you* think?"

"My dear!" Margaret said, distressed. "I cannot believe that any of *our* people would be so unruly. It must have been those scoundrels from across the sea. Why do they send us such good-nothing rascals, signed with the cross, only to make trouble and shed blood? There was not so much sin and wickedness in the days of Godfrey and Saint-Gilles."

Eschiva slid a glance sideways at her friend. Sometimes she suspected Margaret of being compounded more of sentiment than reason. Not that it did her any harm: everyone loved Margaret. Everyone was assured of her readily listening ear.

"How fortunate for Godfrey!" she said, now. "They say that across the sea in France, the name of Acre is a byword for sin and wickedness."

Margaret's veil trembled with horror. "Do you think that any of *our* people could have been implicated in that massacre? But nothing like this has ever happened before!"

"You forget that I am not already half a saint, like you, my dear. Most people are naturally bad. I know I am. But I think the slaughter was too conveniently-timed for *someone*. Depend upon it, if it was looked into, we would find Egyptians at the bottom of it."

Margaret hesitated. "It doesn't matter who stirred up the trouble. Those who wielded the swords are at fault, and so are we, for standing back and allowing it."

"Oh! naturally," Eschiva said. "Such things would never have occurred in the Old Lord's time. That's why I must have one of his own Watchers to advise me."

They left the main road and turned into the network of narrower streets that wound like a labyrinth between the lofty walls of Beirut's houses. The city, it was said, had been underpopulated and poor when the Old Lord received it from his half-sister, Queen Isabella of Jerusalem. John of Ibelin had built magnificent churches and towering tenements as well as his palace. The trading concessions he had made to the Italian merchants had brought the markets to life, while his magnificent building program had gathered artisans and craftsmen from far and wide. Now Beirut was its own little world—an elegant, rarefied city stocked full of people and wealth.

Eschiva turned aside to knock at a gate, and the three of them were admitted to the modest courtyard of a well-to-do house. "Leave your veil," she murmured to Margaret as the merchant and his wife hurried down the steps from the low loggia to greet them. Since she did not trust the merchant not to gossip about his exalted guests, she preferred to make her visit *incognito*.

"My ladies," the merchant puffed, bowing first to Margaret, and then to Eschiva—correctly guessing, it seemed, that two ladies who did *not* remove their veils were likely of greater importance than two who did. "May I know to what I owe this honour?"

"You may," Eschiva said, generously. "Our business is with your esteemed father, in fact. Is he in good health? May we speak to him in private?"

She had already ascertained that the old merchant was well and receiving guests, but it did no harm to be polite.

"Of course, of course! Allow us a moment to prepare him for visitors. And please accept a cup of wine while you wait—or sherbert, if you prefer?"

The merchant exchanged glances with his wife, who gathered up richly brocaded skirts a little too fine for her station and hurried back up the steps into the house, calling for servants.

They had not long to wait before the merchant's wife reappeared and begged them, curtseying, to ascend to the loggia. Although the day was warm and balmy for November, the old man was all muffled up against the light sea breeze. He sat in a curious chair, with two wheels affixed to the front legs and a pair of handles protruding from the back, allowing just one sturdy attendant to wheel him about like a barrow. Eschiva wondered from which far-flung country the clever device had come; she rather thought the style of the richly-carved back suggested it was from as far away as Cathay.

She caught a gleam of keen eyes from beneath the old merchant's bristling eyebrows and wondered whether he had brought it back himself from some long-ago journey.

"You are Arrigo Bandini?" she asked, motioning for the servants—and the rest of the family—to withdraw. "A Pisan name, I believe."

"My father was Pisan," the old man agreed. His accent, like his browned skin, could have made him a native of anywhere in the Levant. "But I am a Beirut man. And two highly-placed ladies did not come all the way to my house to trade tales of Pisa long ago."

Eschiva smiled. "Indeed not," she acknowledged. This was the sort of man who liked to go straight to the point. She approved of such people, although she was not herself one of them: she felt that it put her at an advantage in the conversation. "I was told that Arrigo Bandini was a Watcher in the Old Lord's council."

She didn't expect the look of wariness that at once came into Bandini's eyes. "And if I was?" he asked.

Perhaps he had a guilty conscience. Eschiva shrugged, attempting to put him at his ease. "I am interested in Watchers' Councils of the past," she said. "The Old Lord's council made him the greatest noble, not just in the kingdom of Jerusalem, but that of Cyprus too. If there's anything you can tell me about Prester John or his Watchers, I'll be most obliged."

"*Prester John*. The great noble who fought the emperor for the freedom of all Cyprus and Jerusalem," Bandini repeated, and she thought his voice was almost contemptuous. His eyes flickered up to fix on Eschiva's face, or what was visible of it beneath her veil. "I don't know who you are, my lady," he added, although this was now almost certainly false, "but some of us recall that before the Old Lord went to war with Emperor Frederick, he first seized the kingdom of Cyprus, and not a coin was left in her coffers when he was done."

Beneath her veil, Eschiva felt her skin heat. She *knew*, of course, that in some circles, opinion was divided as to whether her great-grandfather had been a saint, or a fiend. Such disagreements, after all, were difficult to avoid when he had fought a determined civil war against his overlord; it was why the family had had to sponsor a chronicler to write a history making the purity of their intentions known.

But Eschiva had never thought to find such sentiments expressed by one of the Old Lord's own Watchers. She paused a moment, until she had regained her composure: and then, in her laziest tone, she said, "You are a bold man. I never heard of the Old Lord being called a common thief. Certainly not by one of his own people."

"My lady, I never called him a *common* thief," Bandini said. His sinewy old hands were knotted on the armrests of the curious chair; Eschiva noted that he was afraid of her, and she was petty enough to be glad of it. "He was in many ways *uncommon.* But Watchers are meant to do good works; to be the salt that keeps the earth from spoiling. Your—" He caught himself. "Prester John was a great lord, but a poor Watcher."

"In my experience," Eschiva said, for her patience was wearing thin, "all great men have their detractors. I came to learn about the Old Lord's Watcher's Council, not his peccadillos."

"Peccadillos?" the old man demanded, his boldness increasing. "Peccadillos? Is that what you call appropriating all the revenues of an entire kingdom for his own purposes, so that not a groat of them was ever received by the queen he claimed to represent? Is that what you call sorcery?"

Eschiva rose to her feet. "Sorcery? You go altogether too far, old man."

Bandini's lips thinned; she could see the regret in his eyes. He knew that was a great deal too far. One did not accuse other people of witchcraft lightly, even if the accused was no great lord. Even Holy Church discouraged such accusations: in their eyes, it was a short step from believing in witchcraft to practising it oneself.

But Eschiva could never accuse the old man of cowardice. "I'm sorry, my lady," he went on, doggedly. "But you wanted to know the source of the Old Lord's power—and you ought to know that it did not *only* come from his Watchers, or from the blessing of Heaven, or whatever it is that you think. There was a familiar spirit, in the shape of a white snake, bound to the palace at the time when the Old Lord built it. Who is to say it is not there still?"

Eschiva took a deep breath.

"I think we are done here," she said, turning on her heel. Margaret was a soft, fluttering stream of apologies behind her as she stalked through the courtyard and into the narrow street.

"Someone ought to teach that old fox a lesson," Eschiva said, very softly, when Margaret and the knight attending them caught up to her in the alley. "He knew full well to whom he was speaking—and since he could see that I intended my visit to be a secret, he took the opportunity to show unbounded insolence to his own lady."

"He was very bold and very pert; but I think that he was honest. He must have known you were quite capable of ruining him."

"Sorcery!" Eschiva repeated. She was, after all, far angrier than she had thought. "The very idea! My great-grandfather, who lived a Prester of the Watchers, and died a brother of the Temple!"

"I know, Eschiva! But you aren't really going to teach him a lesson, are you?"

"Of course not! I'm not a *tyrant,*" Eschiva said, injured. "No—I'm going to send a gift to his grandchildren. Find me a white python, Sir Ugo, good to keep as a pet."

"Eschiva!" Margaret looked appalled. "A gift like that—he'll take it as a threat."

"I know," she said, with a chuckle as her mood lightened. "Don't mistake me, Sir Ugo—be sure that *is* a harmless snake. I wish to destroy only the old man's peace of mind, not his offspring."

"And now what?" Margaret asked, a little breathless with the effort of keeping up. Remembering her friend's shorter legs, Eschiva slowed her pace.

"I suppose I'll have to find out more about my great-grandfather," Eschiva said, "but not from his detractors." Holding a Watchers' Council was not so difficult, after all. It could be done tomorrow, with whatever younger, less experienced Watchers were left over from her father's council. But Eschiva needed a Council that would *do* things—speak prophecies and work miracles—if the kingdom was to be saved; and she had a vague idea that there was a special process to be followed if she wanted her own Watchers' Council to be favoured in such a way.

Ruffled feathers soothed, her thoughts flew back to the palace and its library. She'd been foolish to stake all her hopes on the last of the Old Lord's Watchers—the man was clearly a trouble-maker. Now the blood of the

Ibelins was up. She would dig out Philip of Novara's history and reacquaint herself with her great-grandfather's honourable life. Perhaps the official Ibelin chronicle might contain the clues she needed.

Chapter VIII.

Eschiva had most afternoons to herself. She might nap, or take her sons hunting, or amuse herself with her ladies in the garden if it was fine, or the loggia with a book of romances if it was not. That afternoon Margaret, tired from her journey and from their expedition into the city, did go for a nap; but Eschiva went into the library. On her way down the loggia, she passed her kinsman Balian, who together with some of his gentlemen was busy chattering, cracking nuts, and ignoring the minstrel who played for them on a lute. Balian rose from his chair as she approached, putting out a hand to bar her way.

"Morrow, cuz," he addressed her, with the informality that always grated upon her. "A word?"

"I am always at your service," she said, imparting a gentle irony to the words that, as usual, passed him by.

"Do not take it too hard, if I disagree with you in council. *In a multitude of counsellors there is safety.* I have only Ibelin's best interests at heart."

Eschiva favoured him with a blank look. What was the purpose of such a platitude? Did Balian think her a novice when it came to chairing council meetings?

"Thank you, cuz, but you need not have said it," she said, smiling graciously after allowing the silence to stretch a little too long. "Being disagreeable in council seems to be a pastime of yours; I'd never dream of depriving you."

"Where are you off to now?" he asked, reddening a little at her mockery. "Casting more horoscopes?"

Balian disapproved of her astrology; he believed that arithmetic was menial work, best left to the servants. Eschiva had long given up trying to explain that she liked the work for its own sake, that the numbers soothed and pleased her, reassuring her that some things in the world, at least, were orderly and predictable.

"I cast yours, once," Eschiva said, lowering her voice. "Would you like to know what I learned?"

"Very much," he said at once, leaning closer, interested despite himself.

"Not a great deal. The stars concern themselves most with the affairs of princes, and you..." She shrugged. "You are not the Lord of Beirut." Balian flushed red as fire, and Eschiva gave him a nod and passed on, into the library.

Perhaps it was beneath her, but it was time Balian was made to understand that she would not have him trying to wheedle himself into power at her expense.

The library was long and thin; on one side was a row of shelves, containing, Eschiva's chamberlain informed her, as many as a thousand books, all of them very precious and some rare. The opposite wall was pierced by a triple arcade of windows looking onto the loggia, admitting plentiful light but no direct sunshine, which might damage the collection. Beneath the windows were three wooden desks with peaked, sloping surfaces, at either side of which one might sit to read a book.

Philip of Novara's chronicle occupied a place of dignity on a stand of its own, its covers carved in ivory miniatures depicting scenes from the Ibelin family's history. A convocation of tiny mailed figures represented Barisan the Old's presence at the council of Nablus, at which the first laws of the Frankish kingdom of Jerusalem had been promulgated. Next came a depiction of his son, the great Prester Balian, carrying the child-king Baldwin the Fifth upon his shoulder to the coronation. Shorter, to fit within the tiny circular frame, a woman stood beside Balian in long robes, girt with a sword—that was his fosterling Marta the Knight, the White Watcher. After this came an image of Balian's son John of Ibelin, the Old Lord himself, meeting with the commune of Acre after that city declared itself free of Emperor Frederick's rule. Eschiva smiled, recalling how the people of Acre had flung refuse and offal to speed the emperor's departure to his native Germany. Although the emperor had claimed the kingship of Jerusalem by right of his marriage to the young queen—the second Isabella—first she, then their son and, finally, grandson had all died as youths without ever setting foot in the East. With the kings distant, and the armies of the imperial interloper chased away, it had fallen to the Ibelins to provide the kingdom's leadership.

Eschiva ran her fingers over the remaining medallions, depicting her grandfather, Balian of Beirut, and her father, John the Second. Five generations of Ibelins; and one last, blank disc which had been left uncarved. By right it should have belonged to her sister Isabella, who had been Lady of Ibelin before herself. But Eschiva always hesitated. Now, she wondered whether she felt ashamed of her sister, who ran from one scandal into another and finished by putting Beirut beneath the protection of the Egyptian sultan.

She would save Beirut first, she decided, before she would have Isabella carved into the book. Or, failing that, she would let the cover go forever unfinished, their line cut short in ignominy.

Eschiva carried the book to the reading-desk and sat down, telling her attendants to wait outside and to bother her only in an hour's time with a cup of snow-cooled wine and an orange. For some time she turned the pages slowly, running the tip of her knife across the page to keep track of the lines, murmuring the words aloud to herself. From time to time she skipped ahead, finding the bright illustrations that marked certain chapter headings—the duel between Aimery Barlais and Anseau of Brie; the confrontation with Emperor Frederick at the castle of Saint Helena; the seizure of Beirut by the wicked Admiral Filangieri.

There was nothing in the book regarding the Watchers, however, and at last Eschiva sat back, biting her lip... What she really wanted was to speak to someone who had *known* the Old Lord. Yet it had been more than fifty years since his death, and there were few now who had known him; Bandini himself had been a very old man, who must have only been a youth when he was part of the Old Lord's council.

She mused on what Bandini had said—*a familiar spirit in the shape of a white snake.* Eschiva found herself biting her lip, tempted. *Perhaps it is still here.* Perhaps the Old Lord's power might yet be hers—

Eschiva shook herself, shuddering. She ought not to entertain such thoughts! Sorcery was not only impossible; it was a sin to boot. And if she was caught dabbling in such things, Isabella's scandals would pale into insignificance.

She was relieved when the bell rang for Vespers, hurrying her away from temptation.

* * *

Eschiva woke with a start. Again, it was a dream that roused her. She was a girl, sitting in the garden beneath the Old Lord's orange-tree, and a white snake had looped its way down the tree onto her shoulder as she amused herself calculating the position of Sirius at midsummer. In her dream the snake was a cool, comforting weight along her arm, coiling around her wrist. It gazed up at her with beady black eyes, and she heard the voice of the young Nubian boy in her head.

"You're making a mistake," the voice said. *"Here, you have added these wrongly. Let me help."*

Dream, she wondered, glancing out the window at the slanting moonlight, or memory?

Bandini's words echoed in her mind. *A familiar spirit in the shape of a white snake.*

Perhaps it is still there.

And the boy: *Let me help.*

And the Egyptian assassins, targeting the Old Lord's orange-tree, which had lived many years longer than it ever should have.

She *had* to know, whatever the risk, because if she did not find out, then Beirut would fall.

Eschiva slid from her bed, pulling her furred robe about her shoulders.

The guard in the loggia overlooking the garden came to attention as she approached, and in the light of the lamp kept burning there by her command, she saw his hands tighten on his spear.

"Be at ease," she told him, pulling her mantle tighter at the throat. "It's I, the Lady. You are dismissed for tonight. Go!"

He scurried off, bowing and averting his eyes from her loosened hair and bare feet. Eschiva watched until he was out of sight; and then she took up the lamp and ventured down the steps that led into the garden. A moment later she stood before the orange-tree, breathing in the smell of sea-salt and citrus, with the words sticking in her throat. At that moment her only thought was that she was being fanciful, mistaking a figment of her own imagination for the instrument of a great deliverance...

"Ibrahim," she whispered, using the name by which she had once called him. The wind stirred in the leaves of the orange-tree; but then, that was nothing to be wondered at. Eschiva bit her lip. She ought to be in *bed.* She had to rise early for prayers, Mass, council, and—

Softly, silently, as though he had only been waiting in the shadows of the branches, a man stepped into the circle of light cast by her lamp.

"My lady," he said hesitantly. "Do you call upon me?"

Eschiva had to look up a long way to see his night-dark face, framed in a loose turban that draped like a hood around his head. He had high cheekbones, a high forehead, and full, curving lips and nose; and Eschiva's mouth went absolutely dry. *Dark, but lovely,* she thought, unbidden. For some reason she had never imagined Ibrahim as a grown man, still less as a handsome one.

"I don't know," she whispered. "Do I? *Are* you Ibrahim?"

"That is still my name," he said; almost as though he regretted it.

"Then I *didn't* imagine you," she said, almost to herself. "But you're not a *mortal* man." And she crossed herself, just to be safe.

Ibrahim watched the motion with a curl of his lips. "I'm half mortal," he said, "or I used to be, when I had a body. I assure you that conversing with me will not harm your soul."

"That's fortunate." A sense of unreality swept over her. Despite the awkwardness of meeting again after so many years, despite the wary look in his eyes, there was something comforting and familiar in their talk. "You taught me how to plot the stars. I should hate to think that I learned at the cost of my salvation. But why…why did you cease your visits?"

More memories drifted back to her. Sitting beneath the orange-tree, waiting for the boy to appear. The lengthening time between his visits. The moment she realised that a whole year had slipped by since she saw him last, so that she began to wonder if he had ever been anything more than a dream or a fancy…

"I missed you," said the lonely young girl she had once been. The moment she uttered the words she regretted them, unseasoned as they were with the careful calculations she made over everything she said.

His lips pressed together. "I've served your family nearly a hundred years," he said, in his soft deep voice. "Believe me when I say that it is better like this. I am a perilous friend to have."

Eschiva calculated that a raised eyebrow was appropriate. "Didn't you promise not to harm my immortal soul? Was it a lie?"

"No, but I can offer you power such as you have never known before. And that is a temptation to ruin kings and undo saints. Why have you bidden me from my slumbers? What is your wish? Command me, if you must, but then forget me."

His voice was bleak. Eschiva shivered; and some spirit of mischief goaded her.

"You first," she said, folding her hands in an attentive attitude. "Have *you* any wishes? Perhaps there is something *I* can offer you, such as you have never known before."

For a moment she thought he was going to laugh at her. "You would offer *me* a boon?"

"I *am* the Lady of Beirut," she said, chin raised. "I will not be outdone by a *servant*."

She watched the understanding dawning in his eyes, that despite her mocking voice, she was in perfect earnest. Then, like a mountain sliding, he fell to his knees.

"Grant me this, Lady of Beirut: cut down my tree. Save a fruit and send it across the sea to be planted in a place with no inhabitants, and then forget me."

She barely understood. "You wish to leave Beirut?"

"An old master of mine knows that I am here," Ibrahim said. "He sent his agents to steal me back; I outmanoeuvred them. But they will return. Promise that you will send me to a place they will never find me."

"You put little faith in my power to protect you," Eschiva said, only half in jest. "Is Beirut's fall so certain?"

"The future is beyond my power to predict, my lady."

"Thus the wish," she acknowledged. "Well: I will see you planted on a lonely Cypriot hillside, if you wish. But first I must save Beirut. Swear me homage, and answer all my questions about the Old Lord, Prester John. And on the day that I hold a new Watcher's Council, I will have all things done as you have asked."

To Eschiva's surprise, he did not greet this offer with the joy she expected. "You might find the truth to be other than you thought."

"Oh?" she asked with heavy irony. "Don't tell me that old Bandini was right in calling the Old Lord a *sorcerer*."

"No, my lady."

"Good," she said briskly, holding out both hands with the palms facing. "Then you can tell me all you knew of him. The main thing I require is the composition of his Watcher's Council. Here: put your hands between mine, and do homage ."

The spirit of the orange-tree sent her a look she could not decipher. But before Eschiva could ask what made him hesitate, he put his hands, palms touching, between hers.

It was then that she knew for certain that Ibrahim was a spirit, for she felt nothing but a little shiver as she closed her hands about his. For a moment she felt another prickle of fear, imagining what her chaplain would say to this, if he knew. Then she asked herself what other choice she had.

This was the grace of heaven, she thought, as Ibrahim repeated the words of homage. To her, appointed by God the Lady of Beirut despite being a woman and the second-born, the task had fallen to revive the ancestral glories. And with Ibrahim as her servant, she would at last have the power to carry out that task.

Chapter IX.

Heliopolis, John thought, surveying the uneven plain beneath a shading hand, was barely more than rubble now. Traces of the ancient walls still formed an irregular rectangle, the mud bricks long since fused with the earthen ramparts on which they stood. What had once been houses, temples, palaces, and workshops had long vanished, anything useful or portable having been carried away to construct the newer city to the south: there were no intact blocks of stone smaller than a footstool, and not many smaller than a mule. Some of the more massive stones remained, foundations for temples or palaces, some of them still crowned with broken columns. The immense, forbidding face of a long-dead king reposed half buried in gravel, one of its eyes half gouged away by some officious hand. As he walked, John had to pick his way between crumbling bits of cornice or wall, long weathered to a dusty sand-grey but still bearing the carvings of ancient kings. The ground, too, was pocked with holes. John could guess who had been digging among the sun god's ruins, and why. From the ancient curios being sold in Cairo's markets—gems, marble panels, scarabs, mummified cats, and canopic jars, many claimed to be good luck talismans used in the rites of ancient magicians—to the enormous amount of ancient columns, slabs, and foundation-stones built into the palaces, mosques, and tenements of the city, the ancient city must have furnished immense quantities of treasure.

A second wall bisected the city, climbing to higher ground on his right. Following a dry streambed or canal, John surmounted a gap in the crumbling wall. It was only then that he felt sure his journey was not in vain.

One edifice on the pockmarked plain remained intact, its pale granite surface still etched with incomprehensible symbols startlingly dark and vivid in the shadows cast by the midday sun: an obelisk, tall enough to dwarf even the gnarled old sycamore tree which grew beside it. John trudged towards it, amazed how the towering needle-like stone seemed to grow even larger as he approached. The distance had confounded his eye, suggesting that the monument was nearer and smaller than in truth it was.

He reached the base of the obelisk and spent some time gazing up at it, thinking wistfully of the old days, the good days in Alexandria when he had been recovering from a certain arrow-wound sustained in the Persian wars, and he and Rahel had gone to visit the obelisks of Cleopatra. They were barely married a week, and because his hand was useless and could not sketch, Rahel had tried drawing the obelisks for him. Now his fingers itched, not for his pen, but for his wife's soft, soft hands.

Then he laid himself down in the shadow cast by the sycamore-tree, cast a fold of his blue turban over his eyes, and composed himself for sleep. He had taught himself to sleep anywhere, any time: he slipped easily into the dream and found Rahel sitting beside him.

"Is this Heliopolis?" she asked, looking about them with eager eyes. "Oh, there is the obelisk of Senroset. How everything has changed! All the great temples and palaces, broken down and carried away!"

"Will it serve?" John asked her, sitting up, and dragging his hands down his face. He felt sleepy: in the dream the midday air had become close and soporific, like the calm before a storm. Despite the absolute silence and emptiness of the landscape, there was a prickle down his neck, as though they were being watched.

"Let me try something," Rahel said, her forehead puckering. "We are in *your* dream now; perhaps we might cross into mine."

John wondered what this meant, but only for a moment. Between one blink and the next the landscape changed, the earth sinking, the tumbled stones and pillars rising. Heart hammering, John rose to his feet, beholding Heliopolis as Rahel had known it. Empty and scarred, with scrub growing from every stony crevice; with paint and whitewash scoured from the stone by the desert storms; with gems and precious metals stripped away by greedy human hands—yet the city itself remained, its ruins silent and echoing.

"The temple of the sun," Rahel murmured. "Do you see it?"

John turned, and the breath dried in his throat. They stood now at the foot of a flight of broad stairs leading up to a great gate, the white towers to either side of it rising as high as the obelisk. The towering double doors of the gate itself had once been covered with sheets of beaten bronze, massive and dark; now one of the leaves was missing and the lower half of the other had been stripped of the valuable metal. Framing the entrance, overpowering in their size and grandeur, were matched pairs of monuments: two sphinxes and two obelisks at the foot of the steps; then, above, two more sphinxes and two massive, faintly smiling statues of the sun god, each crowned with a great horned disc, each clutching crook and flail to his broad, polished chest.

For a moment John's heart failed within him. The sphinxes, the idols, faced each other above the path. He and Rahel must walk the gauntlet of that stony attention. A moment ago he had felt that they were being watched, but now it was as though eyes were everywhere—statues, crumbling friezes, the very eye of the sun itself burning in the naked sky above.

"Come," he whispered, although there was surely no reason to do so. In the waking world, there was only an obelisk, a sycamore tree, and a man asleep at the foot of it. In the dream both of them inhabited, the world seemed suddenly like a blade—thin, and sharp, and ready to turn sideways and cut them...John put a foot on the first step.

At once the glittering sphinx-eyes fastened upon him. John stopped, heart beating. He found that Rahel was praying under her breath: *"Expel by the terror of Thy name the evil one and his legions loose upon the earth..."*

John ground his teeth together and took another step, then another. The air thickened: for a moment it was like forcing his way through waist-deep mud. Then he stumbled; he was up the steps and past the first watchers.

"Let no harm come to them who are sealed in Thy image and let those who are

sealed receive dominion, to tread on serpents and scorpions and all the power of the enemy."

John wiped sweat from his brow. Above him the sun god gazed, remote and smiling, upon the mirrored idols. Above waited another pair of sphinxes, each holding a bird-headed jar between its paws. A quadruple gaze; and he had barely passed the first gauntlet.

"For Thee do we hymn and magnify and with every breath do we glorify Thy all-holy name of the Father and of the Son and of the Holy Spirit, now and ever and unto ages of ages."

He reached out for Rahel. His fingers slipped through her like shadows; but she stopped praying all the same, and sent him a questioning look.

"It's enough," he whispered. "Qeteb is here. Can't you feel him?"

Rahel looked equally daunted. "You'll face him now?" she whispered, as John took a resolute step forward. "Alone? With no one praying and fasting?"

He thought of the callow Brother Simon, of the meek-looking blue-turbaned Christians who bustled through the streets of Cairo by mule and foot, bowing to the proud Mamluk warriors.

"You must fill their place," he told her. Moreover, he could not now go back. He had dealt with Lilith; doubtless he was able to deal with Qeteb. "Give me words."

With that, he stepped deliberately between the images of the sun god.

The force of their attention caught and held him like a mouse on a dagger-point. For a moment John could scarcely breathe, barely think.

Then, behind him, Rahel's whisper.

"Lord, have mercy."

"Lord, have mercy," John repeated, and he thought the attention recoiled a little. He stood a little straighter, although the sweat was running down his body in rivers, and his hands were shaking. Behind him, Rahel whispered on, and John repeated her words:

"I expel you, spirit of uncleanness, who revolted against Adonai, Elohim, the omnipotent God of Sabaoth and the army of His angels. Be gone and depart from this land, for it is become the kingdom of our God and of His

Christ!"

A hot orange light, like coals of fire, began to glow between the broken temple doors. John swallowed and continued:

"I expel you in the name of Him Who created all things by His Word, His Only-Begotten Son, our Lord Jesus Christ, Who was ineffably and dispassionately born before all the ages; by Whom was formed all things visible and invisible, Who made man after His Image: Who guarded him by the angels, Who trained him in the Law, Who drowned sin in the flood of waters from above and Who shut up the abysses under the heaven, Who demolished the impious race of giants, Who shook down the tower of Babel, Who reduced Sodom and Gomorrah to ashes by sulphur and fire—"

Sulphur and fire burst forth from the gate of the temple; John threw his arms over his face as the fire roared over him. When he lowered them, he found that he was on his knees before Qeteb—or whatever his name had been in the days when he was worshipped in this temple. The shape of the god was gigantic and clothed in flame, too hot to look upon. It held a great disc, like an eye, to its chest; now that disc turned and beamed heat down upon him.

"Sulphur and fire," the great creature repeated, with a rolling laugh. "Sulphur and fire I have in abundance, mortal."

John gritted his teeth. "I expel you, Qeteb, by virtue of Christ's baptism in the Jordan, which for us is a type of our inheritance of incorruption through grace and sanctified waters—"

"This amuses me," said the great spirit. "None of my worshippers has ever attempted my *exorcism* before."

For a moment John was speechless. One of *Qeteb's* worshippers? He, John Bessarion?

He waited for Rahel to go on, giving him the words to speak, but she did not. "It's a lie," he hissed, over his shoulder to where she stood with a look of dread upon her face. "He means to daunt us. Go *on*."

"It is no lie," the great voice from above boomed. "I know you, John Bessarion. You have always done my will. Now there is no harm you can do me."

The god reached out a flaming hand. Recoiling, John reached for Rahel again and did not find her. She was gone, whether by the power of Qeteb's gesture or because she had fled of her own accord. At that moment John would not have been surprised by either.

He fell to his knees. Terror had turned his own bones to water.

"Your mortal body lies within my power," Qeteb rumbled, like the distant roll of thunder. "Yet still you have a little usefulness, O votary of mine, and I am not yet ready to dispense with you. Think of that when you lick your wounds, and know to whom you owe your life."

John awoke with a gasp. Around him the dead city had been ground down by time and plunder. The sycamore tree had withered, laying him bare to the scorching sun; the skin of his face was hot and tight.

The moment he opened his eyes, he heard a voice shout. "On him!"

John had a brief glimpse of many black shapes looming over him. For an instant he thought they were gods or images, but then a foot slammed into his ribs and he knew that he had fallen into the hands of brigands. He tried to roll away, to get to his feet, to grab for his crossbows; but some heavy club caught him in the stomach and he curled, gasping, around the agony. Then it was fists and clubs and feet, and hands that plucked at the belt and purse hidden beneath his robes.

A wind sprang up, whipping dust and leaves into the air and halting the beating. Groaning, John blinked the grit from his eyes and looked up to see a flash of jewel-coloured green.

There were shouts of terror from his assailants as the giantess strode nearer, baring her brown right arm, lifting a rock the size of a mule from the earth. Recalling in a flash what had happened at the house of Abdu and Saida, John scrambled to his knees, reaching for his crossbows.

He sought them in vain: they were gone. The sudden movement sent his head into a whirl of pain, and blackness veiled his eyes.

Chapter X.

John fell straight into another dream—a dream of a great white courtyard, and within it a beautiful domed church. An octagonal jewel-box built of white stone, its upper courses were tiled in intricate patterns of cerulean, aquamarine, azure, and cobalt. Its dome was sheathed in red gold, banded about their base with Arabic calligraphy.

There was a measuring rod in his hand, a heavy, elongated cube of some hardened wood taller than himself, marked intricately with units of measurement—digits, spans, feet, and cubits. In his dream John was using the rod to measure the distance from the courtyard gate to the basilica door. He worked quickly, anxious to move nearer, to get a closer look at the great structure. It looked impossible to build—impossible, that is, without the secret that lay sealed within his purse.

Inside, the narthex was cool, shaded from the sun but full of light which reflected off gleaming marble inlay both on the walls and underfoot. As in the imperial basilica, the Hagia Sophia in Constantinople, the great marble slabs had been perfectly split by skilled craftsmen, polished, and then laid side by side. The natural bands of light and dark within the stone created the illusion of shot-silk curtains wavering upon the wall. John measured the narthex, noting the measurements in his mind, and then moved into the nave. The dome rose dizzyingly above him, ornamented with painted frescoes of angels and enormous mosaics of the Christ Pantocrator, the Virgin and the saints. The walls were adorned with more marble revetments, divided by scrolling acanthus carvings and more of the blue tiling that decorated the exterior; across the floor, the marble ripples were like a pool of clear water, banded by geometric stonework that imitated flowers.

Across those flowered meadows, across those rippling waters, one other person walked. In the vast space she was small and distant, using her own rod to measure the altar. John would have recognised her anywhere: Rahel, his wife.

"Rahel," he called, but she did not answer; she was not sharing this dream with him. John ventured nearer and was astonished to behold her as she had been once, years ago, in the days when they were first married—her round girlish face solemn with concentration, her figure soft and slender, her hair dark without a strand of silver.

He already had a notion of what he was seeing. Once, years before, Rahel had awoken from a marvellous vision of a church which, she said, she thought they were meant to build together. She had described it to him in every particular. He had noted it down, made the sketches, and amended them until she was happy. It was then that he had discovered the problem: Rahel's drawing could not be built. The church was too high, too broad, to support its own weight.

"It will need to be smaller," he had told her.

"But in my vision I *measured* it," she replied. "There's a way. There *must* be. This was no ordinary dream; it was a Message. I know it."

Then John had thought of the Hagia Sophia, built a hundred years previously by the Greek geometers Isidore of Miletus and Anthemius of Tralles. Surely *their* structure had been as great; John himself had visited the church and sketched it. The secret of their success was utterly humble: cement. Cement that did not crumble in an earthquake, cement that grew harder with time, cement that could bind a great basilica like this for uncounted generations.

So for years John had searched, inquired, and experimented, mixing batch after batch, experimenting with volcanic ash and quicklime until he had something he thought would be strong enough. People used to laugh behind his back at the young nobleman's passion for cement, for how often he could be found measuring and mixing and striking at the result with a hammer to test its strength. Let them laugh: they would know better when he had built Rahel's vision. For he had found the secret, and it now lay folded into a small, wax-coated packet in his purse.

He took it out now, his fingers trembling as he glanced from the red-dyed wax to the great edifice that surrounded him. This—this, far more than the war, was what called him home. After the war would come the peace; and in the peace he would *build,* things of which the world had never even dreamed.

"Such marvellous properties it has, Rahel," he said now to the ghostly memory of his wife. "Since I added the quicklime, it *heals* itself of fractures. Shake it in an earthquake, and it only becomes stronger."

Dream-Rahel lingered over the altar, the red porphyry of which was carved into great whorls. Her fingertips lingered upon the surface, tracing the stonecutter's marks. John looked closer; to his surprise, they resembled the Frankish marks he had seen everywhere in Acre.

Sudden doubt struck him. Why should there be *Frankish* marks in Rahel's vision?

Why, for that matter, Arabic writing upon the cornices?

Then he felt himself being shaken. For a moment he thought it *was* an earthquake: and then pain pierced the dream, and he remembered.

The confrontation at Heliopolis. The attack.

Soraya, brandishing a stone block as though she meant to fling it directly at his head.

✳ ✳ ✳

John could not have been in a faint for very long—the vision must have taken place in a blink of time—yet his surroundings had changed. He now lay in a dark pool of shade beneath an overhanging block of stone.

John pushed himself to a sitting position. For a moment his head pounded and his dazzling surroundings swam before his eyes. His whole body ached, no doubt shortly to develop a mass of bruises and a raging sun-burn. Beyond the shadow in which he lay, Heliopolis was a sun-whited wasteland of rock and stone and dark sycamore or acacia trees. There was no sign, either of the footpads which had set upon him, or—

A mighty foot crunched into the gravel before his hiding-place, and his bag and belt, together with his stolen crossbows, were flung to the ground at his feet. Soraya—half again the size of a man—knelt down to peer beneath the rock at him.

"Here," she said, offering him a freshly-plucked aloe leaf. "Put that on your injuries."

John's heart leapt. "You remember me," he croaked.

Soraya only scowled. "Tell me: why should I remember *you*, mortal?"

Then she did not remember, after all. For a moment he was speechless with disappointment and loneliness.

"Speak," she growled, dropping the aloe at his feet. "Tell me who you are. Tell me why I *feel* like this when I see you. Tell me…tell me we weren't *lovers*."

"What! No!"

"No, I don't feel this way about any of the people I've gone to bed with," she mused. "Oh, God, *should* we be lovers? Would it stop me *feeling—*"

"*No,*" John repeated, hardly knowing whether to laugh or weep or, perhaps, to skin al-Mukhtar alive for stealing all that Soraya had once known. "No, we were never—we were *friends,* Soraya, like brother and sister." He leaned forward to touch her great shoulder.

Soraya went very still at his touch, and for a moment he thought she almost seemed terrified. "When?" she whispered at last.

"A year ago in Tripoli, before they took your memories."

"In Tripoli," she repeated, as though the words might summon up some memory. But if they did, she kept the knowledge locked behind her wary eyes.

Gingerly, because of his bruises, John took the aloe leaf. Its broken end oozed cool, clear jelly that he knew would soothe his burns and bruises, but before applying the juice, he picked up his wallet and held it out to Soraya.

"There's a gift inside," he said. "I remembered how much you love halwa."

Her eyes narrowed. "I've never eaten halwa."

"Try it," he said, and began dabbing the aloe jelly on the tight skin of his face. At first, Soraya watched him with a wild gazelle's distrustful gaze. Then she opened the wallet and found the paper packet. She sniffed it, glared at him, and finally put one of the crumbs on her tongue.

Soraya's face crumpled slowly. "Oh God," she said, and then the tears spilled over. John did not reach out to her again. Years of marriage and fatherhood had taught him what to do about a crying woman, but this one had barely tolerated a hand on her shoulder.

At length, Soraya wiped her hands up her cheeks as though trying to sweep the tears back into her eyes. "There is sorcery in this food," she growled. "That is enough! Tell me everything you know!"

"As you wish," he said. She might not remember him, but she remembered the halwa; that was enough to go on. "First of all, I know the truth of the vessel which enslaves you. You are the djinn of the Lance—al-Mukhtar's Lance, that he carries with him everywhere he goes."

"I *know* this."

That he had not expected: in Tripoli, al-Mukhtar had Soraya convinced that her vessel was a ring. "You deduced it already?"

"Saif told me."

It was a gesture of trust he would never have expected from al-Mukhtar. "I suppose your master has learned to leaven his lies with a little truth."

"Al-Mukhtar is not my *master*," she snarled. "Our *master* is al-Ashraf Khalil, and Saif has promised to set me free of him."

"He's *what?*" John almost choked. There was a silence. He cleared his throat: "That was me. *My* promise. To *my* friend."

Soraya made a disbelieving sound. "So I *belong* to you."

"I—no!" He dragged a hand down his face. "The Soraya *I* knew, in Tripoli, *loathed* al-Mukhtar."

"Of course *you* would say that."

"Good, so he is not your master, but your friend," John said, keeping his calm with an effort. "Who is it, then, that binds you with his lightest word? Are you capable of resisting him?"

There was another silence, as the obstinacy faded from the djinn's face.

"All right," she said, looking down at the halwa. "Let us say that you *did* promise to free me. How would you do such a thing?"

John opened his mouth, ready to explain his plans for exorcising Qeteb. Then he closed it again.

"I don't know," he said, crestfallen. "Qe—the Hairy One is the one who keeps you bound to the Lance, and you cannot be freed while his power remains. I *tried* to cast him out today. I failed. I don't know why."

He was no worshipper of Qeteb—he never had been. What could have gone wrong?

"That's a shame." Soraya gathered her feet beneath her to rise. "Succeed, and maybe I'll believe that the rest of what you say is true."

"Wait," John begged. "I—I need your help. You know the Hairy One better than I do. I thought that perhaps you might know what went wrong—"

Her eyes narrowed. "Why?" she asked. "Why are you so *desperate* to help me?"

"Because you are my friend. What other reason do I need?"

"We are not friends—not any more. So why?"

He could already hear how the words would sound to her—but he didn't want to be a friend like al-Mukhtar, telling her only what would make her think well of him. Briefly, John closed his eyes. "You made me a promise in return," he said. "I wasn't born in this time, Soraya. I was born almost seven hundred years ago. I have a wife, whom I love, and children who need me, seven hundred years ago. And you promised me that if I freed you from the Lance and restored your memories, you would send me home."

Soraya watched him for a long time, her face absolutely blank. John began to hope. Maybe, just maybe, something he said might have jogged her memory—

She scoffed. "I knew it," she said. "Of course there's something in it for you." Then in a whirl of dust she was gone.

For a while John only sat where she had left him, watching the shadows spread their black fingers across the ground as the sun sank lower in the blazing sky. Then, at last, he climbed to his feet and set out on the long walk back to the mountain, ignoring his body's protests. His bruises would mend all the better for the exercise.

He felt like a drowning man who has just lost his last glimpse of land. For months he had worked towards this day—the day he would cast out Qeteb, free Soraya, and go home. How could he have failed so horribly? Now not only was Soraya still enslaved, but her master had found a far more subtle way to chain her to his side.

John had a sudden horrible vision of the future that awaited them all. Rahel and the children, left behind to fend for themselves in a darkened world. Soraya, trapped forever in a false friendship. And he…John could not even begin to imagine what meaning life would have for him, if he could not find his way home.

The answer, then, was simple. He could not allow himself to fail.

* * *

"John, thank God," Rahel greeted him when he had at last pitched into his narrow monastery bed and fallen asleep. "I didn't know if I would ever see you again. What happened?"

In the dream, they sat side by side in the monastery garden. Rahel shone softly with a nimbus of white light, her eyes attentive as John told the story—the disastrous end of his attempt upon Qeteb; the attack; the rescue; the long journey back to the monastery, where Brother Simon took one look at him and ran for salve from the infirmary.

"Soraya couldn't tell me anything—or wouldn't," he finished, sombrely. "There has to be some reason Qeteb defied us, but I won't let him have the final word. I'll free her and find my way back to you if it's the last thing I do."

Rahel hummed softly, only half paying attention. "He said quite plainly that you were a worshipper of his."

"But *how?* When I have only ever worshipped Christ?"

"My love, I know. But for me it's been three days since I saw you last, and I spent the time in consulting books and scholars. I've learned all that I could about Qeteb the Destroyer. He's associated with midday, heat, fire, and pestilence. His arrows strike with heat and exhaustion. He inspires sloth and accedie…"

"When have I ever been slothful?"

"Never, dear, but listen. He's also worshipped by some as a god, who take him as a principle of masculinity, reason, and above all of order."

"Of order? How can there be a demon of *order?*" The word struck a chord in his memory. "Lilith claimed to represent chaos. I thought that meant that *we*—the Watchers—were the principle of order."

"Perhaps that's the problem," Rahel said, very gently. "You have always revered the commands of your superiors, my love. Sometimes a little too much."

Her words conjured up memories of things he had done, things he would much rather forget. When the emperor demanded he arrest, fine, and sometimes condemn heretics to death, he had carried out those orders, asking himself what right he had to put his own conscience before that of the anointed vice-gerent of God on the earth. Asking himself what chaos might ensue if every man in the empire did what was right in his own eyes.

He swallowed hard, putting a hand to the ghost of pain in his ribs. "I *repented* of that."

"You did," she acknowledged, and this seemed to be as far as her efforts could take them. A leaden silence hung over them before she spoke again. "If Soraya is unwilling to help, perhaps some of the local Copts will know more about this demon."

"If the Copts could have done anything about Qeteb, they wouldn't have lived thousands of years in his power."

"All the more reason they must know him well."

"By that reasoning Soraya is the one who ought to know him best." John ground his teeth. "I could throttle that liar, al-Mukhtar, for driving this wedge between us. But if he thinks I'll take it meekly, he's making a mistake. Soraya *remembers* me. She doesn't yet understand, but she will."

"What will you do?"

He thought about it. Soraya had come to the ruins of Heliopolis to find him; he had asked for no explanation, because she had given him one. *Why do I feel like this?* She remembered too well what he had once meant to her, either to let him alone, or to let him suffer.

"I'll wait," he said grimly. "She will come back to me, even if she doesn't trust me the way she used to. She won't abandon me…"

His voice trailed away. Rahel watched him with sympathetic eyes. "Oh, John. It's hard to feel so alone."

He hadn't meant to let her see that momentary weakness, and now he felt ashamed of it. John had always been advised that it was not good to love one's spouse too much. Truly holy people were able to live as celibates, relying upon God rather than the worldly ties of clan and blood. To live in the world was no benefit, either. He had always known his duty might call him away from her. Worldly affairs of war and rulership had kept them apart often enough.

"Before," he said softly, "I could always count on being able to find my home again." Then he added: "Soraya is pragmatic. If she thinks I can get her free of Qeteb, she'll find a way to work with me. For that matter, I'd offer to make another alliance with al-Mukhtar if I thought it would help."

"Please don't." Rahel smiled wryly. "Remember? He plans to kill you."

"I'll bear it in mind." John let out a breath; now that he had declared his plans, he felt more settled. "Don't be afraid, Rahel; I'll find my way back to you. I *know* it. That vision—your vision, of the church we build—I had it too."

He put out his hand, pale and insubstantial in the darkness, and Rahel placed her equally insubstantial palm against his. Their fingers overlapped without touching, but the combined light of their hands made a stronger light, a pale lantern-glow that swelled in the darkness, silvery and clear.

"I'm coming home to you, dearheart. We'll win the war. And we'll build a new peace together."

Chapter XI.

"One moment," Margaret said, raising a finger, when Eschiva paused. "You said this spirit was *handsome?*"

Margaret always did have very clear priorities.

"My good gossip," Eschiva said, "didn't you hear me before? I don't have time for paramours; I have the name of the Ibelins to uphold. Besides, Ibrahim is a *servant.*"

"Eschiva, he's a—a *djinn,* as the Saracens call them. He has *power.* He's not like any servant you've had before."

Eschiva gave the other woman a flat look. They were standing in church, and ought not to be whispering during the Te Deum; but Eschiva was incapable of keeping the previous night's events to herself a moment longer.

If only Margaret *would* stop dragging the conversation to inappropriate topics. "Margaret," she hissed, "you *saw* what happened when my sister began consorting with that idiot Julian of Sidon; what do you think the Pope would do if *I* was known to be consorting with a *djinn?*"

Witchcraft was still a capital crime, even though Holy Church discouraged accusations. Margaret turned a suddenly serious face upon her friend. "Then paramour or not, I hope you'll be careful."

After that the two of them paid reverent attention to the Mass—externally, at least. Internally, Eschiva's mind kept returning to the previous evening. Having received Ibrahim's oath of fealty, Eschiva had demanded answers to her questions about the Old Lord.

"It would be better to show you than tell you," the djinn had said, hesitantly.

"Show me—how?"

"Wait a few days, until the skies are right."

Seeing that she would get nothing more out of him, Eschiva had changed course. "I want to re-create my great-grandfather's Watcher's Council," she told him. "My father used to tell me stories of the prophets and miracle-workers of those times. And I think I need a Prester also."

Ibrahim was silent a moment. "A prophet is not like a minstrel, to pipe when ordered."

"Naturally not." Eschiva smiled. Illuminated in the light of her lamp, the djinn looked very serious, absorbed in the questions she asked. "My gossip Margaret reminds me that I know of a Prester, John Bessarion. The family has long been connected with mine. Perhaps he might be of assistance?"

She broke off at the look on Ibrahim's face.

"There is a Bessarion here? You ought to have said so before. He is the man you want."

"Then I suppose I'll have to find him," Eschiva said. "I'll bring Margaret to the garden tomorrow." And then, because he was so serious and she felt mischievous, she said: "Did you put on that shape for *my* benefit? The last time we met, you appeared as a child."

Ibrahim blinked. "I'll appear as whatever makes you most comfortable, my lady. A child, if you prefer."

"Oh, for God's sake, no," Eschiva had said, because looking did no harm. "Give me a man, if you please, cast in just this mould."

There was a long silence. She had meant to make him laugh, wondering what a smile would look like on those soft lips. Instead he watched her impassively and at last said, "I live to be your servant, my lady."

Something in the words made her joke seem in poor judgement, and Eschiva did not enjoy being made to feel guilty. "Good night," she said, briefly, and the next morning in church reproved Margaret for suggesting she take a djinn as a paramour.

After Mass, as usual, Eschiva was kept busy at the church door dispensing alms and hearing petitions, and appointing certain gentlemen of her court to look after the requests which could not be answered with a purse of silver or an order to one of her guards. Balian, though he professed himself eager to be of service, was of course never present on such occasions.

There was no council meeting that morning; so at last, having discharged her obligations to the poor, Eschiva got Margaret alone in the garden. "Don't be afraid," she warned Margaret, before calling out: "Ibrahim! Show yourself!"

Between one blink and another, the djinn stepped out from behind the orange-tree.

"There you are," Eschiva said, merrily. "Margaret, here is Ibrahim, the djinn of the orange-tree."

"Where?" Margaret sent her a worried look. "I don't see anything."

Eschiva had a bad moment. "I'm not *imagining* him. Look—there!"

"Would you have me show myself to the entire household, my lady?" Ibrahim asked in a low voice. In the daylight, the reluctance on his face was evident.

Reluctance, she realised, precisely described all his dealings with her in the past day.

"Only to Margaret," she told him, meaning to put his heart at rest. "Is that possible?"

Margaret's soft gasp beside her told her that it was. Then she said, "Good morrow, Ibrahim. I thank you for your courtesy and would gladly return it, as I have the opportunity."

The djinn's face softened in a way it never had with Eschiva—but then, Margaret had the knack of making anyone love her. He bowed to her. "Then I beg you to tell no one of my presence here."

"Neither of us will," Eschiva assured him briskly. "You are a valuable state secret and I will guard you with my life, believe me. Now, Margaret, what can you tell us about the Bessarion Prester?"

Margaret shrugged. "Why, in Tripoli he gave poor Sir Gerard a great deal of trouble, for which I do not blame him. Gerard meant well, and he was following his orders; but he was dealing with a *genuine* demon, my dear. It was a burden off my mind when this Prester John expelled the creature."

"Did he indeed! Then he is the man I want."

"If he's still living, Sir Gerard will know his fate better than I do."

"I'll write to him at once," Eschiva said, making calculations in her head. A fast nava with a good wind could make the sea voyage from Beirut to Acre in a day. Given another day for her servants to find Gerard and wait for him to answer her letter, she would be waiting three days at the very least before hearing back regarding John Bessarion's whereabouts.

"Ibrahim," she said, "I don't suppose *you* could take a letter for me to Acre? I'd wager you travel faster than a ship."

"Not by my own hand, my lady, for the reason that I have no hands." His voice was so serious that Eschiva wondered whether she was being mocked. Then he added, "There is a doorway in this house that leads directly to the Ibelin house in Acre. I might open it for you, if you choose."

"A *doorway?*" Eschiva repeated, before berating herself for her own incredulity. After all, Saracen minstrels told of djinn who whisked their masters about on flying-carpets and mechanical horses. Why shouldn't another operate magical doorways? "Of course! Let me find a veil. Margaret! Will you come?"

Margaret looked aghast. "No, *thank* you! I believe that you are an honest djinn, Ibrahim, but I would rather not be whisked about the countryside by magic, however pure. I shall stay here and tell everyone that the Lady is not to be disturbed."

✳ ✳ ✳

The doorway, to Eschiva's disappointment, was one she already knew well.

"Really?" she murmured, having followed the djinn to the library. "*This* is the doorway to Acre? I would have expected more." Carvings, perhaps, or sigils, as opposed to the wooden door, criss-crossed with ornamental iron strapwork, through which she had been walking all her life.

"That threshold stone was cut in Acre," Ibrahim said, placing a palm against the door. Perhaps it was only Eschiva's imagination that the door rattled as though a wind had shaken it. "There—open it."

Eschiva's heart rose into her throat, but she did as she was asked. One moment she was opening the library door beneath a cloudy Beirut sky; the next she was looking out into a familiar, sunny Acre courtyard. There was no incantation; no feeling of displacement. She simply stepped through and found herself in the loggia of the house she kept in the southern city.

Glancing behind, she saw the grey clouds of Beirut behind her, and heard shouts of laughter from her sons, who had just been released from their books for the morning.

"You will follow me, won't you?" she asked, suddenly feeling a little nervous. Great princes and high ladies—and Eschiva was both—were not well-advised to venture into the narrow streets of Acre alone. "Or should I call for attendants?"

Again, she sensed his reluctance, his weariness. Again, he agreed before she could remark on it. "Of course."

Ibrahim followed her through the door into Acre, and Eschiva closed it behind them. When she re-opened it a moment later, she found herself looking into one of the upper bedrooms of the Acre house, the bed spread with thick cotton to protect it from dust.

"I wonder what other secrets you have been keeping from me," she said, closing the door a second time and leading the way down the loggia. "Did you perform these services for my father?"

"No."

"Why not? My grandfather never thought to mention that there was a *djinn* inhabiting the orange-tree?"

For a deliberative moment, Ibrahim did not answer. "Some men view their sons less as successors, than as rivals. Such was your grandfather."

Eschiva had seen the same mistake made in other families, too often to object when the same accusation was levelled against her own. "So he kept his djinn secret, because he did not wish to share it with his son? But you might have revealed yourself to him, the way you did to me."

"Even a bodiless djinn may long to rest, my lady."

Again, weariness filled his voice. Eschiva said, "I'll take it as a compliment, then, that you appeared to me. I suppose that even djinn feel lonely, at times."

"You were not then your father's heir," he said, very quietly. As though, if she *had* been, he would have remained locked within his tree.

"Regretting it, are you?"

"I told you that I was a peril to my friends."

By now they were at the centre of the courtyard, by the star-shaped trough and fountain that provided drinking-water for beasts of burden. They ought to be hastening through the gate before the house's caretakers happened to see Eschiva loitering where she ought surely not to be. Nevertheless she turned to face the djinn, bringing both of them to a halt.

"Do not regret it, Ibrahim," she said earnestly. "My father was dead and my sister was the Lady, with too many great affairs on her hands to bother with a young sister. I had attendants, servants, *creatures*—but no friends. Until you appeared."

She let out a sigh, allowing herself to remember the long summer afternoons playing in the garden. Sneaking from her bed at night to gaze at the stars together, Ibrahim pointing out the planets, naming the Pleiades and Orion, Scorpio and the signs of the Zodiac.

"It was you who taught me to love the stars," she added. "I must love you for that, if for no other reason."

She wanted to see his eyes warm, the way they had for Margaret a moment ago. Instead, he only looked more guarded—and regretful.

"Rest assured, my lady. I need no additional inducement to perform my bargain."

Eschiva blinked at him, taken aback. "I meant no inducement." To that he said nothing, and she remembered how ill it suited a woman in her position to stand trading words with a servant, let alone in a place where she had no good excuse to be. "Come along," she snapped, turning towards the gate. There was no porter, and she had the key to the place in her pocket, snatched from a drawer in her cabinet. In another moment they were hurrying through the streets.

Acre, as always, was crowded, noisy, and pungent with humanity. As she hurried down the gentle slope towards the great Templar fortress which guarded the harbour, Eschiva must have brushed shoulders with people from just about every nation on earth: bearded Syrian artisans;

pale, sweating pilgrims from France or Scandinavia; sunburned merchants from the Indian Ocean or the trackless African desert; turbaned Egyptian ambassadors like the ones she had at home; Abyssinian expatriates with woolly black hair; Turkish mercenaries not too picky to take service with the Christians of the coast; Damascene fugitives from the sultan's wrath; Bedouin tribesmen bringing wares to sell from the desert; and even black-haired scholars from the Nestorian monasteries far away in Peking, on the furthest edge of Cathay.

Eschiva kept glancing behind to ensure that Ibrahim was with her. A discomfiting question occurred to her: if she were suddenly attacked, would he be willing to run for help?

Did Ibrahim regret their old friendship? She had told him nothing but the truth. As a child, and even now, as a woman, an impassable gulf lay between herself and anyone else who might have been her friend. Her family members, like Balian, and even her dead sister, had always been rivals. As for her servants, they were attentive mainly because it profited them. But Ibrahim was the first person she had ever known who, she felt certain, loved her for herself. Margaret had been the second. There were no others, except perhaps her sons; and they would soon be grown men, eager for a greater share of power…

What had changed? That Ibrahim now had something to gain from her? But all his earthly ambition was a hillside on Cyprus to call his own.

She found herself suddenly in the grip of longing. Because he was bodiless, Ibrahim had nothing to gain from her, and therefore he might been…what? Friend, companion, fellow star-gazer, her other self? But because he had nothing to gain from her, what reason did he have to love her?

He was not a man, and she was not her sister Isabella, and she had promised to send him to that Cypriot hillside when their quest was over.

"Do you know where you're going?" Ibrahim asked, softly, as they approached the gate to the Templar compound. This was an immense, pentagonal fortress at the tip of the promontory on which the city was built, not far from the western mole protecting the harbour. Since the loss of the kingdom a hundred years ago at the battle of Hattin, the Order of the Temple had been forced to make its headquarters here, rather than at the Temple Mount in Jerusalem after which it was named. The walls were massive, as thick as the city wall itself, and the seaward towers bristled with machines capable of throwing stones great distances to threaten hostile ships. Within the vast five-sided courtyard, besides pleasant trees and gardens, were stables, storehouses, workshops, dormitories, churches, kitchens, and refectories—everything needed by so great and wealthy an Order.

Eschiva, of course, was firmly familiar with the place, even though female visitors were kept to a minimum. She sailed in at the gate and was stopped at once by the sergeants guarding it.

"My lady," they said, with a respectful glance at her fine linen cote and the voluminous black veil she wore covering her head and face. "Are you expected?"

She extended her hand, the thumb adorned with the great golden signet-ring of Beirut. "I am on an errand from the Lady of Beirut," she said. "Take me to see Gerard of Montreal, if you please. I have urgent business with him."

There was no arguing with such an impressive weight of gold. At once, the sergeant escorted Eschiva and her silent companion into the courtyard and towards the conventual buildings. The private quarters of the brother knights were situated far from the gate, doubtless with a view to promoting repose and contemplation, in a long building whose nearer side also hosted the cabinets of the Order's officials. A moment later the sergeant showed her into Sir Gerard's own cabinet, and bowed himself away into the loggia.

Eschiva had caught Gerard at his desk, scratching briskly at his paper with a quill. When she was announced, he jumped to his feet, shuffling papers hastily into pigeon-holes.

"Madame," he greeted her, busily concealing papers. "To what do I owe the pleasure?"

Eschiva folded her veil back from her face, unable to forbear a little catlike smile as she did so. "Something to hide, Sir Gerard?"

"Lady Eschiva!" He swallowed his surprise. "You know that the Master relies much upon me to conduct his correspondence, and—"

"Ah, so you're writing to his spies again," she said, pretending to stifle a yawn. "Dear me, *you've* let yourself go. When last I saw you in Tripoli you were dressed like a dog's dinner. Margaret *will* be sad to hear it."

Gerard of Montreal was a man of her own age or a little younger, with a scholar's pale skin, pretty black curls, and a short beard around sulky lips. He might have been handsome, if he did not continually look either petulant or ingratiating. Today, he was also unkempt—it was evidently some time since his beard had been trimmed, and his long surcoat of fine dark-blue wool was both rumpled and stained.

He flushed. "I wasn't expecting visitors, and I've been too busy to scratch myself—but you'll hear the news soon enough."

This was ominous. Eschiva wondered what Beaujeu's formidable spy network might have uncovered this time.

"What brings you to Acre?" Gerard asked, shuffling one last sheaf of papers together, and turning them face-down on the desk. "Are you here to see the Master?"

"No, my friend, I'm here to see *you*. Margaret tells me that in Tripoli last year, you had much to do with a certain Prester John Bessarion. I'm very anxious to see him, for his family has served mine for generations and he is in a position to do me a very great service."

"John Bessarion!" Gerard stared at her, aghast.

"The same. What's the matter? Don't tell me you've mislaid him."

The knight swallowed hard. "Of course I haven't. After the sack, he took service with the Temple. At present his whereabouts are an Order secret."

"So you signed him up to become another one of Beaujeu's spies," Eschiva deduced. Gerard's face told her that she was correct. "Where did you send him, then? Damascus? *Cairo?*"

Gerard's face left her in no doubt on that score, either. Eschiva shook her head in disbelief.

"John Bessarion," she purred. "A Prester of the Watchers. A man under the personal protection of Eschiva of Ibelin…and you sent him into *Egypt* as a *spy*? What was Beaujeu *thinking*?"

Gerard flinched as her voice rose in indignation, but did not say a word. "May I suggest," she said, "that you recall him to the Coast at once?"

"I can't."

"Why not? You were the one who suggested I reinstate my great-grandfather's Watchers—and how am I do to that without a Prester?"

"We need him in Cairo." Gerard had gone scarlet in the face with her tongue-lashing, but on this he seemed quite firm: "You would have found out in any case, soon enough. John Bessarion is in Cairo to watch over the muster of the Egyptian army. We received his report just this morning by a fast ship from Alexandria."

"And?"

Gerard swallowed. "It's confirmed. Sultan Qalawun is preparing for an attack, not on Nubia, but Acre."

Eschiva felt the room become still. In the deathly silence, she heard voices rising from the church, a chant with indistinguishable words. Beaujeu had lost no time: doubtless he already had the Order's priests begging for mercy.

Mercy from heaven, because strength of arms could not save them. How could a handful of isolated cities resist an empire?

Gerard added, "The sultan is getting old and weak, according to this news. Pray that he dies suddenly. As things stand now, only a prolonged struggle for the throne could help us."

Eschiva let out a long, measured breath. "Then it's absolutely certain?"

"Our informant is one of the sultan's most senior amirs, part of his council and highly placed in his army. If anyone knows, he does." Gerard shrugged; she saw now the weariness dragging at his face and shoulders, and regretted mocking him for his haggard appearance. "At present, John Bessarion is our only link to this amir. We need everything he can tell us."

She needed him *here,* on the Coast, saving Beirut, Eschiva thought. But there was no point in saying so, certainly not to Gerard.

"Have him replaced and sent to me as soon as possible," she told Gerard. "Tell Beaujeu about our plan to revive the Watchers. Tell him that this John Bessarion is our one hope for doing so. Tell him it may save us yet."

"How?" Gerard asked, lifelessly. "The stories say that Prester John commands infinite armies. John Bessarion does not. He is not the one you seek."

"Who cares for armies, so long as he may command heaven?" Eschiva beckoned Ibrahim, who waited silently at the door. "I must return at once to Beirut with this news."

"Don't cling to a fool's hope, my lady," Gerard said, his words as measured as a bell's tolling. "Acre will fall, and when it does, Beirut will follow."

* * *

Eschiva emerged from the Beirut library door and came face to face with her cousin Balian.

"Good cuz!" he said. "Where were you hiding? I was seeking you in the library just a moment ago."

"I wasn't beneath one of the desks, if that's what you think," Eschiva replied, with a smile to suggest that that was, in fact, precisely where she had been. The rejoinder rose easily enough to her lips; her mind was still almost a hundred miles away in Acre, fretting over the problem. An invasion which no one believed was coming. The prospect of her own city suffering the kind of horrors suffered last year in Tripoli, and in Antioch twenty years before that. And no Preste John to turn the tide, to rally heaven on their behalf.

"I've been meeting with the Egyptians," Balian informed her, his chest puffed with self-importance. "Demanding an explanation for that incident last month, in the garden. They've refused to hand over the spiesfor questioning."

"Of course they have," Eschiva said. "They can't hand over people whom they've already sent back to Cairo. What? Don't forget that I hear my own spies' reports, cuz."

Balian smoothed over his look of surprise. "I've demanded an explanation, and the Egyptian ambassador will attend on you this evening at sunset. But it's my belief that those spies were after the orange-tree."

That was Eschiva's belief too, but she felt the instinctive need to deflect her cousin's attention as far from the orange-tree as possible. She cast a quick glance behind her; from the look on his face, she felt confident that Ibrahim shared her unease.

"Explain," she said. "Why would you say that?"

"There are stories in the family about that orange-tree," he said, portentously, as though he thought she might have missed hearing them. "Some say it's a good-luck talisman, planted by Marta the Knight after she returned from the battle. Others say that the Old Lord's…servant…dwelt in that tree. A *spirit*."

Eschiva laughed. "Do you mean a *familiar*? Surely you're not accusing our ancestor of *sorcery*, Balian!"

"The Old Lord had excellent reasons for everything he did," Balian pointed out. "You may entrust this question to me, cousin. I'll find out soon enough if there's any way the orange-tree can help us. Only you'll have to inform your guards. Can you believe it? They haven't been allowing anyone but you into the garden for days. Not even me!"

"I'm glad to hear it," Eschiva said. "I gave them strict instructions on the matter."

"Now, cuz, that's hardly sensible! I would never injure the Old Lord's orange-tree, and you clearly need a reliable man to handle it for you."

Eschiva saw the opportunity to give him a little of his own medicine.

"Balian," she said loftily, "I hear what you say, but you haven't proved that that orange-tree is anything more than a symbol of Ibelin vigor and long life. What a fanciful notion, that it might be a dwelling-place of spirits! Now, if you'll excuse me, I have a meeting to attend."

She brushed past him and strode away. When she reached the door to her chamber, she turned aside and hissed, "A word, Ibrahim."

The djinn followed her into the room, a luxurious chamber full of rich brocaded curtains and carpets, with a potted lemon-tree by the windows that overlooked the city and harbour. Today, the sight of them gave Eschiva a pang of anxious longing: the narrow bustling streets, the great buildings in honey-coloured stone with domes of verdigris, the lush palm trees and thickets of masts that clustered by the water's edge.

"Tell me this, Ibrahim: is there a door in this house that will take me to Cairo?"

Her heart sank at his look of reluctance, but she added as gently as she could: "Time runs short for all of us. You heard what Gerard of Montreal said—John Bessarion is in Cairo. If you can open me a door, I might bring him back at once, whatever his duties there."

Still Ibrahim did not answer. "What is it?" she prompted. "I do not fear to walk into the enemy's city alone."

"There is danger for you," Ibrahim said at last, "but more danger for me. Cairo is the seat of my father's power."

"Your *father?*"

"I told you that I was only half mortal."

Only *half* mortal—but then, what of the other half? Eschiva swallowed.

"I'm sorry," she said. "It never occurred to me that a spirit might have… enemies." Which was folly, because two Egyptians had been in her garden, attempting to set fire to Ibrahim's orange-tree. "Is there no way for you to escape your father's attention?"

"There are many," he said, bitterly, "but of them all the most certain is this: to remain here."

Eschiva bit her lip. Impatience had taken hold of her. Gerard had agreed to send John Bessarion to Beirut the moment he was available, but would the Master of the Temple pay any heed to their warnings? It would do them little good if John Bessarion did not return until the sultan was already encamped about Acre.

"Well, then, I'll go to the Master myself," she said. "At once. I'll make him understand he must send someone to relieve his man in Cairo…"

She had wanted to see Ibrahim smile. He did not smile now, but the worried look left his eyes, and that was nearly as good. Eschiva was pleased with her decision for just a moment; and then she cursed herself for her own weakness. How could she justify protecting Ibrahim at the cost of the city, the people, and the Ibelin name?

But there was no going back on her word now. In the meanwhile she must try to make use of the time. Eschiva said, "When will you be able to show me the things you promised, about the Old Lord?"

"Tomorrow night at the soonest," he answered, with a glance at the sky, as though reminding himself of the position of the stars.

With Ibrahim gone, she stood by the window a little longer, gazing into the west where the setting sun painted the sea red.

When the sultan captured Tripoli the previous year, he burned the city to the ground. They said that the isle of St Thomas had been a heap of corpses when the sultan's mamluks were done with the fugitives who had flown there for safety. The sea had been stained red there, too.

Night was coming; it was high time she showed herself to her attendants, assuring them that she had only been taking a prolonged rest in the library. After that she must receive the Egyptian ambassador. She ought, too, to discuss with him the condominium by which she and the sultan shared the rents of her fiefs. Ten barley fields were missing from the sultan's accounts of the incomings of one farm; either by mistake or design, Beirut was being shortchanged. Then she asked herself why she should bother. Soon, the sultan might claim all her land as his own, and there would be nothing she could do to stop him.

Sighing, Eschiva re-pinned her veil in the mirror and went out to see the ambassador.

* * *

It was a clear evening and Eschiva took her custom-made astrolabe, precisely calibrated for Beirut's longitude, up to the roof for a reading of the time. The roof already held her dioptra—a tube fitted with a protractor, mounted on a tripod and used for sighting a star or planet and measuring its height above the horizon. Downstairs in her private cabinet was an armillary sphere, together with her copy of Ptolemy's *Almagest* and endless sheaves of minute triangular calculations with which she was creating her own improved planetary tables for Beirut's longitude. The task had already taken her the best part of four years, and was by no means finished. Tonight's task would help to fill in more of the gaps, as well as providing her with information on the Egyptian campaign.

Hanging her astrolabe from its specially designed hook next to the dioptra, and using Alphecca as her guiding star, Eschiva made a quick calculation of the precise time: twenty-three minutes past eight in the evening.

Would Sultan Qalawun of Egypt indeed besiege Acre? Or would something prevent him—a political crisis, ill-health, death? If Eschiva could accurately calculate the differences between Beirut's latitude and Cairo's, the numbers might contain some hint as to the sultan's fortunes.

Time noted, Eschiva hastened downstairs again to the cabinet where her lamps burned behind shoemaker's globes—glass vessels full of water, positioned to catch and scatter the light. The first step was to set her armillary sphere, according to tables she had already calculated, to determine the position of the seven planets in the sky, according to celestial longitude. The next was then to use the celestial longitude to calculate which house of the night sky each planet fell into, according to the ascendant—her preferred method. Finally, she would create a formula to translate each position into Cairo's latitude. Eschiva sat down, finding her half-completed charts, pinning up the list of calculations that needed to be made, setting her abacus in place and finding a spare piece of waste-paper on which to record her figures.

All these calculations needed to be done perfectly, or the answer would be useless.

Ordinarily, the thing would have been no great challenge. The calculations were complicated, but the chatter of her abacus kept her company and she had done them enough times that she now found it restful, clearing her mind, slowing her pulse, and reminding her of a great central truth: that although the world might *seem* to be chaotic, unpredictable, and frightening, in truth it was no such thing. Two and two always made four; the stars always travelled by predictable courses; and to them was entrusted power over the affairs of men, so that by peering into their mysteries she might share in a little of their power.

Tonight, however, that restfulness evaded her. She could not fix her mind upon her work. Perhaps it was a malign influence of Mercury that made her all thoughts run away from her. For a while she sat staring at a blank page, unable to make herself begin. Ibrahim was in her mind—his soft voice, his watchful silences. She thought of the boy he had pretended to be, pointing out Alphecca in the constellation Corona, showing her how to use her first astrolabe, teaching her the use of the Arabic numerals so much better suited to these complicated calculations than those used by Rome… At last, instead of beginning, she called softly:

"Ibrahim!"

He emerged from the shadows at the edge of the room, stiff and watchful. "What is your will, my lady?"

Eschiva regretted her impulsive summoning at once, but Ibrahim had not only taught her the names of the stars; he had also taught her to use an astrolabe.

"I am trying to cast a horoscope for Cairo," she said. "Perhaps you would like to help me with my figures." He hesitated, and she added, hurriedly: "Or if you do not, there's no harm done. Return to your tree."

"For Cairo?" he repeated, and she knew then that she had caught his attention.

"Yes. And I want to calculate the answer twice. Not just according to the ascendent, but also the meridian. To be certain."

Ibrahim, like herself, had always loved numbers. "Then begin, and I will watch."

She smiled her thanks. This time the numbers flowed easily from her pen, and the two of them began to race against each other to calculate the answers or correct them, Eschiva using her abacus and Ibrahim using his fingers. She was quicker than he was, but more likely to make mistakes. When at last she caught him in a mistake of his own, she shouted with exultation; and then, at last, Ibrahim smiled.

Chapter XII.

The sultan had called the muster at Masjid Tibr—a mosque an hour's ride north of Cairo, built on the edge of the Nile's flood-plains. By now, early in November, the floods had long receded, leaving the ground dark and soft; but at Masjid Tibr the crops and pleasure-gardens that ordinarily bordered the river had given way to the sprawl of a great encampment.

Soraya followed Saif not to the tent that awaited him somewhere within that canvas labyrinth, nor to the sultan's headquarters at the mosque itself. Instead, they directed their horses towards the harder, higher ground on the right, where a large rectangle of flat ground had been marked off with wooden barriers. This was surrounded by a thicket of soldiery and camp-followers, whilst wooden platforms at either side provided a vantage for the great amirs to watch the sport within. Two teams of four horsemen each, in contrasting livery, wielding long-handled mallets, thundered to and fro as they competed to strike a small leathern ball through the goalposts at either end of the playing-field.

"What game is this?" Soraya asked, watching as one of the riders approached the ball at a flat gallop and slung it humming through the air. It shot directly through the goal-posts and elicited roars of approval from the crowd.

Saif sent her a surprised look. "This is polo," he said. "Don't you remember?"

"No." She might have asked him whether *he* remembered that her memories had been stolen—but she was too thrilled, too breathless. "It looks like *fun.*"

Saif gulped. "We're not playing it for *fun*, Soraya. God have mercy. I forgot to make sure you remembered."

Soraya dragged her eyes away from the galloping horses, the swinging mallets, the soaring ball. "Not playing it for fun? Then you are assuredly playing it wrong. I've never seen anything so delightful in my life."

This morning he'd summoned her from a blissful sleep. If God had truly created mankind, it was with a host of bodily pleasures in which to indulge. This one Soraya enhanced by disconnecting the nerves connecting her ears and eyes to her brain. Nothing short of an earthquake could have woken her—or, in this case, one of Saif's own servants, shaking her until she came awake. Reconnecting ears and eyes, she had been greeted only with the instructions to clothe herself in a man's shape and attire for the day's business.

Now she rubbed at the thick black beard on her chin, prickling with anticipation as she watched the play. The pounding of the hooves, the *thwack* of the mallet, the rush of the wind—yes, all of it seemed familiar. "I can do this. I'll remember. What are the rules?"

"You'll *remember*?"

"I remember things all the time," she said, and then the look on his face arrested her. Saif looked positively aghast. "What? It's only by instinct."

"Nothing," he said, pulling himself together. "The aim of the game is to strike the ball between the goalposts yonder, wielding the mallet only in your right hand—that's for safety. Play occurs in seven-minute bouts, and the teams change ends with each bout, or with each goal. There are two mounted umpires, and the team scoring highest wins. Are you listening, Soraya? It's of the greatest importance that we put on a good show in this game. We'll be playing against Turuntay, and you know what that means."

Soraya's thoughts were elsewhere, gnawed by suspicion. Why should Saif look so horrified when she said she remembered things? What was it John Bessarion had said two days ago in the ruins of Heliopolis? *The Soraya I knew, in Tripoli, loathed al-Mukhtar.* He'd been lying, surely. But then, just as surely, Saif had been aghast when she said she remembered.

She ground her teeth. She ought to believe John was lying, ought to be able to trust Saif. She ought to be utterly hostile to a man who only wanted her for what she could do for him.

But he knew her better than she did herself—knew that she loved halwa, knew that her deepest desire was freedom. And Saif, she knew, was a practised deceiver. If he was willing to lie to Khalil, the man he loved and revered above all others, then surely he was capable of lying to her also.

"What about halwa?" she asked him, when he stopped speaking.

Saif blinked at her, evidently at a loss. *"Halwa?"*

"Yes, halwa—the confection. Do I like that, too, as well as polo?"

"How should I know? You like all food. Why?"

She did not want to tell him that she had sought out his enemy, had accepted food at his hands and had left him alive. "What happened in Tripoli?" she asked, instead. "Why did you allow that mortal to live?"

"Hush!" Saif cautioned her, sending a glance at the people milling around them. "We can't discuss that here."

"Then let's go to that sycamore tree and discuss it over there," Soraya said, pointing to the inky-black shade of a lone tree on a rise of ground at the far end of the field.

"We don't have the time. We have to be on the field when the match begins, or Khalil will have our hides."

He turned his horse towards the enclosure where the players awaited their turns, Khalil visible in a snowy white turban and a black linen tunic shot through with narrow stripes of red. Dissatisfied, Soraya urged her horse into a trot beside him.

"You tell me everything else," she said. "Why not this? What makes you so afraid?"

"I'm not afraid! I simply didn't think it was important."

He *was* afraid: of that she was quite certain, and his denials only made her suspicions grow. "It's important to *me.*"

"God have mercy, why?"

"Because I don't understand what is happening to me," she said. "You've warned me against this man, but all I feel when I look at him is—"

She bit her tongue. Saif pulled his horse to a halt; there was naked fear on his face.

"Is *what*, Soraya? Say it."

"*Mawadah*," she whispered. Love—affection.

He swallowed, hard. "I feared it."

A silence lay between them, like an unsheathed sword.

"That's why I need to know," she said, at length. "Because I know that you warned me against him, but my heart tells me something else, and if I'm going to call it a liar I need the *truth*."

"No, you need to *trust* me," Saif said. "Your feelings will lead you astray. However much or little I say, your heart will still deny it. Is there not enough *mawadah* between us for that?"

Perhaps that was the truth. Perhaps she was so blinded by John Bessarion's cunning, that she could never argue herself out of it.

"Man is weak by nature," she said, one of Saif's little sayings, and she saw some of the worry leave his eyes.

"God is merciful," he responded.

But as they proceeded towards the enclosure and Khalil, she could not help wondering: if Saif had always feared that she might love John Bessarion, then why did he say that what had happened in Tripoli was unimportant?

Perhaps, she soothed herself, he meant that it was unimportant for her to *know* the truth about Tripoli—but that was hardly an excuse, either. It was the sort of thing Khalil would do—making decisions, ostensibly for Saif's good, without consulting him. The more Soraya thought about it, the more bitter her disappointment that Saif could be capable of treating her in the same way.

The enclosure gate was thick with jostling onlookers who crowded against the fence to look at the waiting teams and call out their support or predictions. As the crowd parted to let them through, Soraya caught a glimpse of a sunburnt face, a grey beard and iron-grey eyes. Her heart jolted in her breast, but already the man had lost himself in the milling crowd.

There was no possibility of John's recognising her. Not in this man's body she had created, wiry and lean and fine, very different to her customary generous curves.

Then they made it into the enclosure, where Khalil and another of his mamluks were already waiting. To outward appearances, Saif's master was still a young man a few years short of thirty, with smooth skin, dark hair, and aristocratic looks; but his eyes were cold and Soraya did not like to look into them, for the force and power of the spirit within was like a blow from a clenched fist.

"You're late," Khalil welcomed them. "And the slave is wearing the wrong tunic."

Saif had asked Soraya to make her tunic match his, but she hadn't understood the necessity of matching livery and had pleased herself with green stripes rather than red. Now, with a sigh, she willed the stripes to change colour.

"Not in public," Khalil snapped. "Never mind, it's too late now. Husaym, here, will be keeping our goal and I will playing the rear position, as usual. Saif, you'll be scoring and the slave will be your second."

Saif had explained some of this on the way. Apart from the rearmost player, who defended the goalposts, the other three riders would play the offense. Khalil had placed himself in the traditionally third position, one which won little glory in the form of scoring points but was nevertheless the most strategic player on the field, since his long, sweeping shots would determine the angle from which the two forward players—Saif and Soraya— would attempt to score their goals.

It was typical of their master, Soraya thought. In the year she had known him, Khalil had always been happier directing affairs from the shadows, than stepping into the light himself. Power, not glory, had always been his goal.

"Any questions?" he asked, now.

Saif sent Soraya a furtive look, as though warning her not to make trouble. "No, my lord, but there's something I ought to tell you. You warned me once to alert you if I met anyone bearing the name Bessarion."

Soraya realised with dismay that this was the result of her questioning. She had frightened Saif so much that he felt himself obliged to warn Khalil of John's presence.

Khalil seemed equally electrified by the name. "At last! Is it John Bessarion, by any chance?"

"I believe so, my lord. They said he had come to the Coast from Mosul, so I do not know if it is the man you—"

"It's him," Khalil broke in. "At last! What timing!"

Soraya was seated near the fence, and someone reached through to tug on her loose trousers. Impatient, she kicked the hand away without looking down to see who it was or what they wanted.

"I'll bring you his head," Saif offered, and it was as though all the air left her lungs. Her hands were white knots on the horses' reins. She saw John Bessarion's head, hacked and bloody, the grey eyes filmed over, as sharply as though the very sight was before her.

Never. Never. Not while she had breath. She would sooner kill Saif himself—

God have mercy on her! Why would she think such a thing?

"Is he in Cairo?" Khalil was asking, and Saif was saying that he did not know—naturally, for he was only preparing the ground, hedging his bets in case he should not succeed in collecting that head. "Then on no account should you go in search of the man. He will come to us. In the meanwhile, I need you here."

Soraya felt herself able to breathe freely again; and then someone tugged on her clothing again. She looked down. It was, of all people, John Bessarion. Reaching through the fence, he beckoned her to step aside and speak to him.

Between the two of them—John and Saif—her heart was going to give out altogether, and then Khalil would have a very public disintegration to explain to the excited crowd. With an effort, Soraya swallowed her sound of shock and muttered something about checking her girth. Khalil gave her an impatient wave, and she dismounted and led the horse to a post far enough away to prevent them being overheard.

On the other side of the fence, John Bessarion pushed his way towards her. "Who are you?" she muttered, making a show of testing her saddle-girth.

"What do you want?"

"Forgive me, Soraya, but I must speak to you."

She dragged in a sharp breath. More sorcery. "How did you know me?"

"The green," he replied, as though the answer was obvious. "You always have *something* green about you. Where can we meet?"

Soraya looked down at her tunic, at the fine red stripes that had been tiny threads of green not three minutes ago. It didn't mean that he *knew* her, any more than the halwa meant that he knew her. Maybe he'd observed her habits. Or paid someone else to observe them.

"I can't speak to you now," she said, angrily. "I'm busy. If you want to keep your head, you should stay out of sight. Saif was *just* offering it as a peace-offering to al-Ashraf Khalil."

She turned away just as the drum was struck to signal the end of the preceding match. The enclosure gates opened, the sweating horses and men came trotting in, and Khalil led them out onto the field.

Saif came to her side, holding his polo stick upright like a lance. "Try to stay three lengths away from me or more," he hissed. "If I fumble the ball or need to pass it back, you should be there to take it up."

Soraya wanted to laugh at his seriousness over what was, in the end, a mere ball-game. "You think if you win this game, Khalil will save your wife?"

Saif sent her a look she couldn't read and then said "Hush!" The black-liveried team drew up at the centre of the field, facing the opposing team in blue—four mamluks whose tunics were embroidered thickly with golden borders, a brazen display of wealth and arrogance of a kind calculated to provide grist for Friday sermons in mosques all around Cairo. In mortal years, their leader must be at least ten years Khalil's elder. He swung his stick to an upright position and bowed his head, half ironic.

"Al-Ashraf," he greeted. "I wouldn't have expected to see the sultan's chosen heir playing in the third place. I suppose a show of humility befits one who has been proclaimed but not officially invested."

"Play well today, and the sultan may be convinced to favour you with the throne instead, Turuntay."

Khalil spoke serenely, the agitation he had shown in the enclosure wiped away as though it had never been. Soraya raised an eyebrow, but kept her thoughts to herself. The game, then, was not merely a display of equestrian skill and martial ability. Turuntay must be one of the sultan's great amirs, a rival of Khalil's. No wonder the air was tense between them; no wonder Saif had warned her not to think of this as merely a game.

So, the game was to be a rehearsal of the coming power struggle between the sultan's mamluk and his son, an opportunity for the rivals to prove themselves before the sultan and the whole army. Soraya hid a grim smile. She had no intention of helping to burnish Khalil's reputation—even if she remembered how.

A drum sounded, signalling the beginning of the first round of play, and the umpire rolled the small leather ball into the dust between the opposing teams. There came a confused moment in which all the sticks were jabbing at the ball, and there were horses and hooves everywhere; and then Khalil cut the ball out, sending it soaring towards the northern end of the field. Turuntay and Saif dashed off full tilt in its wake. At that moment, as with so many things, instinct took over. Soraya dashed after Saif like a thunderbolt. The horse was a streak of lightning between her thighs, the wind was a shout of exultation against her face, the air was a cloud of dust in her lungs. Ahead, Saif got control of the ball, nursing it along with controlled taps of his stick, but Turuntay was riding him off, stirrup to stirrup, forcing him to the right of the goal, obstructing his shot. Then Saif's stick flicked and the ball abruptly changed direction, cutting back towards Soraya.

Soraya responded without thinking, swinging her stick with a practised flick of her wrist. She felt the solid, satisfying *thwack* of a good hit and instantly shouted "Son of a *shoe*" as the ball shot directly across the field, hummed between the goalposts, and hammered a crack in the barrier fence beyond.

Turuntay and Saif disengaged, their horses circling back towards her as one of the fielders ran to retrieve the ball, tossing it to the mounted umpire. Saif raised a fist in jubilation as he trotted back towards the centre of the field for play to begin again. Soraya ground her teeth and followed him to the line, where even Khalil favoured her with a tight-lipped nod of approval. Instinct, it seemed, was a double-edged sword.

From then on she played a more erratic game. She was too close behind Saif to catch the balls he fumbled or passed back; she incurred a penalty by striking another player, as if by accident; and to crown it all, she struck one ball precisely wide enough that it struck one of the goalposts and rebounded, instead of rolling between them.

When Khalil began to eye her with suspicion, Soraya amused herself by meddling with the field—a form of rebellion he would find more difficult to prove against her. Tiny rocks appeared on the ground, causing the ball to skip and ricochet. Gusts of wind swept dust into the players' eyes at inopportune moments. The ball might grow suddenly lighter or heavier, depending upon who struck it. The game became subtly unpredictable as Soraya held them back, by just a goal or two, from getting ahead. Meanwhile, Turuntay and his men hit goal after goal, crowing over their good luck.

The game was played in four brief periods, the time marked by a sandglass. By the third bout, Khalil wore a tight-lipped smile, and his eyes when they rested upon her were crackling with rage. Soraya decided that it was time to abate her tricks somewhat—though not entirely, lest she increase Khalil's suspicions. She got the ball early in the third period, chasing after it as it approached the side-line. One of Turuntay's mamluks crept up on her left, crowding her further towards the line, seeking to shove her off the field altogether. Soraya flicked the ball into the air a moment before it crossed the line. Saif was beyond the opposing rider, clearly hoping that she would have the chance to pass the ball his way—but the goalposts were near and Soraya was about to be crowded into the corner.

Let Khalil suspect me now, she thought.

The ball soared across the side-line; if it touched the ground it would be out. Even as the horses raced forward, grinding the riders' legs together, Soraya kept the ball in the air, juggling it with three light taps of her stick. When she had it where she wanted it, she struck it from the air. It flew at a sharp angle diagonally across the space before the horses' heads and through the rapidly-narrowing gap still visible between the goal-posts.

There was a breathless silence before the spectators understood what she had done and shrieked in excitement. Soraya disengaged from Turuntay's mamluk and circled her horse. As she rounded and returned, the postures of the other players were imprinted on her mind like miniatures in a manuscript. Saif had an arm flung up in disbelief. Turuntay's man, unaware of what had happened, was reining in more slowly, still scanning the field around him for the missing ball. The other players, who a moment ago had been pelting in a knot behind her, had split apart into gesticulating astonishment.

Only Khalil at the far rear sat apparently motionless on his horse, a black cloud on the pale, starkly lit field. Soraya shivered, feeling his eyes upon her as Saif beat her on the shoulders, shouting congratulations.

"I can't believe you managed that shot! How?"

Even Turuntay could not resist congratulating her. "I've never seen such a goal in all my days," he told her as they gathered again at the field's centre. "What is your name, mamluk?"

"He's not for sale," Khalil said, shortly. Soraya bowed to the other amir, but did not speak.

The points she permitted them to win in the third round left Turuntay still several points ahead. The fourth was a disaster. Saif kept fumbling the ball; once or twice his horse stumbled on suddenly-materialising stones. Turuntay won two goals for each one of theirs and sailed to victory on a tide of the crowd's applause. Khalil congratulated him with another of those furious, tight-lipped smiles as the two teams approached the sultan's throne to make their bows.

Only then did the two antagonists see what Soraya had spotted early in the game: the place of honour at the centre of the box was empty. Instead, a white-bearded amir descended from the box and beckoned to a servant nearby, who stepped forward holding the reins of a magnificent grey horse.

"Well played," announced the amir. "In the name of al-Mansur Qalawun, I award to the victor this Najd-bred stallion, together with its caparisons and its keeper, a slave from Khorasan who is master of all matters pertaining to feeding and physicking horses."

Turuntay leaped from one saddle to another without touching the ground, raising a fist in response to the crowd's acclamations.

Khalil himself seemed unperturbed, his temper soothed by the sultan's absence. "What's this, Bektash? Where is my father?"

"Al-Ashraf," the old amir said, bowing his head. "The sultan remains in his quarters today, indisposed."

"Sick?" Khalil scowled, as though the news did not please him, and then turned to Turuntay. "I wish you joy of the beast," he said. "May he bear you to safety in your hour of need."

"And thence to victory," Turuntay replied, evidently no stranger to veiled threats.

Khalil snapped his fingers and beckoned Saif and Soraya to follow him from the field.

They did not return to the enclosure where the next team was waiting to begin their own match; instead, Khalil rode for the barrier and the guards hurried to drag it open for them. Khalil cut directly through the crowd in the direction of the mosque, striking out with his polo stick at any laggards who remained in his way.

The mosque's gatekeeper saw them coming well in advance and had the gate open when they trotted in. Beyond, Khalil descended from his saddle, tossed his reins and polo stick to Husaym with a command to mind the horses, and beckoned again to Saif and Soraya. They hurried to keep up with their master as he stalked angrily across the forecourt towards the mosque's main entrance. The structure was not quite as grand as some of the mosques in Cairo, but in addition to the prayer hall and the grand central courtyard with its gurgling fountain, there were also some smaller rooms guarded by solemn mamluks in the livery of the sultan's own household. No doubt this was where Qalawun had his quarters.

Khalil stopped at the fountain, turning to face Saif and Soraya. The midday air was hot and clear and there was no sign of life but the bored mamluks congregating about the sultan's rooms in the far corner. The sun was a white eye burning in the sky above, and Khalil was a black cloud of wrath burning in the courtyard below.

For a moment he beheld Soraya with tight-lipped disapproval. Then he turned to Saif. "If this happens again," he said softly, "it'll be you who suffers for it, Saif."

"What! are you blaming *me* for your loss?" Soraya asked, with well-feigned disbelief.

"Show some respect," Saif commanded, turning on her at once.

Soraya felt the command take hold of her; she got rid of the compulsion by bowing, touching a hand to lips and forehead, and saying, "O my lord and O the light of my eyes: is every breath of wind my fault? I am but the canker of incompetence within the blossom of diligence, but you know that no mortal could have played as I did today."

She could not see Khalil from the depths of her bow, but she knew he was not deceived by her pretended obeisance. "What do I care if a wind springs up? I have a djinn as my servant, expressly to dissipate the gusts and smooth the playing-field. You were not *merely* there to strike goals."

"O lord of fragrance, allow the balm of patience to soothe the scorches of adversity. Your miserable servant barely recalled how to play the game. Of any other duties I was, may God have mercy upon me, sadly ignorant."

"Do you think that this is funny?" Khalil asked, at last deigning to notice her sarcasm. Soraya had been half inclined to believe that he was as incapable of understanding it as Saif.

"She's telling the truth, my lord," Saif interposed, reddening. "I forgot to instruct her in her duties. She hasn't played polo since—not for well over a year."

"As I warned you. It must not happen again. All things are now drawing to their culmination, and the slightest deviation might be fatal." Khalil spoke softly enough, but he paused for a long moment, watching Saif mistrustfully. "Do not presume, boy: if you cannot be relied upon, you can always be replaced."

Saif threw himself on his knees.

"I'll set it right," he begged. "What should I do for you? Should I go to Acre and kill their chief men? Should I...should I make you sultan?"

Khalil struck him across the face; Soraya flinched at the sound of the heavy blow, augmented by a heavy gold signet on that hand. Saif recoiled, just managing to catch himself before he measured his length across the pavement.

"Fool!" Khalil hissed. "Do that and I'll have you skinned alive. Qalawun must *live*. Repeat it!"

"Qalawun must live. I hear and obey," Saif gasped, pressing a hand to his reddened face.

Khalil sent Soraya another resentful look. "Keep your women in better control," he snarled, turning on his heel. "If you cannot command the djinn, she had better be kept in the Lance."

As their master stalked away, Saif remained kneeling on the stone, breathing hard—whether from shock or from pain, Soraya could not tell. She dropped to a crouch beside him, and when Khalil seemed to have retreated far enough, she nudged Saif with her shoulder and said, "Think he'd be upset if we assassinated the sultan?"

Then she saw the expression on his face, and the laughter died on her lips. Saif had the look of a young child who does not understand why he has been beaten.

"I've always thought of him as a father," he whispered. "But does he really think of me as a son?"

"Saif," she whispered, touching his shoulder. For days, remembering how easily Saif lied to Khalil, she'd been haunted by the suspicion that he might be lying to her in the same way. But this was truth. She might not trust Saif's smiles, but she trusted his pain.

For a year she'd known him, and although he did not often show her the cracks in his armour, she had glimpsed them enough times to know precisely where his weak points lay. And she had seen Khalil strike at them often enough to conceive a black loathing for their master.

"You would never treat a son of yours in such a way," she murmured, raising her hand palm-out to ward off the evil eye, to ward off *Khalil's* eyes.

"God willing," he said. And then long training must have prompted him to say, "Who can say what I might or might not do in his place? God, who knows all things, has not placed me so highly. I am content."

He stood, dabbing away the blood where his lip had split; the flesh itself had already knitted back together, drawing upon the power Soraya shared with him via the soul tether. In the far corner of the courtyard, the sultan's mamluks stood to attention as Khalil approached them. Saif turned to Soraya.

"How long would it take you to find me John Bessarion?" he asked.

Soraya stiffened. "Why do you ask?"

He was going to make her choose. She did not want to have to choose.

"I have to save her, Soraya."

There was still a smear of blood on his lip. There was still that look of desperation in his eye. Perhaps as recently as a month ago she would have relented at once. But John Bessarion had a claim upon her, too.

Why, she did not understand, and Saif had refused to tell her. It was all very well for Saif to chastise her for letting her feelings guide her—but when he gave her no reason, what else could she rely on? Feelings did not come without reason, after all.

"Don't you understand? Khalil will never relent. No amount of captured spies, or dead enemies, or polo victories will change his mind. He'll just keep you dancing to his tune until Ghaliyah dies!"

Saif had no answer to that. His voice hardened: "Please, Soraya. Don't make me command you."

"No one's *making* you command me," she protested. Saif's expression did not change. She felt icy to her fingertips. He *meant* to command her, she realised. And this was her friend?

"Look," she begged, terrified of what would happen if she did not at least offer him a bargain. "I'll tell you where he is, I swear it. But first you must tell me who he is, and what he did to me in Tripoli. That's fair, isn't it?"

Saif sent a terrified glance in the direction of the far courtyard corner. "You have to forget him, Soraya, and forget Tripoli. I'm warning you."

"Is it a threat, then?"

"No, it's a warning, for your own good! The more you know, the sooner Khalil will take away your memories."

And that confirmed it. John Bessarion was the reason she had lost everything she once knew. It was for fear of him that Saif was keeping her ignorant of her own past.

It was for fear of him that Saif was *lying* to her.

She knew the cracks in his armour, and she fashioned herself a blade of words to cut him.

"You're exactly like him," she hissed. "You wondered how you'd treat your own sons? I take it back. You'd treat them exactly like *that*."

Saif's face went white and pale, and he stamped the Lance on the pavement. *"Enough,"* he hissed, yanking on the soul tether with such force that she lost her grip on her body and flowed back, helpless and eyeless and earless, into the narrow confines of the vessel.

Chapter XIII.

By the time Saif summoned her from the Lance again, something within Soraya had altered to a hard core of bitterness. Saif was lying to her. Pretending to be her friend, when all along John Bessarion had been right: he was her master.

She took form in a column of dust, condensed into her customary female form, and looked about to find herself in a large, comfortable tent, richly carpeted, its hangings woven with lovely geometric patterns. The low divan, with its cushions and soft coverings and the small brazier beside it to ward off the cold, was empty. The armour tree to one side was empty also. Soraya turned and found Saif beside her, clad for a night mission in a black tunic and turban, his armour's chime muffled by the shirt that covered it.

"I'm sorry," he said, not quite meeting her eyes. "Khalil ordered me to put you back into the Lance. I know you don't like it."

She regarded him with speechless disgust. "God be thanked," she said. "It cannot be every djinn's lot to hear such a generous apology."

"Then you forgive me?"

She wanted to strike the hope from his face. She wanted to reach inside her heart and uproot the feelings that still whispered that he was a comrade, to be comforted and protected.

"I thought we were *friends*," she hissed. "I was wrong. The moment I asked the wrong question, you threatened to take away my choices and my memories. Which means that of the two of you, the one who has been telling me more of the truth—is John Bessarion."

John had told her that she had loathed this man, once. She now believed him.

Saif went pale. "I've never lied to you, Soraya."

She snorted. "You let me *believe* a lie. Oh, God! I suppose the rest of it is true, too. I suppose he *is* the one who promised to set me free."

"He might have promised first," Saif said, desperately. "But I promised also, and truly."

"Why? To outbid him for my loyalty? Would it have occurred to you to make that promise if he had not made it first? Do you even mean to keep it?"

"I *do*. I *will* free you, God willing, if it's the last thing I do. The only reason I haven't yet is that I've been trying to save Ghaliyah. I thought you would understand. A man ought to put his own family first."

"Your *family* has served well to shield you from ever having to disobey your master."

His hands clenched on the haft of the Lance, so that Soraya thought that he was about to force her back within. Instead, he said, "I won't kill John Bessarion, if that puts your mind at ease." He took a deep breath. "That's why I've called you. Help me kill Turuntay instead."

Soraya could do nothing but look her disbelief.

"My master will be grateful that his rival is gone," Saif said earnestly. "Then I will ask again for Ghaliyah's life."

She suppressed her incredulous laughter. "This is *ishq*. Love has driven you mad."

"What do you mean?"

"Oh, it is nothing! Far be it from this humble slave to give counsel or advice where it isn't wanted."

"But I *do* want it."

"Is that why you're summoning me and giving me commands, instead of asking, *Soraya, what do you think?* Is that—"

She stopped. Put a hand to her lips. "Oh," she said softly. "Oh. We've done this before, haven't we?"

Saif stared at her, uncomprehending. Then, unbelievably, he smiled. "You always were saucy and pert," he said. As though, now that she was drowning in bitterness and betrayal, he saw a side of her that he had missed.

It was outrageous that he should take pleasure in the just anger he had caused, but the outrage was too raw to put into words. "Command me, then," she rasped. "How should I do this murder? Should I seduce him and feed him poison? Or shall I simply open his veins and bleed him dry?"

"This one I'll do myself," Saif said, as though it was a gift he gave her. "But I'll need a way to get into his presence. Go and steal me Turuntay's signet ring. Use such cunning that he does not notice its absence. Wear a face he will not recognise and do nothing to raise suspicion or let anyone connect you with me. Come back the moment it is safe to do so."

Command mounted upon command, blocking loopholes, lopping off the choices she might have made along the way. Soraya set her teeth, resisting the force of his words for only long enough to choke out a laugh.

"This," she said. "You've done this to me before, too. Bound me up in so many commands that I become your *puppet.*" She spat. "You trust me so little, after all."

"Ghaliyah first," he said, his mouth set in a stubborn line. "Then you. Go."

She went.

Chapter XIV.

John's patience was rewarded about nightfall, when a dusty young boy in ill-fitting clothing emerged from al-Mukhtar's tent and headed further into the camp, towards the mosque. There was nothing in the urchin's appearance to distinguish him from the hundreds of other stable-boys in the camp—nothing but the polished shard of green tile he wore on a simple leather cord about his neck.

John followed the boy silently until they were out of sight of al-Mukhtar's tent. Then he drew level with the boy and said, "Soraya?"

Soraya-the-boy slanted a look up at him "I hoped you would show yourself."

Her voice was subdued, resigned. John felt first relief, then guilt. If she was pleased to see him, it was only because she had been browbeaten into it.

"Can we talk?"

"Not now; Saif has sent me on an errand." She scowled. "Meet me at his tent at half an hour past midnight. You'll know it by its lack of emblems and the—"

"I'm familiar with it," John said. She sent him an inquiring look, and he shrugged. "Tripoli."

"Of course." A weary sigh. "You'll know that it's me by the same sign as ever. Now go."

John did as he was told, finding a kebab stall for his dinner now that he was no longer kept watching al-Mukhtar's tent. For the first time since meeting Soraya in Heliopolis, he felt cautious hope.

He had spent the past few days haunting the street outside al-Mukhtar's palace, waiting for a chance to speak again with the elusive djinn. Only that morning had his efforts been rewarded when she and her master left the palace for the encampment, and of course John had followed. He had taken the risk of changing his blue turban for a dusty white one, knowing how it would appear if a Christian was found loitering about in the sultan's encampment on the eve of an expedition against his co-religionists in Acre. The risk had paid off: all day, John had walked up and down the camp, counting tents and horses, committing them carefully to memory. Preparations must be almost complete, for nearly all the great amirs had now left their palaces to join the sultan in camp, including Beaujeu's highly-placed informant. They were only waiting on the sultan's word to begin their march; and the sultan, it was whispered, was only waiting for a bout of dysentery to clear up.

It must be admitted that things looked bad for Acre—but at least, John thought, the signs were good as regarded himself. If Soraya was willing to speak to him, however reluctantly, then perhaps he could convince her to send him home, after all.

At the hour appointed he approached the al-Mukhtar's tent again, only to halt in confusion when he saw the Chosen himself sitting cross-legged in the tent's opening, methodically sharpening an array of knives and swords laid out on a low table. Al-Mukhtar did not glance up to see him, and at first John thought he should retreat into the shadows and wait for Soraya to show herself. Then he saw the shard of green on the cord about al-Mukhtar's neck.

Soraya's sign, by which he should know her. John's throat went dry. It might be her, wearing al-Mukhtar's face. It might be a trap. Al-Mukhtar could snuff out his life with one flick of the wrist…

He didn't have to put her to the test, he thought. He might turn around, follow Rahel's suggestion, look for a Coptic Watcher to help him. That would be the rational and cautious thing to do.

But then, if Soraya had kept faith with him, and he broke it, how would he explain it to her? He could not claim to be her friend if he did not trust her to protect him.

He stepped before the gleaming array of knives. The *grind, grind, grind* against the whetstone stopped. Al-Mukhtar's face looked up at him. Al-Mukhtar's voice said, "Good. Sit there, out of sight, where we can talk."

John hesitated. He knew that Soraya was able to take on the form of any man, woman, child, or even beast, as she liked. But this resemblance was uncanny. "It really *is* Soraya?" he asked.

"Saif has gone mad and is trying to get himself killed." From the twist of the lips he knew that it was truly her. "Of course it's Soraya."

"And you are covering for him?" John surmised, settling himself within the flap of the tent, where she could see him. "What the devil could he be about? I don't see Saif as the type to break his own sultan's laws."

"You aren't here to ask the questions; you're here to answer them," Soraya said, and the cold tone of her voice was a flood of ice-water on all his hopes. "I need you to tell me what happened in Tripoli. Why Saif wants you dead. What Khalil wants with the djinn of Beirut."

John blinked. "I cannot answer that last one. But the rest of it I will tell you."

Soraya listened with a ferocious scowl on her face, occasionally exclaiming or asking questions—many of which he could not answer. Instead he told the story of how he and al-Mukhtar had forged a reluctant alliance to destroy Tripoli's guardian demon, Lilith, despite the fact that al-Mukhtar had slaughtered his only friends in the Coast. And then, how al-Mukhtar had betrayed and tried to kill him, and only Soraya, who had helped him throughout, had saved his life.

"I still don't know why al-Mukhtar chose to keep my identity concealed from Khalil, rather than revealing it," John admitted, when the tale drew to the end.

"I do." With her finger, Soraya tested the edge of a newly-sharpened blade and laid it on the table beside the others once she was satisfied. "Saif's a coward. There's something he very badly wants from his master, and he's terrified of disappointing him. In addition, if he thinks it will win him what he wants, Saif will do anything—or kill anyone."

John shivered. "Does he have no conscience?"

"There's a point beyond which all consciences fail," she said.

He watched her dark profile—Saif's profile—and wondered what she knew about al-Mukhtar that made her capable of feeling any sympathy for the man at all. As an ally, John must grant, the fellow was obliging and well-spoken, with a certain sense of honour. But he was also more than capable of knifing an ally in the back at the first opportunity. Moreover, he had slaughtered the Zakars in cold blood, and had neither paid for, nor repented his crime.

The silence spun out. John stirred, restless. "Well? Have you any other questions?"

"No," Soraya said, in al-Mukhtar's lowest voice. Then, almost to herself: "Both of you claim to be my friend and champion, but only one of you can be telling the truth. Not Saif. He pretended to be my friend when in fact, he has only ever been my master. In that you were right."

"Then you'll help me?"

She sent him a scowl that was nearly a grimace—a look of unguarded malevolence that he was quite certain had never touched the real al-Mukhtar's face. "Why should I do that? Perhaps both of you are lying to me. Perhaps I'm only a pawn in the game the two of you are playing." Her eyes slid past him into the shadows, the pupils dilated. Her face began to melt and re-form into its accustomed feminine shape. "Son of a shoe," she breathed. "If your story is true he must have had my memories stolen mere days after we parted. If he finds out I've spoken to you tonight, he'll do it again…He's learning. Each time. He gets to start over with an ignorant djinn, and deceive her better each time…"

John had seen that look on the faces of young men in the first moments of battle, on the faces of broken men when they awoke yelling in the night. Its presence now on Soraya's face felt like a desecration, something he ought to protect her from. Instinctively, he reached out to comfort her—but she repelled him at once with an arm as stiff as a bar. Her face firmed again as she watched him out of al-Mukhtar's grey-green eyes.

"Don't," she hissed, "*don't* mistake me for that person you once knew."

He withdrew, heartsore. *"You* may not recall saving my life on the road to Jubail. But I do."

"All I know of *you* is that you are not so different to *him.*" John knew better than to protest. Soraya went on, remorseless: "Al-Mansur Qalawun, al-Ashraf Khalil, al-Mukhtar Saif…they are all the same and you are another like them. You want to go back so that you can make yourself emperor. That is the only reason you care about me at all."

"That's not true," he said quietly, closing his eyes.

"You will never set me free," she said with quiet conviction. "You say you must return to the past to stop the invasion and protect your people. How will you do that without the Lance? Without me, it is only another spear."

"I…" John had no answer to that. He had already repented of failing to free her when he first promised to do so, at Yarmouk when everything first went wrong. But he had cudgelled his wits in vain for some alternative, some other weapon to turn the tide of the war in his favour. "God willing, there will be a way."

"There is only one way, and *you* will not be the one to pay the price," she said with a snarl. Her attention wandered back to al-Mukhtar. "He's been imitating you, I'll wager. Pretending to trust me. Pretending to care for me. Pretending to enjoy my company, all so that he can go on using me."

"I'm not like him, Soraya. I've never deceived you." He was begging now, for her trust. It was all wrong. Trust could only be earned, faithfully, over time. He did not *have* time.

"Have you not? What if I say I will never do as you ask—never send you home? Will you keep your promise and free me, then?"

He could only stare at her in blank dismay. "You wouldn't," he managed, at last.

Soraya uttered a short, scoffing laugh and got to her feet, lifting the small table and the blades upon it. "I think I must," she said. "Each of you claims to be my friend, but neither of you really is. Each of you would dispose of me as best suits yourselves, and pardon yourselves because you say that it is for my good. I've had enough of being ruled over for my good, John Bessarion."

For a long moment he could not move, still kneeling at her feet, looking up into al-Mukhtar's obdurate face in pleading silence. At that moment came shouts in the camp, and a drum beating the alarm.

Soraya flinched as though she had been struck. An avalanche of blades fell from the table in her hands, narrowly missing him.

"Get out of the camp," she hissed. "Run. If they find you there'll be hell to pay."

She dropped the table and staggered into the darkness of the tent, bent as though in pain. Jumping to his feet, John swept the flap aside, letting in a little light from the brazier burning outside. He had seen Soraya react in this way before when al-Mukhtar was pulling on the soul tether, calling upon all her strength. Sure enough: when the red light streamed in, there was nothing of Soraya but a cloud of dust settling upon the carpet.

* * *

John reflected, not for the first time, that for pure chaos on earth one had merely to sound the alarm in a military camp. Hastily armed and terrified soldiers ran to and fro, some on foot and others mounted. Wild rumours were being shouted—the Tartars had attacked, the sultan had been assassinated, a rival faction of the previous sultan's mamluks had staged a coup. When a quartet of foot-soldiers brushed past him, dragging with them a struggling, yellow-turbaned Jew who had been beaten and bloodied, John wondered whether he ought to have concealed himself within al-Mukhtar's tent until the worst of the chaos had abated.

It was too late for that now, of course. Protected by his white turban and the dark scholar's robe he wore, John was passing by the mosque where the sultan had his quarters, aiming for the road to Cairo, when he was caught.

"You there! Stop!" The shout came from behind him, and for a moment John did not realise that the words were directed to him. Then a mamluk on a fine horse cut past and circled to face him, and John found himself surrounded by fully-armed and capable-looking warriors.

"Whose man are you?" the amir asked. "Everyone is supposed to report to his lord and await orders."

John had, of course, prepared himself a story. "I don't have a lord," he admitted. "I'm a scholar from Syria."

"What's your business in the camp, then, Syrian?"

John fished a paper out of his purse. "I brought this. They told me the sultan would be interested in it."

The amir shook the paper open and stared at the diagrams within, turning the paper this way and that. It was a technical drawing which John had been working on in odd minutes of the day recently, and he hoped he would not have to trade it for his life.

"What is this?"

"A spout, my lord."

The amir's eyes widened. "And have you gained admittance to the sultan?"

"Not yet. I was about to ask where he might be found, when all this upset happened."

"Either the sultan or Bektash will want to see this," the amir declared, folding the paper and handing it back to John. "You, al-Shayzari—take him into the mosque."

"What's happened?" John asked, slipping the paper back into his purse. He half expected the amir to ignore him, but the amir sent him a glance over his shoulder.

"An assassination attempt on Turuntay, the *na'ib al-saltana*. Come, the rest of you—with me."

In this way, John found himself trotting to keep up with his mounted escort, who led the way to the great mosque itself. The gate was shut, its guards alert and vigilant—but the name of the amir who had waylaid John quickly gained his admittance. A guard beckoned John with a jerk of his head, and the two of them crossed the forecourt and passed through the shadow of the inner gate leading to the great courtyard—a broad square pavement surrounded by a low portico like the cloister of a monastery, a fountain at the centre. Stars burned overhead, fiercely bright and steady in the arid air. A hush seemed to lie thick over everything, muffling the commotion of the camp.

Drawing a weapon here, on the sultan's doorstep, was sheer madness. He was supposed to be a scholar, not a warrior and not a spy. Yet as they stepped onto the pavement, into the starlight, there was a faint shuffle of sound behind them. John might have left his crossbows behind at the monastery, but he had palmed one of al-Mukhtar's own daggers a moment ago when Soraya disappeared. Now, at the first tiny sound, that knife was in his hand, and he was already turning to use it.

His mind caught up to his reflexes when he saw a dark shape emerge from the shadows of the portico and drive a spear through the guard's back. The man gave one or two soft, dry coughs and then died silently. For a moment John dared not move, not wanting to hurt someone who might, for all he knew, be an ally. Then the dark head turned towards him and John knew from the outline who it was.

"John Bessarion," al-Mukhtar whispered. "Just whom I want to see."

John flung the knife, turned, and ran. There was a stifled groan of pain behind as his knife found its mark. He knew better than to hope that a hastily-thrown knife could kill an immortal, but it ought at least to buy some precious time.

He cut directly across the courtyard, aiming for the light burning in the far corner, a brazier to keep the sultan's guards warm through the chill night. It was useless, of course. Footsteps, light and fleet, echoed behind him. Then a hand fastened on the back of his robe and dragged him to a halt.

John stiffened, expecting to feel al-Mukhtar's blade at any moment tear through his body. His only thought was pity for Soraya, who hated the taste of blood and would soon be forced to drink his.

It was as though al-Mukhtar could hear his thoughts.

"I don't mean to kill you," he said in a low murmur. "I only want to talk, but not here."

"Good," John breathed, and then raised his voice. "Help! Assassin!"

The shout echoed across the courtyard, rebounding from the walls, shattering the silence of the place. Around the distant brazier, black figures pointed and gesticulated and rushed towards them. The inexorable grasp loosened from his belt and John drew a breath which he was half sure was his last—surely al-Mukhtar would think as little of striking him down as he had the guard a moment ago.

Yet no blow came. When he turned, there was no sign of the Chosen in the darkness; al-Mukhtar had melted away as though he had never been. John felt like a puppet whose strings had been cut: a moment ago he had been weaponless, defenceless, staking his life on the terrible gamble that al-Mukhtar really meant what he said.

And he had.

Torches poured into the courtyard from the soldiers in the forecourt. John heard the shout as they stumbled across the guard's body. Near at hand, one of the sultan's personal guards raised another torch, shining the light directly into John's eyes.

"Who are you, shouting and disturbing the sultan's rest? Where's this assassin?" he demanded.

"What's this?" someone else asked. John turned, watching uncomprehendingly as another of the mamluks picked up a scrap of cloth and raised the jewel winking within—a signet of polished emerald.

There was a brief silence as the eyes about him fixed upon the ring and grew wide with understanding.

"That's Turuntay's signet ring," someone breathed. "They say that's how the assassin got at him."

"Here's Ismail, dead, with a bloody knife beside him… Put this man in chains. The sultan will wish to question him."

He had rejoiced too soon. There was more than one way to murder a man, John reflected as they dragged him towards the brazier—and al-Mukhtar was an expert in all of them.

Chapter XV.

Eschiva's own chamber door, as it turned out, led to Cyprus.

Ibrahim had not warned her that they would be travelling across the sea. He had simply appeared within her darkened room, carrying a globe of faint light in his hand in the shape of an orange. He beckoned Eschiva from her bed, past the thick curtain that partitioned her sleeping-quarters from the antechamber, past the slumbering forms of her women, and towards her door. Eschiva's fingers tingled upon the wrought-iron latch with his power: then she had simply opened it and stepped through into the loggia of her house in Nicosia.

As impossible as the thing was, she knew at once that they had travelled across the sea to the island kingdom. Instead of a magnificent view of the Beirut harbour and the orchards, farmlands, and mountains beyond, she was looking into the lush, torchlit garden-courtyard of the Ibelins' Cypriot palace, breathing the distinctive caramel-sweet scent that hung forever in the Nicosian air. Great heaps of refined sugar in the city's warehouses, waiting to be shipped north to the great markets in Venice, Pisa, Genoa, and Marseilles, made the place impossible to mistake.

"Am I asleep?" she asked Ibrahim, in dreamlike contentment. It struck her that she had no memory of awaking.

"Yes," he said. "To see memories of the past, your body does not need to be here; it is enough to dreamwalk."

"Will you show me the Old Lord, then?"

"Look, he is coming now."

Eschiva could not repress a shiver of excitement as two men, who had met at the top of the courtyard stairs, turned to walk towards them. One was a young man, very broad in the shoulders and deep in the chest, with thinning hair and a bronzed, scarred face. The other was older—perhaps in his late forties, tall and grey-haired, wearing a long tunic in cherry-coloured silk. He reminded her so much of her own father that there was no doubt she was gazing upon her great-grandfather: the Old Lord, originator of legends, foster-brother to Marta the Knight: Prester John of Ibelin.

"Was this when he was the *bailli* of Cyprus?" she breathed.

"Not quite," said Ibrahim. "He is soon to become so. At present the *bailli* is his brother, Philip of Ibelin."

A hundred years before, the rich island realm of Cyprus had been seized from its Greek warlord by the king of England, Coeur-de-Lion, and ultimately bestowed as an inheritance upon the house of Lusignan, former kings of Jerusalem. Today, after many impossible twists of fate, the Lusignan king of Cyprus was once again also the king of what remained of the realm of Jerusalem; it was he who had offered Eschiva the hand of his young brother.

Even during the Old Lord's time, the two kingdoms—of Cyprus and Jerusalem—had been closely linked. "There was a time when both Cyprus and Jerusalem required a *bailli,* for their kings were only little children," Eschiva murmured, echoing the lessons she had been taught as a child. "The Old Lord became *bailli* of Jerusalem, for even as a boy he was remarkable for his wisdom and sagacity. Later, he gave up the office in return for the gift of Beirut as his own possession. His brother Philip became *bailli* of Cyprus, an office which he held with honour until his death. Where is my uncle Philip?"

Ibrahim gestured towards Lord John with a shrug. Her ancestor was saying, "He is ill and cannot rise from his bed, but he will see us anyway. We have instructions for tomorrow's duel."

"Ah! I know who the young knight is," Eschiva proclaimed eagerly. "My uncle Philip was appointed to carry out the duties of *bailliship* by Queen-Dowager Alice, until worthless people stirred up strife between them. Queen Alice demanded that my uncle resign his post, and sent to appoint

Sir Aimery Barlais in his place. But Barlais, like the wicked man that he was, refused to consult the High Court of the kingdom or to request their assent to his rule. This knight is that good Sir Anselm who challenged Barlais to battle, calling him disloyal to the laws and customs of Cyprus."

"And fought him, too, although Barlais was a small knight and more a scholar than a warrior."

"What else are knights supposed to do, when one accuses another of treachery?" Eschiva asked, following Lord John and Sir Anselm down the loggia. "Either of them would have been shamed forever had they fled the battle. As Barlais attempted to do." She sniffed, trying to recall how the duel itself had ended. "In any case, it was the Old Lord who descended to the lists and seized Sir Anselm's horse, making peace between them and saving Barlais from certain death, like the prudent gentleman he was."

Ibrahim smiled.

Eschiva followed the Old Lord into a fine bedchamber, where the sugar-sweet smell of the air mingled with the more pungent smell of the herbs used to reduce fever—coriander seeds and garlic. The man who lay there, propped up on pillows and looking hollow-cheeked and weary, resembled her great-grandfather so much that Eschiva knew for certain that she was looking upon his younger brother, Philip.

"Kneel," the sick man whispered. Eschiva recalled what had become of her uncle Philip; this had been his final illness. He had died barely days after the duel.

The young knight knelt at the bedside, like a mountain bowing its head to her uncle.

"Do you remain faithful to your lord, Sir Anselm?" Philip rasped, extending a hand.

"Yes, my lord."

The hand fell back. "My brother speaks for me in all things," Philip said. "Listen to him."

John, the Old Lord, straightened: he had the carelessly blunt way of speaking that Eschiva had seen in great lords before, and some of the same thoughtless arrogance of her cousin Balian. "You did well in challenging

Barlais to battle. We told you then that he would run back to Queen Alice in Tripoli rather than fight you, and indeed he did. We did not expect him to return."

"I do not fear Barlais," said the mountain, with a curl of his lip.

"He is not a man to fear," the Old Lord said. "Barlais knows that he is no match for you in battle. He has only returned to Cyprus and accepted the combat because he hopes that Emperor Frederick will soon arrive to support his claim to the *bailliship.* If Barlais dies the way Baldwin of Bellême died, we shall have trouble explaining it to the emperor."

Eschiva had never heard of Baldwin of Bellême, but the emperor's claim to Cyprus was well known. Because the Holy Roman Emperor had bestowed a crown upon the Lusignans of Cyprus, it was argued that he had sovereignty of the island, and could demand rents and appoint *baillis* in despite of the barons.

"You want me to withdraw my challenge, then?" The kneeling Sir Anselm reddened with displeasure. "That would be to dishonour myself."

"Of course not," Philip said. "Baldwin of Bellême was not enough."

The Old Lord coughed. "Barlais is the man chosen by the queen to rule Cyprus, and if you do not make an example of him, too many of the High Court will go over to him and to the queen. And then there will be an end of all good government in this island. Noble men and wise will no longer be rewarded, and the queen will take all the rents and give them to her paramour in Tripoli."

Eschiva was startled. She had heard such things said before when her sister was the Lady of Beirut. She had heard similar complaints when her barons thought she was not there to hear.

What, she thought, do they, too, think that Alice is incapable of ruling, simply because she is a woman?

Is that why the Ibelins maintained the rule of Cyprus? Was *that* the origin of the dispute with the emperor?

No. No—the Old Lord was not *perfect,* but he went to war with Emperor Frederick for better reasons than *this.* And besides, he had intervened in the duel to *save* Barlais' life.

"Fight Barlais," said John of Ibelin. "When it appears that you have the upper hand, I will descend to the lists and interpose myself between you. Barlais is a timid man and will make peace if I ask it. You must do the same. Honour will be satisfied, no blood will be shed, and no knight or lord in Cyprus will be bold enough to challenge us again."

Sir Anselm frowned, but bowed his head. "As you command, my lord."

With that both the Ibelin brothers seemed to let out a long breath and become more at their ease. "We must save our strength for the emperor, not for Barlais," Philip rasped, and John said, "And you should save yours for getting well, brother." Then the meeting broke up. Eschiva followed the Old Lord into the loggia and stood watching him, speechless, as he bade Sir Anselm good-night.

"That is the end of it tonight," Ibrahim murmured into her ear. "I can bring you back tomorrow to see the duel, if you wish."

"I've seen enough, thank you," Eschiva snapped, turning on her heel. But she did not need to go back through the door. With dream-logic, two steps later, she found herself in the Beirut garden beneath the orange-tree.

She found that her fists were clenched. "What do you mean by showing me this, Ibrahim?" she demanded.

"You asked for the truth about the Old Lord."

That old Pisan—Bandini—had accused the Ibelins of embezzling the rents of Cyprus. Eschiva knew what Ibrahim meant her to learn from tonight's vision. That Queen Alice's rightfully appointed *bailli* had been refused on a technicality by a High Court subservient to the Ibelins, and then run off the island through a campaign of intimidation, all so that the Ibelins could continue ruling the island and parcelling out the rents to their own supporters.

That even the bravery of the Ibelins' resistance to Emperor Frederick was more a question of politics than principle, since he was the one man they feared could loosen their grip on power.

"*All* the East hated Emperor Frederick," Eschiva said. "Why, when the emperor set sail for the west he was pelted with offal as he left. When he sent his admiral to seize Beirut, there was not a vassal or a vavasour in either kingdom who could not read the signs. If the emperor could repossess a man's own fief for a dispute over a *bailliship,* then none of them was safe. If that was not a just cause, then nothing was."

Ibrahim bowed, but said nothing. It was beneath her to argue with him. Eschiva took three steps away, then turned back.

"Who was Baldwin of Bellême? Speak," she added, seeing his reluctance. She was no longer willing to have patience with him.

"He was a knight of Cyprus, who withstood the Ibelins to their face when they quarrelled with Queen Alice about the *bailliship,*" Ibrahim said. "Sir Baldwin said he knew no lord but Queen Alice. Whereupon he was set upon and killed by some of the Ibelins and their supporters."

It was a step too far. Eschiva laughed disbelievingly. "Now you are accusing my family of *murder?* I don't know why you are saying these things. Have we not been good to you?"

There was no answer. "I ought never to have trusted a spirit," she said, turning away again.

"I am saying these things," Ibrahim said in a voice like stone, "because you are the first of the Ibelins I believed I *could* say them to."

Eschiva's laughter stung her mouth, it was so sharp-edged. "What? Did you think me *so* faithless?"

"Then we have both made mistakes."

"How *dare* you—" she began, but her agitation had become too much, and Eschiva found herself sitting upright in bed, breathing hard.

A muffled, sleepy voice drifted from beyond the curtain, where her attendants slept. "My lady? Is something wrong?"

"A bad dream," she said, trying to keep her voice steady. "Go back to sleep."

Eschiva lay back, staring into the darkness. *Baldwin of Bellême was not enough. We must save our strength for the emperor.*

There will be an end to all good government...She will take the rents and give them to her paramour.

The words circled through her mind, preventing rest. It was the Old Lord's complaint against the queen that she found most distasteful. The fact that he evidently believed it was no excuse; her cousin Balian believed the things *he* said, too.

A man capable of domineering over a woman was capable of domineering over other men, too: anyone he saw as an inferior.

But—*murder?*

By now, it must have been an hour since she awoke. Eschiva slipped from her bed, wrapped herself in a robe and stepped through the curtain. Her ladies breathed steadily, once more fast asleep. She slipped into the loggia.

It was a cold night, November having brought the winter. The stars glittered overhead, secretive and silent. Eschiva had had an idea of going to her cabinet to work on her planetary tables, but instead she found herself turning in at the library door.

She pulled down Philip of Novara's chronicle again, reading the description of the duel. There was no mention of Sir Baldwin of Bellême. The account of the duel itself, full of doughty blows and gracious speeches, seemed more a romantic tale tonight than an account of fact. Eschiva put the book back; her hand fell upon another chronicle.

She had always avoided this one, knowing that it had been written by enemies of her house. Tonight she pulled it open, turning the pages in the lamplight until a name leaped out at her. *Baldwin of Bellême.* The chronicle said very little; but it said enough. If Ibrahim had been lying, then it was a lie others had told before him.

And if it was the truth? It was not as though the Old Lord and his brother had been common bandits. They had the loyalty of all right-thinking men. Perhaps, with the peace of the realm at stake, they had been right to condemn a trouble-maker to death.

For a moment the thought was like a breath of free air—but a moment only. Even a traitor had the right to a fair trial by his peers in the High Court.

Eschiva slammed the book shut and went to her cabinet, determined to wrench some good from her ruined night's sleep. But the room seemed oddly empty without Ibrahim. It was strange that she should have lived in such contentment for so many years without him. Now his absence ached like a wound.

She threw down her pen and sat still for a moment, debating whether to summon him. Instead she went out, into the cold and the dew, and approached the orange-tree before softly calling his name.

He appeared, as ever, promptly to her call. "My lady."

Eschiva did not know what to say. "You always come when I call," she said softly. "Thank you."

His jaw ticked. "I swore fealty to you, did I not? I could not refuse, even if I wished."

It was as near as he had come to telling her he did not want to see her. Eschiva felt almost as though he had slapped her.

"Was it the truth?" she asked. "What you showed me tonight?"

"I am no illusionist. I can show you nothing but what I remember."

"Why?" she asked again. She had called him to make amends, but she could not keep the accusation out of her voice. "Do you want to see the house of Ibelin disgraced?"

"Only Ibelin can disgrace Ibelin."

"Should the Old Lord be disgraced for doing only what he thought *best* for the kingdom?" she burst out.

"Power has been a snare to better men than he." Ibrahim was silent a moment. "You think, then, that I wish to tear down the house that has sheltered me for so many years? Why should I wish to do that?"

"Surely *you* can answer that better than me."

Ibrahim looked for a moment impossibly weary. "It is only this, my lady: you wish to bring back the glory of the past. I tell you that if you hope to save the future, you must not repeat the mistakes of your ancestors, but learn from them."

"By condemning a dead man, my own ancestor?"

"By doing better." He sighed. "Why, my lady? Do you not know that good orders have bad members, that good men may have bad impulses? Why cannot I acknowledge the bad, without also meaning to shame the good?"

It seemed a dangerous folly to Eschiva, that the Old Lord's own servants and Watchers should repeat the calumnies of his enemies; but she could see that the djinn was in earnest.

You are the first of the Ibelins I believed I could say them to.

"You could have fulfilled your side of the bargain," she said hesitantly, "by telling me what I wanted to hear, and nothing more."

"But that would not be what you needed."

"That may be debated," she said, coldly. Then, sorry for her tone, she added, "I am sorry for what I said in anger. But all my life I have had a great many people deciding for themselves what I *need,* and I am in no wise inclined to let it pass."

"I am not one of those," Ibrahim said. "I have imposed no course of action upon you."

"I know that you meant well. But all I *need* from you, Ibrahim, is friendship—the friendship we had as children. Can you give me that?"

He was silent a long moment, his face impassive. "Not entirely," he said, at last. "But as much as may be given, you shall have."

"That will be enough," Eschiva said, although she wondered again what difference he found, now that she was grown. "I will listen to you, as you hoped. I will forget John of Ibelin and put my trust in John Bessarion…and in you."

She put out her hand towards him. For a long moment he stared at it, as though he thought it was a snake that might bite him; and then, slowly, he reached out a hand in return.

He was insubstantial to her touch. She had forgotten that. But as his fingers slid through her own, she almost imagined she felt—something. A shiver, a jolt. Not touch, but the desire to touch.

She was still staring at their melded hands, trying to reason it out, when Ibrahim spoke again, so softly that at first she almost thought she had imagined it.

"It is dangerous," he said. "But if you really wish to go to Cairo, I am willing to take you."

Chapter XVI.

"A dagger." The bloodied knife slammed down on the table. "The signet-ring of the amir, Turuntay." The ring followed, so heavy that it made a dull *thunk* of its own. "And this length of blue cloth for a turban. You're a *Copt*."

Gingerly, John tested his bonds. The sultan's guards had dragged him into this dark, torchlit room in the mosque and lashed his wrists to an overhead beam. He had spent half an hour already rubbing his wrists raw, trying to free himkself, before the amir of the guard had stalked in to question him.

"I'm not a Copt," he said now. "I'm Syrian, a scholar from Damascus. I came to offer the sultan a plan for a new weapon. Look at that piece of paper on the table."

The amir picked it up and scanned it. "This is useless. *Our* battlefire needs a match to ignite it."

In better times, John might have found this to be very interesting. So the Egyptian sultan did not have the secret of the true Greek fire, which ignited upon contact with the air. Only a lesser imitation.

"Copt or not, you're still a Christian spy," the amir added. "You have one of their symbols on your wrist. Who are you working for? The Greeks? The Franks? The Tartars?"

"I'm a scholar from Damascus," John repeated. "If you're interested in the weapon, I can add a match to the spout—"

The amir sank a fist into his guts, doubling him over. John's legs gave way, the rope around his wrists taking his weight and making it impossible to breathe. It took him what felt like ages to find his feet again, and his breath.

When he recovered sufficiently to see the room before him, he found that a white-bearded old amir had entered the room and now stood beside the table. This amir wore crisp linen, fine as a spider's web; rings glittered on his fingers. John looked into the shrewd, calculating eyes, and for a moment it seemed that his heart stopped entirely.

"Not only is he marked on the wrist with a Christian symbol, but we found this knife beside the dead guard," his interrogator was saying to the old amir. "The ring had fallen upon the pavement beside him. It's our guess that after attacking the lord Turuntay for his signet ring, this man was hoping to be admitted to the mosque in order to kill the sultan."

"The one they call the Chosen was there—al-Mukhtar Saif al-Din." John wheezed for breath. "I was attacked and forced to defend myself."

"Al-Mukhtar! A *legend.* A story told after dark to frighten children." His interrogator turned to the old amir. "None of us saw such a person, my lord Bektash. This man was alone in the courtyard."

Bektash, the old amir, picked up the knife and turned it consideringly towards the light, its blade red with drying blood. "I have seen this kind of blade before. This is a knife such as the Assassins once used."

The younger amir scoffed. "The Assassins! Where are they now? Their sheikh has submitted to the sultan and their young men now till the earth or hold the horses of our mamluks."

"The tales of al-Mukhtar say that he was born in Masyaf among the Assassins," Bektash said.

"Then perhaps this is al-Mukhtar himself," the amir said. "What, stranger, do you laugh? I will give you something to *weep* about."

"That's enough," said the old amir, standing. "I'll take him. No—leave him fit to travel, for I don't mean to have him carried like a lord."

"*Take* him?" The amir scowled. "My lord, this is a task for the *amir jandar*, not for you. This man has killed at least one guard, and Turuntay may not last the night—"

"I've seen the dead man," Bektash said. "Whatever killed him pierced through his entire body, making an outlet in his breastplate. A sword or lance could have done it, but not this knife."

The was a silence. The amir bristled, "Who else could it have been, then? How many spies do you *think* we have infesting this place?"

"Far too many," said Bektash, throwing the dagger with a clatter onto the table. "There's more to this man than appears. This paper presupposes the real Greek fire, not our imitations. As the lord of the sultan's armoury, I need to question him personally. Hand him over."

"You'll return him when you're done?"

"No, fool." Bektash clapped his hands, summoning a pair of mamluks in the livery of his own household. "I'll hand him over to the sultan, who will know how to make use of him—or an example, if that is preferable."

* * *

John made the three-hour journey back to Cairo stumbling at the end of a rope tethering his hands to the saddle of one of Bektash's mamluks. Exhausted when the long, nightmare journey came to an end, he did not bother protesting when he was thrown into a small cell fitted up for prisoners beneath Bektash's fabulous mansion near the citadel gate. It occupied one end of a long, vaulted undercroft, a barred-off space at one end barely large enough for two to lie down side by side. Bektash's men locked him within, left a lamp burning on the wooden table beyond the bars, and left him alone in the echoing room.

John threw himself down on the thin, uncomfortable mat that covered half of the cell's floor, but there was no possibility of sleep.

Soraya. He'd been so *certain* of her help, so exclusively focused upon finding and freeing her. Now he had found her, and she wanted nothing to do with him, even after discovering the falsehood of al-Mukhtar's friendship.

If they find you there'll be hell to pay. Surely a part of her still cared for him. But if he survived this, if he found her and freed her, what then?

If she did send him home, would he be able to keep his promise to free her in the past, undoing the past centuries of servitude? He'd never had any real idea of what destruction the centuries had wrought upon his people; not until he came here, to Cairo, and saw how the Christians were despised and distrusted here; how persecution and resettlement had whittled them to a vulnerable minority. Now he had experienced for himself how Christians, even when they were not Franks, were suspected of being foreign spies and assassins.

He'd promised to stop the invasion. He'd promised to free Soraya from the narrow prison in which she was forced to drink the blood of every one of the Lance's victims—but was she right? Would he be forced, in the end, to choose which of those promises he must break?

Could he justify freeing Soraya at the cost of so many centuries and so many lives?

Then, al-Mukhtar, who had attacked Turuntay and then pinned the crime upon John. That was more cunning than he expected from the Chosen. Was his presence in Cairo known? What had Soraya told her master concerning him? Was this some gambit of Khalil's, to eliminate two enemies at once? Or was he playing a deeper game?

And finally…Bektash. The sultan's *amir silah,* Master of Weapons. One of the last of Qalawun's brotherhood, the powerful Salihi mamluks who had dominated Egypt for the past fifty years. A man who had much to lose if, indeed, the sultan had tasked him with finding Turuntay's attacker.

Exhausted as John felt, he lay awake worrying at the three-cornered problem until the lamp burned out and the room went dark. At last he slept, but he did not dream of Rahel; instead he found himself walking once more through the great basilica of her vision, tracing out the Arabic words marked upon the wall in flowing mosaic script.

It must have been midday when he awoke to the sound of the door opening. Bektash descended into the undercroft attended by two armed servants carrying lamps. They placed the lights upon the table and withdrew to the doorway, where they stood on guard. Bektash seated himself upon the carved armchair to one side of the table; the stool normally occupied by a scribe was empty.

"It is my custom to carry out my interrogations here," Bektash said, conversationally. "My slaves are both deaf and mute. So you may be certain of one thing, Syrian: no one beyond this cell will hear a sound you utter."

John sighed. "Your pardon, my lord—"

"You might well beg my pardon! Does Beaujeu think I can spend all my days getting his spies out of trouble? Does he think there are no jealous eyes in the sultan's court, watching to encompass my downfall?"

John passed a hand wearily over his eyes. "I've put you in a difficult situation, my lord. I know that."

Bektash grunted. "You had best have a good—a *very* good—reason for being in the camp last night. Or else give me the one who really did attack Turuntay. I won't risk my own neck to save yours."

"I didn't attack Turuntay. I went to the camp for my own ends, not for Beaujeu. There is a friend in the camp, with whom I wished to speak."

He told the rest of the story as it had happened, ending with: "It was al-Mukhtar who killed Turuntay. I saw the blood already on his lance."

Bektash listened impassively, stroking his beard. "God be thanked, Turuntay was not killed."

"I beg your pardon?" John stammered. "How?" It was impossible to imagine al-Mukhtar *failing* in his self-appointed mission.

"A Coptic scribe happened to be passing by Turuntay's tent when the attempt was made," Bektash said. "He ran in to find his master bleeding on the carpet, and stanched his wounds. He saw nothing more than the attacker's back as he fled."

A Coptic scribe? John's scalp. Was Rahel correct, after all? Should he have gone to the Copts for help?

"That's impossible," he murmured.

"What's impossible?"

"Al-Mukhtar doesn't normally *fail*."

"You seem very certain that this spearman *was* al-Mukhtar. Did he introduce himself by that name?" Bektash was laughing at him.

"I suppose you think the Chosen is a story for bad children."

"Oh, no." The amir sent a glance about the room, half-meditative, half-wary. "I know the man exists. The Assassin in black, who strikes whom he wills, where he wills, and his face is never seen? Someone bearing that name and likeness was with us at Antioch, eighteen years ago. And at Tripoli, last year. Yes. I know he is real."

"I was in Tripoli last year, also," John said. "I have looked into his eyes. I have called him by name. It was that man who waylaid me in the courtyard last night and left Turuntay's ring at my feet. If you want the real assassin, you must seek him."

"So the culprit is a man, a djinn, who is little more than a story," Bektash said. "This is convenient for you."

"I'll make it convenient for you, too," John said, boldly. "Al-Mukhtar is not an Assassin, but a mamluk in the service of al-Ashraf Khalil."

"The heir!" Bektash spoke very softly, and his eyes went past John, into a fathomless depth. "That's a very great accusation—but all this past year, al-Ashraf and Turuntay have been like two dogs fighting for a bone."

A mamluk was supposed to remain supremely faithful to his master, and secondarily to the brother mamluks also owned by that master. The great Sultan Baybars had chosen his son as his successor, but the son had attempted to favour his own followers over the powerful mamluks of his father's brotherhood. As revenge, that brotherhood had removed the son and replaced him with Qalawun, one of their own number, who could be trusted to protect their own interest.

Qalawun's choice of an heir might, with a gentle push here and a shove there, turn into another succession crisis like the one which had followed Baybars. And a succession crisis in Cairo might be the saving of Acre.

John said, quietly, "Qalawun is making the same mistake Baybars made before him. Mamluk brotherhood means nothing to al-Ashraf. If he succeeds to the throne, you and your brotherhood will suffer."

"I am too old to be sultan," Bektash said, forbiddingly. But he continued staring into the distance, his ringed fingers linked, the thumbs tapping together delicately. At length, his eyes refocused on John. "Give me this al-Mukhtar, then."

John swallowed. "Al-Mukhtar is the servant of al-Ashraf, and al-Ashraf will never let it be known that his servant carried out a failed attack upon Turuntay. Let it be known that you are holding a witness in your house. Al-

Mukhtar will come to you. You must welcome him and offer him drugged sherbet to drink. Do not attempt to fight him; he is more than a match for you and all your men."

"I'm to use you as bait?"

"I'd really prefer you didn't," John said. "Use the *rumour* as bait. Al-Mukhtar will come to you all the same. But if he finds me here I will be a dead man. Al-Ashraf has a vendetta against my family, and al-Mukhtar has been carrying it out, corpse by corpse. He only allowed me to live last night to distract the pursuit of Turuntay's attacker."

"You must be joking," Bektash said dispassionately. "I am to let you go, before I have al-Mukhtar safely in my custody? My life and position are precious to me, and I think they are precious to the Master of the Temple, also. I do not think he will care greatly if I am forced to sacrifice you—and as much as al-Ashraf needs humbling, I've been ordered by the sultan to ensure *someone* is punished for this crime."

John swallowed hard. "What if al-Mukhtar kills me and then escapes? Then you'll have neither of us."

Bektash rose from his seat. "There's no reward without risk."

"Then, since I am to bear such a great risk, promise me a reward," John begged, gripping the bars of his cell. "Al-Mukhtar always carries a lance with him—a lance he *stole* from my family. Promise me that lance when he is captured."

Bektash considered this a moment. "That is easily granted," he said.

The old amir left the room, trailed by his servants. John dragged his hands down his face and then began to pace his cell, from one wall to another. He may have convinced Bektash that al-Mukhtar was the man he wanted—but he himself was trapped here, exposed, helpless.

"Soraya," he muttered, like a prayer. If she did not save him, then who would?

Chapter XVII.

At last, a command dragged her from the blood-soaked Lance. Soraya had barely finished weaving herself a human form when she spat forcefully on the flagstones and shouted, "Son of a *shoe*, Saif!"

"Don't shout," he begged, pushing a sweating jug towards her. "Here's sherbet to wash the taste of blood from your mouth."

She was sorely tempted to dash the jug to the floor—but the sherbet would be cold and sweet, and it was the least he owed her. Soraya poured out a glass and gulped down the chilled, mint-flavoured liquid.

She swept a glance around their surroundings, instantly recognising the training-room beneath Saif's house in Cairo: racks of weapons, high windows admitting thin streams of morning light, and a smooth stone floor where the two of them trained together when they were between missions.

"Made your escape, I see," she said, slamming the glass beaker back onto the bench where Saif sat, cleaning the Lance with a greasy cloth. The last thing she remembered was speaking to John in the tent, the night of Saif's attempt upon Turuntay. She had no way to measure time within the confines of the Lance, but she was sure that no more than a few hours could have elapsed. During that time the Lance had drunk of blood several times, so that the vile taint of metal and death flooded her strait prison.

"I wonder what the sultan will say," she added, "when they call the roll and find that al-Rafiq Saif is no longer with the army."

"Al-Ashraf will provide an explanation for me," Saif said, polishing the Lance with a flourish. "I've rid him of his rival, and now he can become sultan any time he wants."

Soraya wiped her sleeve across her lips. "Oh yes! I'm sure he will be delighted. Khalil *loves* surprises."

"I'm not sure he does," Saif said, as always missing the sarcasm in her words. "But the Hairy One assured me that it was the master's dearest wish."

"The *Hairy* One?" Soraya nearly choked. "You did this on the advice of an afrit? Are you mad?"

Saif flushed. "Of course not," he said. "When I resolved to do the thing, the Hairy One begged me not to, just as you did."

Soraya ran a hand through her hair. She sometimes thought that Saif's mind must have ceased to age when his body did; certainly his long servitude could not have helped matters. "Why did the Hairy One speak to you at all, Saif? Would you have conceived this madness at all, but for him?"

"I…" Saif's voice trailed off, uncertainly. Soraya laughed.

"He played you like a lute—but t's worse than that," she said, cruelly. "I thought you were a devout man. Now you've put a sorcerer and an afrit on the throne of Egypt. How do you think *that* will look on the Day of Judgement?"

Saif gulped. "God is merciful. Better to have such powers under al-Ashraf's command, rather than running free and spreading chaos."

"You're a greater fool than I thought," Soraya said, contemptuously. "One such as Qeteb will never content himself with being a servant. It would take a saint to resist him, and a saint would never make an alliance with such a creature in the first place. You've doomed Egypt and yourself together. Your passion has driven you mad."

"What would *you* have had me do?" he asked, flushing. "Watch Ghaliyah die?"

"To save her, would you set the whole world on fire?" Soraya paced, unable to contain her frustration. "I told you John Bessarion was in Cairo. You could have joined forces with him to exorcise Qeteb. You could have saved Egypt, rather than dooming it. Whatever evils, whatever terrors, whatever bloodshed lies in store is *your* fault."

He could not meet her eyes, but his voice was small and stubborn. "I don't care."

"At last, some honesty," she said. "No, you don't care. Not about Egypt, not about her, and not about me. And you said I was your *friend.*"

That stubborn facade cracked, and he glanced up at her with quick distress. "Soraya, she's my *wife.*"

"And have you asked *her* whether she wishes to be saved at such a price?" Soraya demanded. Saif's hang-dog expression was answer enough. Weariness flooded her. If this blind obsession was the love between a husband and wife, she wanted no part of it. Yet, what else did life hold for her? She was neither Saif's mother, his wife, nor his sister. And therefore, she was nothing.

Perhaps that was only right and good. Perhaps she should give up wishing for more, and accept what she had. But it seemed hard that she should endure slavery without hope, only because no man shared a name with her.

Suddenly the light in the room changed quality, becoming dim and red, as though smoke had blotted out the sun. Soraya turned and Saif rose to his feet as a pillar of smoke at the centre of the room distilled into the terrifying shape of Qeteb himself—the Hairy One, with a single eye burning in his head and another from the centre of his chest.

"Khalil must speak with you," he said, his voice a torrent of thunder. "At once."

Soraya blinked and the room was empty, the morning sun shining in once more at the high windows.

Saif held up a trembling hand, palm-out against the evil eye. "Is—is he gone?"

Soraya struggled to take a breath; it felt as though a hand had fixed about her lungs, squeezing the air from them. There was a darkness upon her spirit that had nothing to do with the mortal sun. "No," she rasped. "Quickly—the basin."

Saif's hands trembled as he retrieved his silver basin from its place on one of the weapons-racks and filled it with water from the cask in the corner. Even he could tell that if *Qeteb* had been employed as a messenger, something had gone badly wrong with his plan to please his master.

"Do you reckon he's angry with you?" Soraya could not resist needling him.

Saif did not rise to the bait. "I don't care," he repeated, in a whisper.

There was no time for more talk. The water stilled, a light shone from the bowl, and Khalil's icy voice, muffled by the water, said: "Explain yourself."

Saif's throat worked. "My lord?"

"Don't play the fool with me. This attack on Turuntay was *your* doing."

Soraya saw the precise moment at which Saif changed his mind, together with everything that he had been going to say. "Not mine, my lord. But I congratulate you on the death of your rival and the securing of your position as heir—"

"Turuntay is *not* dead," Khalil said, cutting each word very short and clear. "He has not yet spoken, but the *amir silah*, Bektash, claims to have caught a witness who also saw the assassin. And I must decide whether you have now become more trouble to me than you are worth."

"Not dead?" Saif swallowed. "How could he not be *dead?*"

"He had a Healer, you fool. A Coptic servant in his entourage, who snatched him back from the brink of death. Did you think you had done me a *favour?* Before this there was a chance that Turuntay would not make an attempt on the throne, but now it's a certainty. He knows that he must challenge me or die."

"I beg your pardon," Saif stammered, abandoning all pretense. "The Hairy One told me—I thought—"

"I don't keep you to *think*," Khalil snarled. "I keep you to *obey my orders*." There was a moment's silence; and then he added, "You spoke with the Hairy One?"

There was a dangerous note in Khalil's voice. Saif swallowed. "He came to me, my lord, after you left me in the courtyard. *Who will rid al-Ashraf of this upstart Turuntay?* he asked. I believed it was your will."

"It was not," Khalil said, gnawing the final word with wrath. "I will be sultan, but I will be sultan in my own time, not *his*. The moment Qalawun dies I'll be facing a battle such as you cannot begin to comprehend—and all because you let Lilith slip through your fingers…"

His voice died away, leaving an echoing silence in the room. Soraya bit her lip, hearing the things Khalil did *not* say.

It was as she had told Saif: Qeteb would never be content with being under Khalil's thumb. Once Khalil took the throne, Qeteb would try to make himself sole master.

No doubt this was the reason for Qeteb's meddling.

"I was careful to implicate neither myself nor you, my lord," Saif was saying earnestly. "My face was veiled and I had Soraya sitting in the door of my tent in my form. Neither Turuntay nor Bektash's witness, whoever he is, can accuse me. Only Soraya and myself knew what I was about."

He was wrong, of course. There was a third person who knew that the man at the door of Saif's tent last night had not been a man at all, in any sense of the word. Soraya took a little, hissing breath as the possibility occurred to her. Bektash's witness—could it be *John Bessarion?*

It would be just her luck if it was. Soraya did not yet know what she meant to do about the Syrian who claimed to be her friend, but she was never going to let Saif slaughter him.

"It doesn't matter how carefully you covered your face," Khalil said. "Bektash has always taken Turuntay's part. His witness will accuse whomever Turuntay wants him to accuse."

"Should I kill him? Properly, this time."

"On no account are you to touch *anyone* who stands between me and the throne," Khalil snarled. "Go to Bektash's house and eliminate the witness. That won't clean up the mess, but it will be a start."

"Yes, my lord," Saif said hopefully. "But I *have* done you a service."

"Do tell," was the icy rejoinder.

"I left Turuntay alive, with no choice but to challenge you for the throne. Isn't that what you want?"

There was short, charged silence. Soraya winced, but Khalil did not raise his voice. Almost conversationally, he said: "Let me be clear. If you ever do anything on your own authority again, I will have your wife strangled at once. Do you hear me?"

"I hear," Saif whispered.

"It was the Hairy One who deceived you," Khalil added. "Be sure you do not fall for his tricks again. *I* am your master, not he."

The gleam of light from the water was snuffed out, and Soraya drew a deep breath, sure that they were once more alone in the room.

"I told you so," she said. "Khalil wants power more than he wants the throne. He can't permit you to do anything at all beyond what he has commanded you."

Saif scrambled to his feet. "Please don't."

Soraya paid no attention. "You need to stop and *think*, instead of running around like a chicken with its head cut off," she told him. "Khalil threatened your wife. He *knows* that as long as she lingers, dying, he can control you. Maybe he's the one who made her sick in the first place."

"That's ridiculous."

Soraya shrugged. She had not been allowed to see the mortal woman, after all, and could not judge what ailed her. "All right. Think about *this*. Khalil doesn't want to be sultan—or at least not yet—because the moment he does, he'll have a new battle on his hands. He said that it's your fault, because you allowed Lilith to be exorcised in Tripoli, when we ought to have captured her. I can guess why that is."

Saif looked glum. "How so?"

"Maybe I've begun to remember some things," she told him, because for some reason she would rather put herself at risk than John Bessarion. "Khalil knows that once he becomes sultan, the Hairy One will want to make himself the master, and Khalil the slave. He has to rid himself of the Hairy One before he can safely take the throne, but if he does that, he'll be mortal again, and powerless. That's why he wanted Lilith; that's why he sent us to steal the djinn of Beirut. He needs a new familiar; one he can control."

Saif scowled. "How will any of this save Ghaliyah?"

Soraya threw up her hands. "I don't know," she said. "Maybe it will prevent you enraging Khalil further. For that matter, maybe *I* could save Ghaliyah, if you let me see her, and if I had my *memories* back! But I can't get my memories back as long as the Hairy One is binding me to that Lance!"

"If we cast out the Hairy One…" Saif shook himself. "No. He didn't ask me to do that. He's only told me to eliminate this witness of Bektash's."

Soraya felt a lick of dread at the pit of her stomach. "You aren't actually going to *do* it, are you?"

He laughed wildly. "What else should I do? Capture the witness and hold him hostage for Ghaliyah's life?"

Soraya joined in his laughter. Then slammed a fist on the table, making the sherbet jug jump. "Why not? Power is the only language Khalil understands. It should be clear by now that if you want his help, you'll have to force his hand."

With that Saif became solemn again, subdued. "Hush! We shouldn't even speak of such things. We might be overheard."

"If we cast out the Hairy One, we wouldn't have to worry about being overheard."

But it was hopeless.

"We can't," Saif said, picking up the Lance. "Maybe it's as much as any of us can do to survive, Soraya. Come. Let's find this witness of Bektash's."

Chapter XVIII.

Following Ibrahim through the open door, Eschiva caught her breath. A broad terrace lay before them. Grass stretched away to the edge of the platform, beyond which Cairo lay glimmering with faint lights. Beyond that, further still, a golden glow still painted the western horizon. Three massive, sharp-edged shapes stood out against that fading light, and Eschiva caught her breath.

"Are those the *Pyramids?*" she gasped, spinning to gaze about her. In place of the low door she had entered, the door to her own cabinet, she found herself standing in the arcaded porch of a great sandstone palace. "The Old Lord had a door into the very *Citadel* of Cairo?"

"Put on your veil and keep your voice down," Ibrahim told her. "There's only so much I can do to prevent any guards from noticing you."

Eschiva did as he asked, arranging the black silk veil to cover her head and mouth, but not her eyes. Like a shadow, she followed Ibrahim through the shadows of the porch, throwing awed glances upward. It was the night of full moon, and the stars blazed white and clear in the arch of the sky. The constellation of Hercules sprawled above the sunset, reaching out a flailing limb towards the Crown.

"To think that the Old Lord had a door into the sultan's own citadel and never tried to *use* it!" Eschiva marvelled.

"He considered it," Ibrahim said, his voice a low rumble that only she could hear. "But of course it would have been madness, even if there had been no war in Cyprus. The world's greatest city cannot be conquered in a single day by a party small enough to fit through a single door. Hush: here is the door we want."

They turned the corner of the palace and came within view of a gate lit by torches, where two guards stood gossiping. Ibrahim raised a hand, cautioning Eschiva to stop and wait as he approached them.

"They say Turuntay's alive, but I don't believe it," one of them said scornfully. "They're only saying that to prevent a panic among the amirs. We won't find out until Al-Ashraf Khalil tops the sultan and makes himself sultan, and by then it will be too late."

"You're listening to conspiracies again," said the other guard, equally scornful. "If the sultan dies it will have nothing to do with al-Ashraf. He's already on death's doorstep. Had to be carried out in a litter in order to join the army."

Sultan Qalawun, dying? Egypt's amirs, fighting amongst themselves? Eschiva was startled into hope. If the sultan died, then surely the campaign against Acre would be called off; for a year or two, at least.

Ibrahim was at the gate, doing something that she could not quite see. The guards yawned, and a moment later they were slumped against the wall, snoring. The djinn beckoned, and Eschiva hurried through the gate and joined him on a long, narrow, sloping road that ran from the heights of the palace between tall mosques and audience-halls and outbuildings to the main northwestern gate of the citadel, which was defended by massive double towers. By good luck the road was not empty. A man with a cart smelling of nightsoil was approaching the gate, and Eschiva simply followed at his heels with her head bowed low, a silent shadow which the guards waved through.

Then she and Ibrahim were looking out over the largest city, with the tallest buildings, she had ever seen. Its massive, ten-storey tenements—glowing faintly gold about the windows—sprawled on for miles. Its streets were like dark, narrow gorges into which the sun might never shine, except where it opened up about some magnificent mosque or hospital.

"How are we going to find John Bessarion in all *this?*" she whispered, for the first time confronted with the impossibility of their task. And once they had found him, she wondered, how would they return through the citadel? Could Ibrahim get them past the guards a second time?

Ibrahim, who had been muttering something beneath his breath, stopped long enough to say, "I don't know if we can find John Bessarion, but there is one of my own kind who almost certainly knows where to look."

"A friend of yours?"

"God forbid I should claim friendship with one so far above me. But I can find her. Come."

He hurried on in the cart's wake, down the sloping road towards the sleeping city, with its towering tenements, the domes of its mosques and churches, the towering needles of its minarets. As before, a little faint light gathered about him, so that he illuminated her way like an *ignis fatuus*.

As he walked, he continued his muttering.

"Are you reciting *mathematical tables?*" Eschiva asked, hurrying to follow.

Ibrahim nodded. "A friend long ago called it *antimagic,* to ward off unwanted attention. Try not to interrupt."

Eschiva nodded. The city thickened about them, but she joined in Ibrahim's recitations as he whispered the multiplications of the ten first numbers and beyond into mounting complexity. When her chant joined his, Ibrahim sent her a quizzical look, and then, reluctantly, a smile.

A second smile! For a moment, Eschiva felt happiness welling up within her. She clenched her hand, savouring the memory of last night, of the catch in his breath when his insubstantial substance met hers.

Then she remembered that she had promised to send him away to a Cypriot hillside, safely away from Beirut and Cairo and the former master who was determined to recapture him.

The recitation tripped in her mouth and she fell silent. Although she had promised not to interrupt, she could not resist asking, "Ibrahim, how is it that you have an orange-tree, and not a body?"

"Because the Hairy One killed my body and bound me to the orange-tree."

"You can't get yourself another, then?"

"A body?" He shook his head. "My people have not had that power for many years."

"I am sorry."

"Do not be. Trees have pleasures, too."

"As, for instance?"

Ibrahim shook his head with an air of great long-suffering. But after a moment he left off his recitations again.

"The sun on our leaves, quickening the sap. The wind in our branches. The rain, cool and sweet, trickling through our roots. The cold of winter, and the rest it brings, half sleep, half trance." The rich, musical voice hesitated. She looked up and found his eyes on her. "The pleasure on your faces, when you taste our fruit."

Eschiva drew a long breath. Then she heard herself say: "Do you know the story of Orion?"

"He was another of my kin," Ibrahim said. "The son of a mortal and an afrit."

The words died on Eschiva's lips. Of course, Ibrahim knew Orion better than she did herself.

"The Greeks tell it this way," she managed, after a moment. "The demigod Orion was a hunter, beloved of the goddess Artemis. But her brother Apollo slew him rather than see his sister stoop to the love of a mortal. In sorrow, Artemis asked her father Zeus to place Orion among the stars, ever to be remembered."

Ibrahim blinked and said, very carefully: "The story is told differently among the djinn. The Hairy One did bring about Orion's death, but there was no love between the djinn and his mistress."

Eschiva broke the gaze between them. "I suppose that it's impossible for an immortal to truly love a mortal."

There was a long silence, before Ibrahim stirred, restless as a breeze, and said, "I'm not worth it, my lady. I can never touch you."

Eschiva's face heated, but she thought of the king of Cyprus, and the marriage he had offered her with his young brother. She whispered, "To love without return is to be like God, and to love without flesh is to be like the holy angels. If I were offered such a love, I should not despise it."

Ibrahim made no reply, instead continuing his recitations. Eschiva bit her lip. "If I save Beirut," she whispered, unable to help the words any more than she could help the thoughts, "won't you stay?"

His recitations faltered, and for a moment there was only silence and peril.

"What for, my lady?"

"Only to study the stars together," she said. "I'd send you to Cyprus before I died. You would be safe. I swear it on my life."

She ought never to have said the words: she saw that at once. His face shuttered. "I'm your servant, my lady. I will do whatever you command me."

"I don't *want* to command you," she whispered, hot with the sense of rejection.

"Is that why you bound me with an oath of fealty?" There was a sharp edge of resentment in his voice. Eschiva did not understand it: everyone took such oaths. Everyone required a lord—or lady—in turn to take kindly thought for the good of his people.

But his final words, before he turned away and took up his recitations again—those she understood:

"I only want to be free, my lady. Beside that, nothing else matters."

Chapter XIX.

"I *told* you you could not overcome him with force of arms!" John gripped the bars of his cell, staring at Bektash in disbelief. "Al-Mukhtar is no ordinary man."

"What is he, then? A djinn?" Bektash asked.

"He might as well be!"

For a moment Bektash made no response. The only movement in the room was the flickering of the lamps on the table, and the dance of a black moth about them.

Bektash snorted. "You've been listening to fairytales. Djinn don't meddle in human affairs. It's as I said: you ought to be safe here as long as you keep away from the bars. We'll let al-Mukhtar enter from the courtyard, and my men will lock that door behind him. He won't get out. If he tries, he must face all the mamluks of my household."

John closed his eyes to avoid giving Bektash a look the man would resent. "If something goes wrong—and it *will*; you won't recognise him when he comes, or he'll overcome your mamluks—then I'll be dead, and you will have neither your witness nor the real attacker."

"Simpler plans are best," Bektash said, with all the confidence of the powerful. "Keep well away from the bars, and there will be no way he can harm you. I'll see you in the morning."

John pounded a fist against the bars, but it made no difference to Bektash. The amir disappeared up the stairs, into the courtyard. The black moth reeled away from the lamps and disappeared into the shadows.

* * *

Soraya swept dust from the street, expanding in a moment from moth to woman as she alighted beside Saif in the shadows of the alleyway before Bektash's gate.

"It's a trap," she told him. "Bektash has that house stocked with his mamluks, and his witness is the bait."

"No mortal can trap me," Saif said. "Where is the witness kept?"

Soraya ground her teeth. John Bessarion was the bait in that trap… It should mean nothing to her that he had given her halwa. That he had told her about her lost past. But it did, and now the thought of being forced to drink his blood was unbearable.

She bit her lip. "I'll come with you and show you. That will throw them off guard; they'll never expect al-Mukhtar to bring a woman with him."

"True enough, but *tell* me, Soraya. Where is he?"

She was so irritated by the command—thinking or unthinking—that for a moment she tried to resist. But the magic of the Lance tore the words from her lips. "In a cell at the end of a croft beneath the main house. From the courtyard gate, turn left towards the sunken door."

"Good." Saif turned to the house. "The answer is no, by the way. I can't bring a woman with me. They won't admit anyone tonight but al-Mukhtar."

"Saif—"

"You can protect me best in here," he said, rapping the haft of the Lance upon the packed dust of the streets. Soraya uttered a cry of protest, but it was useless; Saif was no longer even pretending to give her freedom. She was torn from her body and returned in the blink of an eye to the Lance.

* * *

The house was as silent as death. John paced his cell. He had not so much as a toothpick with which to defend himself—and even if he had, what good would that do him against al-Mukhtar?

He must make up his mind to die, if that was necessary. But his spirit rebelled, and like milord Saint Abraham, he found himself bargaining. *My Lord,* he begged, *I'm not finished yet. I've failed in everything I set out to do. Let me live a little longer.*

For what purpose? the deathly silence replied.

John threw out his hands. "If I'm to die," he whispered in response, "let it be for my children. Let me give my life for theirs. Not uselessly in a land they will never know."

The silence burned like an invisible fire. John found himself remembering a night in Tripoli, when Lilith had set his children before him, and he had turned his back upon them.

Who are your children? asked the darkness. *Who is your neighbour? What is your land?*

"You *know* my children, Lord," he hissed.

A breath of air touched him. John turned and uttered a shout of terror. Al-Mukhtar Saif al-Din stood, silent and motionless, at the bars of his cell. Blood was spattered across his face and shining on the blade of the knife he carried.

"Who are you speaking to?" asked the Chosen, tipping his head with birdlike curiosity.

The door stood open at the other end of the hall. There was no sound of any pursuit. No sign of Bektash's men. John swallowed hard. "To God," he said.

"You presume that God would listen to *you?*"

John wanted to laugh. "No," he said. "I presume nothing. Have you come to kill me?"

At last, movement from the courtyard—shouts, and running feet.

"That depends," al-Mukhtar said, fastening his hands on the bars. For a moment his teeth showed in the darkness of his beard, and then with a shriek the cell tore open. John stood his ground. There was no point in struggling, just as there was no point in begging.

Al-Mukhtar seized him by the collar and plucked him from the cage, holding John before him like a shield as he hurried towards the steps that led to the door. They were at the foot of the stair when a dark shadow loomed above them and someone yelled, "Shut the door, quickly!"

In one swift motion al-Mukhtar took the Lance from his shoulder and flung it at the looming form. The man crumpled to the threshold. "Soraya!" al-Mukhtar shouted, as more feet pounded in the courtyard. He charged up the stair, shoving John before him.

In the doorway a wind lashed the air, a cloud of dust forming above the dead man's body.

Al-Mukhtar did not slacken his pace as they reached the threshold. Wind and earth stung John's face as a figure took shape within the cloud. Saif thrust John to the side and reached for the Lance.

A slender brown hand shot out and forestalled al-Mukhtar. The last rags of cloud coalesced: Soraya crouched over the dead man, the Bessarion Lance in her hands. Her teeth were bared.

"I'll kill you," she choked at al-Mukhtar.

Saif threw up his hands. "He's alive. Look!"

Soraya turned her head and John looked into eyes wide with happy disbelief.

Maybe she did care, after all.

"Soraya. Give me the Lance," al-Mukhtar ordered. "Take care of the mortal. Get him out alive."

She relinquished the Lance and helped John to his feet. "Stay by me," she whispered. "I'll protect you."

"I know," he said, in a voice thick with emotion.

With a flourish Saif swept the Lance beneath his right arm and stepped from the deep-set doorway full into the view of their enemies. No doubt the courtyard had been empty, save for a token guard or two, when he had broken into it. Now, the space between undercroft and entrance-gate bristled with men and weapons.

"Surrender, al-Mukhtar." Bektash's voice dropped from where he stood unseen at some latticed window high above. "There are a dozen bows trained upon you."

Al-Mukhtar said nothing; only beckoned to John and Soraya, taking a step towards the gate. The armed men before them retreated one step, and then another. The ranks opened before them. Another step. No arrows flew. Another—and just as John knew they would, the ranks of Bektash's mamluks scurried behind them, cutting off their retreat to the cellar. Now they were surrounded on all sides.

This time, when al-Mukhtar attempted to advance, the ranks remained firm. Al-Mukhtar raised the Lance, balancing it in his right hand. The mamluks tensed. There was a moment's absolute silence. Then the air thrummed, and an arrow sprouted in the pavement before al-Mukhtar's feet.

"That was a warning," Bektash called again. "Surrender, or you'll have a dozen arrows to deal with next."

Slowly, slowly, Al-Mukhtar sank into a crouch. Soraya's hand tightened on John's arm. A voice shouted to the mamluks to hold fast. The air thickened, imperceptibly, towards the outbreak of violence.

John ground his teeth. He had warned Bektash, and it was all for nothing.

In the explosive silence, there came the sudden sound of knocking at the gate—a sound which held the courtyard like a spell, entranced.

Then, of all things, a voice drifted to them from the street. A woman's voice, speaking in Frankish.

"There's no answer. Are you sure this is the place, Ibrahim?"

A man's voice answered, deep and musical, the brief words indistinct. Yet Soraya, beside John, stiffened.

"Show yourself, djinn!" she commanded, suddenly, in a voice that tore open the night.

At that even some of the mamluks turned towards the gate, just as a great white shape boiled through it—a mist that thickened and reared up and took on the form of a great white serpent, arching far above them. Its red eyes blinked; its tongue flickered out to savour the cries of terror rising from the men in the courtyard.

John's mouth dried. Soraya was quivering with tension. "Forward, Saif," she hissed.

The great serpent struck downwards at the gaping mamluks. They may have been elite warriors, trained in war since childhood, sworn to loyalty to their amir and their brotherhood. But they had never faced anything like this before. Some swung wildly at the menacing shape, and a storm of arrows tore through it, leaving not the slightest rent in its shadowy form. But most of the men simply screamed and ran, or cowered where they stood, arms raised to protect themselves.

Soraya seemed to take it as the opportunity they needed, for she dragged John forwards, straight into the storm, into the belly of the serpent as it coiled and lashed about the courtyard. John had a whiff of salt-sweet air, redolent with the scent of citrus, as they plunged into a mist in which the quaking forms of men cried or screamed or beat the air. One, wild-eyed, came at John from his left with a swinging sword. Soraya shouted a warning, but she was behind him and weaponless. John raised his left arm, as the limb he could best afford to sacrifice; but then al-Mukhtar appeared in the mist and drove the Lance through the mamluk's breastbone.

"Go!" he shouted, and the three of them emerged from the white fog and found themselves at the gate itself. Soraya did not hesitate: with a burst of motion too sudden for John's slow mortal eyes to comprehend, she hurled herself against the door. The gate burst; the stone of the arch crumbled. Al-Mukhtar seized John and drew him through the dust-cloud into the street.

They found themselves in a cul-de-sac, empty and tranquil between the high walls of the palaces to either side. A veiled woman stood before the gate, the lanterns to either side of it illuminating a strip of pale skin and wide, surprised grey eyes within the shadow of her veil.

Al-Mukhtar skidded to a stop, extending the Lance to point at the stranger. "Who," he panted, "are *you?*"

She pulled the veil away from her face, revealing a face John had last seen in Tripoli on the eve of the siege, a face he had never expected to see in a Cairo street under any circumstances. Pale, clever, and caught somewhere between awe and laughter.

"I am Eschiva of Beirut," she said. "What, John Bessarion? Don't you remember me?"

* * *

"What are *you* doing here?" Saif panted. His eyes flicked to the courtyard and then back again: no doubt he, like Soraya herself, was quickly putting two and two together. The Lady of Beirut was in command of a powerful djinn; that might explain her sudden appearance, as well as the white serpent in the courtyard behind them.

A shard of stone a palm's breadth in size had fallen to the Lady's feet. Unhurriedly, she bent to pick it up, and inclined her head towards the prisoner. "I came to fetch my servant John Bessarion. Hand him over."

Saif merely stared at her.

"He isn't your servant," Soraya snapped, angered by the Frankish woman's unthinking arrogance. "And he promised his help to *me*."

"He belongs to neither of you," Saif put in. "He's *my* captive. And so are you, now, Frank."

John Bessarion only looked a little dazed, but Soraya's attention was already caught by something else.

A quelling sense of dread. An oppressive heat. A probing attentiveness, drawing nearer.

John found his voice, evidently unaware of the threat. "I'd follow you gladly, my lady," he said to the Frank, "but this Saracen woman is right. I have sworn oaths to her, and none to you."

Soraya raised a hand. "Hush." She turned to the Frankish woman, calmly tucking the shard into her purse. "Command your djinn to veil himself. *Now*."

Any practiced sorcerer should have understood. This one merely gazed back at her with parted lips, uncomprehending. Incapable of perceiving what Soraya felt, the swift approach of an ascendant spirit.

"Woe to us," Soraya breathed, as the presence great nearer, more unmistakeable. "An afrit. An afrit is here…"

It was already too late for warnings. That distant presence burst into view like the rising sun, an unbearable blaze of something that was hot and very far from being light. To the mortal eyes of those in the alley, he merely bore the guise of a fine amir, bow in hand, arrows slung at his hip.

Beside her, John Bessarion sucked in a breath. "Qeteb," he breathed.

Soraya did not know with what faculty he pierced the afrit's disguise. Perhaps it was the suffocating sense of hopelessness the Hairy One carried with him. Perhaps it was the way that shape moved, stilted and uncanny, more like a puppet than a man.

With inhumanly quick movements, Qeteb snatched an arrow from his quiver, fitted it to his bow, and levelled it directly at John Bessarion. He turned towards her at the same moment that Soraya reached out to shield him. She realised, too late, that they were both attempting the same thing.

The bow twanged. The arrow flew, and John Bessarion recoiled with a grunt of pain.

Soraya caught and lowered him to the ground, patting frantically at his chest. There was no blood. No wound. No arrow. But his body had gone hot with fever, and he began to pant with shallow, quick breaths, limp and terrified.

"I can't," he muttered. "I can't. I tried. Oh, Rahel..."

Qeteb stalked closer, drawing another arrow from his quiver. The Frankish woman clapped a hand over her mouth, all horrified eyes. Saif stood over them, the Lance ready, but he must know there was no use in fighting such a creature—Khalil's creature. His eyes flickered about the narrow alleyway, doubtless seeking an escape, and finding none. Soraya saw the thoughts written on his face—should he stay with his prize? should he save himself?

Indecision had him in its grip. She felt it herself, a torpor seeking to smother her into silence. And the only person she knew who might *possibly* be capable of saving them was shaking, babbling in her arms.

"John," Soraya whispered. "Look at me. *Breathe.*"

She had heard the words before. *Soraya. Breathe.* John's voice. John's arm about her shoulders. *God, if only I could remember—*

"Ibrahim!" a voice screamed. The Lady of Beirut had found her voice. Far too late.

* * *

All Eschiva had to do was call out, and Ibrahim appeared beside her in the shape of a man. "Ibrahim," she repeated in a sob, hardly knowing what she was saying.

"Yes, *Ibrahim!*" shouted the Saracen archer, who strode towards them on a tide of such impossible terror. "What made you think you could venture away from your orange-tree into *my* city, and not be found? Come, son! Come and pay homage to your father!"

His *father.*

Eschiva caught a glimpse of Ibrahim's face as he turned from her to the archer; remembered the words he had said in Beirut about the demon that awaited him in Cairo if he was foolish enough to venture there.

"No," she whispered, realising her mistake. In her excitement at finding John Bessarion, and the confusion of the ensuing moments, she had forgotten to recite the anti-magic.

"You've been no father to me," Ibrahim now said, with the calm of one who has come at last to face the worst of his fears. "You've been my slave-driver, my captor, the wolf at my door. Never my father."

The demon scoffed. "Is a son greater than his father? I created you to serve *me,* not to be served. I gave you life, and now I take it back."

A shimmer of heat rippled in the air as the approaching shape *changed.* Eschiva choked as a nightmare form took shape. Covered with a thick pelt of hair, the demon wore a helm covering its entire face, save for a solitary glaring eye in the centre of its forehead. A second burned at the centre of its chest. It seemed immeasurably huge, as tall as the stars; yet it also fitted comfortably between the narrow walls of the street. The disparity was nauseating.

Then Ibrahim was before Eschiva, his familiar face filling her vision and restoring her to some self-command, despite the grimace of terror he wore.

"Release me from my servitude," he hissed. "Quickly. *Please.*"

She didn't understand. Ibrahim gnashed his teeth.

"Release me *now*—or I'm dead!"

Eschiva's voice squeaked high. "You're going to *leave* me?"

"I'll come back for you. I *promise.*" Then his eyes widened—perhaps some sense warned him. One moment Ibrahim was there. The next, he had gone.

Qeteb's great clawed hand swiped at the place where the djinn had been. It passed through Eschiva and she recoiled, tripping and falling into the dust of the street. The demon's lips drew back; its mouth opened, jagged with teeth; it howled with rage.

Eschiva looked down a gullet that seemed large enough and ravenous enough to swallow the city and every soul in it. *"Ibrahim!"* she screamed. There was no thought in her head. She was about to die, and he was her only hope.

Ibrahim appeared before her. For a flash she saw the look of betrayal and despair in his eyes and knew what she had done to him. Then his shape stretched and blurred as he began to be drawn into the demon's maw. Swallowed up, consumed by his father.

"Ibrahim!" Eschiva screamed again, but this time, not even her command could bring him back.

* * *

I have you, child. Breathe.

John Bessarion lay muttering in her arms, but his voice echoed in Soraya's memory.

Look up and see your salvation.

He had said such things to her once. Called her his child. Held and calmed her. If only she could remember anything more.

Look up.

Clinging to him in a kind of mindless desperation, Soraya began, stubbornly, to work antimagic. *"In the name of God, the Most Compassionate, Most Merciful. All praise is for God, the Lord of all worlds, the Most Compassionate, Most Merciful, Master of the Day of Judgement. You alone we worship, and you alone we ask for help."*

Slowly, with the recitation, her wits returned to her. She forced her chin up.The Lady of Beirut was in a hasty consultation with her djinn; he seemed to be begging her for freedom. John was helpless, utterly undone by Qeteb's arrow. Saif was still on his feet, but his hands hung nerveless at his sides, trapped in mingled despair and indecision. Releasing John, Soraya crept to Saif and pulled herself up by his arm, moving all the time with sluggish deliberation against the apathy that weighted her body.

She put her mouth against his ear. *"Guide us along the straight path, the path of those you have blessed—not those you are displeased with, or those who go astray."*

Saif heard her—blinked, and came slowly back from whatever dark and distant lands in which his mind had been wandering. Soundlessly, his lips formed her name.

"Recite," she hissed. Qeteb had Ibrahim in his jaws, now. Soraya shuddered, caught in the echo of a long-lost memory. "I'm relying on you."

"For what?"

"Recite," she repeated. "Draw me back before it's too late!"

She did not stay to answer his questions, for if she hesitated she might think better of what she was about to do. In Beirut she had been paralysed by the memory of a rival spirit attempting to consume her, but there was only one way she could think of to trick Qeteb into releasing Ibrahim.

She released Saif. The world moved around her slow and sticky like honey on a cold winter's day as she threw herself between Qeteb and his prey.

Unlike Ibrahim, she did not resist. She was drawn unresisting into his mouth, into heat and corrosion. In one long burst of agony her physical body flaked to ash as Qeteb sank his teeth eagerly into her spirit.

O God, let it work, she thought. And then, *O Saif, don't abandon me.*

Chapter XX.

She must have disagreed with him. No sooner had Qeteb begun to tear apart her spirit than there came a sickening convulsion and Soraya found herself ejected forcefully from the great, dark, seething spirit-light that was Qeteb. For a moment she was a ghost in the ether, surrounded by the spirit-lights of the others—Saif and John's burning low, almost snuffed out; the Lady Eschiva's tinged green with despair. Ragged but still bright, Ibrahim was near at hand, reaching out for her. At his touch, power poured into her. Soraya made an instinctive effort and the next moment, to her complete astonishment, she was sitting up in the gutter, wearing a mortal body again.

Saif stood where she had left him, motionless, helpless. John lay at his feet. Eschiva had fallen back against the wall of the alley with a hand clasped to her mouth.

Qeteb had completely disappeared; there was not even the slightest taint of him in the air.

Ibrahim knelt by Soraya, his intangible hand still overlapping with hers. Soraya looked up into his dark, beautiful eyes and said dizzily, "I know you. I don't know how."

"Lady Soraya, I would be dead if not for you," he said. From the look on his face, he might have been a young soldier looking at a famous warrior.

"Ibrahim," the Lady of Beirut gasped, reaching out a hand. "This was a mistake. Take me home."

She looked as though she might faint, and Soraya wondered whether she ought to offer the mortal woman some kind of assistance. But Ibrahim beckoned her with a glimmering hand and the two of them fled into the night without another word.

Soraya turned to her own mortal charges. John had ceased to move, and for a moment she was afraid that the arrow had killed him. But then he raised his head, looking at her with shadowed eyes into which the reason had returned. She pulled him to his feet with a sob of relief.

Saif's hands still hung slack at his side, but he blinked at her when she turned to face him. "Soraya," he whispered. "What was *that?*"

"*That* was you failing to call me back, even when I was being consumed by a demon," she said tartly. John Bessarion had been willing to step in front of Qeteb's arrow for her, while Saif had not spoken a word to save her. Mentally adding it to the list of things she had learned concerning the two men, she tilted her head towards the courtyard behind them. The confrontation with Qeteb could barely have taken a single minute from beginning to end; now she could hear the voices of the mamluks echoing in the courtyard behind them, and Bektash shouting at his men to seek out the fugitives.

"He tried to consume his son," Saif muttered, still lost and rambling. "What kind of father does such a thing?"

"For God's sake," Soraya hissed. *She* was the one who had nearly been consumed by a demon, and she was in better shape than either of them. For a moment she considered leaving Saif to face Bektash's mamluks alone, but that would not truly free her from him, and might in fact complicate matters. Instead, she tossed John's limp body over her left shoulder, seized hold of the end of the Lance with her right, and dragged both men into the night.

✳ ✳ ✳

Ibrahim made no concessions to stealth on their way back through the Citadel: he merely gave a sweep of his arm as they approached each gatehouse, and the guards within slumped into sleep as they rushed past. Eschiva was shaking by the time they hurried back through the door of the

Old Lord's cabinet and found themselves in Beirut again—cool and wet in the midst of a rain-shower. She slammed the door behind her and turned to watch Ibrahim pass a shaking hand over the latch.

"Is it sealed?" she hissed. "Are we safe?"

He backed away from the door, watching as though it might yet burst open and admit the demon, all reaching claws and gaping teeth, to swallow them.

"Yes," he panted. "I think so. I'm sure."

Eschiva backed away and collapsed onto a low divan that was set in the loggia. "Thank God," she whispered. Then she had all she could do to catch her breath. She had not run so fast, nor so far, in many years.

A lamp appeared at the end of the corridor and she heard the voice of one of her waiting-women. "My lady?"

Ibrahim turned towards his orange-tree. "Don't go," Eschiva hissed in a panic. He stopped, but st the look on his face, her gut clenched.

"I'm here," she called, shoving the guilt away and turning towards the woman. "What is it?"

"Thank God, my lady. We've been seeking you. There's news just arrived from Acre. Your cousin—"

"Lady Eschiva." Balian's voice echoed in the loggia as he brushed past the woman and hurried towards her. "The Master of the Temple sends to inform you of news just now confirmed. It hardly seemed possible, but it is. The Egyptian sultan is shortly to march upon Acre."

Eschiva felt a wild desire to laugh. "You forget, cuz, that I've expected this for some time. Very well. We'll discuss it in council tomorrow morning. You may go."

"You sound breathless," Balian said, halting beside her. The loggia was dark, the only light provided by the lamp some way away. "Is someone with you?"

"*Evidently* not," she pointed out. "It began to rain while I was in the garden taking the time, and I ran up the stairs to avoid a wetting. Good *night*, Balian."

She retreated into the cabinet, not without a moment's doubt as the door opened—but no, rather than pyramids and demons, she found only her books and papers, her abacus and and her astrolabe. Closing the door, she lit her lamps. Then Balian's news sank into her mind and she rested her hands on the table, feeling the darkness press in upon her.

"How can Acre possibly stand against what we saw tonight?" she murmured.

"Have you *more* commands for me, my lady?" Ibrahim asked.

In the lamplight he looked downcast and weary. Once again, Eschiva's heart struck her, but she had no words: only abject guilt. She had failed Ibrahim. She knew full well that Qeteb was a danger to him, yet in that moment of panic she had been ready to fling him straight down the gullet of an angry demon in order to save herself. She, who as far as she knew, had never been in any danger at all.

Had a lord on the battlefield behaved in such a way to one of his vassals, he would be dishonoured forever!

Other thoughts flocked to excuse her—that Ibrahim was not a vassal but a servant, that surely it was a servant's place to give his life for his lord. Hollow excuses, and vain comfort! How many days had she passed thinking wistfully that Ibrahim was the one soul on the earth capable of loving her as an equal?

And yet she had done *this* to him. He was under her command, and she had thrown him away. No wonder he looked at her with mute suffering. No wonder he was reluctant to speak to her.

"No," Eschiva said with an effort. "No more commands. You should rest."

He bowed again—sometimes she thought she saw more of the top of his head than she did his face—and then whisked away between one blink and another. Eschiva sank slowly into her chair, staring at the columns of figures before her in the numerals that Ibrahim had taught her.

She would never have had him as a lover, but she might have had him at least as a friend. And in her selfishness she had destroyed everything.

Chapter XXI.

A fragmented shaft of intense sunlight crept into John's eyes, prodding him from sleep. He sat up, wincing at the pounding in his head. After a long moment the black spots cleared from his vision, allowing him to see his surroundings.

He was in a bare guest-room, its narrow windows covered with a wooden lattice, although the low bed was soft and comfortable enough. There was a jug of water on the floor beside him and John gulped some of it down, hoping that it would settle his complaining head. A closed door blocked any view of the rest of the house. John groaned, massaging his temples and studying the latch-ring. Was it locked? He didn't know whether he was well enough to find out.

He knew he was in Cairo, somewhere in the prosperous suburb between the Bab Zuweila and the citadel, not far from Bektash's palace. He knew they were in a house, the kind belonging to those of modest wealth and noble position. He knew the way in was via a narrow, forbidding door, but that once inside, the courtyard was full of whispering greenery and the tinkle of water. Soraya had dragged him here last night, shoved him into this room, and ordered him to stay put.

For what? Did al-Mukhtar really intend to spare his life, or was he simply too demoralised, after last night's events, to bother executing his prisoner?

John shuddered, his memories of the previous evening mangled and indistinct. Al-Mukhtar had snatched him from the jaws of Bektash's trap, only to be surrounded by Bektash's mamluks. Then events had become exceedingly strange. He recalled the white serpent, the Lady of Beirut, and—Qeteb.

He recalled throwing himself before one of Qeteb's arrows. Then what? Dread and despair had overcome him? This morning he felt the way he had once as a young man campaigning against the Persians in the Sinai Desert—weak and sun-struck. One would expect the arrows of a midday spirit to have such an effect.

John groaned, burying his head in his hands. This was the second time he had confronted Qeteb. The second time he had failed, this time so utterly that he still could not explain how he was still alive.

Presently, as a means of distracting himself from questions for which he had no answer, John got up and searched the room. In the low coffer chest at the end of his bed he discovered, among other things, a sheaf of paper together with a pen and a bottle of ink. This suggested a means of escape, but John hesitated for a moment. Was he better off here in al-Mukhtar's house, or in the house of Bektash?

Until he found his way home, he was trapped in this time, and he must work for the Temple. And so long as he was working for the Temple, he must remain in communication with Bektash. John sighed and sat down, scratching a short message on the paper and shoving it through an opening in the lattice into the breeze. Please God someone in the street would pick it up and take it to Bektash for the promised reward.

He was again considering the previous night's events when a cool breeze stirred the air and a trickle of dust began to run beneath the door. John coughed as it whipped into a cloud that filled the room and then suddenly coalesced into the familiar figure of Soraya in her green veil.

"Soraya," he said. "Thank God you are here. What is going on?"

"You ought to congratulate yourself," she told him, making herself comfortable, cross-legged on the carpet. "Al-Mukhtar has decided that you are more useful to him alive than dead."

Her voice dripped sarcasm. John said humbly, "I have you to thank for that, I suppose. What happened last night? Did Qeteb hurt you?"

She gave a short, self-conscious laugh. "I think I managed to hurt *him*, in fact. What made you step in front of that arrow? You would have been more help trying to exorcise the blighter."

"I thought I could endure it better than you," he said, shamefaced. "But maybe it was all for the best. I could do nothing against Qeteb, but you—"

"I jumped down his throat, and he threw me back up again," she said, truculently. "I don't call that any great victory."

"I promised to *free* you from him. Instead I was helpless. I don't know how I survived."

"I was holding you, remember?" Soraya swallowed. "I think…I think you held me like that, once, when a demon was about to destroy me."

John took a slow breath to calm the hope that was suddenly clawing at him. "I did," he said, "in Tripoli, the night we exorcised Lilith."

"*We* exorcised Lilith?" She raised a sceptical eyebrow. "Or *you* exorcised her?"

"I did," he admitted.

"Then what's the problem?" she asked, as he knew she would. "Why can't you get rid of Qeteb?"

"I wish I knew. Rahel—my wife—thinks he may have some hold over me." John sighed, feeling no better now that the thing was confessed. "I thought you might be able to help me with that."

Soraya got to her feet with a hard little laugh. "If I had the slightest idea how to attack Qeteb, don't you think I would have got rid of him myself by now?"

Another dead end. John shook his head. "Are you leaving me here?"

A snort. "Am I leaving you in a nice, cool, comfortable room where you might have a hope of staying out of trouble for an entire day? Let me consider that."

"Please," he begged her. "I don't want to be *useful* to al-Mukhtar—whatever that means."

"Perhaps I'm considering your usefulness to *me*," she retorted. "What's that look for? Don't you like to be useful?"

He could only send her a despairing look; at which she relented.

"Oh, all right! I don't mind giving Saif a fright. You're upstairs in the house. At this time of day it's pretty much empty up here, so if I were you I wouldn't go downstairs at all. Try the door on the right, and find a window that will let you climb out into the street."

She did something to the latch that made the iron groan before departing, leaving the door pulled to behind her.

John waited until her footsteps had died away. The old Soraya would have been more generous with her help, he thought with a pang. But then, the new Soraya seemed to have softened towards him since last night, and she had always been conscious that helping him too closely might cause both of them trouble with Saif.

He rose to his feet, careful not to jostle his aching head. The door swung open at a touch, and he ventured out into the hushed loggia. This occupied only one of the four sides of the courtyard, the other three featuring large, latticed windows. The whole house had the sleepy, dishevelled air of the sort of morning when the master is in bed with a bad head and should not be disturbed.

From the low divan, a black cat untucked its paws and stared at him with green eyes.

There were two doors to choose from, one to his left and one to his right. The one on his right led to a longer wing of the house. John slipped across the loggia and let himself in, closing the door behind him. The room in which he found himself might once have been inviting: it contained a loom, a writing-desk, and several low divans, but it looked as though it had not been used for many weeks, for the lamps were empty and there was a dusty smell in the air. The window in this room would not serve him, for it looked only into the courtyard. John went on, nearly tripping over the cat which had followed him into the dimness of the room and wove itself about his ankles.

This room led to a second, equally neglected, and equally unsuited to his purposes. Here a low work-bench ran along the wall beneath the window holding bolts of fabric, spools of thread, and one square panel of intricate embroidery, half finished and fuzzy with more dust. Perhaps these had once been the women's quarters. John remembered that al-Mukhtar had mentioned having a wife. Where was she now? She had evidently not used these rooms for some time.

He pushed aside the curtain shrouding the next door and stole within. This must once have been a bedroom, for there was a low divan opposite the door, shrouded with filmy curtains. Here, at last, John seemed to be in luck: the room had broad, latticed windows opening onto the street, allowing the breeze access. John hurried eagerly towards them. In doing so he approached the bed; at which a shadow moved within the curtains.

"Who are you?" asked a quavering old voice.

John recoiled, cursing his mistake. "My lady, I have made a mistake. I beg your pardon. I'll leave at once."

The curtain drew back, disclosing a wizened little woman of perhaps seventy, with white hair and a ring in her nostril. She must be al-Mukhtar's mother, or more likely an old servant of whom he was fond: she seemed unbothered by the display of her face and hair. "Don't you have ears?" she demanded. "I asked who you are. I didn't tell you to go away."

John imagined what al-Mukhtar would say—or do—if he was found trespassing in what were evidently still the women's quarters. "I'm a new servant here," he said. "I was ordered to come sweep up the dust. I didn't think—"

The old lady hitched herself up on her pillows. "That's a likely story," she chirped. Now there was a twinkle in her eyes. "You don't *look* like one of Saif's slaves, and he'd never send a man in here. Should I call for help?"

For a moment John didn't breathe. The cat, which had followed him into the room, used the moment to jump onto the bed and nose curiously at the old woman's face. "Do not fear me. I mean you no harm," he said.

"No, but you do mean to run away before you've told me who you are. Don't even think about it."

John opened his mouth and shut it again. The old lady twinkled at him and made soft welcoming noises to the cat. Since he could not possibly be in any more trouble than he already was, he cleared his throat and said, "My name is John."

He didn't expect the name to mean anything to her—or if it did, he expected her to show fear or anger. Instead, a smile split her face. "John!

That is a *Christian* name! I am Christian too. Look! My parents, they were Copts."

She pushed back her sleeve, revealing the same small Watcher's Mark he had seen on Brother Simon's wrist.

A Christian *here*—in the very house of al-Mukhtar? John blinked down at the woman, and then, slowly, he showed her his own Watcher's Mark.

"I knew it!" she exulted. "Sit down, sit down! I am so sick of being cooped up in this room with no one to speak to!"

"Are you a prisoner of al-Mukhtar's?" John asked.

"Not in the way you imagine," she answered; but the words, and the wistful tone, were not reassuring. "Saif is very kind to me, and there is nowhere else for me now, even if I wished to depart. But he does think I need *rest*." She wrinkled her nose with distaste, and changed her tone. "Tell me, anyway. How did you come to be here? You have the voice of a Syrian."

"Please let me go. I'm not meant to be here, my lady."

She gave a girlish pout. "But you're the most exciting thing that's happened to me in *weeks*."

"Please," he repeated. "*You* may not be a prisoner of al-Mukhtar, but—"

She raised a forefinger in a gesture so imperious that John stuttered into silence. For a moment her eyes were very intent, and very certain, the way Rahel's could be after a vision. "John Bessarion," she said. *"No harm will befall you in this house."*

He had not told her his full name.

Surely she could not *really* be like Rahel. Could she?

Every nerve was shouting at him to make good his escape, but if he did so, the old lady might give him away. The house was quiet, and if it came to the worst, Soraya would be here to back him up.

Best to be patient and give her what she asked. He would get further with her goodwill than without it. And he certainly didn't mean to threaten such a harmless old woman.

"All right," he said, seating himself cross-legged on the carpet. "I am going to tell you a story. You may not believe it. I hardly believe it myself—but you must be the judge."

The old lady clasped her hands, and even the cat sat up to watch him with bright, expectant eyes.

John chose to tell his own story, beginning on the hot day in the Sinai desert when he had stumbled across a young woman being sent into a marriage she did not want, and was obliged to rescue her from Persian raiders. Then he told how after many happy years he had been parted from the woman, now his wife, and hurled many hundreds of years into the future. He made a story of it, omitting any names and embellishing the remaining facts with fanciful touches stolen from ancient folktales. The old lady laughed and asked questions, making of it a sort of game. And John found that he was enjoying himself: there was something healing in taking the hardships he had endured, and weaving them into something he could control, a tale of wandering and persevering love…

"Don't tell me!" the woman cried at length. "The young Assassin's *lance* was the vessel of the djinn woman—not his ring!"

John stuttered to a pause. "How did you know *that?*"

"Oh, because that is where Saif keeps his djinn," she said, unconcerned. John's involuntary movement must have startled the cat, for it gave a startled yowl. "It *is* him you are talking about, isn't it? I *knew* Saif had gone away to the siege of Tripoli. He tries to keep me from knowing these things, you know, but there's no point."

"How?" John climbed to his feet. "Who are you? *What* are you?"

"Hush!" she said, laughing. "Sit down. It's my Gift, of course. I'm a Revealer."

"A *Revealer?* But you're….a Copt," he finished, shamefaced.

"Of course I am," she said. "What? You don't think that you Melkites are the last great hope of Christendom, do you?"

John opened his mouth—then closed it again. Perhaps that was precisely what he *did* think. But if this woman was truly a Revealer…

Before he could say anything more, the woman's eyes slipped past him to the door. "He is coming," she whispered, suddenly. "Hide! There—behind that screen."

There was no sound of footsteps from the room beyond. John hesitated, but the old woman threw a pillow at him. "For heaven's sake!" she hissed. "Do you *want* him to find you here? Didn't I tell you I was a Revealer?"

He obeyed then, darting behind the carved wooden screen and repositioning it to hide him from both the door and the bed. It had evidently been placed here to conceal a low washstand, with a jug and a bowl. For a moment John stood with his heart in his mouth, listening to the old woman flop down on her couch, trying to regulate her breathing. Then silence fell and stayed for a long time.

For a moment he felt foolish, as though he was hiding from nothing. Then he glanced again towards the curtain that covered the doorway. There was a narrow gap between the curtain and the floor, and a shadow was pooled on the threshold—the shadow of a person.

It stood there, motionless, for some time. Then at last it shifted. John withdrew behind the screen again, his heart beating. Had al-Mukhtar been *listening* to them?

Slow footsteps entered the room.

"Saif?" the old lady whispered.

More silence.

"Saif? Is all well?"

Through the screen's latticework, John saw al-Mukhtar's shoulders slumped and dejected. Slowly, he crossed the room to the divan. There came the double thud of knees hitting the floor; a heavy sigh, and—the soft sound of a kiss.

"Saif," the old woman repeated. "Something's wrong. Tell me."

"O Ghaliyah. My darling," al-Mukhtar said in a voice gentler than he had ever heard before. "I've done something very reckless."

John stared at the lattice. *My darling?* He peered around the edge of the screen, just to confirm he was hearing correctly. Al-Mukhtar was on his knees at the old woman's bedside, his arms encircling her, his head against her bosom.

In Tripoli, al-Mukhtar had spoken of his wife. *Ghaliyah,* he had called her. But it was impossible. This woman was at least forty, perhaps fifty years the young man's senior.

Unless al-Mukhtar drew immortality, as well as strength, from the bond he shared with Soraya. A bond which his wife, naturally, would not share...

John pressed the back of his hand against his mouth, strangling a sound of disbelief. For decades, the Chosen had been killing Watchers the length and breadth of Syria—and all this time his wife had been one of them. Did he know? Was that why he tried to keep his mission to Tripoli a secret from her?

"You didn't ask him again to heal me, did you?" Ghaliyah asked, stroking al-Mukhtar's head. "I've told you before, my love. I'm ready to die. I'm not afraid."

Saif shook his head. "But *I* am," he said, woefully. "It is said that there are more women in hell than in Paradise. And if you *will* be a polytheist—"

"Saif," she said, as though weary of a long-standing debate.

"I can *save* you," he insisted. "If al-Ashraf won't do it willingly he must be forced to it. It's a horrible risk, I know."

Ghaliyah was shocked. "You would go against him?

"To save you, I would dare it." Al-Mukhtar made a peculiar sound that might have been a laugh. "Soraya was right. So, too, was al-Ashraf, when he said the two of you would corrupt me. May God forgive me!"

There was a silence; Ghaliyah's lips thinned. "I do not believe that God made you to be that man's slave, and if—" But she got no further. She went into a coughing-fit, disturbing the cat, which leapt down from her bed.

"Where did that creature come from?" al-Mukhtar asked sharply as the coughing subsided. "What is it doing on your bed?"

"Doesn't it belong to one of the servants?" Ghaliyah rasped. "Here, puss!"

"No. It's a stray, and it'll only make you worse. Get away." Al-Mukhtar got up, grabbing for the animal.

John's breath caught. He'd presumed the cat was part of the household— but if not—

The creature slipped between al-Mukhtar's hands and darted towards the screen, towards John. Then it caught sight of him and went into a stiff, arched pose of terror.

"Saif—" Ghaliyah began.

"Something's behind the screen," said the Chosen, and then the screen was wrenched aside and John was staring down the wicked length of a blade.

Al-Mukhtar's lips were thinned, his face furious. *"You,"* he whispered.

"Saif!" Ghaliyah repeated. "I promised—"

She went into a coughing-fit, doubled over. Al-Mukhtar seized John by the collar of his tunic.

"Downstairs," he hissed.

* * *

Tight-lipped, Saif dragged John Bessarion from the room. For a moment, the only sound in the room were Ghaliyah's racking coughs. At length, the spasm subsided and a panting Ghaliyah lifted her head to gaze at the cat.

"This was your doing," she rasped, reproachfully. "Now you had better go and beg Saif not to kill him."

The cat stared back, bland and unblinking.

"Don't give me that," Ghaliyah said. "I've wanted to meet you for a long time, Soraya."

The cat did blink, then. It deliberated for a moment, and then Soraya gathered matter from the dust in the next room and the street outside. There was a strong wind that plucked at the bed-curtains, and then she was sitting cross-legged opposite Ghaliyah, her arms folded and her brow furrowed.

"You save him," she said. "You knew about me, about the Lance, about the killing. *Everything.* Did you know how much of it Saif has done in *your* name? Go down there now, and plead with him yourself."

The old woman looked away, as though evading Soraya's challenging glare. "And let him know that I have a Gift?" she whispered. "I cannot allow al-Ashraf to know of it, to make a tool of me the way he has made of Saif."

Soraya remained silent a moment, her heart contracting. How did Ghaliyah come to this marriage? It could not have been willing on her part; at least not to begin with. *There is nowhere else for me now, even if I wished to depart.* How easy it was to imagine herself in the other woman's place—knowing herself to be in command of a great power, and terrified of losing what little freedom remained to her.

"Saif will pay no heed to me," she said, very gently. "My words are only rain on the stone of his will, but you have the power to move him, now, as you are dying. Will you go to your grave without a word to save him?"

* * *

John staggered down the stairs into the courtyard and turned, throwing up his hands as a furious al-Mukhtar advanced upon him.

"I meant your wife no insult," he protested.

Al-Mukhtar's knife whizzed viciously past him and stuck, quivering, in one of the wooden doors at the other end of the courtyard. "You *disturbed* her *rest,*" he hissed. Another knife stuck in the grass between John's feet. "You *invaded* her *privacy.*" A third knife actually sliced a shallow furrow in his arm as he stumbled back. *"You made her conceal you."*

John yelped with pain. "No! It wasn't like that! I entered by mistake and she begged me to stay!"

"You're lying." A fourth knife was poised in al-Mukhtar's hand.

"Why not ask her?" John insisted. "Even I could tell that she was starved for company and her mind craved new thoughts. She told me you had kept her shut up in that room for months!"

"That's because she is *sick!*" Al-Mukhtar grabbed at the front of John's tunic again. "Give me *one* reason why I should not strike you down where you stand, John Bessarion."

You tell me, he wanted to say. Why had al-Mukhtar not killed him in the house of Bektash? Why go to all this trouble extracting him from his prison and bringing him here?

But it did not fall to John to answer the question. Instead, Soraya's voice descended from the loggia. "Because you want your wife to think well of you."

Al-Mukhtar turned, stiff with astonishment. It was not only Soraya who stood in the loggia looking down upon them. She had her arm around

Ghaliyah, whose thin frame was wrapped in a shawl.

Al-Mukhtar dropped his knife. "Ghaliyah," he said, pleadingly. "This man has insulted you. Of course he must be chastised."

"Saif," she said, wearily. "How many of this man's family have you already killed?"

There was a long silence. John sidled away from al-Mukhtar, partly to get out of reach, and partly to see his slack, horrified face.

"Why do you stare at me? I've always known there is blood on your hands." Ghaliyah waited a moment, but there was no answer. Al-Mukhtar's mouth opened and closed. "For years I used to wonder how you did it," she added. "How you could dip your hands in innocent blood, and then return to me at home with open arms and closed lips. But you never thought you were doing wrong, did you? You thought yourself the most faithful man in the world. All that blood on your conscience, and you were able to tell yourself that you *had* to do it, for your master's sake. That there was a divine order to things, and you were only enforcing it."

Al-Mukhtar pulled himself together sufficiently to point a shaking finger at Soraya. "This is *your* doing," he said, thickly. "When did you tell her?"

"*I* told her nothing, my master," Soraya said.

"It was *you*, Saif," Ghaliyah said, trembling in the wind. "I knew from your face when you killed for him, just as I see now that you are indeed ready to turn against him. God be praised! My death will accomplish some good."

"There you see it, my master," said Soraya, wickedly. "This is for *your own good.*"

"You won't die, Ghaliyah," said al-Mukhtar desperately. "Nor will you drive a wedge between me and al-Ashraf. I'll make him understand that he must save you—that's all."

"I don't *want* to be saved." Ghaliyah sighed. "Not by sorcery. Will you force more of this life upon me?"

"What does *that* mean?" Blades might have no effect upon al-Mukhtar, but those words had struck him to the heart. He hurried up the steps towards her. "Are you really so desperate for company? I've neglected you—I'm sorry. I can bring you people, entertainers, story-tellers. When you're well we might go on a journey. Perhaps you'd like to see Alexandria…"

"No." She put out a hand to hold him off. "Saif, I'm tired. I only want rest."

"Tired of *what?* Of life?"

Ghaliyah pressed her lips together. "I'm tired of loving someone who can never love me the same way."

"What?" Al-Mukhtar choked. "I do love you. I would burn the world for you."

"I know." Ghaliyah touched his face. "You've never been able to have love. Not the real thing, and it eats at you like a vulture. That's why you've spent your whole life killing to get it from that master of yours."

"Why would you say that?" Al-Mukhtar caught her hand, shaking his head. "Al-Ashraf's been like a father to me."

"Open your eyes, Saif," she rasped. "Al-Ashraf *is* your father."

Al-Mukhtar blinked. "My *father?* What do you mean?"

"I mean he's the one who begot you!"

John's eyes met Soraya's, wide with shock.

"That's impossible," al-Mukhtar insisted, but Soraya let out a bitterlaugh.

"Oh, of course it's true. Of course Khalil would craft himself the perfect servant. He'd leave nothing to chance, not even the birth. Oh, your poor mother!"

"No. No. Why would you say such a thing?" Al-Mukhtar was backing away from his wife now, backing towards John.

With grim enjoyment, John said, "Your wife is a Revealer, al-Mukhtar. Such secrets are hers to read."

"Why would I lie to you?" Ghaliyah demanded, pushing away from Soraya, stumbling towards her husband. With her white hair flying, she looked like an ancient sibyl. "Do you not know me by now?"

"No!" Al-Mukhtar grabbed John, holding him before him almost like a shield against the arrows of Ghaliyah's words. "Take her back to her room, Soraya! *Now!*"

Soraya had to obey—of course she did; but as she supported Ghaliyah back into the women's quarters, she turned a triumphant grin over her shoulder. Al-Mukhtar was panting as though he had run a race. John's mind was an uproar.

Al-Mukhtar—the son of Khalil ibn Hassan. Of course. Of *course* Khalil would never hand over Soraya to *anyone* not bound to him directly by blood.

Of *course* Khalil would not allow even his son to know of their link, to imagine that he could succeed him.

Al-Mukhtar's wife. He'd imagined her as one of a string of young women, nubile and interchangeable. Instead, she was an ancient and powerful Watcher.

"Do you really think you can silence her, merely by locking her away?" he asked now.

Al-Mukhtar yanked John to face him. "You never answered my question," he hissed. *"Tell me why I should not kill you."*

This time, John had an answer.

"Because we both want our revenge on Khalil," he said softly.

Al-Mukhtar stared at him, lips parted.

"Revenge," he said, as if tasting the word for the first time.

"That's why you didn't kill me in Bektash's house," John pressed. "Because we can help each other."

Al-Mukhtar's eyes focused on John again. "I brought you here to be of *use,*" he said. "Not because I wanted to *help* you." He nearly yanked John off his feet, dragging him once again to the room at the back of the loggia. The door slammed, the broken latch jumping. John caught the door to keep it from rebounding; outside, he heard al-Mukhtar calling for his guards, ordering them to keep a constant watch upon the door.

John turned and sank to his haunches, back against the door, grimly smiling.

Al-Mukhtar, the son of Khalil. Of course.

Such a vicious son could only come from a vicious father.

Chapter XXII.

Soraya said little as she helped Ghaliyah back to her couch. Saif's voice echoed in the courtyard, summoning guards. The old woman sank into her pillows with a sigh, her exhaustion witnessing to the toll the confrontation had taken upon her.

"Thank you," she whispered.

Soraya hesitated, but Ghaliyah said nothing else; her eyes fluttered closed. Soraya felt the bite of guilt. She'd used the woman with ruthless disregard for her health, intending only to strike back at Saif by exposing his true nature to the wife he loved. Instead, Ghaliyah had with a few words torn out the cornerstone of Saif's existence. Soraya herself was half terrified by what might happen next.

Saif had finished shouting at his guards and was now shouting for her. For once, she was glad to answer the command, marching out of Ghaliyah's room to meet Saif in the antechamber.

Saif closed the door behind him, muffling their voices from onlookers. He was white to the lips with wrath.

"This was *your* doing," he hissed. "I thought we were *friends.*"

A moment ago Soraya had been half regretful for her actions. At his words she forgot all that.

"We were *never* friends," she hissed. "Friends don't deceive each other. Friends don't command each other. You know full well that you've only ever been my master."

Saif's face worked. She expected a scolding, but none came. "I'm leaving the house," he said instead. "You are in command here. Do not leave. Watch over Ghaliyah. Supply her with food, water, medicine, and physicians as necessary. Protect her with your life. Keep John Bessarion in his cell and don't bother me unless it's urgent."

Soraya stared at him. Saif, leaving? Why? She didn't for a moment imagine that he was leaving her in command because he trusted her. He preferred her only because he could tie her down beneath a web of commands.

"Saif." A weak voice echoed from beyond the curtain.

Saif startled. "That's Ghaliyah," he said, almost accusingly.

"Are you afraid of her?" Soraya taunted.

But the mockery seemed to stiffen his resolve, because he sent her a resentful look and stalked across the workroom to his wife's chamber.

Ghaliyah was kneeling on the carpet as though she had struggled to rise from her bed, but had lost the strength. Saif swept her into his arms. Soraya watched their faces close together, age and wrinkles beside youth and beauty.

It had never occurred to her that Saif's beloved wife might be *old*. That she might be dying of age, not sickness. And yet.

"You're leaving," Ghaliyah whispered, putting a hand to his cheek. "Kiss me good-bye, beloved. One last time."

Saif stiffened, peering down at her with a worried furrow between his eyes. "Ghaliyah. It will only be for a day or two."

"I know."

He kissed her. Soraya stood forgotten in the doorway, but she could not look away. She had never seen a man kiss a woman like this—sweetly, gently, because she asked him to.

How much of what Saif felt for his wife was real? Did he hold onto her because she was one of only a few things that he could control—or was there something deeper at work?

It didn't matter—it wasn't her place to wonder. She owed him nothing and could make her escape whenever it suited her. Soraya was glad, then— fiercely glad—that *she* was not the woman in Saif's arms.

Saif helped Ghaliyah back onto her couch and stalked away. He made a threatening gesture at Soraya as he brushed past her—promising some dreadful fate, no doubt, should she fail in her assigned task. Then they heard him crossing the courtyard, calling for his horse. Ghaliyah turned her head, beholding Soraya with wide-open eyes.

"Tell him," she whispered. "When the time comes, tell him that I loved him."

Soraya was no longer a cat, but she could feel the hairs prickling on the back of her neck. "You aren't going to die before he comes back, are you?"

"No," Ghaliyah said sadly.

"Good. Then you can tell him yourself."

Soraya was about to turn away, but a thought had been growing in her mind ever since Ghaliyah had looked at her and called her by name, when she was wearing the body of a cat and it should have been impossible to identify her as a djinn. "You're truly a Revealer. Can you perform exorcisms?"

"Probably," Ghaliyah said, almost as though she had expected the question. "Should I exorcise you?"

Soraya shrugged. "Why not? Although I don't think it would help. I'm not a demon; I'm a djinn. I must have been half mortal, once. How long have you been married to Saif?"

"Fifty-five years," Ghaliyah said. "When they first came to Cairo from Khorasan, his father gave him leave to choose a wife. Saif chose me. And suffered for it. A Coptic slave girl was not the kind of wife al-Ashraf meant."

"From Khorasan?" Soraya opened her eyes wide. So, Saif and Khalil had been in Egypt less than sixty years. She wondered how long before that they had been in the great Tartar empire. Whether that empire would have been so great if not for Khalil and his familiars.

Whether Khalil's defection to Egypt had anything to do with the abrupt halt of that empire's expansion.

"We have never had children," Ghaliyah added, quietly recalling Soraya to the present. "Al-Ashraf made sure of that. It did not bother me, at first. A mamluk was not the kind of husband I would have chosen for myself, or as a father for my sons. Now, I wish…"

Her voice trailed away. Soraya watched her with curiosity. "What changed?" she asked.

"Nothing changed," Ghaliyah said, with a sigh. "In this life, we can only make the best of what we have. Saif gave me no choice, but since then he has loved me as well as he knows how. And I have loved him as far as he has allowed it. I might have fared worse."

Soraya put a hand over her mouth to stifle her disbelieving laughter.

"What is the joke?" Ghaliyah asked, not at all put out.

"To hear Saif, one would think that the two of you were Leila and Majnun, sharing the forbidden love of ages," Soraya said. "Did you not hear him declare his love? He would burn the world for you!"

Ghaliyah laughed, and if there was pain in the sound, there was also fondness. "That is not love, but sentiment."

Soraya fell silent. For longer than she could remember, she had felt like a starving beggar hearing the sounds of lutes and feasting from within the courtyard of a rich palace, and wishing in vain that such bounty might be hers. All this time, Ghaliyah had been within the palace, the guest of honour at the banquet. And yet she was starving too, her feast a painted show.

Somehow that made it all worse: Soraya felt curiously bereft. "Then what *is* love?"

"*Greater love hath no man than this,*" Ghaliyah quoted softly, "*that a man lay down his life for his friend.*"

"I haven't asked anyone to die for me," Soraya said, unable to keep the hurt out of her voice. "Only to free me. To put me, just *once*, before himself. Can such a love be found on the earth?"

Ghaliyah put a hand to her breast; her eyes glimmered. "Perhaps only here," she said. "*Love bears all things, believes all things, hopes all things...* Perhaps I ought to have spoken to Saif sooner, despite the cost. Perhaps I have already left it too late. If I had died without speaking..."

"Then it would have been no more than he deserves," Soraya said, although her voice was husky. Drearily, she brought her thoughts back to the task at hand. Saif was gone; God only knew where. Perhaps to run an errand for his master, or perhaps to lick his wounds in the wilderness. John, meanwhile, was no use at all. Twice he had faced Qeteb, and twice he had failed.

At this point, there was no use in looking *there* for help.

Not when she had Ghaliyah.

"You want to set Saif free?" Soraya asked. "You want to cut his ties with Khalil for good—even if it means laying down your life?"

Ghaliyah's eyes grew large. "Of course," she whispered. "Tell me how."

Chapter XXIII.

"Can you imagine treating your own son in this way?" John stifled an incredulous laugh. "Here is al-Mukhtar, devoted to his master and pathetically grateful for any scraps that fall from Khalil's table. And now it turns out he is that master's son, and the table itself is his own by right. "

Rahel listened placidly from her seat beside him on the bed. The two of them had not ventured past John's small guest room tonight; he had had his fill of wandering the house, at least for the moment.

It had not escaped him that in advising his escape, Soraya had sent him directly towards Ghaliyah's room.

"What will he do now, I wonder?" Rahel mused.

"Ghaliyah hopes that he'll turn against Khalil," John said. "But he won't. That young man comes of a bad stock. He's suffered too much in his master's cause to give him up now. And he's been instilled with a strong sense of filial piety. If anything, he'll take his father's part more stubbornly than ever before."

Rahel looked worried, but she did not tell him to be careful, or beg him to make good his escape. Instead, she said: "You should stay long enough to speak to Ghaliyah, at least. Who could have guessed that al-Mukhtar would have a Gifted Watcher in his own house?"

John shook his head, still scarcely able to believe it. "As his *wife,* no less. How can she love a man like that?"

"I don't know," Rahel said, with a glimmer of humour. "Perhaps the same way I could love a man like John Bessarion."

"I was *nothing* like al-Mukhtar."

"Not in degree," she acknowledged. "But you have both been heretic-hunters, my love. And I gather she did not pretend that it had been easy for her—or pleasant."

"That woman was forced into a marriage with a heretic," John said, his voice vibrating with rage. "She has lived her whole life with someone who tells her that she is going to hell. Had she had had any children, they would have been taken from her to be brought up in a different faith. *You* did not have to endure that. I will do everything to ensure that my children do not have to endure it, either."

"Oh, John. Are you God, to protect us from what may happen to anyone? We have a King greater than any sultan. Whether we are uprooted, or whether we remain, it will be *his* doing and not the deed of any mortal."

John felt sickened. He thought of Ghaliyah calling al-Mukhtar her love, asking for his kiss—when it was his people who had occupied her country and subjected her people.

Then he thought of bands of calligraphic Arabic girdling the domes of a church, of Frankish masons' marks on an altar.

"The church in my vision," he said, slowly. "It wasn't what I expected. There were Arabic words written upon it, and the altar had been built by Frankish craftsmen. I saw their marks carved upon the stone." He watched Rahel's face. "Did you see these things too?"

"I don't know about the stonecutters' marks," Rahel admitted, "but yes, the calligraphy was always there."

"Why didn't you tell me?" he burst out. "It's *our* land, Syrian land. Why should you and I build a church with the help of Franks and Saracens? They have their own lands. Why can't they stay there?"

"Because it's beautiful," Rahel said. *"The kings of the earth do bring their glory and honour into* the New Jerusalem; why should they not do so for our churches?"

"The kings of earth may pay us tribute as they wish," John muttered. "But why should *they* build my church?"

Rahel laughed. "Does it matter who builds the church?"

"Yes, it *does*," he insisted. "It matters to me. *What if it means I never find my way home?"*

Rahel's laughter died.

He had concealed this fear, trying to keep both their hopes up. But there was no point in hiding it from her any longer. "I don't know if Soraya will ever take me home. She's changed towards me. In Tripoli I was her friend. Now…" He wiped a hand over his eyes to catch the tears. "Now I'm only her tool."

"She doesn't know you yet, my love. Not the way she did in Tripoli."

"Perhaps," he said. The silence stretched out, somehow accusing, until he added: "Or perhaps this time she sees me more clearly. Once, for the sake of my family and my people, I was willing to break a promise to her. Now she believes I'll do it again."

"Will you?"

"No," he said, hotly. "When I go home to you I'll break the Lance, and Soraya shall be free for as many centuries as she was bound, no matter what it means for *us*. But first she must send me home."

For a long moment Rahel said nothing, allowing his words to echo in the silence, before she said, softly, *"Must* she?"

John had known she would say that; but he wished she had not said it in *that* voice, the patient voice he had heard her use with the children when they were being demanding. He bit his lip, holding back the excuses that would have come pouring out—that any wrong he might do Soraya would be undone by the undoing of this future. That if she was freed in the past, she would recall no suffering in the future.

"That's Khalil's error," Rahel went on slowly. "You can't do people good by force. You can't do *Soraya* good by force. We made the same error in the day of the great persecution; don't you remember?"

He did. He had thrown people into prison, beaten and threatened them, partly on the orders of the emperor, it was true. But also because he had really believed that he was doing them good in turning them away from heresy that would injure their souls. If he truly repented of that error, he could not do the same by Soraya.

"Beware, John," Rahel added, after a moment. "Qeteb left you alive for a reason. He is plotting something. Be sure you do not play into his hands."

He scraped a hand over his head, knowing better than to protest. "Is that a Message?" he asked.

Her answer was only a whisper. "I don't know. Perhaps."

* * *

Soraya came to him the following evening, which was more than John had dared to hope.

"Still here?" she greeted him, having dismissed the guard at his door. He had heard her voice around the house, evidently relishing the chance to order al-Mukhtar's soldiers about for once. "I thought you would have attempted another escape by now. Especially after I fixed the lock for you."

"I didn't fancy my chances against a fully armed mamluk guard," he said. Soraya, with her infinitely repairable bodies and her magically augmented strength, had perhaps an inflated notion of his abilities. He took a deep breath and said, "I ought to thank you. Al-Mukhtar was about to cut my throat in the courtyard yesterday before you and the Lady Ghaliyah appeared."

Soraya looked, for a moment, surprised. "You're thanking me?"

Perhaps she was thinking of the way in which she'd provoked that same confrontation in the first place. "You helped get me out of Bektash's prison alive. You stood by me when I was pierced with Qeteb's arrows. And then you sent me where I might meet Ghaliyah, a powerful Watcher and possible ally. Indeed, I have much for which to thank you."

"I did it for my own ends," she said gruffly.

He tried not to flinch at that. "You owe me nothing after the suffering I have caused you." She did not speak, so he went on: "You asked me a question which I never answered. The answer is yes. No matter whether you send me home or not, I made you a promise. I may not be able to do it myself, but I *will* find someone to free you from Qeteb's control."

Soraya's expression hardened. "So that's how you think it will be? You will speak sweet words to me and banish Qeteb, and then perhaps I will relent and send you home. Where I will be utterly in your power, and all of Palestine with me. I suppose it is worth the gamble."

"Soraya," he began, and stopped, finding himself choking upon his own rage and sorrow. Al-Mukhtar did this to her, making her believe that she could trust no friends, making her believe that she would only ever know betrayal… "Soraya," he said again, in a voice that concealed nothing, "I want to hold my wife and kiss my children. Send me back to them and it will be everything I need. I'll do as I promised in Tripoli, and I'll free you in the past. All these centuries of blood and slavery will be undone. *Please.*"

That stony expression cracked; Soraya put a hand across her mouth. "I wish I knew whether it's really your family you love, or power."

"It's both," he said, because there was no escaping the truth now. "I won't lie to you, Soraya. Not like he does. To my shame, it's both."

"Truth." Soraya shook her head. "I am not your family, John Bessarion, and so for you I will always be second. I must content myself with the scraps of your love and the scraps of what power you can spare me; I understand that. But if no one will feed me anything but scraps, I must feast at my own table. I must put myself first, and I must put *you* second. Do you understand?"

He wanted to say that she was wrong. He wanted to say that love need not be measured out, that there was enough of it to redeem the world. That although he must always consider Rahel first, he was still called to love all his neighbours as himself, regardless of blood or nation.

But if he said it, she would laugh in his face, and tell him that his actions did not bear it out. And he would be unable to protest, because he had treated her as less than she was—as nothing.

"I understand," he said, instead. Trust must be earned; it could not be demanded.

Perhaps Soraya sensed his thought, for she sent him a suspicious look. But she said, "I came to tell you that Ghaliyah and I will try to cast out the Hairy One ourselves. We have no need of you."

"Ah," John said. "No more you do."

Soraya's chin tilted up. "You may come, if you like, and observe."

Last night, as he spoke with Rahel, John had envisioned himself putting the notion to Ghaliyah himself and himself presiding over Soraya's liberation. Now he felt utterly superfluous.

Does it matter who builds the church? Rahel had asked him.

"I should not be there," he admitted now, bowing his head. "The Hairy One has some hold over me which I do not understand. I might only hamper you as I did the other night."

"Please yourself," Soraya said with a shrug, turning to go.

If Soraya meant to free herself, if there was no going home for him, then what could he do?

"Wait," he said. "I might yet help. You don't recall what it was like when we cast out Lilith in Tripoli; she fought to stop us. The Hairy One will likely do the same. Let me go, and I'll return to Heliopolis and confront him there, as a diversion. Then it will be easier for Ghaliyah."

Soraya looked surprised, but shook her head. "I can't," she admitted. "I've been commanded not to let you go—and there's no way I can disobey that command, even if I want to."

At that moment, from the courtyard, there came a sound of hammering at the gate, and confused shouts. Soraya hissed with annoyance and departed, leaving the door ajar behind her.

John waited, but the commotion did not die away. He heard Soraya's voice again, now deep and masculine, as footsteps and jingling armour burst into the courtyard. He heard footsteps leave his door—his guards were gone. John got to his feet and ventured out into the loggia, for he had a suspicion that he knew the meaning of this commotion.

The westering sun was a yellow glow at the edge of the sky, but the courtyard lay wrapped in its own shadow, hot and stifling. A band of mamluks stood below, and Soraya—now wearing a man's body—waited on the loggia steps facing them. Five of al-Mukhtar's guards surrounded her, swords drawn. The gate stood open, and the gatekeeper was slumped against the wall with splayed legs and a bloodied pate.

"How dare you attack the house of al-Rafiq and injure his servants?" Soraya demanded of the intruders. "Who sent you?"

"You're holding a man prisoner here," the leader of the mamluks declared. "I have orders to retrieve him."

Strife, John thought. This must be the answer to the letter he'd thrown into the street. What was Bektash thinking, responding with an invasion? Hadn't he learned his lesson after the disastrous confrontation with not one, but *two* djinn and a demon the night before last?

A hand tugged at his sleeve, and John looked down into Ghaliyah's bright eyes and wrinkled brown face. A maidservant hovered watchfully behind the old woman, but she was leaning on a staff and looking far livelier than she had yesterday.

"This is your chance to go," she told him. "I'll distract Soraya while you escape."

Bemused, John glanced at Soraya, who was once again demanding to know on whose orders the intruders had come. "Did...did she put you up to this?"

"Of *course* not," Ghaliyah said, but she grinned widely.

Soraya had always had a genius for finding loopholes in her orders, and she was evidently not the only one.

"Quickly," said Ghaliyah. "Don't you wish to leave this house?"

He did, although he was not entirely sure he wished to do so as the prisoner of Bektash. But what would they do if he resisted? Would Soraya be able to stop them ransacking the house? And how would Ghaliyah fare at the hands of these men?

"Do they mean me harm?" he asked, instead.

"Whatever they mean," Ghaliyah answered, "they will do you none."

John sighed. The sooner he dealt with this incursion—which, after all, he had incited—the sooner Ghaliyah and Soraya could carry out their exorcism. He would be out of the house, as he had promised. Ghaliyah would be safe. And if he proved unable to distract Qeteb, at least he could re-establish himself in Bektash's favour.

"I promised to free Soraya," John told her in a low voice. "That promise is yours to keep now."

Ghaliyah reached for his head, drew him down, and left a kiss upon his forehead. "Trust in God, John Bessarion."

He bowed his head to her, then strode to the loggia railing and dropped down into the courtyard, where the intruders were now preparing to rush the men on the stair.

"I am John Bessarion, the man you are looking for," he told them, raising his hands. "I surrender myself."

Chapter XXIV.

John's mamluk escort hurried him through the dusky streets and in at the now-repaired gate of the palace he had left barely two nights before. In the half-light of sunset, Bektash al-Fakhri awaited him in the peristyle that surrounded the courtyard. At first a dark and indistinct figure seated with others beside a low, glowing brazier, he left the firelight and came forward to meet John at the centre of the courtyard.

"John Bessarion," the old amir said gravely. "You are yet living."

There was something wary in Bektash's face and tone of voice. John glanced uneasily at the men who waited in the peristyle, but they too were in shadow: a small knot of mamluks standing to attention, and their master visible as little but a gold-limned gleam of jewelled scabbard and richly-woven linen, and booted feet stretched out towards the brazier.

John bowed to the old amir. "My lord, peace be upon you. I am grateful for your help in freeing me from the place where I was held. Is there somewhere we can speak in private?"

"Speak here," said Bektash, waving his mamluks further back.

John lowered his voice. "The house from which you took me, my lord, is the one belonging to al-Mukhtar—or al-Rafiq, as he is more commonly known. This is the evidence you needed. Now, if you will allow me to go in peace—"

"To what end?" Bektash asked.

Again, there was that wary look. John's gut knotted. "I'm trying to help you," he said. "Have your loyalties altered so soon, my lord?"

"They have," came the answer, but not from Bektash. John turned, once again, to the peristyle and the man who sat there, guarded by shadows from the dying light of the sunset. There was a glimmer of light on steel as the man rose and faced him, still in darkness.

"John Bessarion," said that soft, deadly voice. "Qeteb told me you had been seen."

With that, he knew who he was facing. How long had it been—months or centuries—since he had faced Khalil ibn Hassan in the lost city of Oliveta? It had been dark then, too; his enemy at first little more than a soft, menacing voice in the shadows. That voice was both familiar and not; deeper, huskier than it used to be. But the cadence was the same.

John felt his whole body turn to ice.

"Bektash," he whispered, half in reproach.

"Bektash is *my* servant now," Khalil announced. "As you are *my* prisoner."

There was a silence. John's skin prickled, suddenly clammy in the breathless calm. The air, which in this city was always laden with dust, seemed thick and grey and hard to see through. He heard his own voice speak:

"Did Qeteb tell you he spoke to me himself, five days ago in Heliopolis?"

That surprised his enemy. "He did not," said Khalil.

"I wonder why he would have concealed it from you." John took a deep breath, forcing himself to think. Ghaliyah had promised him they would not harm him. Al-Mukhtar had spared him; perhaps Khalil, too, could be convinced to keep him alive. "Isn't he supposed to be your servant? Perhaps you should speak to him about it."

"I will," said Khalil, "but you will not live to see it." And he drew the sword at his side.

It was here that he would die, if Ghaliyah was wrong, if he failed to save himself. John's hands itched for his cross-bows, but they were still at the monastery and he had nothing else, not so much as a pen-knife, with which to defend himself. But Bektash's mamluks hung back as Khalil stepped forward; and there was a gate behind him.

John turned and hurled himself at it. Bektash's startled mamluks moved to intercept him, but Khalil cried a warning and they fell back. John hit the gate, a solid door set in a wall of stone, impossible to climb over. The lock had been set, and the porter stood amidst Bektash's mamluks clutching his great wooden key.

John shook the gate, half believing that he could snatch it off its hinges, or that if he could not, Soraya would. "Open," he panted, throwing a glance over his shoulder. *"Open,* damn you!"

By some miracle, the door opened.

In his surprise, John nearly fell back upon the point of Khalil's sword. But then he caught at the door and hurled himself through, slamming it behind him with an echoing crash. Abruptly, the sounds of shouts and scuffling feet from the courtyard were shut off.

John dragged in a huge gasp. He was cold. The air was cold. The pavement was cold and smooth beneath his thin sandals. He looked down and saw a rich geometric pattern of polished marble underfoot. Then a shadow fell over him, blotting out what little light still glowed in the east.

"John Bessarion," said a voice as rich as honey at his side. "Peace be upon you."

This voice, too, was familiar, he thought, blinking at the figure beside him. It was the other djinn, the one for whom Soraya had nearly sacrificed herself two nights before in this very alley.

No—he was in no alley now. The very air was different, sweet with citrus, salty with the sea. The door through which he had fled stood not in a street, but a palace loggia. Facing it was an arcade of round arches, and through them he beheld the sea, and a far rim of fire where the sun sank beneath it.

John stared. "Where am I?"

"You are in the house of John of Ibelin," said the djinn, "in Beirut. It is fortunate that you knocked when you did, at the sunset, when my power is greatest and the doors of my house open easily to my friends."

"And to Khalil?" John asked, eyeing the door suspiciously.

The djinn—Ibrahim, he had been called—made a growl deep in his throat. "Never to Khalil," he said. "Not even the Hairy One has the power to force an entrance here. That is why he had to send his mamluk."

John let go of the breath he had been holding. At the same moment, a little way down the loggia, a door opened. It admitted a shaft of golden light and a bevy of women, gleaming in silk and jewels. Speaking in low, contented voices, they went away from John, not seeing where he stood in the shadows.

"See where the Lady of Beirut goes to her supper," Ibrahim said, tilting his head in their direction. "She has sought you long, and at great risk, John Bessarion. It is a great good fortune that you have come to us."

John blinked. The Lady's presence at Bektash's gate, the night of his rescue—or capture—by al-Mukhtar had completely escaped his mind, overwhelmed by everything else. "What does she want with me?"

"That she can best explain herself, when she returns from her supper. Come with me; I'll show you where you can wait in privacy."

Wait—in safety and comfort, to speak with a prince who did *not* wish to kill him! John let out a harried laugh. "I cannot," he said. "I made a vow to a friend, and I must keep it. You must send me back to Cairo."

"I will, if you wish it," said Ibrahim, "when you have spoken with the Lady."

"No," John insisted. It was impossible to remain still: he had locusts in his veins. Soraya and Ghaliyah would soon conduct their exorcism—might already be about it. He needed to travel to Helopolis, to summon Qeteb, to keep him from noticing the true threat in Cairo. How could he do that in Beirut? "You must send me back now, this moment."

"Now? When Khalil is hunting you?"

John squeezed his eyes shut. "Yes," he said, and even to his own ears his voice was strained. "I can only bait them now; that's the best I can do for all of us. Whatever the Lady wants of me can wait until Qeteb is cast out."

"You mean to cast him out?" Ibrahim breathed. "Then you are right. You must return at once—but not by this door. Follow me."

The djinn led him down the loggia to another door, across which he passed his hand. "This will take you into the citadel," he told John. "Hurry. The gates are closed at sunset, with the blowing of horns. You may be in time."

There was no time to say more. "Thank you," John told the djinn, and stepped from the cold of Beirut to the warmth of Cairo. There was an echoing ring upon the dusky air: the ringing of the horns.

John did not wait, did not look back, did not linger to gaze upon the distant Nile or the tall shapes of the pyramids beyond. He threw the door shut and dashed in the direction of that sound.

* * *

The streets of Cairo were alive with mamluks. John caught his first glimpse of them not three steps from the citadel gates, stopping a man in the black robes and blue turban of a Coptic official who had emerged from the citadel ahead of himself. They dragged him away, protesting, and John felt a cold certainty trace down his spine. Surely they were looking for *him.*

Three more of Khalil's men moved towards him through the press of traffic in the street, holding a torch aloft and peering into the faces of those they passed. John tucked himself into a crouch at the foot of a wall, hastily pulling off his blue turban and his black robe. Just as quickly, unseen in the twilight, he tore off the white sash he wore at his waist and fashioned it into a makeshift turban. Within moments he rejoined the flow traffic, transformed into a sturdy Mahometan craftsman.

Still, it would take only a glance at his wrist, and the Watcher's Mark inked there, to give him away. John turned his face away as the torch swept by. Then the danger was past for now; but as he turned aside into a narrower street, he saw more mamluks ahead of him, with more torches.

Khalil was seeking him with a vengeance. Despite having shed his scholar's robe, John felt the prickle of sweat on his breastbone as he ducked again into the flow of traffic. What now? He would never make it to Heliopolis like this—for that he must somehow walk the entire length of the Qasaba, or "throat"—the long, narrow, gorge-like street that bisected Cairo—without being caught. It was impossible.

He needed help, but from whom, now that Bektash had betrayed him?

No sooner had the thought crossed his mind than he had an answer. Turuntay, the na'ib, whom Saif had attempted to murder. If anyone would be willing to shelter him, it was Khalil's rival. The amir might even agree to send him to Heliopolis with an escort—and his house must be near at hand.

A water-carrier directed him to the house of Turuntay. John kept to the shadows and pulled the loose end of his turban across his face as he knocked at the gate, guessing that Khalil must have spies watching his rival's house, quite apart from the search for John Bessarion himself. Still, he was surprised when the gate opened abruptly, and he was without warning yanked roughly inside.

"What do you want?" asked the gatekeeper, a burly man and well-armed. "Speak, or I'll throw you out again, and al-Ashraf's dogs can have you."

"You'd better not do that," John said, almost laughing despite the threat. "It was al-Ashraf's dog that nearly killed your master. That's what I want with the na'ib."

"Five in your eye," the gatekeeper breathed, astonished. Then he raised his voice in a shout, and in the time it might take to recite the Creed, John was hustled through the house and into the hall beyond. Here a stream of water flowed from the far wall into a channel lined with gorgeous geometrical mosaics, feeding a burbling fountain in an octagonal pool at its centre. Near it, on a divan where he had evidently been listening to the strumming of an oud-player, sat the gorgeously-clad figure of the na'ib himself. John found himself beholding Khalil's opponent in the polo game—a lean, vigorous man a few years older than John himself. White bandages peeped out at the unbuttoned neck of his tunic, but despite his wound, the luxurious surroundings only served to make the man seem like a sword in a jewelled scabbard: all the more keen and dangerous.

Turuntay did not speak until he had dismissed the oud-player. Only an attendant in a blue turban remained.

"Who are you?" the na'ib asked then, with a narrowed glare. "You do not look like an Egyptian."

John bowed his head. "I am John Zakar, a scholar from Syria. Pardon my disguise, but al-Ashraf has his men searching for me. He knows that I can witness to his complicity in the attack upon you."

It was true, as far as it went. In Acre John had been briefed on Turuntay's position, and his enmity with the sultan's heir. If he could not go to Heliopolis to distract Qeteb, then he might at least keep Khalil's hands full, stirring up strife between the two rivals to the throne of Egypt.

"They say Bektash had a witness in his keeping," Turuntay said. "But he was stolen away by al-Ashraf's people."

John answered the implied question: "I am that witness, my lord."

"Is it true, then? Was it al-Mukhtar, the Chosen, who dealt me this wound?"

John hesitated, knowing that if he committed himself, he might win a new ally for the Temple, now that Bektash had bowed to Khalil. Perhaps even a new Egyptian sultan with a debt to Acre. But that would be dangerous: a witness must speak publicly.

"I'll swear to it," he said. "And al-Mukhtar does all things by his master's command."

"Good. Are you willing to make me sultan, Syrian?"

John did not like to make any Saracen lord of Egypt. "I am a Christian, my lord," he said. "I do not know whether my word is worth anything in Egypt, against that of great lords like al-Mukhtar and al-Ashraf."

"It is not," Turuntay said. "Not in a court of law—but that's not how Bektash meant to use you." He beckoned to a servant who stood waiting just out of earshot, near the doctor. "Send a man to Bektash. Tell him to wait upon me, for I've found what he lost two nights ago."

"I don't advise it," John said. "Bektash has gone over to al-Ashraf. I barely escaped from his house."

Turuntay went as still as a stone; for a moment he sat with his hands clenched on his knees like the statues in the dead city of Heliopolis, with something of the same deadly purpose radiating from him.

"Bektash can afford to play either side, or both, as it suits him," said the na'ib at last. "*He* will not perish, even if al-Ashraf takes the throne! …So, then. We have lost Bektash. But you, Syrian, will get me new allies, and many more of them."

John bowed in assent. "As you wish, my lord. But I have urgent business in Heliopolis. If you will provide me with an escort—"

"Heliopolis is in ruins," Turuntay said with a flick of his hand. "And if you step outside that gate, escorted or not, al-Ashraf will be on you like a falcon on a mouse. You will stay."

It was not an invitation, but a command. John ground his teeth, but he bowed again.

"Nufir!" Turuntay added, beckoning to the blue-turbaned attendant—an older man, grey-bearded and soft-spoken. "I am putting this man in your charge. Take him away and see that he has a bed and food."

There was no other choice. John followed the Copt—Nufir—into the warm interior of the house. Once in the servants' quarters, Nufir opened a door on a small cell where three or four sleeping-mats were rolled against the wall with other belongings.

"You may have this mat, next to mine," said the Copt. "No one will disturb you here."

Between that mat and the one beside it was a low desk and writing implements. John's heart leapt as he recalled that it had been one of Turuntay's scribes, a Copt, who had saved his life.

He touched his left wrist and the hidden Watcher's Mark that lay there. "Tell me," he said softly, "were you the Healer who saved the na'ib?"

Nufir sent him a guarded look. "I was."

John hid his elation. A second Gifted Watcher, one who might help him if Ghaliyah failed. "You prefer Turuntay to al-Ashraf, then?"

But the old man only shrugged. "Not particularly," he said. "Both are the thieves who stole this land from us. But it is the Lord who gives life and takes it away; I did not see why an assassin should have that right."

Nufir departed. Left alone in the dormitory, John rolled out his mat and sat upon it, cross-legged. It was not Heliopolis; but it would have to do.

"Qeteb," he breathed, daring to use the demon's true name for the first time since his first attempt, with Rahel, had failed. "Qeteb, I am here. Come and face me, if you dare."

A hot wind, like a long sighing breath, puffed through the stifling air of the dormitory and faded away. Qeteb had heard him. But no matter how long or loudly John might call, the demon did not answer.

Chapter XXV.

Al-Mukhtar Saif al-Din knew—because Soraya never allowed him to forget it—that sorcery was forbidden by the Prophet (may peace be upon him). That those who consulted with afrits would have no share in the Hereafter. That only the worst kind of fool, knowing this, would break the habit of a lifetime and go to the ancient obelisk in Heliopolis, calling on the name of Qeteb himself until the demon appeared.

Al-Mukhtar Saif al-Din was caught up in a kind of madness. He was like a stone knocked from the mountainside, rolling helplessly down the slope, spinning and splintering as it went.

Had he ever truly known his wife? All this time, while he thought he was the one protecting her, was she the one protecting him?

"Is it true?" Saif was on his knees, the pebbly dust making his knees hurt. He could not look the Hairy One in either eye, but he had to ask the question which had preyed on him for a night and a day as he tried and failed to find solace in the peace of the desert, the rush of the hunt. "Is al-Ashraf my father?"

It was not the only question to torment him. Saif had always thought of al-Ashraf as a father. Why was he not overjoyed to discover that it was true?

Why did he feel sick at the very thought?

The whole landscape wavered about him, drunk with heat, as Qeteb considered his answer. A nightmare landscape, where nothing was solid, nothing was real.

"Why ask me?" the afrit rumbled. "Al-Ashraf will do. Use up a little of *his* time asking foolish questions."

Saif's face was hot. "Counsel me," he said. "What is so very foolish about my question?"

"You were a mistake when you were made," Qeteb said. "And you have been a disappointment ever since. Do you imagine that you can persuade al-Ashraf to make you his heir?"

"That is *not* why I—"

But the afrit had already lost interest. "Summon me again, and *I'll* summon a host of khaphra beetles to eat the flesh from your bones."

With that the afrit vanished. Feeling the hot glare dissipate like the sun going behind a cloud, Saif pounded a fist into the dust. What else had he expected from Qeteb? He'd seen how the afrit treated its own son, three nights ago in the alleyway that led to Bektash's mansion.

Coming here was a mistake. In that, Qeteb was right. Why had he not gone directly to al-Ashraf?

He swallowed, wetting his dry, dust-caked throat.

This was why: because if Ghaliyah spoke the truth, then Khalil could have chosen to have a son, and instead he had chosen to have a slave.

Saif staggered to his feet. No. How could he think such things of al-Ashraf, his greatest benefactor? He should go directly to his master. Al-Ashraf would tell him what it was good for him to know, and with that Saif would need to be content.

Yes. That was the best thing to do. Turning on his heel, Saif hurried back in the direction of Cairo.

* * *

The house of al-Ashraf was always silent, and there was always a feeling of unquiet in the air, as though every shadow hid a wild beast waiting to spring. Having asked to see his master, Saif stood in the peristyle waiting to be summoned. He could not help recalling a thing that had happened shortly after Khalil had taken on the form and identity of the sultan's son, shortly after the real al-Ashraf was buried secretly in the desert in the tomb of an ancient king. He was waiting in the peristyle in this very spot when a woman had burst out of the women's quarters, unveiled and frantic.

"What have you done with him?" she screamed. "Ghoul! Djinn! What have you done with my husband?"

The Nubian eunuchs who guarded the women's quarters had caught her and dragged her back inside, where her shrieks remained, echoing faintly from the window-lattices. Khalil had emerged from the house to give Saif his instructions, then, and had not seemed at all bothered by the commotion. But Saif never heard a woman's voice in that house again. Only silence lay thick on the place.

If Khalil was his father, Saif wondered, then who had his mother been? Khalil once told him that she had been stolen away by the Franks—was this the reason for his father's hatred of that people?

"You're wanted, my lord," a servant announced, holding open the door that led to the room beneath al-Ashraf's house.

Saif descended the stairs with a knot of worry in his guts. The undercroft of his own house was devoted to training with weapons. That of Khalil's had been converted into a place for the practice of magic: its shelves were filled with books, instruments, and all the paraphernalia of a sorcerer's craft— a unicorn's horn, knives, deadly herbs, sticks of chalk. A sigil had been painted upon the floor, hemmed in with words in an intricate calligraphic script which had been made intentionally difficult to read. Otherwise the room was scrupulously clean and austerely bare. Khalil sat slumped behind his desk, his chin on his hand; and Qeteb stood giving off shimmering heat within the sigil.

"What do you want?" al-Ashraf snapped at him, when Saif entered.

Saif felt Qeteb's mocking smile, al-Ashraf's impatient glare. *Are you my father? Have you been lying to me all these years?* The words stuck in his throat.

He shouldn't need al-Ashraf's reassurance; he should trust him. How could Ghaliyah really know these things, anyway?

If Khalil was truly his father, were there not surely excellent reasons for keeping it a secret?

"It isn't urgent," he stammered. "I came to report on my raid on Bektash's house, that's all."

"That was two nights ago," al-Ashraf snapped. "I've already been in communication with Bektash."

Saif bowed his head. "It's as I said—I didn't think it urgent, my lord."

"It's beside the point now," al-Ashraf said. "John Bessarion is in Cairo."

Saif's heart stood still. Qeteb, pacing his sigil, smiled.

"Did *he* tell you so?" Saif asked, pointing at the afrit.

"And then I confirmed it," said his master. "*You* don't seem surprised to hear it. Did you know of this?"

What did it mean, this game Qeteb was playing? Informing Khalil of the Bessarion's presence, but not of Saif's own complicity? Saif sent the afrit a wary glance, but Qeteb gave him no signal.

He knew he ought to confess. He had no right to keep any secrets from this master of his—but there was still Ghaliyah, and it was not as though Khalil was *really* his father.

Instead, he bowed. "I heard that John Bessarion had been seen in Mesopotamia, my lord. As you recall my telling you."

Khalil stroked his beard, eyes narrowed. At last he said, "The Bessarion must die. You will bait a trap for him."

"Yes, my lord." Saif's mouth went dry again, conscious as he was that John Bessarion was presently occupying a locked guest-room in his own house. If he was going to trade the man for Ghaliyah's life, then surely now was the moment to reveal his advantage, to make his demands.

Demands. Of al-Ashraf Khalil, lord and master. Saif swallowed hard, feeling the sweat thicken in his palms.

Before he could gather the courage to speak, Qeteb forestalled him.

"John Bessarion will need to be taken care of eventually. But at present he is powerless, and therefore negligible."

"As his daughter was?" Khalil cut in, with a snarl.

Qeteb shimmered with heat. "*She* was no votary of mine. Do not allow yourself to be distracted from the great opportunity."

"And that is?"

"The throne of Egypt," Qeteb said. "You told Bektash that it was as much as his life was worth to throw in his lot with Turuntay. With Turuntay wounded, that gives you the upper hand. And the sultan is ailing anyway. No one will be surprised if he dies."

"The answer is the same. No."

"Are you waiting for Turuntay to recover his strength and strike back, then?" The Hairy One gave a mirthless smile. "Be glad I am not like Lilith, who would already have transferred her loyalty to Turuntay."

Al-Ashraf snarled, half rising from his seat. "Do not use lofty words with me! You cannot dispense with me—"

"*Yet*—I cannot dispense with you *yet*," Qeteb hissed, showing all his teeth in return. The words fell like a stone from a great height, shattering all Khalil's bluster, crushing him back into his chair.

It had never occurred to Saif that his master might be acquainted with bluster. It had not occurred to him that Soraya might be *right* in predicting a coming struggle between the afrit and his master.

"That throne is *mine*," Qeteb said. "Be grateful for the privilege afforded you, mortal, of being my instrument in its capture. Now, pay heed to what I say. Egypt is now a fruit ripe for plucking. Seize it now and it falls into your hand. Delay, and Turuntay will forestall you."

"*I* will see to Turuntay," al-Ashraf said, flushed with rage. "You may be power, but I am wit, I am sinew, I am blood. You will *never* be able to dispense with me. And for that reason, you will wait for *my* word to take the throne."

The whole room rippled with heat, and the Hairy One put a hand to the quiver of arrows at his hip. "Who says that I must dispense with your *flesh?*" he began, but then ceased speaking with a gasp, as though he had just taken one of his own arrows.

"What has happened?" al-Ashraf rose from his chair, wrath forgotten.

Qeteb frowned. The look of astonishment on his inhuman face was unexpected, almost comical. "Someone is trying to *cast me out*," he said, in tones of offended dignity. "*Agai—*"

The afrit never finished speaking the word. One moment he was there, ringed by the sigil.

The next, he was gone.

For a moment neither Saif nor Khalil moved, staring at the void where the afrit had been. Khalil recovered first. With an explosive oath, he rose to his feet, knocking over his chair, grabbing for blades and bundles of herbs and sticks of chalk and candles.

"Light these," he said, thrusting the candles into Saif's hands. "Quickly!"

He went down onto his knees, adding strokes and words to the existing sigil.

Saif hesitated. "What are you doing, my lord?"

"Summoning Qeteb back, of course," al-Ashraf declared. "Don't dawdle! If I can catch him before he is utterly cast out—"

Saif had swallowed his words twice already today; now he stammered, "But he's planning to *possess* you, my lord."

His master's hand faltered. Al-Ashraf glanced up at him; there was a haunted look in his eyes.

He was afraid, Saif realised. Al-Ashraf had made unspeakable bargains with evil spirits. And now he was afraid.

A moment—a blink of the eye—and the fear passed.

"I need him for the siege of Acre," al-Ashraf snarled. "I'll dispense with him after that, and no sooner. Get out if you don't mean to help!"

Saif was only too willing to leave that dark room, with its stink of candles and incense and bitter herbs, behind him. A moment later he stood in the street, all blazing midday sun and glaring whitewashed walls, stifling dust and inky-black shadows. His head whirled. How could al-Ashraf be mad enough to summon Qeteb back, once free of him? He had always believed that Khalil must have been ignorant of the evil he dealt with when first he called upon the afrits. Now that he knew the extent of their malice, how could he summon one *back?*

Despite the heat of the sun, Saif shivered. He found himself hoping, fiercely, that the exorcism would work. For al-Ashraf's sake. For his own. For Soraya's—

Then, like the bottom falling out of his guts, he knew exactly who was performing this exorcism, and why.

Saif took to his heels, angling through the streets towards his own ungoverned house.

Chapter XXVI.

It turned out that an exorcism was a ridiculously simple matter.

Ghaliyah had prepared herself with a day's fasting. Soraya, afraid of seeing her condition worsen, had remonstrated, but the old lady had asked, "What are you afraid of? I'm already dying, and we're already planning to infuriate my husband." After that she let Ghaliyah please herself. Soraya had enough on her hands, anyway, what with strange mamluks forcing their way into the house and absconding with the prisoner. John Bessarion had evidently intended to leave with the strange mamluks, and she had been glad to make use of the loophole in her orders which instructed her to keep him in his room, but not to prevent someone else letting him out. All the same, she wished she had been able to leave the house. She had recognised the servants of Bektash, and found herself wondering what the amir silah wanted with the Syrian scholar.

"It's midday," Soraya said, once she had been summoned to Ghaliyah's quarters the following day. "Isn't it dangerous to attack the Hairy One during his time of power?"

"Only if you are *beneath* his power," Ghaliyah said, apparently unconcerned. "Which *you* are, my dear, but not me. Take my hand."

Soraya did as she was told, but she felt the overwhelming desire to laugh. Ghaliyah sat cross-legged on her divan, looking very frail and bent despite the twinkle in her eye. She had drawn no sigils, lighted no candles. It would be a miracle if she could summon any afrit like that; still less contain him.

"Are you ready?" Ghaliyah asked, and when Soraya nodded, the old woman took a deep breath. "Hail God of Abraham!" she cried out in a startlingly loud voice. "Hail God of Isaac! Hail God of Jacob! Jesus the Christ, the Holy Spirit, Son of the Father, Lord of Hosts! Let your power emanate from this Soraya, until you cast out the unclean demon Qeteb, who oppresses her!"

Soraya gasped, for her sight slipped at once half into the spirit-world. Ghaliyah was before her a seethe of blue-hot light, too bright to look upon. About them, Cairo was a sphere of fires, souls as innumerable and lovely as the stars of the night sky. And among those fires she was conscious of hot attention fastening upon her, full of rage and malice.

She needed to speak, to warn Ghaliyah of the wrath she had awoken; but the little woman had both her hands locked tightly in her own, and continued her declamation:

"I adjure you, Qeteb, wherever you are, by the God of armies. Come out, wherever you are, and stay away from Soraya! Now, *now,* quickly!"

There came a flash, a smell of unbearable heat—and Qeteb was with them in the room. Soraya's gut clenched at the sudden sense she had of something larger than the earth itself fitting itself into that tiny space.

"Presumptuous mortal!" Qeteb bellowed. "Do you know who I am? I am the god of Egypt!"

"You *used* to be one of them," Ghaliyah retorted, unabashed. "Do you know who *I* am? I sit in the heavenly places with Christ. And I bind you in unbreakable chains of adamant—"

"Wait!" Qeteb demanded in quite a different voice. "Do you want Egypt given over to chaos? Cast me out, and seven others will take my place, worse than me!"

"Then I'll cast them out, too," Ghaliyah said. "That's enough. Go into the outer darkness!"

It turned out that it was that easy. One moment Qeteb was bending over them, bellowing threats. The next he was gone.

Soraya gave a sob as the world returned to normal; no longer did the room seem simultaneously a few paces and a few aeons wide. No longer was Ghaliyah bright enough to scorch her vision. The light in the room cleared, and a breath of cool air blew through the windows from the courtyard, fresh and somehow laden, deliciously, with spices.

"That's *all?*" Soraya asked, scarcely able to believe it.

"Mm, I think so," Ghaliyah said. "I have never done this before. Are you free now?"

Soraya could still feel the drag of the soul-tether binding her to Saif—she could *always* feel the soul-tether. "Not yet." Her voice was breathless in her own ears. "Not while the Lance remains. We can break it now."

"Where is it?" Ghaliyah asked, and Soraya felt her mouth slacken.

She had never quite believed that this would *work*. Now that it had, she was completely unprepared. "I don't know," she said, dizzily. "Did Saif take it with him? Where did he go?"

"Don't ask *me,*" Ghaliyah said. "Where does he keep it when he's at home?"

"The undercroft," Soraya said, starting up and taking to her heels. The sparring-room below the house was locked and she was obliged to break in, but there was no sign of the Lance among either the wooden practice weapons, or the sharps from which Saif equipped himself when he was on a mission. She hurried upstairs again, across the courtyard, and let herself into Saif's own quarters. She had never seen inside his room before, and she let out a huff of laughter at the sight of it: the place was bare and almost completely impersonal, save for the unusual number of luxurious blankets on the bed. Otherwise, the only sign of individuality was the low table on which a few of his knives, with the means of polishing and sharpening them, were set out.

It took her little more than a glance to determine that the Lance was not here, either. Groaning, Soraya lifted both hands to her head.

"You didn't think I could do it, did you?" Ghaliyah asked from behind her. Soraya turned, seeing that the old woman had followed her into the loggia and was now leaning in the doorway eating a contented flatbread.

Soraya ran a hand through her hair, increasingly frantic. "Son of a shoe! What am I going to do?" John would have had a plan. As it was—she didn't know where Saif was, and she could not go in search of him because she was bound to the house. Ought she to send a servant? But what would she say when Saif had returned? The longer he was away from the house, the likelier it was that he would have caught wind of what she had done by the time he returned—and then he would be on his guard.

"What am I going to do?" she asked again, Then a strong gust of hot wind bore down upon them. For a moment Soraya's eyes and throat were full of dust. She flinched, choking, in the hot glare of—

Oh.Oh, *no*.

She blinked the grit out of her eyes. Al-Ashraf Khalil, white-lipped and furious, stepped down from the loggia baluster onto the floor. Behind him there was a ripple of hair, the blink of an eye from the centre of a great chest.

Qeteb had returned.

She had only a glimpse of him. Then Qeteb had vanished.

Ghaliyah pointed at the thin air where the demon had been a moment since. "I cast him *out!*" she protested, her voice high with indignation.

Khalil strode forwards, teeth bared with rage. "So! You confess!"

Ghaliyah began to say something, but it was already too late. Khalil raised a short pipe to his mouth; with a puff of breath, a needle-thin dart shot from it and struck her in the neck. Ghaliyah was like a candle snuffed out. For a moment she swayed; and then her knees gave way beneath her, and she pitched into the carpet.

Khalil turned upon Soraya, reaching out a threatening hand. Soraya saw his lips part. Knew that a string of commands would follow.

Reached for the knife at her waist. Pinched out the nerves that might deliver pain, and dragged the steel across her guts.

She saw the loggia fall sideways, saw Khalil standing over her, heard the faraway sound of his voice. And then she came free of her fallen body and was whisked away, into the distant Lance.

What had happened? Qeteb had been cast *out.* Had Khalil summoned him back? She ought to have known it could never be so simple.

But then how would she *ever* be free?

Saif, as she hoped, felt the shock of Soraya's arrival along the soul tether and instantly summoned her forth again. She took shape and found herself in a crowded street, surrounded by staring passers-by.

"This way!" Saif's voice drifted back to her, and Soraya caught a glimpse of him elbowing through the crowd ahead of her. She hastened to follow, leaving the pedestrians muttering and raising their palms against the evil eye behind her.

"What have you done?" Saif growled as she drew abreast of him. "You were supposed to *watch* the Bessarion and prevent him making a nuisance of himself! Not to assist him in performing *exorcisms!*"

He was bound to learn the truth, sooner rather than later. Soraya laughed. "You think that was John Bessarion?"

"Wasn't it?" Reaching the gate of his own house, Saif staggered to a halt, gazing at her in dawning horror. "No. Not Ghaliyah. What were you *thinking?* Don't you know what al-Ashraf will do to her when he—"

"I know what he's *done,*" Soraya interrupted. "That's why I—"

"*No,*" Saif groaned. He slammed the butt of the Spear against the stones, whisking her back inside as he threw open the gate.

* * *

Soraya could not have been inside the Lance for very long. She had only time to reflect upon how terribly angry Saif was bound to be. John Bessarion had escaped, Ghaliyah was hurt, and even the house had been breached not once, but twice, by different intruders. To cap it off, she had brought him into a mount of trouble with Khalil.

Good, she thought, mutinously. If one good thing was to come out of this disaster, a greater wedge driven between Saif and his master would be it.

Then Soraya felt the pull of his summons and made herself another form; rather wearily, since she was tired of losing bodies.

She was in the loggia. There was no sign of Ghaliyah. Saif sat cross-legged on the divan, hands hanging limply over his knees. His gaze was thunderstruck. Unfocused.

Soraya's gut clenched. "Ghaliyah," she said. "She isn't—"

"She's alive," Saif said, fixing his eyes upon her with apparent difficulty. "No thanks to *you.*"

"Oh, no," Soraya said fiercely. "Don't you blame *me* for this. Ghaliyah knew the risks and accepted them."

"You *used* her," he said, rising to his feet.

"She is a grown woman," Soraya retorted. "And one who sees further into the future than most! Why else did she call you back for a kiss? Why else did she ask me to tell you that she had always loved you?"

"She—what?" There was a silence. Saif's eyes were enormous. "She said that?"

Soraya's gut contracted again. Almost, she felt sorry for him. "What has happened, Saif? What did Khalil do to her?"

He dragged a hand down his face. "She is asleep and will remain so," he said. "Qeteb has done something to her, and now Al-Ashraf has promised that she will awake only once I have delivered John Bessarion into his hands."

"You were fool enough to tell him that John was *here?*"

"No! That must have been the afrit." Saif threw up his hands. "I *meant* to use him as a bargaining-chip. I could have traded him for more years with Ghaliyah! Now, because of you, I am bargaining just for the chance to *speak* to her again."

"Oh, you had *plenty* of time to drive your bargain with Khalil. But you never had the courage for that, did you? You're a *coward.*"

The words were like an arrow loosed at random, but they must have hit the mark. "And *you* are insolent!" he bellowed, raising a hand. Soraya flinched, but he was only pointing a finger at her.

His hand, the threat of violence, hung between them a long moment; long enough for Soraya to marvel that she could ever have considered this man a friend. Then Saif muttered something under his breath and turned away, his shoulders slumping. He looked utterly despairing.

"You ought to have *told* me what you meant to do," he whispered.

"You would only have stopped us," she retorted, and saw his shoulders cave in further. "You won't really do it, will you? You won't hand John over to him?"

"With Ghaliyah in that state, what other choice do I have?"

"There's another way to arouse her," Soraya said. "Khalil has no power of his own; *you* know that. Exorcise the Hairy One, and she'll awake. You weren't there, Saif; you didn't see how *simple* it was. We failed only because we were not prepared to exploit our advantage. If we had been able to depend upon *you*, we might have arranged for the Lance to be broken and Khalil to be attacked—killed or kept busy until the Hairy One was gone beyond recall." It was her turn to jab a finger at him. *"It can be done,* Saif. We can all of us be *free.* We don't have to go on being trampled on."

Saif was pale and hesitant. "It's not my place to question al-Ashraf."

"He's your *father,* Saif. And the only reason he's decided to conceal it from you is that he prefers you as his slave."

"We don't know that for certain—"

"Are you calling Ghaliyah a liar, then?"

"O God!" Saif threw up his hands in despair. "I don't know what the truth is."

"Ghaliyah knows it," Soraya said, ruthlessly. "And speaking of Ghaliyah, you don't still plan to make Khalil prolong her life, do you? Not after she told you to your face that she doesn't want it?"

There was a long silence. Then, at last, Saif wiped an angry hand over his eyes and said: "She was right. She has always loved me more than I loved her. I thought I was sparing her the burden of knowing my true nature, but she knew. She had to bear not only that burden, but also the burden of my lies."

Soraya sniffed. *"I* would not have done so." Moreover, she was absolutely determined to carry no burdens at all. Not for Saif—and not for John.

"I meant it for her good."

"You always do," she said wearily. "Even Khalil means what he does for your good. But that doesn't make it any better, does it?"

"This isn't about al-Ashraf. It's about Ghaliyah's wishes." Whatever al-Mukhtar's true age, he wore suddenly the weary, sagging features of an ancient man. "I've visited death upon more mortals than I can even remember, but I've met few who wouldn't grasp for life. It isn't normal, or right—but if it's truly what she wants—"

"She doesn't want to *die,*" Soraya said. "She only wants the choice to lie in God's hands, and not Khalil's—or yours. Aren't you a devout man? How can you interfere with such a wish?"

"Why should God spare a polytheist?"

Soraya snorted. "God has never spared *me,* no matter how much I pray. I'm not convinced that he cares about us at all, to be honest. And if he doesn't, then you ought to respect Ghaliyah's wishes all the more."

"And I will," Saif growled. "You were right. I was wrong. Is that enough?"

"You know that it isn't," she snarled back at him.

There was a moment's silence. Slowly, slowly, the anger faded from his face.

"I meant to be a better friend to you," he said at last.

Soraya resented the part of herself that wished to pity him, to be grateful for this limp acknowledgement of his failure. It wasn't real. He might be able to acknowledge the paucity of their friendship, but evidently he didn't repent it enough to *change.*

Instead, she said, "Well? If I can find another Watcher to cast out Qeteb, will you help me to finish the job this time?"

Saif looked half afraid, half longing. "Another Watcher? Do you mean John Bessarion?"

Soraya shrugged. "Or one of his friends. Does it matter?"

"Where *is* John Bessarion?"

"Oh, he isn't here," she said. "Some mamluks came to teach you a lesson, and Ghaliyah released him to them. It was the only way to make them go away."

"What! *Whose* mamluks?"

She shrugged. "Bektash's, I believe. Who else? He would not have given up his witness so easily. Anyway, you can easily get the Bessarion to help you. All you need to do is offer him your help in destroying the Hairy One and Khalil together."

Saif hesitated, evidently conflicted, until Soraya added, "Didn't Ghaliyah say that she only wanted you to be free of them?"

"She did," he admitted, and dropped his head into his hands. "Very well.

If that's all I can now do for her, then so be it."

Chapter XXVII.

"Speak up, Syrian," Turuntay commanded. "Tell these amirs what you told Bektash."

John straightened from the humble bow with which he had greeted the assembled company—all of them stately men in costly robes, glinting with jewels and precious metals at their necks and belts and on the hilts of their knives. His pulse quickened, warning him that he was surrounded by his enemies, men who would disdain him purely on account of his religion.

True to his word, Turuntay had not brought him before a court. What John faced tonight was a conspiracy—a group of amirs Turuntay hoped to win over as his supporters. Those who wished to listen to him would do so, despite his religion, the na'ib assured him. And those who did not, John supposed, would have an easy way to discount his testimony and demand his punishment as a traitor and spy.

He tried not to look into their eyes, knowing that to do so would be an assumption of equality they would not endure. But he knew the type: men of the warrior class, accustomed to govern and command. He had been one of them himself, once.

Now they saw him only as a tool, to be used up and discarded as it suited them to do so. That he was merely a pawn of Turuntay's had been driven home by the three days he had spent shut up in the servants' quarters, forbidden to leave the house or even to send a message. In the end he had begged Nufir, the na'ib's Coptic servant, to seek news.

"My friends meant to cast out the Hairy One, and I promised to help them as much as I could," John had told Nufir, forcing himself to speak the humiliating truth. "But the Hairy One despises me utterly and now I do not know whether they have succeeded, or failed, or not even made the attempt."

Nufir had asked no questions. "If they tried it, they failed," he said. "Such go not out but by prayer and fasting. The Hairy One is still in Cairo; his roots go deep in this city. Do you think the thing has not been tried?"

"Then perhaps we had better both be in prayer and fasting," John had retorted, angered by the Copt's words.

"Perhaps," Nufir had said, quietly, as if to himself. "Perhaps it is time the thing was attempted again."

Now, facing the assembled amirs, John drew a deep breath, reminding himself that he might yet turn this meeting to his own purposes, and find a way to destroy Khalil and save Acre.

Then his eyes stopped on a coat of rich damask, woven with threads of glowing green silk. Faintly smiling, the amir held his gaze. There was nothing in the bearded face to recognise, except the expression. Still smiling, the amir reached forward to the platters that stood on the low table around which they all sat, selecting a crumbly block of halwa.

John glanced around the room, his pulse quickening further. In the courtyard, visible through the open door of the room, the amirs' personal attendants congregated around braziers, chatting and laughing. One of them sat a little apart from the others, his eyes fixed on John. A spear leaned casually against his shoulder as he sat whittling a block of wood.

His face was in shadow, but John recognised al-Mukhtar's silhouette as readily as Soraya's smile.

"Speak, I said," Turuntay prompted, as the silence lengthened.

Forcing a smile, John turned back to the na'ib. If nothing else, al-Mukhtar's presence made his story simpler to tell, and far easier to prove.

"The one who attacked the na'ib was al-Mukhtar Saif al-Din, better known as al-Rafiq," he proclaimed. "He did it for the sake of his master, al-Ashraf Khalil."

"Your proof?" one of the amirs asked. "The sultan has men to swear that al-Rafiq was in his tent when the attack happened."

"I have three items of proof," John said. "First, when the attack took place, I was in al-Mukhtar's tent, speaking to the person who sat there. It was *not* al-Mukhtar, but one of his servants who resembles him. Second, after the attack I was being escorted to the sultan's rooms when I met al-Mukhtar himself in the courtyard. Whether by mistake or design, he dropped the signet of the lord na'ib at my feet."

"Then the culprit was not, in fact, yourself?" Turuntay prompted.

"No, my lord. That is my third item of proof." John swallowed, wondering what destruction he might be about to incite. "Al-Mukhtar knows that I am the one person able to tell the truth about what happened that night. That is why he came to the house of Bektash and snatched me away. And that is why he is sitting there, in that very courtyard."

A blank silence greeted his words. Turuntay rose to his feet, a hand going to the hilt of his sword, his eyes roving the darkness. "Are you mocking me?"

"He is not," the mamluk in the courtyard announced, slowly putting down his carving and rising to his feet. A ripple of fear ran around the circle of seated amirs as the Chosen stepped, wary and graceful, to the door of the room. Some of them rose to their feet, seizing weapons. Others remained seated, as though congealed in terror.

Turuntay must have made some invisible signal, for the mamluks in the courtyard leapt to attention and hurried to surround al-Mukhtar.

He was already in the doorway, two paces from John—no distance at all for a man armed with the Lance. John's throat went dry, but he made himself hold his ground. It was Soraya who sat at his back, Soraya who had given him the signal confirming her presence. She would protect him—or, if she had given up on him, then he might as well die here.

Al-Mukhtar sent John a wry smile as he halted on the threshold, but it was Turuntay he addressed.

"The Syrian is telling the truth," he announced. "It was I who attacked the *na'ib al-saltana* in his tent that night, and nearly killed him. But I did *not* act on the orders of al-Ashraf Khalil, who has disciplined me for my presumption."

Turuntay scoffed. "You don't expect us to *believe* that?"

"Why not?" al-Mukhtar asked. "I did not *need* to come here alone, to put myself in your power and admit to my mistakes. I might have come with a body of the sultan's own mamluks. Al-Ashraf Khalil is his heir, and by plotting against him you plot against Qalawun."

"What do you want?" asked the sceptical amir, who earlier had asked for proof.

"A moment of your attention," al-Mukhtar replied. "I came to tell you that al-Ashraf is like his father, fair-minded and lenient. He will not persecute you, merely because you have had doubts about his ability or goodwill. In addition to this, he is energetic and has a martial temperament. In the saddle or on the battlefield he is the match of any trained mamluk. I came to ask you not to throw your lives away on Turuntay's greed, at least not for my sake."

"This is *my* house," Turuntay said. "*I* am speaking now! My lords, don't listen to messages al-Ashraf sends to entrap us!"

"Al-Ashraf knows nothing of this visit," said al-Mukhtar. "I've acted without his approval again tonight—but if it prevents Egypt being destroyed in a struggle for the throne, it will be worth all the punishment he can mete out to me."

The amirs began to exchange doubtful looks. Turuntay's teeth ground together. John stepped in: "He'd punish you for doing this—his most loyal servant? Is this his fair-mindedness? Is this his leniency?"

"It is more grace than I merit." Al-Mukhtar's voice rang with humble sincerity: there was nothing slippery or smooth about him at all. "My lords, don't allow one man's ambition to destroy the empire Saladin himself built, more than a hundred years ago. Can't you see that this is what this Syrian, this *Christian,* wants? Better to leave now. Allow al-Ashraf to reward your faithfulness, and not your treachery."

"Is this true?" another of the amirs asked, turning to face Turuntay with great indignation. "Is this witness of yours a Christian?"

Turuntay's face darkened. "He was telling the *truth.* Even Al-Rafiq cannot deny it."

"Tell me, Turuntay, can *you* deny this?" al-Mukhtar rejoined, seizing John's arm and stripping the sleeve back, so that the whole company could see his Watcher's Mark.

There was nothing else that could be said: the whole assembly was terrified by al-Mukhtar's appearance, tempted by his offer of leniency, and eager to dig their way out. "A Christian!" said the indignant amir. "My lord, you are much to be censured, relying on the word of such a person!"

With that he gathered up the skirts of his robe and hastened out into the courtyard, summoning his own mamluks for departure. One by one, the others rose to their feet and followed, with muttered apologies to both Turuntay and al-Mukhtar. Just as Soraya, who had remained silent the whole time, made to follow suit, Turuntay seized her sleeve.

"How did al-Rafiq gain admittance to this house?" he growled. "Did he not follow *you,* al-Aswani?"

"I never told you that my name was al-Aswani," Soraya said. At some point, with all eyes on Turuntay and al-Mukhtar, she must have transformed back to a woman. Turuntay released her with a hiss of shock.

"A *djinn!*" he whispered. Then, as Soraya moved to stand beside John, his eyes narrowed. "This was *your* plot," he seethed, pointing an accusing finger. "You have been in al-Ashraf's pay all along! This is what comes of allying with the Temple!"

John glanced to either side of him, realising how he must look standing between al-Mukhtar and Soraya. "No," he protested, seeing all his hopes crumble about him. "Neither the Temple nor I have anything to do with this man."

In a low clear voice that Turuntay could not possibly miss, Soraya said "Humour us, John."

He could not help sending her an incredulous look. Whose side was Soraya on, anyway? She might not care to save Acre herself, but couldn't she respect his desire to protect his coreligionists?

"This man belongs to me," al-Mukhtar said, addressing Turuntay in the same even tones. "I am taking him back, and I would advise you not to interfere."

John saw the calculations flickering behind the na'ib's eyes: the four of them were alone in the room, al-Mukhtar with levelled spear. Turuntay's own men, clustered at the courtyard door behind, were tense and expectant, but if al-Mukhtar chose to finish what he had begun, they could not save their master

Turuntay's conclusion was evident, even before the na'ib himself acknowledged it.

"Go in peace," he said at length. "But know that I never forget. The hour I see any of your faces again will be your last."

The journey across the courtyard to the street gate was interminable, watchful, terrifying—Turuntay's mamluks followed them the entire way like hungry wolves. But at last they backed into the street and lost themselves in the shadows of the narrow, gorge-like alleys; it was in one of these that al-Mukhtar came to a halt, and Soraya turned on him with a furious gesture.

"We were only going to get him *back,*" she said, jerking a thumb in John's direction. "But oh, no, you had to take Khalil's part and explode the conspiracy against him. Fair-minded and lenient, my *shoe!*"

"What else ought I to have done?" al-Mukhtar protested. "You would have preferred me to kill them all?"

"You're mad," Soraya said, contemptuously. "I should have tracked him down myself."

John himself was seething. Trust al-Mukhtar, that spawn of the devil and Khalil, to undo all his efforts and manoeuvre him into use as a pawn of Khalil's. And now Turuntay would not work with the Temple again, either. "Now Khalil will certainly become sultan."

"Nothing is certain in politics," said al-Mukhtar. "Turuntay would never have given you up without bloodshed, John Bessarion; not while you were still useful to him."

"*He* was useful to *me,*" John protested. "I had a chance to do more good as his prisoner than I could as yours."

"That's not the case," al-Mukhtar said with a wave of his hand. "Don't you *want* to cast out Qeteb and destroy the Lance?"

The words died on John's lips. He cast Soraya a questioning glance. She was little more than a pale shape in the darkness, but he saw her nod.

"He wants to help," she confirmed. "Our first attempt failed. Khalil was quick, and recalled Qeteb before he could be completely banished from the world. Now Ghaliyah is in a deep sleep, and there is no waking her."

John could say nothing. It was as though all their efforts were cursed.

Soraya sniffed. "Next time, we must be better prepared."

"Is there a place we can speak together?" al-Mukhtar asked. "Not my house; al-Ashraf has it watched."

John hesitated, worried for the monks if he brought these two back to the monastery. "Can we really trust him?" he asked Soraya.

From the rustle of her clothing, he thought she shrugged. "He knows you'll make him suffer if he betrays us," she said, but there was more bravado than certainty in her voice.

"We," John said, an implicit promise that he would not abandon her. "*We* will make him suffer."

He took the lead, then. Soraya and al-Mukhtar followed silently at his heels. John found himself in the grip of nostalgia, recalling the stormy night in Tripoli when for a few brief hours the three of them had shared a common cause and a common enemy. For a moment he would have given anything to go back to that night—a night when he was strong enough to defeat his foe, when al-Mukhtar was merely an enemy who had for the moment agreed to help him, when Soraya *believed* in him.

But had John deserved that faith? Or had he been only a little less cruel to her than Saif had been? She had forgiven him once for the promise he had broken after the battle of Yarmouk, but did she really comprehend then what that broken promise had meant for her?

It was a confession he would need to make at some point. Not now, in the presence of al-Mukhtar. All the same, perhaps his own guilt was the reason why, when he had gained permission for a male guest and a hooded falcon to enter the monastery for a visit, and when he had lit the lamps in his cell, and when Soraya had scraped together enough earth and moisture from the garden to resume a human body, the first thing he said had nothing to do with their plans for Qeteb.

"There's a price for my help," John declared, crossing his arms, and fixing al-Mukhtar with the icy glare that in the old days, in the emperor's armies, had made young captains quail and stammer. "You've been lying to Soraya about what happened in Tripoli. About *us.* Now you will tell her the truth."

Al-Mukhtar flushed. "She knows the truth," he hedged.

"She needs to hear it in *your* words."

"*Enough*, Syrian," Soraya cut in. "I know enough of the truth, or do you think I'm a fool? I know that *he* is a liar, and you are not."

"Then why help him? Why stand by that *hellspawn?*"

John did not raise his voice, but he did raise an arm to point, accusingly, at the Chosen. Al-Mukhtar batted it aside with contempt.

"Save your breath. Soraya might not listen to me, but she certainly won't listen to you."

"Stop wasting time, both of you," Soraya said in a cracked voice. "What do I care about his lies when I'm bound to obey his lightest whim?"

John's laughter faded into renewed guilt. Here were he and al-Mukhtar, squabbling over Soraya like infatuated boys, when he had vowed to be her friend.

"I beg your pardon," he said. "You're living the worst kind of servitude, and I'm making a game of it with al-Mukhtar. Forgive me."

Soraya sent him a startled look, but was calmer when she spoke again. "Qeteb has cursed Ghaliyah, and she will not awaken from her sleep. We need to find another Watcher like her, someone to cast out the Hairy One. This time we must be ready to break the Lance before al-Ashraf can call him back—and then at the very least I will be freed."

"We can do better than that," John said. "Al-Ashraf will be vulnerable while the Hairy One is gone. If we attack him then, we might kill him altogether, or at least keep him distracted long enough that the demon can be banished, beyond the world and beyond recall."

"No!" Soraya scowled. "You've both promised to free me from the Lance. Don't be distracted trying to murder Khalil. Qeteb can eat him alive, and most likely will."

John shook his head. It was for the good of the world that that infernal alliance needed to be broken up, that Khalil must die.

"All this could be done in the past," he said. *"I should have done it in the past—"*

"That's why it has to be done *now*," Soraya said, interrupting. "That's why *I* must do it. Do you disagree, John Bessarion?"

She held him in a challenging gaze. John dropped his eyes, a gesture of submission. Had he not promised to serve her first, and himself second?

"No," he said. "We'll do it your way."

"Soraya is right," al-Mukhtar put in, looking eager to be of help. "Al-Ashraf will be upon his guard now more than ever."

"Why now?" John asked. "If he's put Ghaliyah into a slumber, he surely has nothing to fear from *her.*" Then a thought occurred to him, and the bottom dropped out of his gut. "You told him I was in Cairo, didn't you?"

For a moment the room was in complete silence. Light and shadow flicked across al-Mukhtar's expressionless face a moment; then he said, "No. It was Qeteb who informed him. Al-Ashraf has ordered me to set a trap for you."

John wanted to laugh; instead, he kept a watchful gaze on the other man's face. "And will you set a trap for me? Is that what this is?"

Al-Mukhtar's gaze slithered away. Soraya said sharply, "Answer the question!"

The Chosen took a deep breath. "I must do this for Ghaliyah," he said. "If we cast out Qeteb, Ghaliyah will awake."

That had the ring of truth. John glanced at Soraya, and she slanted a shoulder upward in response.

And what other choice did they have?

"All right," John told them. "But I am sorry, Soraya. All this trouble is because I failed. I should have been able to cast out Qeteb myself."

Al-Mukhtar was stone-faced. "At the house of Bektash, you stepped in front of one of Qeteb's arrows. Had you let Soraya take the blow, had you cast out Qeteb yourself, she might have been free by now, and my wife would be with me."

"I'm afraid you've overvalued me." John sighed. "I took the arrow because

I had already tried to cast out Qeteb. He only laughed at me. I knew I was useless."

Soraya said, not unkindly, "Don't blame yourself. Enlisting Ghaliyah's help was *my* idea."

She put a hand on his shoulder and John, after a moment's hesitation, covered it with his own.

"Don't blame yourself, either," he told her.

For one aching moment, he might almost have believed that the lost past had come again. Then Soraya drew her hand away, watching him with distrust in her narrowed eyes. To distract himself from the loss, John said, "The Copts speak with pride of their miracle-workers. I know a Healer of great power whom I am sure will be able to cast out a demon, or who can point us in the direction of another who can."

"Swear to it," Soraya said, putting up her left hand, palm outwards. The right she kept tucked against her heart. "Swear, both of you, on your honour and on the life of the one you most love, that you will cast out Qeteb and free me."

"I swear on my honour and Ghaliyah's life," al-Mukhtar said, raising his hand. "God willing, I will free you, Soraya."

"I swear by my honour and by the love I bear Rahel Bessarion," John said, following suit. "As God is my witness, I will free you, and no thought of my own gain will stand in the way."

Perhaps that meant he would be trapped forever in this hostile future. In that case, *this* was the day in which it had been ordained that he should live. *Now* was the time to free Soraya.

Now was the time to bring Khalil to justice.

"Look for a Gift among the Copts," Soraya told him. "Saif and I will return tomorrow night for news."

As Soraya turned to the door, al-Mukhtar hung back.

"You swear on your wife," he said, pointing to Soraya, "but you take an arrow for *her*. What is she to you, John Bessarion?"

Soraya stilled with her hand on the latch, listening for his answer.

John remembered something Rahel had said to him once, before he found that Soraya might be capable of returning him home. *Don't be a wanderer, John. Wherever you are, I want you to find a home.*

"Soraya isn't one of my children by blood," he said, addressing that still figure at the door more than al-Mukhtar. "But in this time, she's the nearest thing I have. I think of her as my own."

Soraya did not move. After a moment, al-Mukhtar scoffed and muttered, "Would that we could all find a father so easily."

John did not say anything to this. If the Chosen wanted a father, he knew where to find one.

Chapter XXVIII.

Will John Bessarion survive his mission to Cairo? Will he return to me? In the days since Eschiva's disastrous visit to Cairo, such questions plagued her relentlessly. She had undergone all that difficulty and danger, had covered herself in dishonour and had not even succeeded in having that brief word with Prester John, summoning him back to Beirut for the saving of the Coast.

Now she stood fidgeting with her astrolabe on the roof of the Beirut palace, staring at the stars above her and remembering the verdict of the horoscope she had cast for Cairo last week. Her calculations had shown that at the time of asking, Jupiter had occupied the Eighth House. The planet of kings in the house of death and misfortune was an unlucky sign, but for whom? Did it portend the death of the ailing sultan? Or something else—the fall of Acre and with it, the lordly house of Ibelin?

Eschiva was drawn to astrology for its numbers and calculations, which in a world of chaos felt so neat, so predictable, so *certain.* But even once she had the positions of the heavens calculated to the nearest fraction of a second, she had still to guess at what those positions *meant.* She still might be entirely wrong.

There was a way to be more certain; and that was to make an interrogation. The notion was a tempting one—but astrologers were not supposed to make interrogations themselves, because they would be certain to influence the results by asking their question at a time they guessed to be auspicious. Eschiva knew that she was only tempted to ask the question *now,* because at this moment, Mercury was in the ninth house and not in retrograde, while the sixth and eighth houses denoting sickness and death were likely empty. It was probable that this moment was highly auspicious for a successful journey.

For a moment, just now in her cabinet, it had seemed to her that she *ought* to ask the question now, to wrest a favourable answer from the stars and ensure John Bessarion's safe return.

Each moment she lingered risked squandering the auspicious moment. Eschiva raised the astrolabe towards its hook, the silver rēte glinting in the starlight.

She could not. It was one thing to read the heavens for predictions of earthly affairs. It was another to think that an earthly creature could impose some future upon the heavens. Ashamed, Eschiva lowered the instrument. Astrology was close enough to magic as it was. If she did this—if she sought not merely to predict but to govern the heavens—she would be crossing a line.

She ought not to seek power that did not belong to her.

Abandoning her purpose with a sigh, Eschiva returned her astrolabe to her cabinet and hurried towards her chamber, where her ladies had the lamps burning and her fool waiting with a song or a tale to take her mind from her cares. Eschiva dismissed the fool, but she accepted the posset of spiced wine her ladies had waiting for her and sat down to let them comb her hair from the braids in which it lived, coiled above each ear.

She had trod pretty close to the line already, she reflected. Six days ago she had carried home from Cairo, from the doorstep of Bektash himself, a shard of stone the size of her palm. Ibrahim had told her that the doors in her palace were given their power by a stone placed into the threshold from some other city, some other land. It had seemed to her at the time that if she brought the shard home, it might form a new doorway into Egypt by which she could come and go more easily than by the door in the citadel.

But the excursion had gone badly, and after that she had been reluctant to call upon Ibrahim for his instructions. Instead, she did the thing herself, first prying up another of the threshold-stones to study the carved marks on its lower surface. Here was a sigil like a round wheel with a little carved sun in its centre: Eschiva recognised it at once as a horoscope. She went up to her cabinet and calculated the horoscope for that night in Cairo, as near as possible to the very hour and latitude at which she had taken the stone. Once the calculations had been checked, and checked again, she had the horoscope inscribed upon the stone, and the stone embedded into another of the thresholds of her house. There it remained, unused. She was not quite bold enough to ask Ibrahim for his help again.

There came a knock at the outer door and Plaisance, another of her ladies, entered. "My lady, there was a petitioner at the church door this morning, who begs to see you. The matter is regarding an officer whom he claims has been demanding too high a tariff at the harbour and pocketing the excess."

Unhappy with the interruption, Eschiva closed her eyes. "I told Prince Balian to see to it. He was going to round up the accused and some witnesses, and bring them to me."

"This man claims that the prince is implicated in the embezzlement, my lady."

Eschiva opened her eyes. If Balian were truly caught in some misdeed, she would have an excuse for banishing him from the city. She might send him to Cyprus, where he would be King Henry's problem.

"Bring him in," she ordered, reaching for a mantle and sweeping into her anteroom.

The man entered with his head humbly lowered. Although he was well-groomed and wore fine clothing, he walked like a sleep-walker, his feet dragging a little.

"You had a petition to make," Eschiva drawled. "I was of the impression that I had granted it."

Glassy and unfocused eyes rose to meet Eschiva's. Her heart constricted. Something was wrong with this man; how could Plaisance have missed it? There was a minuscule speck of spittle in his greying beard, and his mouth pulled into a mirthless smile. Eschiva controlled the sudden icy-cold shaft of fear that went through her. *Ibrahim,* she nearly called, but then stopped herself. Last time she had called upon the djinn, it had almost destroyed him.

"This man is drunk," she said, although she was very much afraid that the trouble was worse than drink. "Call a guard at once, Plaisance."

In answer the man lurched forward, hands reaching. Eschiva threw herself back, but the wooden partition that separated her sleeping-quarters from the antechamber stopped her. She vaguely heard a shriek from her ladies, and saw one, Héloise, throw her arms around the man's neck, attempting to hold him back. The man seemed not to notice. He surged forwards, implacable, and his hands fastened on Eschiva's throat.

She might have tried to fight him, but her limbs were still tangled in the folds of her mantle and her dagger had been put away for the night.

"Guards," Eschiva rasped, but with that crushing grip on her throat there was nothing left of her voice.

The petitioner's face was close to hers, and there was no expression on it at all. He removed one hand from her throat to pluck Héloise from his back and run her head against the partition beside her. Wood splintered and she fell into a motionless huddle at Eschiva's feet.

At once the crushing grip returned to her throat, cutting off the flow of blood. Eschiva's head seemed almost to have lifted free of her body. Where were her guards? she wondered, dizzily. But almost at once the grip faltered again. Eschiva blinked through the firebursts occluding her vision and saw Ibrahim's familiar face hovering behind her attacker's shoulder. His shadowy hands were buried deep within the man's body.

"Help me," she begged, but only her lips moved.

Ibrahim tore an oily black shape from the man's body.

Instantly the throttling hands slackened. Eschiva tore herself free and lurched away, gulping air in a shallow, agonising whoop. She caught a single glimpse of Ibrahim locked in battle with a black, tarry shape that resembled nothing human, before the two shades burst through the wall and vanished. Her attacker was on his knees on the carpet, gazing at his hands and shaking violently. The door stood open and both her remaining ladies had fled. Eschiva staggered through it into the loggia and at once ran into Margaret, who caught her in her arms and helped her to stand upright.

"Eschiva! What happened?" the Lady of Tyre begged. "What's the commotion? Where are the guards?"

"We couldn't find any," said Plaisance, wringing her hands. "Agnes has run to the guardhouse, but—"

"Cousin!" a man called, and Eschiva turned to see Balian hurrying down the loggia towards her—with, thank God, five guards at his back. "Where is he? Where's the assassin?"

Eschiva drew breath but the words could not get out. Instead, she pointed in at the door, where her attacker was still sobbing on the carpet. The guards entered; just a moment too late, Eschiva thought better of what she had done. She tried to move, but Margaret still held her. She let out a weak, croaking sound just as the shouts erupted; just as the wet, heavy blows of falling blades began.

Balian returned to the door splashed in blood, pale and grim. "Take her away and have a doctor see her," he told Margaret. "She doesn't need to see this."

Whatever she needed, there was no longer any reason to stay. Furious, Eschiva turned her back and fairly dragged Margaret away. Once in the room assigned to the Lady of Tyre, she brushed away her clinging ladies and threw open the coffer where pen and paper were kept. Only once she had penned a peremptory note summoning the captain of her guard did she allow Margaret to give her the hot, sweet posset of wine that had been prepared for herself. Sweet and spicy, the drink soothed her throat. Eschiva sat and drank it quietly as Plaisance told Margaret what had happened.

"He didn't seem drunk to *me,*" Plaisance insisted, wringing her hands. "Only once he entered the Lady's presence did he go mad!"

"Héloise," Eschiva whispered. Her throat must be horribly bruised, but at least she could get a word out.

"She was already waking when we brought you away," Plaisance said. "P-prince Balian wanted her for questioning."

Eschiva hissed low under her breath and considered storming out of the room now that her trembling had subsided. If her guard captain would not come to her then she would go to him. She did not trust her cousin; there may no longer be hands around her neck but Eschiva wondered whether there might not be, soon, a knife in her back.

She was about to rise when a knock came at the door and her captain did, indeed, enter.

"My lady," he said, going to his knees. "It is my fault. I deserve death for failing to guard you as I ought."

"Why," Eschiva rasped in a whisper, "were there no guards in the loggia?"

"They had left their posts, my lady. A rabid dog had got loose in the courtyard and they went down to help catch it."

A rabid dog. A rabid man. Guards not at their posts. None of it seemed like coincidence. And Prince Balian ready to profit from all of it.

"Where is the body?" she whispered.

"Prince Balian ordered it to be quartered and displayed on the gate, my lady."

"Absolutely not." Eschiva choked on her own words and took another mouthful of wine to soothe her throat. "Is Prince Balian lord here, or am I?"

"You, my lady, but—"

"Have the prince sent back to his lodgings. See that the palace and town are secure. Leave the body in peace." She drew a careful breath, trying to think what else needed doing. "Take orders from no one but me or the lady Margaret. That is all."

She did not listen to his further apologies as he left. In his absence, the sense of danger faded a little. Margaret and her women, she knew, could be trusted. And her guard would obey her commands.

Margaret watched her thoughtfully. "Do you really think your cousin had something to do with this?"

Eschiva shrugged and got up.

"Shouldn't you stay with me for tonight?" Margaret inquired. But Eschiva shook her head. There was another person to whom she must speak tonight.

She went back to her chamber, where the bloodied carpet had already been rolled up and taken away. Only the splintered panel in the partition-wall remained as evidence of the deadly attack. Signalling her attendants to remain in the anteroom, Eschiva passed into her own bed-chamber and found Ibrahim sitting on the chest at the end of her bed, scowling at his loosely linked hands. When he saw her, he jumped to his feet.

"Ibrahim," whispered Eschiva. To her horror, she found her face crumpling around the word.

"Are you hurt?" he asked.

She had the back of her wrist pressed against her mouth to avoid letting her women hear her cry. But she nodded her head and gestured to her bruised throat.

"You should have called me. If I hadn't come to find you…"

She shook her head and rasped, "That man had a—a spirit inside him. I didn't want it to hurt you."

A long silence followed. Ibrahim said, softly, "That was one of Qeteb's servants, a being of far less power. It could not possibly have hurt me."

"Qeteb," Eschiva repeated. "Was this his doing? Did he have help from—within the palace?"

Ibrahim was evidently startled by the question. "I didn't ask," he said. "Shall I go after the spirit? It may still be lingering in the city."

"No!" Eschiva tried to clutch his sleeve before remembering that he could not be caught. She swallowed painfully. "Please don't go."

He gave her a look of pity that reminded her oddly of Margaret. Then he said, "You should not be here tonight. Come."

He made her put on her mantle and roll up some of her bedding, and then the two of them opened the door in the partition. Eschiva caught her breath at what lay beyond: instead of the antechamber, she stepped out onto a broken pavement. The ruined columns bordering the pavement to the east were the only thing obscuring the stars—a river of light arching above her. A broken archway at the end of the pavement led down a series of shallow steps onto a lonely hilltop plain. The air was icy; Eschiva could tell that they must be high in the mountains. As far as the eye could see there was no light of lamp or smell of hearthfire or trace of another building; only this lonely, ruined villa.

"Some of the stone in your floor must have been quarried among these ruins," Ibrahim told her. "I like to sit here when I can. There is no better place to watch the stars."

Eschiva sank down onto the stone, pulling one quilt over her knees and the other around her shoulders. Ibrahim hesitated a moment, but then sat beside her, an airy presence that somehow comforted her better than anything else could have. There were no walls here to hem her in, no mortals to choke the life from her.

"Is Qeteb really your father?" she whispered, to distract herself from the possibility that someone might be trying to kill her.

Ibrahim shrugged. "So he claims. Perhaps it is true. My mother never knew my father's true name."

"Then why does he hate you so much?"

She heard a whiff of laughter. "Qeteb hates everything he does not control. But it goes deeper than that. He's the familiar of an ancient sorcerer. They made an alliance long ago to build an empire together. You and I both stand in their way, and so do the Watchers."

"John Bessarion," Eschiva whispered.

"Yes."

"That is why you are helping me to save Beirut?"

"Our deeds will accomplish little, one way or another," Ibrahim said. Eschiva sent him a startled look, but the djinn added serenely: "The sorcerer's days are numbered. Qeteb and Khalil may both desire an empire, but they don't intend to share it. They'll tear each other down soon enough. You don't have to fear, my lady, because men are not gods. Even the gods are not really gods."

Eschiva was silent, wanting to believe Ibrahim, but doubtful. *He* was not mortal. He did not stand to lose home or possessions if he were wrong.

"When is a god not a god?" she asked, at length.

Ibrahim pointed towards the west, tracing a line across the ecliptic from the constellation of Taurus. "Do you know the story of the Pleiades?" he asked, softly.

Eschiva shrugged. "The Greeks say they were the daughters of a Titan and a sea-nymph."

"The truth is different," Ibrahim told her. "They were sisters not by blood, but by choice."

That stirred her curiosity. "You speak as though you knew them."

"Not in those days. I was not yet born, but I heard the tale from my mother, who was learned in all that lore. In those days there were many of us, the demigods. The world was younger then, before the great Flood, and full of mighty wonders. The demigods communed with their divine parents and taught mankind to worship them. In this way the gods received worship and obedience. Among mankind, great kings and sorcerers received the power to achieve all they could imagine. And we, the demigods, received wealth and fame and power beyond all reckoning. It was a great victory—for all but the weak. Do not marvel that so many of us fell to that temptation.

"The seven sisters alone did not. Maia was the first of them to rebel against the self-styled gods, their makers. The others followed her example: together they took oaths to provide a refuge for as many as should flee to them for help. One day a Messenger came to them, warning that the earth must be cleansed by water. But it was granted to them to take on aetherial bodies and ascend into the heavens, there to take their place among the holy stars until the world should be remade. All seven of the sisters accepted gladly. They ascended into heaven and dwelt among the stars."

"But there are now only six of them," Eschiva said. "We counted them together when I was a child, I recall."

"I'm coming to that," Ibrahim said. "Because the sisters had chosen to ascend to the heavens of their own free will, they retained the power to take up their mortal bodies again at will. Six of them were content in the heavens, watching over the earth from afar. The youngest of the sisters, however, was not. A new race of djinn had arisen after the Flood, and they quickly mixed with mankind. Their children and grandchildren were not so mighty, nor were they always obedient to the gods who had sired them. Those who remained faithful to their ancestors were thrown into the forefront of their battles; they perished by sword and spear and even by the slings of shepherd boys. Those who rebelled began to be hunted—enslaved or sacrificed by their own kin. Merope burned to rescue them. Her sisters counselled her against it, but she would not be dissuaded. She descended once again to the earth and took on a living form. But there she lost her way."

Ibrahim stopped speaking. Eschiva blinked at him. "And? How does the story end?"

"I will tell you that when Merope finds her way back home."

"Do you mean that she is still here?"

For a moment Ibrahim did not speak. At last he said, "So the story goes. But no one has heard of a demigod of that name in many long centuries."

For a while they went on gazing up at the bright stars. Eschiva felt questions bubbling up in her brain, but before she could give voice to any of them, Ibrahim spoke again.

"Do not worry about John Bessarion. He has friends who can protect him better than either you or I can."

Eschiva sent him an inquiring look.

"I saw you on the roof with your astrolabe," he said, apologetically. "I guessed what was troubling you."

It took her a moment to remember this—that indeed she had been up on the roof a while earlier with a mind to try wresting answers from the stars. The attack had driven it from her mind.

Yet, in future days, when she remembered this night, it would not be the attack that would first come to mind. It would be sitting on a mountaintop with Ibrahim, listening to tales of the stars.

"You are a far better friend to me than I deserve, Ibrahim," she said softly.

"Let us not talk of *deserving,* my lady,."

She could not allow him to deflect her confession. "In Cairo, I ordered you back so that I could throw you into the jaws of your maker. I was willing to sacrifice you for my own good. What love can be merited by such a mistress?"

Ibrahim was only a shadow in the darkness, curiously still and alert. He said, repeating her own words to her: "To love without return is to be like God. If such a love should come to me I will not flee it."

Eschiva was speechless. She had never before imagined that gentleness could be as bruising as cruelty.

"You asked that night whether I would stay in Beirut with you," Ibrahim added now. "The truth is this. I was conceived in rebellion and born in iniquity. If I could, I would take the choice of the Seven, and leave this world behind. Since I cannot, I wish only to escape my masters, and to sleep peacefully where they will never find me again. There is nothing else to desire any more."

A younger, more foolish version of herself urged her to speak, to tell him that there was yet joy and sweetness in the world; that life was still a gift. But such words would mean nothing to Ibrahim, who had lived far longer than she, amidst far greater sorrows.

She was so accustomed to being the great lady, able to rescue her lessers with a commanding word or a purse of gold. Here was something she could not cure, for it was the weariness of a life lived too long in a world of grief.

In that moment it felt like a personal affront that this one thing should be so far beyond her power to cure.

"I am sorry," was all that she said. "I wish that we had met in happier days."

He said nothing. For a while they sat in silence, watching the slow turn of the stars. *I have found the one my soul loves,* she thought. *But it is all far too late for both of us.*

Wearily, she turned her thoughts back to the business at hand. To the one thing she *could* control: to John Bessarion.

"Is there any way I might return to Cairo without putting you in danger?" she asked.

"You would need to travel alone, and that would put *you* in danger."

"I was nearly strangled in my own bedchamber," she reminded him. "Send me back. The guards will not trouble me. I have a better door to use, I think."

"The shard," Ibrahim said, as though he had watched her prepare it. There was a silence. "Is that your command?"

"No," Eschiva said. "That is a plea. *This* is my command: that no matter what happens, this time you must not come for me."

"I would dare it," he said, in a level, expressionless voice.

Eschiva stood, brushing her hands against her thighs. "I know that you would," she said, more softly. "Thus, the command."

Chapter XXIX.

John sat on a bench in the monastery courtyard, failing to pay any attention to the scroll unrolled on his knee. It was a favourite book of his, Athanasius' *On the Incarnation*, and he had the words by heart: *When did the deceitfulness and madness of demons fall into contempt, save when the power of God, the Word, the Master of all these as well, appeared on earth?*

The day had been warm, the evening was still and stifling, and the words mocked his impotence. Had the irrepressible young Athanasius lived in this troubled time, would he have been able to speak with such boundless hope?

Look for a Gift among the Copts, Soraya had told him. With Khalil's mamluks no longer searching the city, it had been easy to arrange a meeting with Nufir away from Turuntay's indignant eye.

"It is time we tried again," Nufir had said, but he seemed subdued somehow. John recalled his words: *this kind comes not out except by prayer and fasting.* He was fasting now; but for once, the bodily discipline had brought him no spiritual peace.

John heard a muffled knock at the monastery gate and leaped to his feet. By the time the elderly doorkeeper had shuffled from his cell to attend the door, John stood eagerly beside him. Soraya and al-Mukhtar had promised to return tonight, and John was eager to share his new plans.

Instead, the wicket gate opened to show a woman swathed in a black veil. Taller and thinner than the body Soraya habitually took on, she wore no telltale glint of green.

"Peace be upon you," she said. Her Arabic had a northern accent. "I am here to see John Bessarion. Will you call him?"

John considered the possibility that this might be a trap; but that was unlikely. If he was betrayed to Khalil it would be by al-Mukhtar, not by a strange woman who evidently was not even Egyptian.

"I am here," he said.

"Marvellous," the lady declared, sailing through the gate without waiting to be invited. "A word with you, Prester John."

The gatekeeper stammered a protest, but John said in an undertone, "Better let me speak with her" and hastened after the lady, who seated herself on the bench and picked up his discarded scroll.

"*On the Incarnation*," she read. "I'll consider that a good omen. I believe you remember me, John Bessarion."

She lifted her veil and looked up at him with the clear grey eyes and catlike smile of Eschiva, the Lady of Beirut.

John was rendered momentarily speechless. The Lady Eschiva, again! In Beirut four days ago the djinn Ibrahim had told him the Lady wanted him—but how could she behave so rashly?

"My lady," he said. "What are you doing in Cairo? You ought not to be wandering here alone."

"Neither should you, when you are so urgently needed elsewhere." Eschiva smiled at him, all charm. "Sir Gerard of Montreal told me to look for you at this monastery. I believe you're aware that the sultan is gathering an army to attack the Coast. This has come about because I have allowed the Watchers' Council of my forefather, John of Ibelin, to lapse. You are a Prester, John Bessarion. Return to Beirut with me and revive the Watchers. Succeed, and nothing you ask will be too much."

She sounded like himself in Oliveta, little more than a year ago—so sure that a Watchers' Council could change the course of an entire kingdom at the moment it was already sliding into the depths of disaster. For a moment, John wanted to laugh. Almost cruelly, he said:

"Do you think there were no Watchers in Tripoli a year ago, my lady?"

Her smile wavered. "*I must try*," the Lady said, with concentrated force. Then she regained her composure and added, "Why waste yourself in Cairo when you might be a lord in Beirut?"

A lord! John found his heartbeat quicken at the word. Ever since arriving in this time he had had to humble himself, to be a servant to every man. He had not complained, even in his heart. When he thought of the extent to which he had fallen from the state in which he was born, he told himself that Christ had done the same and that surely he was no greater than his Master.

Yet it was easier to be content when this humiliation seemed a temporary condition. Now that Soraya refused to return him to the past, John's hopes had contracted to a mean and friendless existence in a hostile new world. What the Lady offered him was a future. If Soraya remained adamant there were worse ways to live than as a vassal of Beirut.

In a flash his path unrolled before his feet. As Prester he would occupy a position of great influence. He could gather allies, build power, and do something better for his people than this unmanly sneaking for the Franks. He could be back in armour, fighting *real* battles, bringing Khalil's ambitions to a decisive end.

John dragged his vision away from this beguiling thought to find the Lady smiling at him.

"I thought so," she said, as though his heart was so very easy to read. "Come with me to Beirut, Prester John."

A knock sounded at the gate, and this time, John knew that it would be his allies.

"My lady, I am here in Cairo on Watcher business," he told her, regretfully. "I have a chance to stop the invasion before it ever leaves Egypt. When that is done, then I will come to Beirut—if I am still living."

A year ago in Tripoli, Eschiva had been offended when he refused to follow her to Beirut. Today she only inclined her head. "To put a stop to the invasion would be a great boon for us all, but do not linger overlong. Time grows short."

A sharp exchange of words had erupted at the gate. Now, Al-Mukhtar shoved his way past the gatekeeper and stalked towards John with his head lowered and shoulders tensed—looking, for a moment, like a wild beast about to charge.

There was neither a companion with him, nor the Lance. John's hand found his crossbow beneath his robe.

"Stay back," he cautioned the Lady as she rose to her feet. Then he addressed al-Mukhtar. "What's wrong, friend? Where's Soraya?"

"What's wrong? Everything's wrong," al-Mukhtar hissed. "Al-Ashraf took her. He took the Lance."

John's mind, which had been furiously calculating how to save himself and the Lady from an immortal attacker, stuttered to a halt. "He *what?*"

"He repossessed the Lance," al-Mukhtar repeated. "He said that it was bait, that you would come to take it as you did at Yarmouk."

"And you handed it over to him? You handed *Soraya* over to him?"

"Ghaliyah lies in the palm of his hand," al-Mukhtar growled. "Of *course* I gave her up."

"Of course," John repeated, scoffing. "Ghaliyah is your wife, but Soraya is only your slave."

Al-Mukhtar flushed. "You would have done the same."

John ground his teeth. *No,* he wanted to say, *I would not trade in lives at all. I would have found a way to save both of them.*

But would he? Truly?

Al-Mukhtar transferred his gaze to the Lady of Beirut. "Who is this woman?" he demanded. "Her veil is Egyptian, but her shoes are Frankish."

"How very observant you are," said the Lady. "Al-Mukhtar Saif al-Din, I believe. Ibrahim told me much of you. And speaking of my djinn, I take it that the al-Ashraf you speak of is the sorcerer who takes such an interest in him."

Al-Mukhtar gaped in astonishment. Suddenly his hand was on the hilt of his dagger, and John's crossbow was under his nose.

"The Lady of Beirut!" he hissed. "What are you doing here? No Franks are permitted south of Alexandria!"

"Watch yourself, friend," John said, although he was equally curious as to how the Lady had, for a second time, appeared in Egypt.

"You wouldn't believe me if I told you," the Lady said in lazy unserious tones. "But if it makes you any happier, Egyptian, I have come to *your* house with even fewer attendants and weapons than *you* brought to mine."

Al-Mukhtar glared at them both and then thrust his dagger back into the sheath.

"Where is Soraya now?" John asked.

"Al-Ashraf has her at the army camp. But I'm telling you that it is a trap. He believes that you will come for her."

"So does she," John said. After all the ways he'd failed Soraya, he could never leave her in the sorcerer's hands like this. "Don't you understand? We cannot cast out Qeteb while Khalil has the Lance in his possession, or while he has the leisure to call back Qeteb. That would only repeat our first mistake."

"Evidently," al-Mukhtar said. "We should take back the Lance and *then* perform the exorcism." A though lit up his eyes. "Al-Ashraf was able to summon back the Hairy One because he did so at once, before the afrit had left the world entirely. And *that* was possible because the afrit was speaking to him and warned him. If we staged the exorcism at the moment of stealing the Lance..."

"Then, with good fortune, Khalil would be too busy chasing after the Lance to pay any heed to Qeteb." John paused a moment, thinking fiercely. Success would require perfect co-ordination: they must steal the Lance and stage the exorcism at the same moment. No, but what if Khalil perceived their gambit? "No. Khalil is a man of great foresight, who will likely choose Qeteb over the Lance. We must attack in three directions simultaneously: Qeteb, the Lance...and Khalil himself."

Al-Mukhtar frowned. "What do you mean?"

"I have found a Gifted Watcher, a Healer," John said. "He will perform the exorcism. We'll need him nearby, as close as possible without letting him be seen. I will take the Lance, and the moment it's in my hands I will send Soraya to Nufir to signal the exorcism. You must attack Khalil himself and keep him engaged until the exorcism is done and Qeteb can no longer be called back. Are you willing?"

Al-Mukhtar was silent, and John was conscious that the moment of choice had come. He had asked the mamluk not merely to plot against his master, but to confront him.

"It's the only way," he prompted, as the silence stretched out. "It takes an immortal to fight another immortal. As soon as the exorcism is done, your father will be mortal and powerless. Then we'll break the Lance. You'll be free, and Ghaliyah will be free, and Soraya will be free."

At last al-Mukhtar said, "If I do this—if I lift my hand against my father—I won't kill him. And I won't have you kill him, either."

John felt his hands clench at his sides; he forced them to relax. "I understand," he said.

He understood—but there would be a moment when Khalil was mortal, when al-Mukhtar left him and ran. And then John would try what he could do. A scratch with a poisoned blade, perhaps, so that al-Mukhtar would never suspect John of killing his father?

"Swear," he said to al-Mukhtar, raising his hand. "Swear that as long as this enterprise lasts, you will obey me; that you will play your part, and that when Qeteb is cast out and al-Mukhtar is mortal again, you will break the Lance and free Soraya."

Al-Mukhtar raised his hand. "I will do so, God willing."

In the shadows, the Lady of Beirut also raised a white hand, recalling John to her presence. Turning towards her, he said, "You see that we are in the midst of a desperate enterprise, my lady. You ought to return to your people."

"Ought I?" she asked in that voice of perpetual amusement.

"You are in danger every moment you remain in Cairo," al-Mukhtar told her.

"Thank you; I didn't know," she replied, with light raillery. "Good fellows, it has been impressed upon me lately that I am not such a great person as I have sometimes believed myself to be. I have decided that the world will get along without me if it must, and I am willing to hazard myself upon this adventure with you. Moreover, I might be of very great assistance to you, since I am in possession of something which the sorcerer Khalil desires very greatly."

"What is that?" John asked, since she evidently meant him to do so.

"My djinn," she replied, with a smile.

"God is great," al-Mukhtar breathed. "It is true. Al-Ashraf sent me to Beirut to capture it."

"Take me to this sorcerer," said the Lady. "I will offer him some kind of trade or alliance. I'll ask to see this—Lance, isn't it? —and that will give *you* fellows the chance to seize it."

John glanced at al-Mukhtar. "Will this work?" he asked.

Al-Mukhtar tilted his head. "Yes," he said. "She is our excuse to seek an audience with al-Ashraf. I will escort her in. You will pose as her guard. I will give you a helmet to cover your face and no one will be any the wiser."

Unless you betray us, John thought. How much could he really trust al-Mukhtar? It was true that he had warned John against putting his head into Khalil's trap, but that might be a ploy to gain his trust. The only real loyalty the man had was to his wife.

The Lady seemed to have no such doubts. "Then it's settled," she said briskly. "Is your exorcist ready, Prester? Then we should lose no time."

"My lady," John protested, "are you certain of this? We are strangers to you, and in the hands of a sorcerer you might be a very great weapon."

Eschiva hesitated, and for a moment her front of raillery cracked again.

"I also have a friend I must protect from him," she said. "Come, Prester. Let us not tarry until the stars turn against us."

Chapter XXX.

The guards at the Masjid Tibr informed them that Al-Ashraf Khalil was keeping watch at the sultan's bedside. It seemed that after all, the rumours of the sultan's ill-health were true.

"Perhaps al-Ashraf will come out to speak with us," al-Mukhtar told the guards, persuasively. "Tell him the mistress of Ibrahim is here to speak with him."

John scanned the great courtyard from the shadows of his helmet—a conical cap with a straight nosepiece and openings for the eyes, from which a veil of chain-mail hung, concealing his features. Al-Mukhtar had also fitted him out in armour and a silk surcoat, together with a sword to hang at his hip, so that John looked the model of a high-born Egyptian knight.

He was glad of the sword. On his previous occasion in this courtyard he had been thoroughly defenceless.

Now, although every nerve was on the alert for danger, although he could not quite convince himself of al-Mukhtar's sincerity, John felt oddly elated. Soon he would be facing Khalil again for only the second time in his life. Soon Khalil would be mortal, and John would have the satisfaction of seeing the colour of his blood.

He recognised the source of his elation, then. The blood-drinker that lived within him, that had made his name on the battlefields of the Persian wars when he was young, was stirring again. John took three deep breaths, warning himself not to let that beast escape. It had brought him to shame more than once, and tonight it would only impede him. Tonight he ought to hide behind his mask and remain silent until al-Mukhtar could secure the Lance. After that, his task was merely to break the weapon, and so doing, to free Soraya. Anything else—ending Khalil, escorting the Lady to safety—was secondary.

At length an official appeared and asked them to follow him. Al-Ashraf would receive the lady, so long as her guard laid aside his weapons. Reluctantly, John complied.

He was surprised to be shown into a lamplit bedchamber. Whatever purpose this room had once served in the mosque, it had now been re-furnished with spartan luxury: a low broad bed shrouded with curtains of fine muslin, an armour-tree holding a burnished suit of armour and a gilded helm, and lamps burning bright within chimneys of coloured glass. In the bed an old man lay asleep. A sickbed odour pervaded the room, ripe with the fumes of fever and doses.

They had been ushered into the sultan's own chamber.

A young man, who had been sitting beside the bed, now rose to meet them.

"Eschiva of Beirut," he said, in a voice that was horribly familiar. "I always suspected that the Old Lord had doors opening into Cairo from Beirut. Now I know."

"Al-Ashraf Khalil," the Lady greeted him, inclining her head. "The sultan is in good health, I trust?"

John realised with a shock that this must indeed be the man he saw in Oliveta wreaking sword and fire upon the populace. It had not been clear in the courtyard of Bektash, but Khalil must have altered his appearance to impersonate the sultan's son. The change was somehow disappointing, as though revenge would lose all its sweetness now that the man wore a new face.

"My father's fever has broken," al-Ashraf said with a thin smile. "He will live and thrive, as I am sure you will rejoice to hear. Now tell me what folly brings the Ibelin daughter to the heart of my empire."

The Lady made a humming sound in her throat, but did not answer at once. Instead she approached the bed to gaze down upon the sleeping sultan. "Does he know you consider his kingdom to be your own, I wonder?

Perhaps he does. My informants tell me that your position as heir is not so secure as you should like."

"Then you were misinformed," Khalil said. "State your business."

"Mm," the Lady hummed. "I believe you want something that belongs to me."

"The djinn Ibrahim." Khalil watched the Lady with thinly veiled contempt; he evidently cared little for the games she played. "Speak plainly."

"Ibrahim," the Lady confirmed. "You sent your servants to steal him from me. That caught my attention. Your father is old and weak, and you will be the sultan soon enough. I came to propose an alliance. I'm not prepared to give up my djinn, but I am prepared to swear allegiance to you, and to place both him and myself at your service."

"In exchange for the uninterrupted command of Beirut?"

"Among other things." The Lady took another pause. In the lengthening silence, John felt the atmosphere thicken with anticipated violence. He wished he had warned her: Khalil's patience was apt to run out without warning.

"Knowledge is power," the Lady said at last, "and that is what I seek. My djinn is unable to answer certain of my questions. He believes that a djinn in your service, whom he calls Soraya, will be able to do so. Let me speak to your djinn, in your presence if you wish, and we shall have a bargain."

"Is that all?" Khalil asked, grimly ironic.

The Lady sent him a broad smile. "That, and the uninterrupted command of Beirut, of course."

"I need not bargain with you. Inside a year Beirut will be ours, and so will your djinn."

"Why should the djinn remain in Beirut so long?" the Lady asked, gently. "If I must flee to Cyprus, then I will of course take my djinn with me. All you will inherit is ashes. Or, you might allow me to speak to Soraya tonight."

Khalil frowned, but then he snapped his fingers. "Fetch the Lance," he told the servant who answered. John allowed himself a deep breath and a glance towards the door where al-Mukhtar stood with his arms folded, a vigilant guardian. Khalil seated himself once more beside the sultan, and the Lady favoured him with a bright smile.

"You won't regret it, my lord," she told him. "The world of the spirit is perilous and requires constant vigilance. A prince has many cares to distract him. When you become the sultan you will be glad of another sorcerer to guard you from surprise."

Oddly, Khalil responded to this with a smile of his own. "I am counting on it," he said.

There was something terribly wrong with that smile—a peculiar and alien peeling of flesh from teeth. The elation John had felt in the porch was now fast ebbing before the face of this monster. The passing centuries had shaped his old enemy into something entirely beyond his ken.

Footsteps approached the doorway. A servant carried the Lance into the room and, at a command from Khalil, placed the weapon into the Lady's hands.

"What is this?" she asked, feigning surprise.

"That is the vessel of the djinn Soraya. While you hold the Lance you command her. Summon her forth."

"Soraya," the Lady called, and in the blink of an eye a whirlwind of dust appeared, which quickly resolved into his dark-eyed friend.

Soraya blinked at the Lady and narrowed her eyes. "Five and Thursday," she said, unimpressed. "Who are *you?*"

"Do not move or speak," Khalil commanded, "except to answer this lady's questions."

Soraya stiffened, and John ground his teeth in frustration. Here was an unexpected complication. Nufir was stationed outside, hidden in a shadowed corner of the great masjid courtyard, waiting to begin his exorcism. This was the moment in their plan at which the Lady ought to have commanded Soraya to find and signal him. Al-Mukhtar, by the door, stood coiled and ready; John's hands itched to seize the Lance—and yet none of it could be done, since Soraya had been forbidden to move.

Only Soraya's eyes retained their expression and movement. At first they widened in alarm. Then she threw a wild look at al-Mukhtar by the door as though trying to communicate with him.

Perhaps she had not known that Khalil had repossessed the Lance.

"My question is this," said the Lady, after a pause that seemed endless. "I am seeking a djinn named Merope. Do you know her?"

Soraya scowled. "Of *course* not."

"And why is that?" the Lady asked.

She must be playing for time, waiting for John and al-Mukhtar to solve this conundrum. John sent al-Mukhtar a furious glance, trying to signal him to go find Nufir himself; but all the mamluk's attention was on his master.

Was this al-Mukhtar's game? Had he simply decided to follow his orders, and deliver both the Lady and John Bessarion to their enemy?

"I don't know your friend, because *he's* taken all my memories," Soraya said, turning accusing eyes upon the man on the divan.

"Silence," Khalil said. Soraya's mouth closed firmly; she glared daggers and sent another pleading glance to al-Mukhtar. Khalil addressed the Lady: "You see what an unruly servant she is. Only the repeated removal of her memories prevents her rising against me in earnest. But you are a sorcerer yourself; you know how it is."

"I'm not sure I do," said the Lady with the same calculated insolence, "as my djinn has no desire to rise against *me*. Perhaps you would be good enough to restore her memories, my lord. Her knowledge may be to the advantage of us both."

Although no expression crossed Khalil's face, the seething atmosphere of the room intensified. "You delude yourself," he said. "All djinn want freedom. What is sorcery, but the art of bending other wills to your own? Perhaps you are only a dabbler, who has inherited a djinn from her mighty ancestors and fancies herself a great Power. What use should I have for such an ally?"

The silence in the room thickened, almost to suffocation. Hidden behind his mailed face-covering, John slid his eyes towards the Lance. Only an enchanted weapon like this could possibly hurt an immortal sorcerer, and here it was, practically within reach. The Lady held it loosely in upturned palms. Al-Mukhtar had not moved from the door. One step, and John might snatch it for himself. An over-arm cast and he could drive it through Khalil's body, all before the sorcerer had the chance to rise from his seat upon the floor.

Khalil must surely know that the Lady was only here to cozen him. That was why John should act now—because in another heartbeat it would be too late.

"I have heard of your wisdom and experience in these matters," the Lady said, before John could make a rash decision. "Indeed the half was not told me. There are, perhaps, things which we could learn from each other."

"Perhaps," said Khalil, with another frightful smile. "But first, prove that you are what you claim to be. Draw the circle, Lady of Beirut, and assist me to harvest the memories of this djinn."

John's heart stood still. The Lady sent a glance towards the bed where the sultan lay sleeping. "What, here? Now?" she asked.

"I have seen to it that my father will not wake," said the sorcerer, inexorable. "Draw the circle. Perform the chant. Or is it possible that you have come here to cozen me, when you know that I will take your life's blood in payment?"

"Not at all," said the Lady, lightly. "Yet I do not see how it will benefit me to destroy the very memories I seek. I am not your Assassin, to do myself an injury at your command."

"Do you wish to keep Beirut?" Khalil asked, flat and menacing.

Soraya stood like an image, but her eyes were full of despair. At the sorcerer's words the Lady went stock-still; and in that stillness John read the truth that even someone like Eschiva of Beirut might have her price.

For a moment it seemed that no one in the room breathed. Then the Lady said, "A circle is easily drawn. Bring me chalk."

Soraya must have tried to cry out in protest, but no sound left her lips; the command lay heavily upon her. At the look of despair on her face, John's self-command deserted him. Whatever the Lady was playing at, whatever her plans to extricate them from this trap, John could not stand meekly while Soraya's memories were taken.

John took that single step and snatched the Lance from the Lady's grasp.

Shuddered with the power that rushed into him.

Yes, said the blood-drinker that had slumbered for so long within him. *Yes!*

It was at that moment that al-Mukhtar, finally, did something. "Wait," he said. "Something is not right. This is not—"

But he had waited too long. John tore off his helmet, throwing it on the floor at Khalil's feet.

"Do you remember me?" he asked. He had been mistaken, before. Whatever semblance Khalil wore, this was every bit as satisfying as he had imagined.

Khalil's face was a mask, like a dead man's. "Yes," he whispered, but he drew out the word almost lovingly. "I knew it."

Al-Mukhtar was shouting. John did not hear the words. "Die," he said, and flung the Lance with all his own and Soraya's strength. It left his hand like a thunderbolt.

Where Khalil sat was suddenly a cloud of smoke. The Lance passed through it and struck the old man on the bed. There was a wet thud; a sudden choking, gasping sound from the sultan; a high-pitched, wordless scream from Soraya.

The cloud of smoke coalesced, and there was not Khalil, but a giant covered in hair, an eye in his forehead and another in his breast.

John's hands fell, trembling, to his sides. His throat had gone dry.

"For this reason I kept you alive," said Qeteb in a voice that echoed within his mind. "Did you really suppose that you could use *my own weapons* against me?"

With that he was gone. Released, Soraya turned upon John with white lips and flashing eyes.

"Son of a *shoe!*" she hissed. "Where are your wits? Couldn't you tell *that wasn't Khalil?*"

John was conscious of little but the body on the bed. The blood; the old man's rasping breaths and fluttering hands; the staring eyes that turned towards him. Behind were the sounds of running feet and clashing arms; Soraya's warning shriek had undoubtedly summoned the sultan's servants.

What the Lady and al-Mukhtar might be doing, he had no notion. All he could do now was watch as the life faded from the sultan's eyes.

Khalil had never been in the room at all. It had only ever been Qeteb. Qeteb, who wanted the sultan dead and Khalil on the throne. Qeteb, who had goaded John into lashing out.

His own fault, for allowing the blood-drinker once more to awaken.

"What is the meaning of this?" a voice demanded behind him, and John turned with a feeling of grim inevitability to face Khalil—the real Khalil, a flesh-and-blood man who cast a shadow as he passed the lamps by the door, whose fury twisted his face into an all-too-human snarl. His mamluks fanned out around him, seizing John and the two women.

Al-Mukhtar was still by the door: motionless, speechless and weaponless. He dragged his eyes away from the dead sultan. "My lord!" he stammered, pointing towards the bed. "This was Qeteb's doing!"

Khalil went white. For a moment he said nothing, only shoving past his mamluks and halting at the bedside where the sultan lay, bloodied and dying.

John said nothing. Indeed, had he attempted to do so, he might have choked on his own self-reproach. The Lady sent him a censorious glance, but he hardly needed Eschiva of Ibelin to tell him that if he'd only allowed her play to along with Qeteb a little longer, Khalil might have come face to face with his own double, winning them a swift and uncomplicated retreat.

Now he had ruined everything, and everyone who knew of Khalil's true nature was neatly trapped in this room, virtually red-handed.

All but one.

"Soraya," he hissed, grasping her wrist where she stood beside him. "Quickly—there's a Watcher in the porch; go to him. He will know what to do—"

"The Watcher will do *nothing*," said Khalil, very softly, as he closed the sultan's glassy eyes. "Bring him in."

Nufir appeared, caught and held securely between two of Khalil's mamluks. All hope at last died. For a long moment there was only silence. John did not know what to do. Nufir, who had put his trust in John and was about to suffer for it, closed his eyes; his lips moved and John, to his surprise, heard the words of the Creed, faint but clear: *We believe in one God: the Father, the Pantocrator, who created heaven and earth...*

"Well?" Khalil rasped in a dangerous whisper, rising to his feet. "Was this *your* doing, al-Mukhtar?"

"My lord!" the young mamluk cried, falling to his knees. "Did you not order me to entrap John Bessarion? The guards will tell you how I brought him into your presence, but it was that deceiver, that afrit, wearing your face! My lord, would I be so foolish as to risk my Ghaliyah's life?"

"She had best hope not."

Al-Mukhtar wrung his hands. "My lord, the Hairy One cannot be trusted."

Khalil grunted. Nufir had finished saying the Creed and now began a new recitation. *Hail God of Abraham! Hail God of Isaac! Hail—*

Khalil drew the Lance from the sultan's body with brutal force. Soraya screamed a second time. John barely understood what was happening, even as the air hissed near his cheek. Then the Lance struck Nufir, silencing his invocation. The Healer's eyes opened wide. There was a horrible gasp. John was conscious of throwing himself against the hands that restrained him, but there was no escaping Khalil's men. Then Nufir was nothing more than a huddle of bloodstained robes upon the floor.

There was absolute silence. John stared down at the lifeless Watcher. In the silence of his horror he thought, *It should have been me. I should have been the one to die.*

"An exorcist." Khalil scoffed, then strode past him, retrieved the Lance a second time, and handed it to al-Mukhtar. "Get up, boy, and don't bandy words with me. I want the Bessarion locked safely away. Allow no one to see him."

"Yes, my lord. Right away," al-Mukhtar whispered, staring at the corpse as though he had never seen one before; as though he had never made a hundred such corpses. After a moment the mamluk rapped the Lance against the pavement, and the white, stricken Soraya beside John fell away into a pile of sand. The Lady made a startled sound.

"Wait," Khalil added. "This woman is Frankish."

The Lady must have been utterly terrified, but John was impressed by the effort with which she repressed it. "I am Eschiva of Ibelin, the Lady of Beirut," she said in a voice that shook only a little."I came to deal with al-Ashraf Khalil, but I found an imposter. As for this man—"

"Leave her with me," Khalil ordered al-Mukhtar. "Take the Bessarion away and have him shut up securely. If he escapes, *you* will not be the one to answer for it."

"I understand," al-Mukhtar stammered, seizing John from the mamluks that held him.

John sent one last glance over his shoulder at the Lady of Beirut, who now stood alone and ringed with swords before the wrathful Khalil. If Eschiva meant to disavow him, he could not fault her for it. Al-Mukhtar, though— al-Mukhtar he could fault, and would; that traitor, who had promised faithfulness in two directions, and who would change loyalties as easily as he changed his shoes.

Then the warm night air opened to receive him.

News of the sultan's death must not yet have spread, for the mosque's vast courtyard was silent and empty. Al-Mukhtar propelled John hastily through the dark portico, chanting beneath his breath, evidently long passages of his holy writ. John could not fathom why, unless it was some penance he laid upon himself.

"It was a trap all along, wasn't it?" he growled at last. "I ought to have known, when you did not go to Nufir the moment we had the Lance."

Al-Mukhtar's only reply was more muttering. He propelled John into a dark passage which pierced the thick walls of the mosque and ended in a small, unguarded postern-gate which looked out upon the mass of tents, animals, and livestock that surrounded the building. Seizing the gate, he forced it open; they ventured out into the camp.

John remained silent. An insane hope had come to him.

Al-Mukhtar's tent stood where he remembered it. Nearby, a boy held a pair of magnificent grey rounceys, saddled and bridled for a journey. With a curt nod to the youngster, al-Mukhtar propelled John into the tent and broke his chanting mid-sentence to call, "Soraya!"

In a blink Soraya was with them again; she was speaking even before her body finished taking shape.

"Could *neither* of you tell that was the Hairy One? There he was sitting there like a bad puppet-master, *black* with malice, forbidding me to speak, and you thought it was *Khalil?* Now what?"

"Yes. Now what?" John echoed, his voice hollow in defeat. "The sultan is dead—and so is Nufir." Then words failed him. The Lance could not be broken, now. Soraya could not be freed. He was forsworn. Again.

"Now you do what you ought to have done weeks ago," al-Mukhtar shot back. "Take that horse and get out of Egypt." He turned to Soraya. "You, stay with him and protect him. See him safely to the Coast."

There was a long silence before John really heard what the Chosen had said. Then he took hold of the tent's central pole to steady himself. Soraya said shakily, "You aren't really going to defy Khalil. What about Ghaliyah?"

"He won't lay a finger on her," al-Mukhtar said. "Now more than ever. She's his only defence against the Hairy One."

John scraped words together. "But Khalil—"

"Khalil is my father," al-Mukhtar said, in a voice that was as soft as thistledown, and as hard as a stone. It halted John at once. "My father, and yet he has taken everything from me—my memories, my family, my dignity. He'll never free Ghaliyah. And he'll never treat me with respect. Not unless I force him to do so."

Soraya snorted. "What? After all this, do you still believe that his respect is something you can have?"

Al-Mukhtar swallowed, hard. "He's all the father I have, Soraya. Family is family, no matter what they're like."

She blinked. "You're still deceiving yourself, then."

"Stop arguing, Soraya. Go *now*." Al-Mukhtar pointed the Lance at the horses waiting outside. "There's no time to find another exorcist. If you fall into Khalil's hands, it will all be over."

John cleared his throat. "What about the Lady? She's trapped because of me. I won't leave her."

"I'll take care of the Lady," he said, stubbornly. *"Go.* I need you off my hands, don't you see?"

Soraya slid John a resentful glare. "You certainly do," she said. "Come on, *Prester* John."

Chapter XXXI.

Implicated in the death of the sultan, and forced to confront his successor, a powerful sorcerer, alone—Eschiva felt that she had wandered into a nightmare. Except that one might awake from a nightmare. Probably only death could free her from this. If she was fortunate, that death would be as instantaneous as the Coptic Watcher's had been.

One consolation remained to her. With the sultan dead, al-Ashraf must move instantly to secure his right of succession against all rivals, mortal or immortal. The invasion must be delayed, perhaps even called off completely.

That was a price worth her life—worth even Prester John's life. Eschiva would die, then. She would not summon Ibrahim, even if it meant her own death and the loss of Beirut and the whole Coast to her family forever. Margaret would see the djinn removed to Cyprus according to his wishes.

She had lost the gamble, but she had always known she might.

Now, with the treacherous al-Mukhtar dragging John Bessarion into the night, she sank into a deep, ceremonious bow. "Hail, al-Ashraf Khalil, sultan of Egypt," she said. "Long life to your lordship."

The man's mouth twisted, making it clearer in retrospect how absolutely unnatural the demon's phantasm had been. "What do you want from me, Eschiva of Ibelin?"

She marshalled her thoughts. "I came to offer an alliance."

"We already have an alliance with Beirut."

"A marriage alliance," she amended, making her final gamble. "You would gain full control of Beirut and everything in it, without losing a drop of blood. In return, you will confirm my sons in possession of the fief." She let that sink in, watching the calculations flicker in his eyes, before adding: "A succession crisis has already begun. I can give you help both seen and unseen. Even if things go badly for you, there will always be Beirut to fall back upon."

"Things will not go so badly," al-Ashraf said, as though speaking to himself. "Turuntay has lost all support. There remains only the afrit…" His eyes focused suddenly upon Eschiva, cold and daunting. "Why should I offer you anything, when you are here in my power?"

Eschiva shrugged. "You had better kill me if you don't mean to deal with me," she said. "Ibrahim has hidden nothing from me concerning his history in your house. What do you think that young mamluk, al-Mukhtar, will say if I tell him the truth of his birth?"

She had as warning only the ugly look that darkened al-Ashraf's face before he dealt her a stinging slap across the cheek. The blow made her stagger.

"That was a warning," al-Ashraf said coldly. "Spread any more such tales and you will learn how heavy my hand can be."

Eschiva fought bitterly to control her tears. "I am not your wife *yet*," she drawled. "Keep your hands to yourself, and think about my offer. If I don't hear from you within three months, I suppose I shall go to Cyprus instead, and take my djinn with me."

She turned towards the door, only to find her way blocked by mamluks.

"If I don't return to Beirut by dawn," she said, turning, "then my djinn goes to Cyprus on the first tide."

There was a long, fraught silence. Again, she watched the calculations flit through al-Ashraf's empty eyes.

"You shall have my answer," he said, "when I come north with this army. Go in peace—for now."

Eschiva dragged her eyes away from the sorcerer. The wall of bodies between herself and the door dissolved at Khalil's gesture. Perhaps there was another sign from him, for one of them followed her, silent and vigilant, into the courtyard. Eschiva drew her veil once more across her face.

When I come north with this army. Al-Ashraf's words echoed in her mind. He meant, then, to go ahead with the invasion.

Let not him who puts on his armour boast as one who takes it off, she told herself. All the same, she found that her heart was racing, her hands shaking with terror. She tried not to think, only putting one foot in front of the other. Back in the city, she dismissed her escort and returned to Bektash's door; it opened at a touch, and she stepped into the loggia at Beirut.

Eschiva found Margaret waiting with Ibrahim in her chamber.

"Eschiva!" Margaret cried, rushing to hug her. "God be thanked, I thought you would never return. You promised to be only a couple of hours, and look, it is dawn!"

Eschiva collapsed into a chair, pushing away Margaret's anxious fluttering hands. "I'm alive," she said, but she laughed a little as she looked up at Ibrahim, who stood above her brooding like a thundercloud. "I think I'm going to have nightmares about *this* night, too."

Margaret had left her only momentarily; now she came back with a blanket from the bed. "I'm warming a posset for you," she said, pulling it around Eschiva's shoulders. "Now for heaven's sake, tell us what happened."

"I delivered my message and I came back safely," Eschiva said. "What else is there to know?" But both of them gave her a stern look, and meekly, she obeyed.

"So the sultan is dead," she finished, "but al-Ashraf plans to continue the invasion."

Ibrahim looked horrified. "You might have been killed. My lady, you ought to have called me."

Eschiva began to laugh. Perhaps she should have called the djinn. Had she died, what would it have accomplished, but to deprive Beirut of their lady in the face of an invasion? What had become of her, that she was willing to burn down the Ibelin legacy, the very thing she sought to save, for a servant she fancied?

"I want to rest," she said, stopping the laughter with a gasp.

Margaret looked at her, then at Ibrahim, and seemed to understand at once what was wanted, for she kissed Eschiva on the cheek and departed.

Ibrahim, less perceptive, bowed and turned away.

"Wait," Eschiva said. Ibrahim halted, looking back at her inquiringly. She touched her tongue to her lips, suddenly unsure what she meant to say. She ought to be tending to Beirut, not pining for a man she could never have in any of the ways that mattered. And he—he ought to be finding what peace and rest he could, not putting himself in danger to save her.

"I think," she began, but she could not finish the words. *I think you love me,* she had meant to say. But what was the use? He loved her, and she knew it, and he knew that she knew it. But if she said the thing, then what? She was mortal, and he was not. She was living, and he was not. She was mistress, and he was not. In this life they would never meet on an equal footing; and therefore she could ask nothing of him, not even an answer.

He waited, expectant. Eschiva bowed her head in defeat. "I think I had better send you to Cyprus," she said. "Soon. As soon as the Egyptian host begins its march."

Chapter XXXII.

As morning rose in the sky, Soraya led the way south from the army encampment along the road that bordered the river. On any other day, John would have found it a pleasant ride. Both the road and the horses were in perfect condition; the day was mildly cool, the light breeze was at his back, and the sun shimmered rose and gold from the broad sweep of the Nile. Strands of mist crept through the green pleasure-gardens to his left that stood between the river and the distant towering tenements of the city. It was a beautiful sight, yet all he could think of was his own folly.

From her stiff, unspeaking back and the punishing pace she set them, that was all Soraya could think of, too. Not until the port suburb of Babylon came within view did she ease the pace to a walk, allowing the magnificent horses to cool themselves and enabling John to draw level and speak with her.

"I am sorry," he told her.

"Oh, are you?" she demanded. "You played right into their hands. You put Khalil and his afrit on the throne of Egypt, and now you're having to flee the country. And now when will I be freed?" Her voice broke, and the sound of it went through him like a blade.

"I've been a fool," he said bitterly. "Qeteb played me like a stringed instrument. I thought I was saving our necks, Soraya. I thought I was saving *you* from losing your memories again."

She gazed at him in disbelief. "But *why?* I could have done without my memories for a day or two! I would have had them back, all of them, when I got my freedom!"

"Soraya..."

"Don't," she said. "If you cared for me as much as you pretend, you'd free me. Oh, God. What is wrong with me, that I cannot be loved so much, even for a moment?"

"The fault lies in me, not in you," he said bitterly. And he rubbed his eyes, wishing that he could rub away the image that lingered, of Nufir's eyes as he died.

Neither of them spoke again after this until they entered the town and John blinked at the destruction around him. Babylon—now also called Fustat—was a city that had been hollowed out from the inside: ruins, some of them still bearing scorch-marks from long-ago flames, sprawled like a mouthful of broken teeth from the riverbank. At the heart of the city, along the water's edge where quays still lined the river, the rubble had been gathered and built up again into new buildings, fewer and smaller than those that had once been.

"What happened here?" John marvelled

Soraya slanted him a disdainful look. "Your Franks happened," she told him. "Amalric, the father of the Leper King, was the first to dream of conquering Egypt. As his army approached Cairo, Vizier Shawar had the port emptied and burned to prevent it falling into the enemy's hands. Now most of the river-traffic has moved north, opposite the capital. But here in Fustat we should be able to find a ship to take us north, and we'll attract less attention."

"There ought to be a caravanserai kept here by a Copt named Mikhael, who works for the Temple. He may be able to find us passage—unless..." John swallowed. "Soraya, we could try to find another Watcher..."

Soraya remained almost expressionless. "I'll find one myself when I return from Beirut."

"But if we both waited a day or two—"

"I *can't* wait. I'm under orders." She forged ahead of him into the jagged streets. Silently, John followed. No doubt it was only right to step aside and let Soraya achieve her own freedom, since he had done nothing but harm.

An odd mood hung over the city this morning. People milled restlessly, gossiping on the street corners rather than going about their business. John overheard snatches of their conversation as he passed by.

"Trouble in Cairo?"

"Messengers between the camp and the citadel."

"Turuntay arrested."

"But if it was a natural illness…"

"Khalil."

"The sultan."

"Assassins…"

One of the mutterers broke off to point them towards the caravanserai they wanted—a new but modest hostelry consisting of two levels of tiny, cramped rooms surrounding a small courtyard. Here an unexpected meeting awaited them. Having paid for a room and had a word with Mikhael, John was stretching his cramped legs in the courtyard when a voice boomed out, "John! John Zakar!" and John turned to see Abdu, the pottery merchant, bearing down on him with outstretched arms.

"God wills it that I should find you here, rather than in Cairo!" Abdu exulted, slapping his back. John sensed the relief that flowed from him. "Saida and I were about to seek you in Cairo. Come—we have a message for you from the Master."

John and Soraya followed the merchant and sometime spy upstairs to the loggia before Abdu's room, where a pair of battered cushions faced each other across a small, low table. "Be seated," Abdu offered, before gesturing towards the door. "As for the woman, perhaps she would like to enter…"

"I don't think your wife would be pleased to see me," Soraya said.

Abdu gave her a closer look than he had dared hitherto; his face turned grey as he recognised her. "Oh, peace!"

John had forgotten that Abdu had met Soraya before. "It's all right," he said, hurriedly. "She really is a friend."

Soraya now appeared tired and glum. "I'll step away," she muttered.

"No, no, it's all right," Abdu assured her. "Sit down, both of you. Let me find some food to offer you, and have a word with my wife. But what brings you here, John Zakar? Were you expecting us?"

"No," John said. Despite his hunger, he did not take the proffered seat; he felt that the less time he spent in Abdu's company, the better it would be for the merchant and his wife. "We won't stay long. I ran into a spot of trouble with al-Mukhtar, and he's sent me back to the Coast."

Abdu gaped at him. "My friend! You ran afoul of *al-Mukhtar*? Are you *quite* sure this escape isn't some sort of trap?" And he gave Soraya a distrustful glance.

John hesitated. "Not entirely sure, no."

Abdu threw up his hands. "Oh, God."

"Don't worry." Soraya spoke directly to the merchant, disregarding etiquette. "It's not a trap. But we'd best put as much distance as possible between ourselves and Cairo before al-Ashraf manages to set hunters on our tracks."

That hardly seemed to comfort the merchant. John cleared his throat. "You said the Master had sent a message for me. You've been to Acre, then?"

Abdu expanded. "The story," he said, "is as follows. We arrived at Acre after five days' sailing—no. I will come to the point. The Master informs you that your work in Cairo is done. You're to go at once to Beirut, where you'll report to the Lady Eschiva and the Temple commandery there."

Soraya sniffed. "The Temple wants you back in its wallet very suddenly," she said to John. "I suppose they have the same ideas as Lady Eschiva."

John recalled how anxious Beaujeu had been to secure the help of Katsaros, the old man whom Lilith had used as her mouthpiece in Tripoli. "I suppose he imagines that if I can save Beirut, I can save Acre as well."

"What's the matter?" Soraya taunted him. "You don't like being used as a tool by the powerful?"

John took the gibe without complaint. "Thank you, my friend, and farewell," he told Abdu. "I would say, until we meet again—but I doubt we have such days of peace in store."

* * *

A ship would take them north up the swiftly-flowing Nile at a little past noon. With several hours to pass, John and Soraya shut themselves inside the room they had hired, and while Soraya kept watch, John wrapped himself in his mantle for sleep.

He seemed barely to have closed his eyes when Rahel appeared in his dream.

"John," she greeted him. "What news, beloved?"

The room was warm and close, filled like a globe with warm sunlight that shone through the parchment-covered window like a lamp. Soraya sat cross-legged with her back against the door, eyes closed. John's dreamself rose to his knees and drank in his fill of Rahel's wistful face. In the light he saw for the first time that the dark waves of her hair were rimed a little with silver strands.

At the sight, he wanted to break down. "No news but bad," he said. "I failed. Again."

"Tell me," she said, softly.

He did: it was the best comfort he could find. "Everything I touch turns to evil," he ended. "I thought I was killing Khalil, but I brought about the death of two men I never intended to harm."

Rahel said nothing; only she watched him with troubled eyes, as though she knew there was more to be said.

"That isn't the worst of it," he acknowledged. "When our plans went awry, Nufir turned to heaven. What did I do? I tried to kill a man. I thought I was a child of heaven, but it turns out that I am only a tool of Qeteb's."

"He *did* warn you not to use his own weapons against him," Soraya said, from her place near the door. John jumped. She opened her eyes and said, "Yes, I *can* walk in the world of the spirit, just as you do. Is this your wife?"

"Peace be upon you, Soraya," Rahel said warmly. "It is good to see you again, whatever the circumstances."

"Again?" Soraya blinked. "Have we met?"

"You will remember it one day," Rahel told her. "Take heart. This is no empty prophecy, but true."

There was sometimes in the words of Rahel the Messenger an authority like that of the oracles of God. Soraya made no sound or movement, but she must have felt that absolute certainty: there were suddenly tears rolling silently down her face. She bowed her head.

"The Lance was made by the power of Qeteb," John added. "Of course it could not be used against him."

"The Lance? That's the least of it." Soraya wiped her sleeve across her eyes and sent John a weary look. "He was tempting you and you succumbed—tempting you to seize power. That's what he's the demon of, after all: *order*. And you have no defence against that."

"I thought so," Rahel said. "We've been looking at it all wrong. Even at Oliveta, we debated whether or not we should be kind to those under our command. We never stopped to ask whether—"

"—whether we ought to be in command at all," John finished, glumly. For a long moment none of them spoke. Was Soraya right? he asked himself. If he was truly sorry for what he'd done, for how he'd carried out the emperor's persecutions, would he be trying to return to make himself a ruler once more?

"No," he said in a thick voice. "*Someone* must be in command. It is the way of the world. If not Christians, then who? I have seen what has happened to the Copts—their endurance is great, but so is their suffering. I was there when the Persians took Jerusalem and slaughtered the priests, calling them agents of the Roman emperor."

"Christians will be treated as imperial agents so long as we demand—and receive—preferential treatment from the empire," Rahel said softly. "But what if we broke that bond?"

"The bond *cannot* break," John pleaded. "What of Christ's kingdom? Aren't the saints meant to judge the world?"

"*His kingdom is an everlasting kingdom, and his dominion endureth throughout all generations,*" Rahel recited softly. "But have you forgotten that it is a kingdom not from this world, not built by human hands? If we rule, it is not rulership as the world understands it, dominating each other, even for good."

It sounded a great deal like what Soraya had told him. It sounded dangerous. It sounded terrifying.

"Will that kind of power protect us from armed and mounted knights?" he asked.

Soraya sniffed, derisive. "Surely the better question would be whether it might protect you from Qeteb."

With that she got up and left the room. Perhaps it was the question, or perhaps it was the slam of the door behind her. John's sleeping body awoke, dragging him too soon from an unrestful sleep. He sat up, rubbing his gritty eyes. Rahel's words seemed foolish to him—but was not the foolishness of God wiser than the wisdom of men? And how could he tell her that she was wrong, when Qeteb had so easily mastered him?

Chapter XXXIII.

Soraya returned to the room two hours later with food: taamiya balls and halwa. She had spent the intervening time in the shape of a hawk, riding the winds far above where she could keep a sharp eye not only on the caravanserai but also the network of roads leading between Cairo and the ruined port. She had seen the dust-clouds of riders creeping from the capital towards the camp and some of the more important outlying towns—no doubt Khalil's agents and rivals tightening their grip on the reins of power. But she had hoped, none of the messengers had yet bothered with Fustat.

She tried not to think about the fact that now, while Khalil was preoccupied with the succession, would have been the perfect time to stage a second attack on him and Qeteb. But of course it was no use making an attempt when they had no exorcist, and al-Mukhtar would never have permitted it. Perhaps it was not in his interest to let her bring about his father's downfall; only to keep them all tumbling in the balance like juggling-balls while he tried to repair his wife's fate.

Can I not be loved so much? she had asked, but another wistful part of her said, *For whom should he burn the world, if not his own wife?*

Now, returning to the small room where she had left John, Soraya felt herself in a more resigned mood. There was no point in blaming others for doing what was only natural to all men.

"Eat," she announced, entering the room and setting the cheap tin plate on the floor before him. John sat gazing into the air; he startled a little when she spoke, like a man coming out of a dream.

"There's something I ought to tell you," he said.

Oh no, Soraya thought. She sat down facing him and took up one of the taamiya balls. "Go on, then."

John's gaze fell to the plate. "I first met you in the reign of the emperor Heraclius," he said, "at the defeat of Yarmouk, when you helped me to steal Khalil's Lance from him. You helped me to do that for the sake of a vow which I made, promising to break the Lance and set you free once the battle was done. It was a vow I wilfully did not keep. And because of my sin, you have endured more than six centuries of servitude."

Soraya lowered the food from her lips. In her state of mind it would only taste of dust and ashes. "Why are you telling me this? Do you mean to taunt me with what I have lost?"

"No," he said, hunching a little with shame. His pale silver eyes were intent in his sun-browned face. "I mean to tell you that I am sorry. I truly meant to do you good, but I only ever thought of you as a child and not an equal… I dare not ask forgiveness. Only the chance to make amends, by serving you as you desire."

Soraya had never heard a man deliver such an apology—never to an inferior, never to a woman. For a moment she was torn between wonder and outrage. "It's too late to make amends," she said, but her voice betrayed as much sadness as wrath. "The opportunity has passed. You cannot free me now."

"Lady Eschiva wants me to revive the Watchers of Beirut," John said heavily. "No doubt one of them will be able to handle Qeteb."

"It's no use unless we have Saif at our side, ready to break the Lance," she told him. John made no answer.

Neither of them had touched the food. She took out a clean cloth to wrap it in. "Come. We're expected aboard our ship."

They muffled their faces and ventured out. Soraya's whole body felt leaden and tired, bowed down by the sheer weight of her disappointment. All the rage had gone out of her, leaving her an empty husk. The trouble of it all was that she truly believed him to be sincere. In his own way, John Bessarion loved her and wished to help her. And yet he could not, because he had no notion how to love without ruling.

They had left the caravanserai courtyard and ventured into the street beyond when a shout was raised behind them, ordering them to stop. Soraya threw a glance over her shoulder and saw two mamluks in al-Ashraf's livery spurring their horses into a trot.

"Son of a shoe," Soraya muttered, catching John's hand. It was just her luck that the new sultan's men should have arrived at the moment she stopped watching the roads. "Run!"

They slipped down the nearest alleyway. The port's streets were narrow and ill-planned, winding between the rubble-heaps that were all that remained of the old city.

Soraya threw a glance over her shoulder, seeing one of the mamluks dismount to follow them on foot. The other was nowhere to be seen.

"This way." John pointed down a narrow gap that had opened between two high walls. Fustat still boasted one or two buildings that had escaped the blaze, including a pair of towering tenements at least ten floors high. To Soraya, the dark passage smelled like a trap: there could be no way out but ahead. But it was already too late. John plunged into the darkness, running for the glimpse of open sky, palm-fronds, and ship-masts that glowed in the midday sunlight at the far end.

They were within five strides of the opening when the light dimmed. Ahead, the second mamluk appeared atop his horse, his sword drawn, awaiting them.

John flowed smoothly from a run into a watchful crouch, but despite the armour with which Saif had supplied him, he still lacked a weapon. Soraya turned, throwing a glance behind her. Sure enough, their dismounted pursuer had come to the other end of the alley and was advancing upon them. She threw a despairing glance upwards at the blue stripe of sky above, knowing that despite all her strength she could barely climb that sheer gorge alone, never mind carrying John with her. And Saif had commanded her not to leave him.

A shadow blinked across that distant blue slash. Soraya gasped, and her hands fastened on John's sleeve even as he coiled to spring.

"Wait," she hissed. There was a sickening pull on the soul tether, which nearly dragged her from her mortal body. Then a dark thunderbolt fell from the sky above. Horse and man fell as though poleaxed and rolled away from the opening. John made a muffled sound of terror.

"Now," Soraya said, through her dizziness.

They staggered through the opening and found themselves on the lush river-bank, dazzling in the glare of the noonday sun. The quays were downriver, a little to the right. The mamluk and his horse lay twitching athwart the path, a splash of bright blood forming a pool beneath the man's cut throat. Neither man nor beast were quite dead, but surely would be within moments.

There was no sign of the attacker, unless he had vanished in at one of the dark, open windows that gave onto the river-front. Soraya glanced into the darkness from which they had emerged and saw the dismounted mamluk go down with a faint cry beneath the tigerish leap of the same dark shadow.

"It's *him,*" Soraya breathed. "Go, go, go."

They arrived at their ship just as the captain was preparing to cast off. A hut stood on the deck; Soraya dragged John behind it to hide, before allowing herself to slide into a crouch and recover her breath.

John dropped beside her. "Al-Mukhtar?" he panted.

Soraya shuddered, thinking of that ten-storey drop. "Who else?"

"Then there's no hope at all," he muttered.

All Soraya had been able to think, in the moment she saw Saif falling like a thunderbolt from the sky, was that she must not allow him near enough to countermand her previous orders. She realised now how foolish that fear had been. "If he wanted to recapture us, he'd only have to drag me back along the soul tether and then give me new orders."

"Then why hasn't he done it?" John muttered. "Is he still trying to force his father's hand?"

"No," Soraya said. There was an unaccustomed taste in her mouth: hope. "There isn't a chance. If Khalil is sending his mamluks after us, it can only mean that he knows Saif defied him by releasing us. Yet he's still protecting us."

John hummed quietly. After a moment he reached into his robe and withdrew the crumbly packet of halwa which had slipped her mind as they left their rooms at the caravanserai. Thoughtfully, methodically, he unwrapped it and offered Soraya a piece. As in Heliopolis, the taste of the sweet flooded her heart with emotion; yet this time there was less of longing, and more of happiness to it.

She did not know whether she trusted the feeling.

"You think he's changed sides?" John asked, at length, when the halwa was eaten. His voice was almost incredulous.

"There's no going back from this. I just don't know whether Saif knows it yet." Suddenly it felt as though her heart might burst. She pressed a hand to her chest.

"What is it?" John asked. "Is he pulling on the soul tether?"

"No," she said, dropping her hand. "It's nothing." Saif had resisted with all his might, but perhaps at last he was behaving as the friend he had always claimed to be. She should not feel as though two broken halves of herself were coming together again. She should not imagine that she could be whole.

"He's still a killer," John said, watching her. "He still lied to you and used you."

"Do you think I need reminding?" she snapped. "But this is still to our advantage. As long as Saif has the Lance, we need him on our side."

Chapter XXXIV.

Two days later, in the port town of Damietta, their shadow returned. John and a heavily-disguised Soraya were returning to their caravanserai after an unprofitable trip to the quays. Because of the impending siege no Egyptian ships, fast or otherwise, were travelling to Acre. The streets were busy, but Soraya, adapting her eyes to the darkness, nudged John with an elbow.

"Up on the rooves," she whispered. "Saif is following us."

"Let him," John said. He unclenched his jaw with an effort. "If we can't go north by ship from Damietta, we must walk west, to Alexandria, and find passage on an Italian vessel. If al-Mukhtar wants to speak with us, he can do it on the road."

They set out the next morning on the Alexandria road. There they would be able to find Christian merchants in plenty, since it was the only port in Egypt where their ships were permitted to dock. The land lay quiet and expectant, waiting for the sultan's army on its northward march. No one this far north had yet heard of Qalawun's death. There was no sign of any follower on the road; yet when John woke at dawn the next morning and made a circuit of the camp, there were a set of footprints muddling the dust at the foot of one of the palm trees that grew by the wayside well—footprints which certainly had not been there on the evening before.

Soraya growled when she saw them. "I'll keep watch tonight with a cat's eyes, not a woman's."

They continued their journey between sea and land—the land on their left, sandy and speckled with shrubs and palm trees; the sea on their right, an intense blue that shone brightly enough to make mortal eyes ache. The monotony of the road was broken only by the cisterns that had been built to mark the road. Walking was warm work, even at the threshold of winter. They passed a caravan hastening from Rexi and found themselves once more in solitude.

That night, having kindled their fire and eaten their slim ration of bread and dates, Soraya sat with her back to the blaze looking back the way they had come. Her eyes scanned the shadows without ceasing; she told him of the passing creatures she saw, jackals and owls like grey shadows.

On Soraya's orders, John was whittling at a dry block of wood. "Anti-magic," she had told him. "This will prevent Qeteb listening in." He did not understand why this was supposed to work, but he recognised that she must know better than himself.

It was a different thing that he was compelled to question.

"Are you sure about al-Mukhtar?" he asked.

Soraya scowled into the darkness. "What's the point of doubting him, when there's nothing we can do to free me without him?"

"Agreed." John hesitated before continuing. "Do you think he's truly capable of helping us? Couldn't we take the Lance from him and hide it until it's ready to be destroyed?"

Soraya scowled. "You're forgetting that I am bound to him, and that it is bound to me. No! Better to have his help."

Silence followed; John wondered whether to recall her to his true question. Then she added more slowly, "Saif has done great evil all his life. If there's now even the slightest chance that he might leave his father's service, shouldn't we do what we can to help him?"

John considered this for a long moment. If it had been anyone else, he would have been the first to agree with her. Devil take it, he would have been the first to make that precise argument. But this was Khalil's son, Khalil's *tool*. *If a man does evil deeds,* he thought, *doesn't that make him evil by nature?*

With what judgment ye judge, ye shall be judged, another thought told him, *and with what measure ye mete, it shall be measured to you again.*

John shuddered, knowing that this was a test he himself could not abide.

Instead he said, almost accusingly, "You are fond of him, aren't you? You *want* him to change."

"I'm fond of you, too," she growled. "Hush, now: he's coming."

"Should I try to get behind him?"

"No, I'll do that. *You* keep working." She got up, but after a moment sighed and said, "There's hope for him, I know it. He *sees* that Khalil oppresses him. He just doesn't know yet what to do about it."

With that, she circled the fire and melted into the darkness. John continued to work, as he had been told; the knife he had purchased in Damietta scraped at the wood, crafting a hair-pin, the image of one Rahel had often worn.

Soraya was right. Deep down, he knew that the instinct to punish al-Mukhtar was part of the same disastrous temptation that had driven him to fling the Lance at Khalil.

It was a temptation he must resist, so that one day, when he faced Qeteb again, he would not fail.

* * *

With John working steadily at his task, Soraya took a great circle into the night, always keeping her eyes on the pale shape that had seated itself at the foot of a palm-tree half a bow-shot from the campfire. Shifting into the form of a snake, Soraya crept up on her master out of the dark. He did not know she was there until she whipped up a dust-cloud and reached newly-formed fingers around his throat. He gave a strangled noise as she pressed her thumbs against his windpipe and the vocal cords beneath.

"Do you come in peace, al-Mukhtar Saif al-Din?" she whispered into his ear. With her cat's eyes, she could see his hands raised in token of submission. The Lance lay on the ground between them. If he reached for it or tried to draw a knife, she would squeeze the voice from his throat, at least for as long as it took her to escape beyond hearing.

Soraya was desperately tired of being commanded. But Saif neither reached for a knife nor tried to speak. Instead, he only nodded.

"Into the light," she said, releasing him. He did not try to countermand her then, either, simply preceding her meekly to the campfire.

"Keep working," Soraya told John, when he heard their approach and rose to his feet.

He obeyed, but did not relax or resume his seat. The three of them shifted to stand equidistant about the fire, wary and distrustful.

John's gaze shifted from his work to Saif's face. "Why do you follow us, al-Mukhtar? Are you with us or against us?"

Saif's jaw worked, and he held up the Lance. "We had a task to complete," he said.

"If you meant to help us, why not join us openly?" Soraya put in. "Do you still deceive yourself? Do you think you have a future with Khalil?"

"Do you plan to carry us back to him when he promises to release your wife?" John put in.

Saif swallowed. A resinous stick of wood on the fire snapped, sending a shower of sparks into the air. Shadows danced across his face.

"Answer him," Soraya said.

Saif looked at John almost pleadingly. "You understand that a man must put his own blood above any other consideration."

It was time for John to look uncomfortable, but he answered steadily: "Not if it means treating another person as a *thing*. If you want our help, we will give it. But we won't be your bargaining-pieces."

He said it as though he meant it. Soraya wanted, so much, to believe that he did mean it. She swallowed hard and said, "Make your choice, Saif. Throw in your lot with us. Be free of him. We can help you."

His gentle face became stubborn. "What, side openly with *you*? Then I might as well bid my Ghaliyah farewell."

This part, Soraya had determined as she and John walked the long road through the desert. She put out her hand. "Then give us a different guarantee. Give us the Lance."

Saif's hands clenched possessively on the weapon. "He'll *know*."

John slid Soraya an eloquent look. She set her lips. "He already knows, surely, or he'd never have sent his mamluks after us."

"I told him you'd had help escaping," Saif said. "I told him I'd go after you. If I return without the Lance, he'll *know*. And I'll be defenceless."

"It will be for a few weeks only," John put in, quietly calm and confident, as ever. "In Beirut we will find a Watcher to cast out Qeteb. We'll break the Lance the moment the thing is done. It's up to you to prevent Khalil recalling Qeteb. After that it won't matter *what* he knows or doesn't know—and you'll have your Ghaliyah back, for what remains of her life."

Saif's hands were white on the Lance's haft, and his face was sheer naked yearning.

"But he's my *father*," he pleaded.

"No he isn't," Soraya said. "He may have sired you, but he *chose* to own you as his slave, not as his son."

"Be *quiet*," Saif snapped. Soraya's lips sealed. Saif turned his back on them, but didn't move away from the fire. His shoulders heaved.

Soraya sent John a look of fury, indicating her stopped mouth. John said, very mildly, "That was unmannerly, Saif. Among friends, we *ask*, we don't command."

"I'm sorry," Saif muttered, and Soraya felt the lock on her mouth loosen. He added, "I don't know what to *do*. Will *you* guide me when al-Ashraf is gone? You, John Bessarion, a polytheist who does not know the truth? Or *you*, Soraya, who know the truth but live as you please?"

"If your father had any regard for the truth," said John, "would he have lied to you all your life?"

Saif turned towards them again. His throat worked. "It is permissible to lie in the service of greater ends."

Soraya snorted. "It was he who told you that, wasn't it?"

Saif flushed.

"That's his fatal miscalculation," John added, sadly. "People cannot be forced into belief. Hearts cannot be changed by a king's decree. But force is all Khalil knows. That idea lost me an empire, centuries ago. It will cost him his kingdom, too."

Saif put a hand to his face. "No—it will be my fault if the kingdom is lost. What impiety is this? Soraya was right. My love for Ghaliyah has sent me mad."

He seemed to be speaking more to himself than to them. Soraya could not help pitying him. If he had deceived her, he had been in turn deceived by Khalil. If he had oppressed her, he had been oppressed himself, too.

"You have your silver bowl, don't you?" she asked, softly. "Khalil must be expecting a report from you soon. Call him up. Tell him what you have learned. Ask him why he withheld the truth from you. I'm sure he must have his reasons."

Saif looked at her, aghast. "He'll be angry that I doubted him."

Soraya shrugged. "If it was a son of yours, wouldn't you rather he come to you for an explanation?"

"Yes, but…" Saif's voice trailed off and he glanced up at the sky above, where the waxing moon was little more than a bright patch behind the clouds . "Oh, God," he said helplessly, and then he picked up the bowl and walked away from the firelight, into the scrub. Soraya readjusted her eyes, watching his grey figure bend down and kneel. Khalil must have been waiting, for within a few moments, a gleam of silvery light flashed in the darkness.

Soraya turned back to the fire to find John watching her quizzically.

"Was that wise?" he asked.

She let out a snort. "Saif is only feeling guilty because Khalil isn't at *present* giving him any nonsense. Give them a little time together. You'll see."

Chapter XXXV.

"Where have you been?" Saif's master demanded. "Do you think I have nothing better to do with my time than wait on your reports?"

"I'm sorry," Saif said, humbly. It was a bad beginning to the conversation. "The stars are hidden; I had to guess at the time."

"Then you should have been early," al-Ashraf said. "Now that I'm sultan, I have hourly rituals to perform. People to arrest. Other reports to hear."

His father's—his master's—eyes kept flickering from the connection to something in his hands. He gave an irritable flick, and a white speck went flying through the air. Saif glimpsed a small knife and a piece of wood and realised, with a sense midway between awe and hilarity, that al-Ashraf Khalil was performing antimagic.

Antimagic, and hourly rituals. Was he so frightened of Qeteb?

"It's a nightmare," Khalil finished, irritably. "Have you found John Bessarion yet?"

Saif forced himself not to glance in the direction of the campfire. "I'm working on it, my lord."

"You're taking too long. I need you back in Cairo. Turuntay is popular with my father's mamluks, and I don't know whom I can rely upon for support. I don't care what the difficulty is; kill the Bessarion and return to Cairo."

Saif swallowed hard, tempted to do as he always had done—to obey at once and return with Soraya in tow. But that would not help him recover Ghaliyah. Nor would it show his father that he had grown old enough, now, to merit the truth.

"I can't, my lord," he said, so quietly that he almost hoped his master had not heard.

Khalil's hands stopped working abruptly. "You *can't?* What's the matter? You've never lost a trail before."

Saif cleared his throat unhappily. "I haven't lost it now. John Bessarion is sitting within a stone's throw of me."

There was a long silence, and then Khalil said, dangerously soft: *"What has he told you?"*

"Nothing," Saif said. Suddenly, the words came out in a torrent. "It's Ghaliyah. I asked you to give her back to me, and you refused. She isn't a passing fancy, my lord. I want her back."

There was a long silence. Khalil's jaw twitched. "Come back to Cairo," he said softly, "and we'll talk about it."

"Then it's true. You mean never to free her."

His father made no reply.

Saif's heart sank into his guts. What could he say? *You lied to me?* His father would ask what duty he had to confide in such an unprofitable servant.

Soraya's advice, which had seemed so good a moment ago, seemed useless now.

"I don't doubt that you have your reasons," he said, humbly. "I have never asked for anything else. I have always counted myself happier as your slave than as the son of the emperor of Tartary. I only ask one thing—that you'll give me back my wife. Let me watch over her for what is left of her life, and I'll serve you faithfully ever after."

"Spoken like a true and loyal servant," Khalil said, and although his face and his tone were stiff, Saif thought he might die happy now that he had heard these words with his own ears. "Come back to Cairo, Saif. Bring the Bessarion, or what's left of him. Then we'll discuss whatever you want."

Saif opened his mouth to agree, but at that moment he sensed a hovering presence and looked up with a start to see Soraya standing over him.

"No," she said, boldly. "The truth, *now.* Otherwise maybe you'll never see the three of us again."

"Why is she out of the Lance?" Khalil asked Saif wearily. "I don't have time for this. I told you that I have a ritual to perform every hour. The slightest deviation, the least oversight, could destroy me."

"Good," Soraya said. "Then you'll just have to keep it short and honest."

Khalil scowled, and the approving words from a moment ago sounded suddenly hollow and unconvincing in Saif's memory. His father had called him a fool, a boy, a weapon that could be discarded if it proved to be more trouble than it was worth.

"Please," he whispered, begging for—he did not know what.

Khalil sighed. "Turuntay's rebellion is the least of my worries. The Hairy One means to rise against me, as you know—and Ghaliyah is the only one who can stop him. I cannot let her out of my hands, even for you."

All Saif wanted was Ghaliyah. And all al-Ashraf Khalil wanted was protection from the afrit he had summoned and to which he clung, stubbornly, for the sake of power.

Perhaps it was wrong of him, but Saif was tired of suffering for the sake of his master's power.

"Come back to Cairo," Khalil repeated for the third time. "We will make a new bargain, you and I. What is it that you wish? Turuntay's post as na'ib? Formal adoption as my heir?"

Abruptly, the clamour in Saif's mind stilled. His whole body went cold. "Your *heir*," he whispered. "You would do all this for me?"

"All this and more. Why not? As sultan, there is nothing I cannot offer you." Khalil paused. A smile touched his lips, but not his eyes. "I like the idea of adoption," he said. "You know that I have always considered you as my son."

"How can you?" Saif asked, nearly choking on the words. He was so angry, he barely saw the widening of Khalil's eyes. "I *am* your son!"

His shout rang in the still air; not far away, some nocturnal animal, frightened by the noise, rush away with a scrabble of paws. Saif barely heard.

"I am your *son*," he repeated, "and you took *everything* from me. My name. My wife. My memories. I never even knew my *mother*."

Khalil made no reply. Above Saif, Soraya stood like a demon goddess, her arms folded and her face set in a mask of grim triumph. Yet he had no anger to spare for her tempting words which had drawn him into this trap. All his soul was taken up with rage at Khalil.

"You've always told me how kind you are," he rasped. "How much I should thank you for taking me in when my own father sold me. You've only ever taken from me, and taken, and taken. My memories, my mother… God forbid—*do I have children?* Has Ghaliyah ever borne me a son? How should I know?"

"You have neither son nor daughter," Khalil said, coldly flicking another chip from his wood-carving. "Calm yourself."

"I am calm," he retorted. It was not the truth, but what of it? Khalil lied all the time. Saif gasped for air. "All right," he said. "I thank you for one thing, at least: that you'll keep Ghaliyah alive and safe for as long as she will be of *use* to you. As for me, I'll be going to the Coast. And I'll be taking the Lance with me."

"Wait—*Saif!*" Khalil thundered, but it was too late. Saif picked up the bowl and upended it on the ground. The water spattered his feet.

Saif sat with his hand splayed across the bowl's foot, breathing hard and trembling.

Above him, Soraya took a long, deep breath.

"*To* him, Saif! Well said!"

Her voice was fierce, exultant. Saif could not bear it. He buried his face in his hands and sobbed like the child he had always been.

Chapter XXXVI.

John caught his first glimpse of Beirut from the deck of the fast nava which took them north from Acre. After the weeks he had spent in Egypt, the landscape was a riot of startlingly cool colours—purple mountains and green slopes beneath blue-tinged fortresses of clouds. Against this backdrop the city glowed like an opal—honey-coloured stone, whitewashed walls, and domes of turquoise and gold. As the ship approached the harbour, John remained at the rail drinking in the sight of warehouses, tenements, and churches. There was a great basilica at the heart of the city. John's eyes fastened upon it with a professional interest; and then understanding ran through him like the first bite of a snow-cooled fruit on a hot summer's day.

The Beirut merchant who owned the ship stood nearby, watching his home drift nearer. John turned to him, pointing.

"That *dome*," he breathed.

"That's the cathedral," the merchant said, nodding. "The Old Lord John of Ibelin built it, modelled on the Hagia Sophia."

John could see that. The immense dome was poised gracefully on a curving arcade of windows, allowing light to penetrate the interior from any angle. Calculating the massive weight that must be balanced so delicately upon that thin row of pillars, John felt his scalp prickle with wonder. It ought to be impossible. That secret was lost.

"I must see it nearer," he said. His curiosity grew. Who had this Old Lord been, this powerful Prester who built impossible things?

"You'd best hurry, then," the merchant said drily. "They're saying that the sultan's death has only postponed the invasion, not prevented it altogether. That's why I'm clearing out my warehouses and moving my goods to Cyprus."

Deeming it wise to put off his visit to the basilica until he had spoken to the Lady, John called Saif and Soraya to disembark. Their way was not hard to find. The citadel, a grey watchtower, loomed over the harbour on a rugged promontory of rock. The newer palace was visible as a white arcade of round arches lining the wall leading to the tower. A terrace beneath the arches held what seemed to be a garden. John breathed in the scent of citrus and was reminded suddenly, painfully, of Tripoli before the sack.

He felt in that moment that he must at any cost try to save this city.

John and his companions were quickly admitted to the courtyard of the palace, a compact ring of stables, storehouses, and barracks at the landward end of the fortress. When he told the porter at the inner gate that he had come to see the Lady, however, the man looked him up and down with suspicion. Indeed, his dusty clothing and the blue turban that marked him out as a traveller from the sultan's lands must have done little to recommend him. Nor could his companions have inspired much confidence. Saif had appeared downhearted and sullen ever since the conversation in the desert. Soraya, on the other hand, was loudly calling his attention to the bit of wall the two of them had scaled to infiltrate the palace on a previous occasion. Both, even more than himself, were visibly Saracen.

"Tell the Lady that John Bessarion is here," John told the porter, pushing up his sleeve to show the Watcher's Mark tattooed there.

"I can't bother the Lady at this hour," said the porter. "Come to the basilica tomorrow morning and you may have the chance to petition her."

"But she's expecting us," John protested.

"What seems to be the matter?" a voice asked, and John turned to see a tall, dark-haired man in rich clothing.

"Prince Balian," the porter said, bowing. "This fellow demands to see the Lady. Perhaps you can find out what he wants."

The prince beckoned grandly. "Follow me. I'll speak to the Lady on your behalf."

Sending Soraya a quelling look, John followed, the prince's knights bringing up the rear.

The steps led to a long arcade that looked down upon the harbour—the same row of white arches they had seen from the ship. From this vantage, John could see down into a garden, lush and green, scented with herbs and citrus. There was a huge old orange-tree at the far end, and there, walking across the grass with their heads bowed close together, were two women he recognised. John hesitated, wondering whether he should call out to the Lady, but a servant threw open a massive door on his right.

"Wait in the audience-hall," Prince Balian directed. "I will see you shortly."

A glimpse of the interior drove all thought of the Lady from John's head and he entered the room with a breath caught on wonder.

It was less like entering a hall, than a garden. Two high galleries of windows marched down either side of the hall, filling it with light and soft breezes and the scent of citrus. A stream of water issued from the wall at one end, falling into a shallow channel that delivered it into an octagonal pool beneath the high central cupola. At the centre of the pool was a fountain where the porphyry image of a dragon reared up, lifting a threatening claw, as the water bubbled from between its jaws. Its segmented tail lashed to and fro, driven by the fall of the water.

John's mouth went dry; he felt that he had wandered into Paradise before the Fall. The hall was alive with shifting light reflected from the fountain. The floor was made of a softly-coloured marble, split by skilled masons into panels whose mirrored patterns resembled the ripples of water, so that John felt though he trod across the surface of a clear sea. More vivid red-and-white marble revetments upon the wall resembled silk curtaining. The basin of the fountain itself was a mosaic of intricate geometric knotwork, so that the water ran without ceasing over the flowers of a deathless meadow. Mighty pillars upheld the groin-vaulted roof, the central dome of which was painted in concentric rings: at the centre was the Sun in his chariot, surrounded by allegorical figures representing the minutes, the hours, the signs of the Zodiac and the four winds.

Beyond the fountain, separated by the stream from the great doors, stood an empty chair. In that hall, it seemed that all of heaven and earth came to wait upon the great Ibelin lords of Beirut. John turned from it, once again marvelling at the wealth, the power, the sheer beauty of what the Old Lord had built.

Al-Mukhtar and Soraya, too, were wide-eyed at the sight. "I'm walking on water," Soraya breathed, smoothing a toe across the floor.

"We developed that technique in Constantinople," John said, absent-mindedly. "But I've never seen anything like the dome. One could calculate any time down to the minute."

Al-Mukhtar stirred himself from his apathy long enough to say, "We have ceilings like this in Cairo. Astrologers sometimes find them useful, but an astrolabe is better."

Apart from the ceiling, John thought, it was very like the basilica in Rahel's vision. The arches of the doors, the towering pillars—those were Frankish. The light-and-dark banded stonework of the castle's exterior was the work of Christian Syrian stonecutters. The painted ceiling, and the geometrically intense starbursts on the carved wooden doors, must have been done by Saracen craftsmen. The place was not just a declaration of the power of the lords of Ibelin: it was, far more deeply, a harmonious blending of East and West, of Frank and Saracen.

John felt that his heart had stopped, leaving him suspended like a fly in amber. This—*this* was the future Rahel had envisioned: this blending of different peoples, this fruitful mixing of arts…this wrenching away of his own dominion.

No, he thought. He was meant to go *home*. If he did not go home, then how would any of this be possible? None of this could be built without the secret he carried safe in his wallet. Without that secret, a dome so immense would collapse like wet paper in any of the earthquakes to which Syria was prone.

Still, he had to be certain. Putting a hand to the dagger he carried, John hurried to the door again. It wouldn't take much; only a little testing of the cement binding together that lovely *ablaq* stonework.

A moment before he crossed the threshold, the November day was grey and overcast. The moment after, it was sunny and warm. John stopped, his errand forgotten.

It was as though he'd walked straight into a vision. He stood still in the palace loggia, looking down upon the harbour of Beirut; but the city was smaller now, the dome of its basilica a tangle of half-completed scaffolding. A cluster of workmen with their cranes and engines were visible at the far end of the loggia, the tapping of their hammers ringing harshly in the morning air. In the terrace below, the earth was being tilled and raked, planted with bushes and tender saplings.

To his left, a familiar voice spoke in delight and wonder.

"John! It's *beautiful.*"

John turned and saw his daughter, Marta.

Last time he saw her, she had been a delicate girl of fourteen, all dark eyes and banked inner fire. Now he saw her as a grown woman; not tall, but wiry and vigorous. She was older than him now, and the hair which had once been thick and black now shone like silver above the black eyes and brows, and the smooth olive skin of her face.

She had still that banked inner fire, but there was both mirth and strength in her eyes. She walked leaning on the arm of a younger man, tall and dark, whose resemblance to the Lady Eschiva suggested that this was the Old Lord himself.

"Come inside and I'll show you the stonework," he now told Marta eagerly, proving that she had not been addressing John himself.

"First we must see Ibrahim settled into his new home." Marta turned, indicating the four workmen who followed her, carrying between them on a frame of crossed sticks a wooden tub in which grew a young orange-tree. "Is that your garden?"

"Yes, and I have a place marked out for the tree," said the Old Lord. He came to a stop, looking down into the face of the older woman. "Are you sure about this, my sister? This is a great power. Don't you want to keep it?"

"Him. Not *it.*" A shadow fell over her face. "And no—I don't desire such power. Beware, my lord. Power is a two-edged sword, which can always be taken away and wielded against you. That would be unfortunate for you, but a tragedy for *him*. Promise me that this secret will only ever be known to you and your heirs."

"John Bessarion!" another voice called. John blinked; the bright vision faded. He stood once again in the loggia on a grey November day, and the Lady of Beirut stood before him, flanked by her attendants. "You came," she said. "I had wondered."

"Answer the Lady when she addresses you," Prince Balian demanded, as John blinked in confusion.

"Don't be unmannerly, cuz," said the Lady, in her sleepy drawl. "What is it, Bessarion? You look as though you've seen a ghost."

John swallowed hard. Perhaps he had. "My lady, was there ever a servant of your family named Marta Bessarion?"

Surprise flickered across the Lady's face. "By our Lady," she said. "You really don't know?"

Wordlessly, John shook his head.

"Marta Bessarion was known as Marta the Knight, the White Watcher. She was raised as the Old Lord's foster-sister. No?"

"The *knight?*" John shook his head. "Do you mean that she rode into *battle?*"

"Many a time. They say she was invincible. That she wielded a holy lance, blessed by the Emperor Heraclius himself. Without her the Ibelins would never have survived the great defeat."

A holy lance, or *the* Lance? John put a hand to his head. Just when he had given up seeking news of his lost children, he stumbled upon one of them. A *knight?* What could have possessed Marta to do something so reckless?

"What became of her?" he asked.

He already guessed the answer, even before the Lady replied. "After the death of Saladin, she settled in Cyprus. Her descendents live there still. Why do you ask?"

"I *saw* something," he said, unable to answer more clearly. Apparently the Lady found this a satisfactory explanation, for she went on speaking, perhaps of those very descendents—*his* descendents. John barely heard.

Marta had found a family in this time, had grown old, had died. What did it mean? Would he never find his daughter again? Never reunite his family?

"You see now why I went to so much trouble to bring you here," the Lady added. "The Old Lord had a Bessarion among his Watchers, and she saved him, woman though she was. How much more can *you* do?"

"Don't pin all your hopes on me," John begged, but his thoughts were half elsewhere. If he brought Marta back to Rahel, what would become of the Lady? What would become of this city, which he was attempting to save? Would Marta herself consent to return?

The thought tasted oddly like despair.

"God knows my hopes are faint enough," the Lady said gently. She turned towards the doorway where al-Mukhtar and Soraya waited, listening wide-eyed to their conversation. Evidently, the name of Marta the Knight was known to neither of them.

"Your friends from Cairo?" the Lady inquired, indicating the pair.

"I'll vouch for them both," John said hastily, knowing that she, too, must recall al-Mukhtar's dubious loyalties.

All the same, John's attention lingered on the Lance worn over al-Mukhtar's shoulder.

He had left the Lance in the crypt of Antioch, and now it was carried by al-Mukhtar. For the first time, it occurred to John to wonder how it had travelled from Antioch to Cairo—and which hands had wielded it along the way.

"Good," said the Lady. "Go now and rest. I'll have some rooms prepared for you. In the morning I'll summon my Watchers to council."

In Acre, John had received orders to report to the Temple commandery in Beirut: the Master, it seemed, was keen to keep him under his eye. John considered but then dismissed the thought. His journey had left him weary, and he had much to occupy his mind. There would be time enough, tomorrow, to make his report to the Temple.

Before then, tonight, he must speak to Rahel. At last he had news of one, at least, of the children.

Chapter XXXVII.

"Maybe you don't bring the formula home, John." Rahel broke a long, heavy silence. "Maybe you simply pass it to me."

"What?" John's own voice was blank with confusion. He'd spent the whole day reasoning himself back into hope. Perhaps the reason Marta had grown old in this time was merely that in this telling of the world's story, she had not been offered the opportunity to go home. Or, even if she *had* been offered the opportunity, she might have chosen to refuse it. Who was John to refuse her the choice of a life of her own making? Knight-errantry, after all, might suit her better than the life of a Roman matron. It would be a wrench to leave her here, but in this time it was plain to see that she was both happy and honoured—Rahel had shed tears when he told her this. None of it necessarily meant that *he* would not find his way home.

"If you entrust the formula to me," Rahel repeated, gently, "then you may be sure that all these things will be built, whether you find your way home or no."

"But who will build them?" John asked.

"You may need to leave that to me—and the children." Rahel angled a shimmering glance up at him. "Would that be so very bad?"

It would, he wanted to tell her. *He* was the architect. It was *he* who had magnificent plans in his mind, plans that took shape every time he was able to find a precious scrap of paper, a drop of ink. He wanted to create something as marvellous as John of Ibelin's palace, something by which the world would always remember his name.

He could not imagine surrendering that dream to anyone else, not even to Rahel.

Suddenly, Rahel stiffened. "John," she hissed. "Something is wrong. Wake up."

The tone of her voice warned him not to linger. John pulled himself back to his body and rolled from his bed.

The Lady had housed him in one of her stately rooms, the kind a lord or knight would be given. He had a whole bedstead to himself, a shocking luxury after the past months of nameless wandering. Al-Mukhtar and Soraya shared the room, too, sleeping on mats unrolled on the floor. Or at least, al-Mukhtar was sleeping. Soraya was a shadow looming in the darkness before him.

"It's *him*," she whispered, withdrawing the hand she had put out to shake him. "The Hairy One."

* * *

Soraya, a moment before, had been walking in her own dreams. She had found herself again in the great, beautiful audience hall of the Ibelin palace, gazing up at the celestial figures in the dome overhead. She knew at once that this was no ordinary dream: it was far too vivid and clear.

She turned, expecting to see John and Rahel in one of their nightly conversations. But there was no sign of them—no sound of voice, or flicker of movement.

At once she was alert, tense with fear. She turned again and saw the slow glide of a lithe body where the mechanical dragon surmounted the fountain. Soraya moved without thinking, plunging into the water and pinning the white serpent to its perch with her left hand. A blade of ice sprang from the fountain into her right.

The serpent twisted in her hand and then a moment later took the shape of a man—a djinn—taller than herself and dark as a Nubian. He looked down at her hand on his chest with eyes that had gone wide with shock. "You," he said blankly. "How can you *touch* me?"

"You!" Soraya said in the same moment, dissolving the blade of ice that had formed in her hand. She remembered now: the lady Eschiva had a djinn of her own, Qeteb's offspring… For a horrible moment she had imagined that something much worse than a fellow djinn had disturbed her sleep.

She retreated a step, but the other djinn caught her hand.

"Blessed Lady! It *is* you! Grant me a boon. Set me free. Destroy the Hairy One."

Soraya could not help it; she glanced over her shoulder to see who else he could be addressing. *Blessed Lady?* "You have mistaken me for someone else," she told him. "Set you *free?* I cannot even free myself."

"You can do it," he urged, his hands tight on hers. "You were always the stronger one. I am only his son, and he and the Poison Mother were able to destroy my body and bind me as a slave to the orange-tree. But you—"

"I have *tried,*" Soraya burst out, wrenching her hands away from the other djinn. She stepped out of the fountain and paced away, covering her face with her hands. The peace she had known the past week, the hope that came from having two friends pledged to her aid, broke like a glass vessel.

As much as she had done, as far as she had come, even her success mocked her. She was still enslaved to the Lance, and now this other djinn clasped her hands and begged her to free him. Blessed Lady? *Cursed* might have been nearer the mark. If God knew her name, it was only to punish her.

"I know what you have suffered," she said now, turning back to face Ibrahim. "Believe me, I would free you if I could. But I have *tried,* again and again, and I have only failed."

Ibrahim's attention was no longer upon her. Stiff with alarm, he raised his eyes to the high windows that let in the moonlight. The light was silver, but the arcading that admitted it was now faintly rimmed with gold.

"Try again," he said, with a shudder. "Qeteb is here. He has come for me at last."

* * *

"Qeteb?" John felt all the hairs on his body prickle and stand upright. Strife, he ought not to have spoken that name aloud. It was too *soon.* He couldn't face Qeteb when he had no Watchers. He was utterly unprepared.

Soraya gave him no time to make more preparations. "Come," she said, grabbing his hand. "I know what he wants."

Outside the full moon shone in a clear sky, edging every pillar and arch with silver. Below in the terrace, a fire raged silently at the foot of the gnarled old orange-tree which Marta the Knight had planted so many years ago. The whole tree was wreathed in flame, and the dark shape of a man stood before it.

"That doesn't look like Qeteb," John muttered, but Soraya said, "He's *here*. I can tell!"

At once she vaulted the baluster and fell like a thunderbolt into the garden.

Down the loggia, a door slammed. The Lady emerged from her own chambers. At the sight of the burning tree, she clapped a hand over her mouth in horror.

By the time Eschiva began calling for her guards, John was hot on Soraya's trail, halfway down the narrow stair leading to the garden. The tree was like a torch, casting a yellow light across the whole terrace. By its light John saw Soraya pounce and seize upon the man who stood there.

"Prince *Balian?*" John gasped, recognising the protesting man despite his undignified posture.

The Lady must have followed close behind him, for she heard what John said and brushed him aside. Her hand flew, striking the prince open-handed across the face.

"What have you *done?*" the Lady hissed,. John had not thought her capable of looking either frantic or murderous. "Devil take it, Balian! *Who put you up to this?*"

The prince sent the Lady a furious, tight-lipped glare. Soraya, seeing it, bent and whispered into his ear. He tried to wrench away from her, but she forced him to his knees, apparently without effort.

"*Answer* me!" the Lady commanded in a voice like thunder.

"This should all be *mine!*" the prince burst out. "The djinn, the lordship, all of it! He said that if I destroyed the tree the djinn would be mine!"

The *djinn?* For the first time, John saw that another silent figure had joined them, standing beside the Lady Eschiva. In shape he resembled a tall Nubian clad in rich silks, his face a mask dull with resignation.

The djinn. Marta's djinn, brought to Beirut in the form of an orange-tree. Eschiva's djinn, who had carried her to Cairo and helped to spirit him from Bektash's courtyard not once but twice.

"Who told you these things, cuz?" the Lady demanded.

The prince's face glistened with perspiration. "He said that his name was—"

Ibrahim stiffened, perhaps sensing a danger that was hidden from the rest of them. "Don't say it," he began.

Too late.

"His name was *Qeteb*."

There was a silence like death.

There was a blast of hot wind.

Streamers of yellow flame roared towards them from the dying tree. Out of the fire the Hairy One appeared, clad in full panoply of armour: in the centre of his chest his lower eye glared red through a grille of iron. The garden, the air, groaned to contain him; beneath the imprint of his foot, John half expected the terrace to crumble, falling into the sea below.

In that moment words came to him—the exorcism prayer Rahel used. *"O Eternal God, Who has redeemed the race of men from the captivity of the devil, deliver Thy servant..."*

No. That wasn't right.

"Me," he whispered, closing his eyes. *"Deliver* me *from all the workings of unclean spirits..."*

* * *

The prince collapsed, and Soraya let him, instead turning slowly to face the newcomer. Qeteb's shadow fell over them, black as ink and edged with flame. She felt the shudder that ran through all of them and concentrated in the djinn Ibrahim.

"It's time, child of mine," the afrit said, laying an arrow to his bowstring.

"Give yourself up."

Soraya felt a blaze of indignation. She might never know what Ibrahim had endured in the long years of his servitude, but she could guess. His mortal body had been destroyed, his liberty taken from him, and now he was being wrangled over by two would-be masters and the father who hungered to consume him.

It was a foolish thing to do when she could not even find her own freedom. But Soraya stepped between the other djinn and his enemy.

"Try it," she challenged Qeteb. "I'll do what I did last time, and jump down your throat. You'd like that, wouldn't you? Sacrifice is poison to one like you."

A pace away, John Bessarion had his eyes shut, whispering under his breath. Soraya hoped that it was an incantation of great power, but she could not rely on him. She had learned that lesson.

"Step aside," the great afrit said, his voice bubbling with wrath. "Don't you know that you are my slave? I can destroy you, body, and soul, as I destroyed Ibrahim."

Soraya scoffed. "You've already done all you can. Do you mean to take my memories again? It makes no difference. I'll remember who my enemy is. I *always* remember."

The shadow seethed, but did not advance. Ibrahim spoke to her in a whisper. "Don't, Blessed Lady. I'm dying anyway."

"Die if you like," she said, "but I'm not letting *him* consume you."

"We don't need to be enemies." Qeteb's voice was a hiss for her ears alone. "What if you served me willingly? What if I freed you from the Lance? Then you could make all of them your slaves. Khalil. Saif. This Bessarion."

Soraya blinked up at him, struck momentarily speechless. The afrit pointed to the grass withering beneath his feet.

"Kneel," he whispered. "Swear homage. Speak the words: *Qeteb is Lord.* No one has ever said that I do not reward those who bend the knee."

How little he knew her, if he thought such an offer could tempt her. It was that chain again, she thought, the one that bound the world. By means of that chain, each man was given leave to lord it over the ones beneath him.

And Qeteb was willing to offer her a higher place on it, not understanding that it was the chain itself that she loathed.

"Wonderful," she told him. "I am to be just as much a slave as ever; except that I am to have the privilege of enslaving others in turn? I want to be *free*. Neither serving nor mastering anyone."

"Is that all?" Qeteb smiled thinly. "I can give you *that* with a word. *My* power made that Lance. *My* power is binding you to it. How many times have you tried and failed to get free? There's no way but this. Speak your words, and I will speak mine. Then you may depart to any corner of the earth or the heavens, as free as the souls in bliss."

Soraya tried to laugh, but the sound was more like a sob. She had underestimated him, after all. If there was one way to tempt her, it was this.

"Do it," Qeteb said. "Three little words and freedom is yours. You certainly won't get it any other way."

She tried not to listen, but his voice had woken another in her head. Qeteb was right, it told her. All attempts at escape had failed, because there was no one to help her. All of them, even John Bessarion, were part of the chain. They loved it too much to give up the privileges it lent them.

She could not break the chain, but surely she could escape it. The only price would be giving up Ibrahim to capture and slavery.

A hand slipped around hers. The warm, firm pressure broke her spiralling thoughts into fragments. Soraya looked up and saw John Bessarion beside her, his eyes very gentle and sorry.

"You mustn't say it," he told her. "There is another lord, and he is not Qeteb."

"I am already lord in every way that matters," Qeteb proclaimed. "I know you, John Bessarion. You would make yourself lord in the name of your God, whatever bodies you must tread upon to do so. Whatever blood, and warfare, and chaos you must wreak upon the earth. Surely it is more righteous to withdraw than to wreak such destruction."

John's jaw flexed, as though he wished to speak but could not. He returned to his mutterings. Soraya drew a deep breath.

John had a faith that she did not. For all purposes, Qeteb *was* lord. It was her friend's touch, rather than his words, that had restored to her a clear mind and purpose.

"It doesn't matter," she said. There were tears on her face. "If I can never escape, then I will be a slave forever. But this djinn is kin to me, in servitude if not in blood. I will not abandon him."

Qeteb growled and drew his bow, his arrow pointing directly at John's heart. "This is your last chance," he told her. "Refuse a third time, and this time your mortal friend will die."

John's voice lifted, the quiet words now perceptible. *We beseech Thee, O Almighty God—peaceful, untempted King. Stretch out Thy mighty hand. In Thy watchful care look down upon us. Send down upon us a peaceful angel, a mighty angel, a guardian of soul and body that will rebuke—"*

Soraya had only time to doubt whether God knew or cared about anything that was happening in this garden, before a pillar of white-hot light sprang up on her right hand.

Then on her left.

Then to either side of the orange-tree.

Then behind her.

Light so hot she could hear it. Light so bright that she could taste it. Light that resolved as quickly as it had come into six woman-shapes, bright and fierce, winged and gigantic, their hands gripping blades of pure light. Light and wings, hair and robes streamed away from them, as though they still raced through the starry sphere of the sky. As though they must chase, tirelessly, everlastingly, just to remain in this garden.

Heaven only knew what the mortals thought of it; they had fallen to the ground in a swoon.

"Fly, Qeteb," said a voice from somewhere behind Soraya. "Your time is determined, and your days are short. Fly, and prepare for the wrath to come."

Just like that, there was only a burning orange-tree where Qeteb had been. A burning orange-tree, and six mighty women with wind in their wings who now advanced, converging upon Soraya and Ibrahim.

"God have mercy," Ibrahim whispered in a muffled voice. Soraya felt it too: the stifling weight of everything she had ever done wrong. Qeteb's threats had not frightened her half so much as the fire of these women's eyes, the scorching holiness that could unravel her being in a moment.

She put out an arm to protect Ibrahim—as though she *could* protect him from so much light and power. Seeing this, the women halted. One of them stepped forward, sheathing her sword.

"Merope," she said, putting out her hands. Tears trembled like diamonds in her eyes. "Sister. At last we meet, beyond all hope."

Merope. Soraya's lips parted, all the breath stolen from her. She had felt this bone-deep recognition only once before, when John Bessarion had greeted her. This, she knew in her guts, was a name by which she had once been known.

"Sister?" she breathed. The shining woman stood before her, waiting. Soraya backed a step, eyeing those glittering hands in doubt. If they touched her she would burn, she knew it.

"I'm half afrit," she whispered. Half earth, and half evil. "I'm no angel."

"We were the same, long ago," said another of the women. "But we were given the choice—death, or immortality. We chose immortality and were taken up into the heavens. *You* were taken up into the heavens. It has been long since you departed again, sweet sister. But we have kept your place for you, if you will have it."

Her place—in the heavens! Soraya backed another step. "Have you come to take me back?"

Seeing her terror, the woman before her lowered her hands. "Only if it pleases you," she said, and there was something so gentle, so wistful in that voice that Soraya wanted to weep. There was love shining in her eyes— neither pity nor lofty compassion, but true affection. After Qeteb's bullying ways, and the way his servants had treated her, she felt like a traveller reaching a well in a desert.

It never occurred to her to doubt that the woman could do as she promised. Whatever hold Qeteb had over Soraya, it was no match for these creatures of pure light.

Merope. Soraya. Wayward djinn, or heavenly angel. Which to be? She opened her mouth to give her assent, but shame pierced through her. It was a way of escape they had offered her, to leave the world and flee into the heavens, and in that moment it was too much like what Qeteb had offered.

The world was yet full of those who would benefit from her help. Ghaliyah. Saif. John. Ibrahim, and those few of her kin still trapped and enslaved. What good was it, to deny Qeteb the title of lord, but to fly away and leave him to his wickedness?

She glanced behind her. Ibrahim's spirit was less vivid than it had been a moment ago, as though it was burning up more quickly in this heavenly blaze than it had in the conflagration set by the mortal. He did not speak; only met her eyes with a look of terror.

"Why did I descend from the heavens?" Soraya asked.

In a way, it was no surprise when the women replied, "To rescue those of our kin still left upon the earth."

Soraya closed her eyes. "Please," she said softly, "this djinn has suffered more than me, for he remembers all of it. Take him, instead. Leave me here to do what I came to do."

The woman stepped away from her, relieving her mortal flesh a little of the intensity of her presence. "This we will gladly do, sister." She stretched out a white-hot hand to Ibrahim. "Put your hand in mine."

Ibrahim shuddered. "I cannot."

"You must."

"I will burn."

"You will burn," the woman agreed. "That is now your only hope."

"Not here, sister," said yet another of the women. Soraya marvelled that none of them seemed to take precedence over the others. "Remember the mortals."

A weak voice spoke. "Go with them, Ibrahim. You must."

The Lady now knelt with her face pressed to the ground, prostrated as though for prayer. John, beside her, had a hand pressed over his eyes. Tears trickled through his fingers.

The Lady added, "I cannot protect you, beloved, nor hide you. Go with them and be free."

"We will still hold your seat for you, our sister," Soraya was told. "There is room among the stars for all of us."

Restless, preparing to return, the bright women drifted a little in the unseen wind that bore them.

"Wait," John gasped through his trembling fingers. "Don't go. Soraya is still bound. Can you not cast out Qeteb before you go?"

"John, John," said the woman with the sheathed sword. "This world is no longer ours to rule. That task has been given to you, the heirs of Adam and Eve."

"You have your freedom," said another of the women. "We may shine. We may speak. We may even descend. But we no longer rule."

"Once we stood between God and men," said a third. "But no longer. Therefore, daughter of Beirut, do not ask us to govern or predict your fate. That is in the hands of the King Above."

"You are fading, brother," said a fourth, looking at Ibrahim. "Come away to the great dance."

"Another question," Soraya blurted out. "Why didn't you come *sooner?*"

"There is not time," said the fifth. But the sixth said, "Follow a little way with us." Catching the end of her girdle, she tossed it to Soraya. Soraya caught hold of it, startled by how little it burned her. Then it was as though a bowstring snapped, restoring the world to its right course. The women ceased in their race, and the garden hurtled away from them like a ball that has been tossed downhill.

Chapter XXXVIII.

One moment the garden had been full of impossible creatures. The next it was only two terrified mortals and the dying flames that consumed the orange-tree. John could not repress a sob of relief as the stars whisked away their kin.

Stars. And angels. And sisters. And somehow Soraya—angry, prickly, bold Soraya—was all three.

Be not forgetful to entertain strangers: for thereby some have entertained angels unawares. Not all of Soraya's scoldings could have made him feel more wretched than he did at that moment, for in his distrust of those who were strange to him, he had betrayed the only angel he had ever known.

Beside him there was a muffled sob from the Lady of Beirut. John could not see her: his eyes were still too dazzled to see anything beyond a smudge of red from the fire.

"My lady," he said, reaching out to steady her. "I'm here. It's all right. All is well."

"No, it isn't," Eschiva gasped. "I have lost my only friend, and all my power."

All the same, she found his hand and grasped it. It was there that al-Mukhtar found them a moment later.

"What's going on?" he asked, sleepily. "I woke up and saw lights outside."

"You!" the Lady exclaimed. "Where are my guards? I was shouting for them a minute ago."

"They're all asleep," al-Mukhtar said, with a voice like a shrug. "Are you hurt? Why are you on the ground?"

"Because I can't *see*," the Lady drawled. "Here, John Bessarion—help me up."

There was no way to explain to one who had not been there. Getting shakily to his feet and helping the Lady to rise, John said in the direction of al-Mukhtar, "Qeteb tried to attack the Lady's djinn. He failed, and the djinn has ascended to the heavens."

"And Soraya?" al-Mukhtar asked at once. There was a note of anxiety in his voice.

"Don't worry; she'll return presently," John said. What was it the star-woman had said to Qeteb? His days were numbered? That brought him a great sense of relief. Whatever his own faults and mistakes, at least Soraya would soon be freed.

Saif guided them up the stairs and went, at Eschiva's bidding, to rouse her guards and send them to her. As the men ran down into the garden to seize the Lady's treacherous kinsman, John retreated to the quiet of his room. A lamp burned there, its light clear enough to let him pick out the shapes of the furniture. Relieved, John let out a sigh. He had not been entirely sure that his eyes would recover.

Al-Mukhtar joined him a moment later. "This is good news," he proclaimed. "Khalil sent us to Beirut to steal the djinn and return him to his old master. Now Ibrahim is forever beyond reach. My father must now bend all his attention to one thing: protecting himself from Qeteb."

"He won't be able to do that," John said, glumly. "From what I know of Khalil, he has the same vulnerabilities I do. Qeteb can have the empire the moment he so chooses."

"Someone ought to warn him," al-Mukhtar said after a moment.

John shook his head. "Khalil had the opportunity to be free of Qeteb, and he called him back." His eyesight was still blurred, but he could see the tunic al-Mukhtar wore, black with golden spirals and starbursts ramping across it. It was odd and beautiful, and if he could see it more clearly he might be able to say more clearly what it reminded him of. "Who made that shirt?"

Al-Mukhtar looked down at it. "I don't know. I've always had it." He touched the golden embroidery. "Odd that you should ask. Tonight I dreamed that it was being woven by a woman who unravelled her work each night."

John remembered his vision of Marta, and wondered whether Ibrahim had sent al-Mukhtar a dream, also. Or perhaps the Chosen had only heard somewhere the tale of the Queen Penelope, who put off her fate by each day unravelling the shroud she was weaving for her father-in-law. Perhaps that old story had found its way into his dreams.

"It will be dawn in another hour," al-Mukhtar said, getting to his feet. "I'd better get some sleep before it's time for prayers."

"Go on," John told him, but he did not seek his bed. His mind was too full even to speak to Rahel. Instead, he ventured out again into the loggia, silent and empty now that the excitement had died down and everyone had gone back to bed. He found a bench and sat down, watching the slow dawn creep up from behind the Lebanon mountains.

He'd begged for help from the heavens, but had he really expected the heavens to answer? Had he ever really expected the heavens to answer? Was not that the reason for his desperate need to rule, which had made him so vulnerable to Qeteb?

John was still there, reflecting, an hour later when Soraya returned. He did not see where or how she came. One moment he was watching the dawn sky, and the next she settled, softly and lightly, on the bench beside him.

John watched her face, almost expecting her to be altered in some way. She was not, save for an absolute stillness that shone from her nearly as brightly as the starlight.

"Ibrahim is safe," she said. "One of my people, at least, is better off because of me."

"Soraya," he said, holding out his hand. She took it, gazing down at the pale outline of their clasped fingers.

"Thank you," she said, very softly. "Thank you for calling upon them."

"The first time I ever met you," John said, "on the battlefield at Yarmouk, you told me you were one of seven sisters. I did not imagine *which* sisters."

"I could not possibly have imagined, and now..." She bit her lip. "I still don't know what to think. Qeteb told me that I should look to him for my freedom, because there was no other way to defeat him. He was lying. Perhaps God is closer than I dreamed, and kinder than I dared to hope."

John was startled to find that her thoughts chimed so closely with his, but he said nothing. The revelation which had come to them both was still too great to put into words.

There must have been a chapel nearby, because he heard the faint distant voices of the canons singing Prime. A door opened and a yawning al-Mukhtar emerged from their room, dragging a mat with him. He faced south, threw down the mat, and began to make his prayers.

"Aren't you going to join him?" John asked after a moment.

Soraya gave a wry smile. "You know, it turns out that Saif's wrong about some things."

John laughed—softly, so as not to disturb al-Mukhtar's prayers. "Well?" he teased. "Should we go to sing Prime instead?"

"I don't know," she repeated, more solemnly. "I think you're wrong about some things, too."

John laughed, and after a moment Soraya joined him. The mountaintops were turning gilt in the light of a sun they could not yet see. John leaned his tired head back against the banded black-and-white stones of the wall. It would be a big day: he must chair the Watchers' Council. He would get up in a little while, and go to prepare in the great audience-hall where the meeting would take place. For now, he was at peace. They were both at peace—he and his immortal sister.

Chapter XXXIX.

"On second thought," Soraya said, watching two elderly Beirut merchants bicker over which of them should have the seat nearer the Lady's own chair, "I don't think we'll find what we need here."

Surveying the collection of knights, ladies, and merchant princes ringing the fountain of the audience-hall for the first meeting of the Beirut Watchers' Council, John could not help agreeing with her. This looked like a meeting of local dignitaries, not a council of true Watchers. The Lady said that she had summoned nearly all of her father's Watchers, who had been eager to come—but if the two squabbling merchants were any indication, he feared that these men would be no better able to face Qeteb than himself.

"We'll just have to do it ourselves," Soraya said, patting his shoulder. With that, she walked serenely out of the hall, the peacefulness which had come upon her that morning perfectly undiminished. John watched her go, feeling that his own peacefulness was wearing decidedly ragged.

If so, he was the only soul in the room feeling downhearted—save possibly for the Lady, who sat to his left in her imposing seat. Across the stream of water, the knights and lords of Beirut were excitedly discussing the news of Sultan's Qalawun's death, and the rumour that the invasion had been halted, the troops marched back to Cairo as the new heir tightened his grip on the reins of power. Some even spoke hopefully of a new truce with the new sultan, and a reprieve that might last years.

The Lady's mouth drew tight, and she glanced sidelong at John. "They're wrong, you know," she told him. "Al-Ashraf himself informed me that he would be riding north."

"Then we'd best begin," John told her, trying for a hope he did not feel.

The Lady clapped her hands and a hush fell upon the assembly. "My thanks for your attendance," she announced. "Since it has been many years since the last Watcher's Council was held in the lifetime of my beloved father, John the Second, it seemed good to me to ensure that this ancient custom did not lapse. To that end I have brought hither John Bessarion, formerly a Prester of Tripoli, to act as our Prester in Beirut. Prester John, we hold ourselves ready to do your commands."

John took a deep breath, unable despite the very different setting to forget what had happened at the last great Watcher's Council he had chaired. He felt guilty, too, at having allowed the Lady to describe him as a Prester of Tripoli. The only person in this room who resembled the humble, sincere Watchers who had taken him under their wing in that doomed city was the young pageboy who was pouring a glass of wine for a wealthy knight. And he was not one of the Watchers.

Ordinarily a meeting began with a prayer and a discussion of business. John found that none of the things he wished to confide to the heavens were things that could be said before this crowd, and so he simply recited the Our Father.

An expectant hush settled upon the assembly. John cleared his throat and dealt with the most pressing order of business.

"My brothers and...sister. The Lady has asked me to reconvene the Watchers of Beirut, and therefore I must give you all a reminder of what a Watchers' Council *is*. Watchers are, quite simply, a body of laymen who have committed themselves to the service of God in their secular lives. This doesn't mean that we sing and pray over our work: it means that our work itself becomes a means of serving God. Those of us who are lords must dispense the Lord's justice, and not our own. Those of us who are carpenters and shoemakers—" not that there were any carpenters, or any shoemakers, present today, but he had contemplated his words before seeing what he had to work with— "must shelter the houseless and shoe the barefooted, always bearing in mind that in doing so, we may be clothing and sheltering Christ and his angels, and that our work is holy in consequence. It is in this way that we become the salt that preserves the earth, the righteous men for lack of whom that great city, Sodom, was destroyed. My friends, do you pledge yourselves to this task?"

"We do!" cried one of the merchants. A knight said, "In token of this pledge, I will endow a new monastery to sing masses for the preservation of the city." The others murmured their approvals.

Soraya was right, John thought. These people were not the Watchers who could save Beirut. He sent a pleading glance towards the Lady, who returned it hopefully.

It was like Oliveta all over again. Yet he had promised the Lady to do what he could.

"Hear the word of the Lord, ye rulers of Sodom!" he cried out in a voice that made everyone jump. *"To what purpose is the multitude of your sacrifices unto me? Bring no more vain oblations; incense is an abomination unto me. Yea, when ye make many prayers, I will not hear: your hands are full of blood. Wash you, make you clean; put away the evil of your doings from before mine eyes; cease to do evil; learn to do well; seek judgment, relieve the oppressed, judge the fatherless, plead for the widow."*

He paused. But what could they do to him? Hang him?

He pointed at the two merchants whom he had seen squabbling earlier. "Stop wrangling for the high honours. *Do* what Our Lord commanded. Humble yourselves. Bring to God the sacrifice of a humble and contrite heart."

The merchant who had won the honour reddened, visibly indignant. For a moment there was absolute silence in the room. Although he had spoken nothing but the truth, John was left ashamed of having scolded them. They did not know him; they did not understand him. He could not make them understand in a moment.

He was hardly one to teach them how they ought to conduct themselves. He had been saying these things to himself for so many years, and had failed utterly to do them.

Sighing, he turned towards the Lady. "Is there a Messenger present? Let us hear from him."

The Lady sent him a look of wordless reproach, and then indicated the man he had scolded.

Of course, John thought, feeling himself redden. He cleared his throat. "Sir, have you a Message for us?"

The man rose from his seat with a self-important clearing of his throat. Closing his eyes, he raised his hands. A deep hush fell on the company, measured out only by the gurgle of the water in the fountain, and the soft metallic sounds of the dragon's lashing tail.

John was used to Messengers' vagaries. At one Watchers' Council he had attended, the assembly had waited almost an entire night for the Message to arrive. This looked like being one of those days—until the moment that a clear, young voice broke the silence.

"Hear the Message of heaven," proclaimed the young page. He could not have been older than thirteen or fourteen years. John turned and found that the boy's eyes were fixed upon him, intent and a little terrified, as though he did not understand the strange compulsion that had come upon him.

The old Messenger dropped his hands, his face turning absolutely white, aghast that the Gift had departed from him. As for John, a sense of deep foreboding had come upon him. At Oliveta a child had also prophesied.

"Out of the south, a calamity shall come forth," the boy proclaimed. "For God has called together all the peoples of Egypt to march against this kingdom. They shall set up engines at the gates of Acre, and encamp around her and all the cities that put their trust in her. For a judgement has been proclaimed against us concerning all our wickedness—concerning the slaves who cry out for freedom, and the innocent blood we have shed, and the work of our own hands, in which we put our trust."

"Silence, boy! What are you saying?" someone hissed, but the Lady raised her hand. She was as white as paper.

"Can't you see that he is weeping?" she asked. "Go on, child."

The boy drew a sobbing breath. "The land is taken away from you and given to the sultan, the king of Egypt. And the guardianship of this council is taken away from you and given to—to al-Mukhtar, my Chosen son, your awaited Prester. Welcome him when he comes."

John's hands clenched on the arms of his chair as an echoing silence filled the hall. It was impossible. He must have misheard.

"Who?" the Lady asked, blankly.

The boy covered his mouth with his hands and fell to his knees, trembling. "Pardon me, my lady! I don't know why I said those things!"

The whole room filled with indignation.

"What presumption! Have that child taken out and beaten!"

"What did he say? *Al-Mukhtar?* Isn't that a Saracen name?"

"It's as I always say—God loves the Saracens more than us. Anyone can see *that.*"

John remained silent, dimly conscious of an ache in his fingers where they clutched the chair's arms. Al-Mukhtar? That spawn of Khalil? *How?*

"Then it's confirmed," said the Lady, and if her voice had not lost its laziness, her eyes and her posture had stilled to an unbearable sharpness. "Our reign is over and done. No longer will the house of Ibelin rule in the East."

"Eschiva, gossip," said Lady Margaret faintly from her place behind the Lady's chair. "You mustn't despair."

The Lady sent her a sidelong glance. "What, then? Should we fight against God?"

"Obedience to the will of Heaven is never a counsel of despair, my lady," John said. Oh, he was well practised in preaching what he did not believe. Al-Mukhtar! The killer of the Zakars, the traitor of Tripoli, Soraya's tyrant. *Why?*

He stood with his ears full of indistinct sound—the rushing of blood, the wrangling of the assembly. "Give me leave to go," he begged the Lady. "I must go to speak with the Chosen."

The Lady's eyes widened with understanding. *"That* man?"

"Let me speak with him," John repeated, and fled into the loggia without waiting for permission.

The gallery was clogged with guards and attendants. John forced his way through and passed through the door that divided the public area of the loggia from the private quarters beyond.

God loves the Saracens more than us, one of the Beirut knights had said, in tones of despair. Was it the truth? Had John been mistaken all this time?

At this hour, with all the palace's attention on the audience-hall, the place was quiet and hushed. In the garden, a thin wisp of smoke still ascended from the stump of the ruined orange-tree. Al-Mukhtar must still be in the sleeping-quarters they shared. Bursting in, he found al-Mukhtar shouldering his rolled-up belongings, evidently ready to set out on a journey.

John came to a halt, speechless in the face of this new surprise. He had rather expected to find al-Mukhtar in the act of spying out the land: ransacking the Lady's cabinet for secret papers or searching for postern-gates that might be betrayed to the enemy. Not preparing to *leave.*

"Where are you going?" he demanded. "Don't you know that you're wanted here?"

Al-Mukhtar swallowed, hard. "I spoke to al-Ashraf again. He's agreed to release Ghaliyah."

The world stopped spinning and John was left clinging to the wreckage. "You're going back to him?"

"I can't abandon her," al-Mukhtar said, defiantly.

It was a trap, of course. Khalil could not risk losing his most prized mamluk to the Coast—nor the Lance and the djinn bound within it. If al-Mukhtar returned to Cairo he would never be heard of again. Khalil would kill him and repossess the Lance. With both Ghaliyah and Soraya—the lost star—under his command, not even Khalil would any longer have a reason to fear Qeteb.

The thought was horribly tempting. All John had to do was keep his mouth shut, and al-Mukhtar would go away to his doom, to the fate he so richly deserved. The Message would fall empty. He would remain a Prester of the Watchers, with all the honour that entailed.

The Coast might yet be saved.

John could no longer deceive himself with such thoughts. If it was true that God ruled over the kingdoms of men, he would only injure himself if he tried to thwart the divine will.

He took a deep breath, reminding himself of the scene in the garden last night when he had given up trying to battle Qeteb in his own strength, when the stars had fallen in answer to his prayer. The heavens were not blind, he reminded himself, nor pitiless. The King was with his people, even now, invisible.

"There's something you ought to know, before you go," he told Saif. "I've just come from the Watcher's Council. A Message was received— a prophecy. You have been appointed a Prester of the Council, with the guardianship of the Coast."

Al-Mukhtar's response, gratifyingly, was little different from that of the council. He blinked. "Me? Are you joking? I'm no Watcher."

"Believe me, I know," John said, closing the door behind him. "Beyond which, you're a liar and a killer and a tyrant."

He couldn't help the angry words that spilled out of him, but possibly nothing else could have convinced al-Mukhtar that he was in earnest.

"I don't understand," he repeated. "A Prester? What does that mean?"

"It means teaching and warning," John said. "It means living a sober, restrained, and upright life. It means setting yourself up as an example of goodness, so that when others wish to know what kind of life they ought to live, they may look to you for guidance."

Al-Mukhtar looked stunned.

"Or at least," John added, "that's what I thought it meant, until this hour. God help the Coast. Maybe it means you become the sultan and spend your life in spreading your father's empire and grinding the faces of the people. Or maybe it means that you become like Ghaliyah, a helpless pawn whose only help is in heaven. Either way, all this talk of a great Prester of the East—it doesn't mean the Old Lord, John of Ibelin. Not any more. And it doesn't mean me, John Bessarion. It means *you*."

"*I* am Prester John?" At that, al-Mukhtar laughed, and the look of terrified awe retreated from his face. "Your Message got tied to the leg of the wrong bird. It makes no difference. My wife is alive and waiting for me. I must return to Cairo."

"It's a trap," John warned him. "Do you really imagine that your father has had a change of heart? You forced his hand: that is all. Whatever he's promised you is a lie."

"I know that," al-Mukhtar said, pulling the door open. He let in a clamour of voices. Half the Council must have been gathered in the loggia, eager for that door to open, for a look at the man whom the Messenger had, truly or falsely, named their Prester. Al-Mukhtar closed it hastily. "It's like I told you," he added, going to the windows at the opposite side of the room, the windows that looked down upon a deep moat and the green orchards beyond. Throwing open the casement, he stepped up to the sill and crouched there, looking down at the sheer wall beyond. "All the family I have is in Cairo. I can't abandon them."

Them. After all this, did he still think of Khalil as his father?

"Tell her I'm sorry," al-Mukhtar added. "If I make it back I'll apologise properly."

"Who?" John asked, but the window was now empty. "Strife," he said. By the time he got to the window and leaned out, al-Mukhtar—the Chosen— the unlikely Prester—was already picking his way across the moat below.

John was still watching when the door opened, letting in more clamour— together with the Lady of Beirut.

"Where is he?" she asked wearily.

"Gone," John said, pulling his head in.

"He went out the *window?*" The Lady brushed John aside and quickly spotted the runaway Prester as he picked his way up the far side of the moat. "What an efficient young man," she said. "But the Council is determined to have a word with him, and so am I for that matter. I'm sure we can catch him."

She left as hurriedly as she had come. From the sound of it, the clamouring crowd followed her, leaving the loggia in peace. John took another glance out the window, satisfying himself that al-Mukhtar had already disappeared within the groves of mulberry-trees that grew there. Almost he wished he might follow. If the Council failed to get a word with Saif, they would be only too eager to tackle John next. He stuck his thumbs into his belt, letting out a deep sigh.

It was in that moment that his eyes fell upon the Lance, still leaning in the corner behind the door.

He stared at it a long moment in complete bewilderment. When he snatched it up, he felt the familiar, tell-tale hum of power: the soul-tether that connected the Lance with Soraya. Al-Mukhtar must have somehow forgotten to take it with him. What stroke of luck was this?

The door opened a third time; this time it was Soraya who strolled in, looking as sunny and contented as she had all morning. "Where's Saif?" she asked. "Whatever he's doing, he's pulling on the soul-tether and I keep feeling faint."

Al-Mukhtar was bound to Soraya and able to access her power, even when he wasn't directly touching the Lance. He must have used a fair bit of her strength to descend the wall and cross the moat unhurt.

When John turned and Soraya saw the Lance in his hands, her jaw dropped, and her eyebrows rose. For a moment they beheld each other in utter bafflement.

"What is going on?" she asked at last. "Why do *you* have the Lance? He never lets it out of his hand."

Tell her I'm sorry. It was no mistake, he realised.

"He's gone back to Cairo," John blurted. "And he left this behind."

Chapter XL.

Eschiva expected her knights to find and recover the Saracen within the hour, but he was still missing by sunset. She called off the search and had John Bessarion summoned to the audience-hall, where she paced by the stream. Margaret occupied her own seat, watching her with placid eyes.

"Don't wear out the pavement, my dear," she said.

Eschiva gave a hard laugh. "What a riddle is this! Beirut is taken from me and given to this al-Mukhtar, an Egyptian mamluk. A servant of al-Ashraf. I suppose he is the man who will rule in Beirut when I am gone."

John entered the hall with the other djinn, Soraya, at his side. Eschiva was surprised to see her, but pleased. "Perhaps *you* can answer my questions," she said, letting them feel her displeasure. "What does all this mean? A Saracen, the new Prester of Beirut?"

John shook his head wearily. "One guess is as good as another, my lady."

"You couldn't find him, could you?" the djinn surmised.

Eschiva pressed her lips together. "We found one man who said he saw a Saracen of al-Mukhtar's description at the harbour about midday. That's all. We presume he's taken ship already."

The man and the djinn exchanged a look. "He said he was returning to Cairo, my lady," John said.

"Don't worry," the djinn put in. "He's meant to come back. So he will."

"Yes, but how?" Eschiva snapped. "At the head of the sultan's army?"

"He'd better come back *somehow*," Soraya said. "He owes me a proper apology."

John, at least, seemed to grasp the seriousness of the matter. "One thing is certain. My lady, I'm sorry, but so far as I know anything, I know that it was a true Message we heard in the council this morning. The Coast is no longer our responsibility."

Eschiva wanted to lash out and strike him, demand he take the words back. If only she'd secured al-Mukhtar before he could get away from her, then she might still retain the mastery in Beirut by retaining the mastery of the Prester...

Then she might be no better, indeed, than the Old Lord.

Eschiva closed her eyes and took a long, slow breath. The sound of flowing water was a ceaseless music in the air. This was her *home*, the city which her forefathers had built. She thought she would rather die than leave it. Surely the sultan could not really do to Beirut what had been done to Antioch, to Tripoli, to a hundred smaller towns and fortresses up and down the Coast?

To ask the question was to answer it. She must leave Beirut, or this palace in all its splendour would become her tomb.

"I will give the order," she said, sighing. "Everyone who has goods and children in the city must be warned to send them to Cyprus." *And I*, she thought bleakly. *To purchase refuge for my people I shall have to marry King Henry's young brother.*

Margaret rose to her feet "Eschiva," she said, appealingly, "is it really so serious? Is it really the end?"

"Do not think of it as the end, my lady," John Bessarion put in. "Think of it, rather, as a chance to begin anew, saving what you can from the ruin." Yet, as he glanced about the beautiful palace which the Old Lord had made, Eschiva thought that he could understand a little of what she felt. "You will leave a rich inheritance behind you," he said, sadly. And then in words that rang like a memory of long ago: *"Peace be with you, O Syria! Such a beautiful land you will be for the enemy!"*

There was no more left to be said. Eschiva summoned her chancellor and gave orders for the decrees that must go out tomorrow, advising the people of Beirut to set their affairs in order. She sent her marshal to the Mamluk garrison with orders commanding them to depart the city. And she ordered her seneschal to travel at once to Cyprus, where he might inspect the Ibelin properties there and buy whatever new ships and warehouses might be necessary for the coming move. If nothing else, she had a treaty with Egypt; al-Ashraf might yet choose to honour it. But if it came to the worst, Eschiva would not be destitute. As much as she and her predecessors had clung to Beirut, they now owned more property in Cyprus than on the mainland.

It was well after Vespers by the time she finished her arrangements, but Eschiva did not feel like seeking her bed. Instead, she went into the cabinet where her planetary tables awaited her. What she needed tonight was the click of her abacus, the soothing predictability of her figures, the sheer relief of abstracted thought.

But the moment she spread out the stack of papers, it struck her. The tables were useless, having been calculated for Beirut's latitude. In Cyprus she would have to do all the work again. Moreover, the stars themselves had forbidden her to inquire of them. *Your fate is in the hands of the King Above.*

Eschiva let out a little sound like a whimper. The next moment she swept up all the papers and took out a knife, ready to shred them into pieces.

Her whole life's work had been fruitless. Why should she not destroy it? Why should she leave any inheritance to the enemy?

A smell of burning filled her nostrils.

For a moment she wondered if she had been careless with her candle. But this was not the scent of paper scorching: it was somehow cleaner, clearer, purer. It reminded her of the hot smell of the star-women.

Eschiva leaped to her feet. The next moment light burst upon the room. Ibrahim stood before her, his dark skin shining like a jewel, the span of his unfurled wings too great to be contained in the room. He was pure, smokeless fire.

Eschiva threw up her hands to shield herself. All that glory, all that beauty. She was afraid that to look upon him would break her utterly; not with fear, but with longing.

"Ibrahim," she gasped. "You returned."

"Only for a moment. Only to say farewell." For a moment neither of them knew where to look. Then he said, "My lady, do you fear me?"

"Yes," she gasped. "Don't go. Speak to me."

"And say what?"

"I don't know. They usually begin with *Be not afraid,* don't they?"

She had never heard a star laugh before. That allowed her the courage to take her hands away from her eyes and look upon him.

It was as bad as she had thought. She wanted this—this light, this glory, this bliss. To be perfected with him. In that moment nothing else seemed to matter. Her city, the great culmination of all the craft and wisdom of the world, all the beauty and all the glory, was yet but a faint shadow of what might one day be.

There had been lovely things before. There would be lovely things again. How prodigally generous the world was, that it could generate a thousand new glories each morning, in a thousand new hues. What though evening came and faded? There would always be a new morning.

"Are you casting horoscopes?" he asked her, and Eschiva dropped her eyes to her papers, bathed in the golden light of this visiting star.

"No," she said, with a wry smile. She smoothed a hand over the papers, knowing now that although they might be useless to her, she could never be so mean as to destroy them. "I am forbidden to do it."

"You are free now to forge your own fate," he told her.

She bit her lip. It had always given her a measure of comfort to think that the stars ruled her life. They were far away. She could tell herself comforting stories about them: use them to bring herself good fortune. Don't set out on a journey when Mercury is in retrograde. Don't go to war under a comet. Do nothing dangerous at all after an eclipse.

And the numbers. How she loved the numbers! Their abstract beauty, she now saw, carried an echo of the perfection that dwelt only among the stars.

"I don't want to," she whispered. "The stars have always been my guide. What will I do without them to rule over me?"

Ibrahim bent down until his great, glorious face filled her vision. "Can you not love them for their own sake?"

Eschiva looked up at the nearest thing she had ever had to a true love. He was going away from her now, into the skies. From now on he would be to her a happy memory, a distant glimmer, and the elegant calculus by which she tracked his path.

"I suppose I can." She managed a smile. "You are happy, Ibrahim. It makes me glad to see you attain better than you ever desired."

"Or deserved," he said. "Farewell, Eschiva of Ibelin. May you also find your way to the heavens."

Chapter XLI.

"It's strange," John mused. "It made me remember the words of Emperor Heraclius, when he left Syria. *A beautiful land you will be for the enemy.* At the time it felt like forever—but it wasn't. The land was taken away from us and given to others. It was taken away from them, too. Nothing is forever."

"Perhaps it is a blessing," Rahel reflected. The two of them sat side by side in the loggia, looking out at the silvery sea across which the setting moon painted a path towards the west. "There is no constancy beneath the moon. All things change and fall into decay, but who would desire their mistakes to be preserved forever?"

"I would," John said, ruefully. "I have been mistaken in so many things, Rahel. I always thought that lordship was a matter of imposing our laws upon the unbelievers and the unrighteous. I thought that it could be done benevolently, kindly for their good. But that isn't what Our Lord proposed, was it? Soraya troubled me because she said there is no way to make such lordship benevolent. If the greatest of all is the servant of all, then true lordship is no more power than that wielded by the meanest slave."

"Like a pageboy giving a Message?" Rahel said. "Like an old woman casting out the great Qeteb from her sickbed?"

John bowed his head. "That was why I was never able to overcome Qeteb. I always accepted that power was an end in itself. I despised the Copts for losing the power they had, not seeing that they had remained faithful and gained a truer strength. All my life I have been fighting to impose my own lordship, not Christ's. And I have used Qeteb's weapons to do it." The bitter, lingering taste of disillusionment filled his mouth. "And now I have lost the same land twice."

"It is hard to repent when you're sitting on a throne," Rahel said. "But the fault ran further and deeper than you, my love."

"I have done with being part of the fault," John said. He had fallen asleep clutching the little wax packet, and now he held it up. "For so many years I've been keeping this hidden and secret against the day when Palestine would be ours again. But why should we build only things that will benefit ourselves? The house of God is large enough for all peoples, and his kingdom is not from this world; it goes on growing even when all earthly rulers are against it. I want you to use this, Rahel—you and the children, no matter whether I come home again, or no. Use it. Build. Believe. Work. Thrive. *Live,* no matter who rules, because in the end there is only one King that matters. His kingdom is an everlasting kingdom, which no earthly power can touch. And he is nearer to us than we imagine."

He shivered, remembering the star-women. Rahel watched him, biting her lip to conceal her smile.

"What is it?" he asked.

"I miss you," she told him, fondly.

"I miss you, too." He heaved a sigh. Marriage had always been a way for the great of the world to forge alliances and create an order that favoured them. He wished, intensely, that he had been able to learn his lesson sooner, before Rahel had been taken away from him.

"Where is Soraya?" she asked now.

"Asleep," he said. "She came to me today for instructions on how to care for a body she meant to keep for a while. The idea of regular sleep, food, and water was strange to her."

"And al-Mukhtar?"

John shook his head. "I still don't understand. For now, he has returned to Cairo. But Soraya is right. It isn't the last we'll see of him."

"And you, John?"

He heaved a deep sigh. "We have done all we can in Beirut. The Master of the Temple wants me back in Acre. Soraya wants me to help her cast out Qeteb, and then we'll finally be able to break the Lance. Beyond that...I don't know. I can only hope that Soraya will relent."

"It will be all right," she told him, softly. "Not all partings are forever."

He nodded, but the thought still brought him a pang. He held up the packet again.

"The formula is this," he told Rahel. "Three parts volcanic ash. One part quicklime. And when you slurry the lime with water, mix it over a furnace until it becomes as hot as glass. That is the secret I searched all the libraries of Constantinople to find. The mortar that results will dry fast and set hard—hard enough to withstand any but the most disastrous shaking. Even when it cracks, it heals again, stronger than before."

"A just and fitting image," Rahel told him, impishly. "Of Christ, the true mortar."

John laughed, tucking the packet away again. He had loosened his grip upon nearly everything he wanted—his wife, his lordship, his basilica. He ought to feel bereft; but he was conscious only of a great relief. He had laid down his burdens. They could rest now upon a strength far better able to carry them.

Epilogue

Al-Ashraf Khalil, sultan of Egypt, was pleased to learn that his mamluks had seized the former na'ib, Turuntay. He had his prisoner dragged to meet him on the terrace of his citadel, overlooking the great city which his former rival had lost.

Turuntay fell to his knees before Khalil, his breathing harsh and distressed. Blood flowed down his face from a cut above the brow. Khalil handed the hooded hawk that had been riding his wrist to its falconer and looked down on his rival with a thin smile.

He didn't like this terrace; he didn't like the way the sun beat down on his unprotected head. It reminded him too much of the long years he had spent as a captive, half stone in the dead city of Oliveta. But with Turuntay at his feet, he felt different. Turuntay was the captive, now. And this citadel would be his torment.

"I believe I overestimated you, Turuntay," Khalil observed pleasantly. "I expected you to pose a greater threat."

The other man made no response. Perhaps he saw that he had lost, and was only concerned to face his death in dignified silence. Or perhaps he was still befuddled from the beating Khalil's men had given him.

"You must have mismanaged your conspirators," Khalil added. "Few of them stood by you. One of them gave me the location of your refuge. It doesn't do, you know, to allow yourself to look so weak."

Turuntay spat blood on the stones. Khalil sighed and beckoned to his guards.

"Take him to the prison," he commanded, waving for his mamluks to drag the man away. "I never want to see this man again."

"Let me eat him." Qeteb's spoke in his ear and Khalil felt as though he had fallen into the snow of Lebanon in the middle of winter. If he had not been accustomed to keep such a tight rein upon himself, he might have flinched or cried out.

Khalil glanced down at his feet, at the sigil in which he was standing. Every stroke was still crisp, every line still in place. Naturally. He had made it clear to the attendant he had charged with following him around, chalk in hand, that if the sigils were ever drawn with less than perfect clarity it would not only be he who paid with his life.

He was safe—for now—but felt far from secure.

"Qeteb," he murmured, waving his attendants out of earshot. The afrit had taken up his place at the border of the sigil, like a greedy lion watching a deer from behind the bars of its cage. "Where have you been all this while? Report!"

"Peace be upon you, O Khalil, sultan and lord!" the afrit replied mockingly. "I have been in Beirut, watching over your affairs."

He could not allow Qeteb to see his anxieties. "And?"

"O fount of all magnificence, it's bad news. The djinn Ibrahim has departed his vessel and ascended into the heavens."

"How is that bad news?" Khalil demanded, intrigued despite himself. "You mean the Lady freed him? Surely we can summon him back!"

"Not from the heavens, O king of kings."

"But you're his father." He became aware that he was sounding desperate, and swallowed.

"In the heavens they recognise no fathers." Qeteb heaved a sigh. "True it is what the mortal, Nizam al-Mulk said: *One obedient slave is better than three hundred sons: for the latter desire their father's death, the former long life for his master.* Now let us speak of *your* son. I told you when he was born that he was a dangerous mistake. Now he's a disobedient mistake. You ought to let me have him."

Khalil waved an irritable hand. "You can have Turuntay. Saif is still useful to me. I promised that I would return his wife, and he took the next ship for Alexandria."

Qeteb's voice took on its accustomed stony quality. "What? I hope you don't mean to *reward* the boy for his rebellion."

Khalil forced himself to take a long, slow breath. Of course he didn't. But he couldn't very well admit this to Qeteb.

"Qalawun was not a perfect ruler, but he was wise," he said. "He did not merely punish those who disobeyed him. He also rewarded those who served him. I will punish al-Mukhtar in some other way, but his wife I will return to him. See to it that the woman Ghaliyah is permitted to awake, and ensure that she is in strong health and fit to meet him."

There was a long silence. "Well?" Khalil demanded. "Will there be a problem?"

"O lamp of eternal wisdom," Qeteb said. "I'm sorry to tell you that that will be impossible. The woman Ghaliyah died in her sleep. Alas! My attention was distracted while I was in the north. No doubt you will see fit to punish me for this oversight."

Khalil stared at him, disbelieving. The afrit stared back, unblinking. If he had been a mortal, there might have been a smile on his face to go along with the mockery of his words. There was nothing on Qeteb's face, no expression in his voice but the lust of an insatiable hunger.

With Ibrahim and Soraya both beyond his reach, Ghaliyah was Khalil's last line of defence against that hunger. And now she was gone, because he had had no choice but to entrust her to the keeping of the very thing that hungered to destroy him.

It was Saif's fault. If his mamluk had only done as he was told and captured Lilith instead of casting her out, he would still be able to balance his afrit allies against each other.

Saif, he thought, his heart sinking. Of late the boy had been stubborn, rebellious. His loyalties no longer lay entirely with Khalil—and that was dangerous.

What would Saif do when he knew that his woman was dead?

S.D.G.

EPILOGUE

*John Bessarion will return in **A Wall of Fire***

Watch out for the next Watchers of Outremer book
A Covenant of Salt

Historical Note

This book posed a particular challenge for me because of the paucity of English-language sources on the thirteenth-century Bahri Mamluk sultanate based in Cairo, Egypt. There is only one scholarly book in the English language that focuses on the reign of Sultan Qalawun: Linda S. Northrup's *From Slave to Sultan,* which is out of print and available only at a few academic libraries scattered across the world. It feels like a special dispensation of Providence that a copy recently surfaced at the University of Melbourne's Baillieu Library, enabling me to read it just in time to write this book.

As always, I have included fictional representations of many real historical people in this book: Eschiva of Ibelin, Margaret of Tyre, John of Ibelin and his brother Philip, Sultan Qalawun, al-Ashraf Khalil, Turuntay, Badr al-Din Bektash al-Fakhri, William of Beaujeu, Gerard of Montreal, and others.

The final years of the medieval crusader states were characterised by a slow but steady loss of territory to the Mamluk sultans of Egypt. In 1268, the sultan Baybars seized Antioch in a bloody slaughter. In 1289, a year before the events of this story, his successor Qalawun levelled Tripoli to the ground, leaving the isle of Saint Thomas where some of the townspeople had taken refuge heaped with corpses. The city of Acre, a wealthy, bustling trade centre, was now one of only a few crusader enclaves remaining on the mainland. Notably, these included Tyre, ruled by Margaret of Antioch-Lusignan, and Beirut, ruled by Eschiva of Ibelin.

The kingdom of Cyprus now served as an offshore stronghold and asylum for refugees fleeing the wars on the mainland. Seized from its Byzantine warlord by Richard I Plantagenet nearly a century previously during the Third Crusade, the island had been handed over as a sort of consolation prize to the former king of Jerusalem, Guy of Lusignan. Although the island therefore became Guy's property, in order to take the title of king it was necessary for him to receive a crown from the Holy Roman Emperor. This would cause trouble later.

Life expectancy for the warrior class being what it was, the Lusignan dynasty of Cyprus quickly ran into dynastic troubles. In 1218, Alice of Champagne, the widowed queen, assumed the bailliship (or regency) on behalf of her young son, Henry I. Alice delegated the day-to-day ruling of the kingdom to her uncle, Philip of Ibelin; but the Ibelin regime soon raised hackles as Philip and his powerful elder brother—John I of Ibelin, the Lord of Beirut—were accused of enriching themselves and promoting their own supporters at the expense of the established Cypriot nobility. Ultimately, the Ibelin brothers quarreled with Queen Alice and intimidated or even assassinated those of her supporters who tried to remove them. Once Philip of Ibelin died in 1227, Ibelin supporters in the High Court conferred the bailliship upon John of Ibelin. It was shortly after, in 1228, that the Holy Roman Emperor, Frederick II, arrived in the east on crusade. Frederick, by dint of marrying the young Queen Isabella II of Jerusalem (who quickly died in childbirth), now claimed not only the rulership of the kingdom of Jerusalem in right of his infant son, but also that of the kingdom of Cyprus based on his father's having originally granted the crown to the Lusignan dynasty. Frederick's high-handed behaviour, laying claim to both thrones and challenging the power of the respective High Courts in each kingdom, outraged many of the nobility, who chose to fight back.

So began the War of the Lombards, which would last until 1243 and bring the Ibelin dynasty to the peak of its power. When the war began, John of Ibelin was the lord of Beirut and bailli of Cyprus, a controversial figure whose ties to the ruling family of Jerusalem had enabled him to richly feather his own nest. Within a few years, however, John had become an emblem of popular and baronial resistance to the emperor and his hated Lombard enforcers. The Ibelin family had solidified its role as the kingmakers of the crusader Levant. And John's position was further bolstered by the official family history, written by Philip of Novara, which cast all the Ibelins' doings in the best possible light.

By the time *A Stranger in the Land* takes place, John I of Ibelin is long dead and the Ibelin dynasty has lost power along with the rest of the crusader states. In 1264, the Old Lord's great-granddaughter Isabella succeeded to the lordship of Beirut. Her career would be dogged with scandal for what contemporaries called her "notorious lack of chastity." In 1269, shortly after the sack of Antioch, Isabella concluded a treaty with Sultan Baybars of Egypt. By this time, the crowns of Cyprus and Jerusalem had been united under the rule of King Hugh III, who considered himself to be Isabella's overlord. In 1273, therefore, after the death of Isabella's first husband, she was effectively kidnapped by Hugh and taken to Cyprus, where the king planned to have her marry a knight of his own choosing who would rule Beirut on Hugh's behalf. Isabella's response was to claim before the High Court of Jerusalem that she was not a vassal of King Hugh at all, but of Sultan Baybars. Baybars supported her claim, and the High Court ruled in favour of the sultan. Isabella was thus free to choose subsequent husbands on her own terms; but Beirut was thereafter under the authority of Cairo, with a small Mamluk garrison stationed in the city collecting much of the lordship's incomes for the sultan. It was this delicate and unstable political situation which Isabella's younger sister, Eschiva, inherited in 1282, at the age of 29.

Little is known of Eschiva's character and rule. In describing her daily life, I consulted Christina de Pizan's 1405 book of instructions for noblewomen, *The Treasure of the City of Ladies,* for a typical day in the life of a medieval noblewoman. The historical Eschiva married Humphrey of Montfort, the lord of Tyre, in 1274 and gave birth to six children, only two of whom survived to adulthood. Humphrey died in 1284. In 1291, shortly after the events of this book, King Henry II of Cyprus arranged Eschiva's marriage to his younger brother Guy. She was thirty-eight; Guy was at the very oldest sixteen. The couple had two children, before Guy rebelled against his brother the king and was executed in 1302.

Perhaps the most illuminating episode of Eschiva's life came afterwards, when she travelled to mainland Greece claiming the vacant crusader duchy of Athens in right of her mother, Alice de la Roche of Athens. The High Court of Achaia decided in favour of a rival claimant, according to the William Miller's 1908 book *The Latins in the Levant: A History of Frankish Greece*: "on the ground that he was a powerful and gallant man, while the Lady of Beyrout was not only a woman but a widow. When Eschive heard the sentence of the Court, she knelt down at the altar of the church of St Francis at Glarentza, where the barons had met, and prayed the Virgin that if her judges and her opponent had wrought injustice, they might die without heirs of their bodies. Then she departed to her own home..." Reading this, I was struck by the contrast between Eschiva and her great-grandfather. Could Eschiva have been so *very* poor and humbled, even after having lost Beirut, even after her husband's treason, that she could not have remained in Athens—pursuing her claim, seeking baronial support and making life difficult for her rival? I'm not enough of a historian to say, but I choose to imagine that in choosing to withdraw, she was showing a measure of wisdom her exalted ancestor did not.

Certainly, I found no evidence to suggest that the real Eschiva of Ibelin took any interest in astrology. This element of the story was inspired, however, by Wilbrand of Oldenburg's vivid description of the Ibelins' magnificent palace at Beirut, which contained—in addition to design elements contributed by craftsmen from across the region—a domed ceiling depicting an astrological scheme of the heavens and seasons. Investigating medieval astrology further, I learned that for medieval people, there was no distinction made between the astrological interpretation of the heavens on one hand, and the disciplines of mathematics and astronomy which today form a branch of science, on the other. Medieval astrology was considered to be quite prosaic: a science that not only used complex trigonometric calculations to pinpoint the positions of the stars but also (albeit with less certainty) attempted to predict their influence upon the careers of princes and kingdoms. Like many medieval courts, the Ibelins of Beirut would have employed court astrologers to interpret the heavens, diagnose their illnesses and advise them on the auspicious timing of important events.

Scholarly consensus on the final years of the medieval crusader states, at least so far as crusader historians have been concerned, has traditionally been as follows. The Mamluk sultans who ruled both Egypt and Syria were anxious about the rise of the Tartar, or Mongol, Il-Khanate at Baghdad, which posed a significant military threat to their empire. Of particular concern was the possibility of a military alliance between the Mongols and the crusaders, potentially even with the addition of the kingdom of Nubia south of Egypt, which might then attack the Mamluk empire from three directions. It was for this reason that Qalawun planned to eliminate the remains of the crusader states by targeting Acre. He was given his pretext in August 1290, when newly-arrived crusaders from Western Europe rioted in Acre, slaughtering Muslim merchants as well as Syrian Christian farmers who had entered the city to sell their crops. The bloodstained clothing of the victims was taken to Cairo and presented to the sultan, prompting him to seek the support of his amirs in mustering an army for an attack on Acre.

However, when I located Linda S. Northrup's biography of Qalawun, *From Slave to Sultan*, I read a different take on the facts. According to Northrup, Qalawun had little to fear militarily from the crusader states— realistically, there was very little the crusaders or the Nubians could contribute to a Mongol attack on the Mamluk empire, even if all parties could be persuaded to agree to such a thing . What truly worried Qalawun was something quite different: the possibility of a trade embargo.

The Mamluk regime was powered by slavery. High-ranking amirs would purchase slaves from Central Asia and train them in corps of elite soldiers, who ultimately would be freed and take high rank in turn under their former masters. These elite soldiers formed the core of the Egyptian army, as well as a tightly-knit system of patronage and brotherhood that in many ways replaced family amid the ruling classes. Qalawun himself had become sultan after rising from slavery to become a powerful amir, and most of the Mamluk sultans and their highest officials followed a similar trajectory. The problem was that the whole system depended on a steady supply of male slaves from Central Asia.

Meanwhile, the trading empire run by the Italian city of Genoa had recently defeated its rivals, Venice and Pisa, in a couple of long-lasting naval wars. Having gained dominance over all the trading cities of the eastern Mediterranean and the Black Sea, Genoa now virtually controlled all the trade routes that flowed from Central Asia to Cairo. By late in the century, Genoese merchants were negotiating with the Mongol Il-Khan at Baghdad to extend their trade as far as the Persian Gulf. Should this trade agreement be consolidated, Genoa would gain the power to cut off the slave trade to Cairo altogether.

There was one vulnerable point in this cordon: the crusader city of Acre, a trade hub that played host to a major slave market. By capturing Acre, the sultan could blast a gap in the Genoese cordon, open up the possibility of capturing more trade cities such as Ayas in Cilician Armenia, and cut the Genoese link with Baghdad and beyond. *This*, according to the world's foremost English-speaking expert on the reign, is what impelled Qalawun to snuff out the last remnants of the crusader states in the mainland Levant. His urgency to do so, moreover, must only have been increased by the fact that the Muslim merchants targeted by the 1290 Acre riots were slave-traders from Damascus.

Qalawun's son and first choice of heir, al-Salih 'Ali, had died in 1289. This brought to prominence his second son, al-Ashraf Khalil, who in reality was *not* being impersonated by a shapeshifting immortal sorcerer. The historical al-Ashraf Khalil was known for his vigorous leadership and his skill in horsemanship and archery. He was designated as his father's successor during Qalawun's lifetime, but the legal diploma confirming his position was never finalised—a peculiarity which leads Northrup to conjecture that Qalawun felt threatened by his son's ambitions. This uncertainty may also have influenced the behaviour of Husam al-Din Turuntay al-Mansuri, the na'ib al-saltana, who had been a close supporter of al-Salih. Conscious of his danger as the supporter of a dead prince, Turuntay spent the final year of Qalawun's reign feuding with Khalil. When Qalawun died of illness before his expedition against Acre could set out in November 1290, one of Khalil's first actions was to arrest Turuntay, confiscate his wealth, and torture him into disclosing any hidden treasure. The polo game, and Saif's assassination attempt, are my own inventions; but in reality Turuntay really did die of his injuries shortly after being released from prison, leaving the coast clear for Khalil's rule.

I'm disappointed that I wasn't able to spend more time in this book on the spy network run by William of Beaujeu, the Master of the Temple. What we know of the Temple's intelligence-gathering comes from the chronicler known as the "Templar of Tyre"—in reality a secular knight in Beaujeu's service who likely handled his correspondence, and who appears as a character in this book under the name of Gerard of Montreal. According to the "Templar", the high-ranking Mamluk amir Badr al-Din Bektash al-Fakhri acted as an informant in the pay of Beaujeu in the years leading up to the siege of Acre. It was Bektash who informed Beaujeu about Cairo's impending attacks on Tripoli in 1289, as well as on Acre in 1291. Information on crusader intelligence-gathering activities was kept secret, of course, because of the nature of the work; and little to no scholarship has been done on the topic. What I have included, I have more or less invented. Centuries before intelligence became recognised as a basic necessity of the modern state, Beaujeu was evidently aware of the value of his highly-placed informant at Qalawun's court; this marks him out as an exceptionally prudent and well informed leader.

The Egyptian Copts are, like many indigenous Christian populations of this region, underrepresented in fiction and nearly invisible in contemporary discourse. Partly this is for theological reasons going back to the ecumenical church council of Chalcedon in AD 451. At Chalcedon, the Incarnation of Christ was declared to be both divine and human: "acknowledged in two natures without confusion, without change, without division, without separation." *Contra* Chalcedon, some oriental churches proclaimed that Christ's humanity had been subsumed by his divine nature; this was the heresy known as Monophysitism, and it became a label used throughout history to delegitimise the Coptic church. In fact, Copts adhere to Miaphysitism, a view that many theologians now argue differs only semantically from the orthodox definition of Chalcedon: while claiming a single nature for Christ, Miaphysites affirm that Christ is both fully divine and fully human, without confusion, mixture, or separation.

As the original inhabitants of Egypt prior to the seventh-century Arabic conquest, Coptic identity has been forged over the centuries by Christian faith, persecution under both Roman and Muslim regimes, and the retention of the Coptic language, even if only as a liturgical tongue. At the moment in history when this book is set, Coptic Christians still formed likely around twenty percent of the Egyptian population. They had not yet suffered intense or systematic persecution, but the centuries had seen large numbers convert in order to access the better social and economic opportunities reserved for Muslims. The fourteenth century, with its climate change, pandemics, and other disruptions, would soon also witness severe persecutions of Copts in Egypts, as of other religious minorities across Europe and Asia. Nevertheless, Coptic faith and practice remained strong then as it does today. I hope that, despite my limited understanding of Coptic theology, culture, and history, I have managed to pay homage to the legacy of which they are so justly proud.

Many purely fictional characters and elements remain in this book: John Bessarion, al-Mukhtar Saif al-Din, Soraya, Ghaliyah, Ibrahim and his orange-tree, and of course, Eschiva of Ibelin's adventures through the supposedly magical portals of the Old Lord's house.

The song John and Soraya hear in the Tentmakers' Market is a paraphrase of "Sawwah", a hauntingly beautiful 1972 release by the Egyptian singer Abdel Halim Hafez. As such it could not possibly have been sung in 1290; however, the moment I heard it I thought of John Bessarion, and I couldn't resist including it. Perhaps other songs like it were being sung at that time.

As always, I would like to acknowledge the many people who have helped in the writing of this book. Particular thanks are due to Helen J. Nicholson for sharing what she knew about Templar spies; to Jamie Wheeler and Beverley Twomey for tracking down copies of *From Slave to Sultan* in order to send me scanned pages; and above all to Manal Chalaby for an unforgettable hour sharing her experience of growing up Coptic in Egypt, telling me the stories of her people, their martyrs, and their miracles. Thanks, as ever, are due to my beta and sensitivity readers for their generosity in giving of their time and expertise: Christina Baehr,

Rosamund Hodge, Naomi Kewley, Leila Ammar, and Joy Chalaby. Finally, I am endlessly grateful to my wonderful cover designer, Jenny Zemanek.
Suzannah Rowntree
July, 2025

Further Reading

For this, the second book I have written set in the late thirteen-century Levant, I revisited a few standard works: Paul Crawford's translation of *The 'Templar of Tyre', Part III of the 'Deeds of the Cypriots'*, still the most important Crusader chronicle of the final years of the medieval crusader states; Christopher Tyerman's *God's War: A New History of the Crusades;* David Nicolle's *Acre 1291: Bloody sunset of the Crusader States;* and Robert Irwin's *The Middle East in the Middle Ages: The Early Mamluk Sultanate, 1250-1382.*

Other works, as ever, helped to put the history of the period into a broader perspective: John Man's *The Mongol Empire;* John of Joinville's *Life of St Louis;* David Nicholle's *The Mamluks, 1250-1517;* Piers Mitchell's *Medicine in the Crusades;* Adrian J Boas' *Crusader Archaeology: The Material Culture of the Latin East;* Jonathan Riley-Smith's *The Atlas of the Crusades*; Christopher MacEvitt's *The Crusades and the Christian World of the East: Rough Tolerance;* and *Medieval Feudalism* by Carl Stephenson. Adam Simmons' *Nubia, Ethiopia, and the Crusading World, 1095-1402* provided a helpful perspective on the geopolitical activity of Christian Africa at this period. As always, for inspiration in my fantasy world-building I have leaned upon van der Toorn, Becking, and van der Horst's *Dictionary of Deities and Demons in the Bible*, and Amira El-Zein's *Islam, Arabs, and the Intelligent World of the Jinn.*

I also took advantage of this opportunity to broaden my reading and acquaint myself with more of the extant scholarship. For the Egyptian setting, Linda S Northrup's *From Slave to Sultan: The Career of Al-Mansur Qalawun and the Consolidation of Mamluk Rule in Egypt and Syria (678-689 A.H./1279-1290A.D.)* was a priceless resource in acquainting myself with the reign of and motivations of Qalawun himself. Max Rodenbeck's *Cairo: The*

City Victorious provided me with much vivid detail on the city, its history, and its daily life during the medieval period. Above all, Philip Jenkins' superb book *The Lost History of Christianity: The Thousand-Year Golden Age of the Church in the Middle East, Africa, and Asia—and How It Died* provided essential background on the long history of the Coptic church, as well as endless food for thought which prompted many of the foundational themes of the story. If you read only one of the books mentioned in this note, make it this one.

For the crusader settings, particularly the tangled history of the Ibelin family, I made plentiful use of two excellent books by Peter W. Edbury: *John of Ibelin and the Kingdom of Jerusalem* and *The Kingdom of Cyprus and the Crusades, 1191-1374.* I also dipped into William Miller's *The Latins in the Levant: A History of Frankish Greece (1204–1566)* for details on Eschiva's claim to the Duchy of Athens. For a study of the Ibelin's Beirut palace, I am indebted to Lucy-Anne Hunt's wonderful article "John of Ibelin's Audience Hall in Beirut: A Crusader palace building between Byzantine and Islamic Art in its Mediterranean Context". Malcolm Barber's article "Was the Holy Land Betrayed in 1291?" also provided helpful insight to the actions of William of Beaujeu and the Templars in the months before the 1291 siege of Acre.

I knew very little about medieval astrology when I decided to explore the possible implications of the Beirut palace architecture. Hilary M. Carey's article "Astrology in the Middle Ages" and J.D. North's article "Scholars And Power: Astrologers at The Courts of Medieval Europe" helped me to get my teeth into this topic. Seb Falk's fascinating book *The Light Ages: The Surprising Story of Medieval Science* provided essential details on how mathematics and astronomy were practised in the middle ages, as well as helping me get my head around astrolabes. And Alexander Boxer's book *A Scheme of Heaven: The History and Science of Astrology, from Ptolemy to the Victorians and Beyond* was a readable and very helpful history of astrology that helped me grasp how medieval people would have understood and practiced the art.

Finally, readers of CS Lewis will notice strong echoes and references to his work in Chapter 38 of this book. Some of these are certainly intentional; but given how strongly Lewis drew on medieval cosmology for his fiction, it's fairly difficult to write such a scene, in such a book, without evoking his work. If he is aware of this evocation, I hope that he finds it flattering.

About the Author

Suzannah Rowntree lives in a big house in rural Australia with her wonderful family, drinking fancy tea and writing historical fantasy fiction that blends real-world history with legend, adventure, and a dash of romance.

You can connect with me on:

🌐 https://suzannahrowntree.site

Subscribe to my newsletter:

✉ https://subscribepage.io/srauthor

Also by Suzannah Rowntree

The Prince of Fishes
The Bells of Paradise
Death Be Not Proud
Ten Thousand Thorns
The City Beyond the Glass

Non-Fiction
How to Write a Fantasy Battle